# If Not Now . . .

Bestselling author Denyse Devlin lives in Cork with her family. *If Not Now* . . . is her fifth novel.

WITHDRAWN FROM STOCK

# If Not Now . . .

DENYSE DEVLIN

00538689.

WITHDRAWN FROM STOCK

PENGUIN
IRELAND

PENGUIN IRELAND

Published by the Penguin Group
Penguin Ireland, 25 St Stephen's Green, Dublin 2, Ireland
(a division of Penguin Books Ltd)
Penguin Books Ltd, 80 Strand, London WC2R 0RL, England
Penguin Group (USA) Inc., 375 Hudson Street, New York, New York 10014, USA
Penguin Group (Australia), 250 Camberwell Road,
Camberwell, Victoria 3124, Australia (a division of Pearson Australia Group Pty Ltd)
Penguin Group (Canada), 90 Eglinton Avenue East, Suite 700,
Toronto, Ontario, Canada M4P 2Y3
(a division of Pearson Penguin Canada Inc.)
Penguin Books India Pvt Ltd, 11 Community Centre,
Panchsheel Park, New Delhi – 110 017, India
Penguin Group (NZ), 67 Apollo Drive, Rosedale, North Shore 0632, New Zealand
(a division of Pearson New Zealand Ltd)
Penguin Books (South Africa) (Pty) Ltd, 24 Sturdee Avenue,
Rosebank, Johannesburg 2196, South Africa
Penguin Books Ltd, Registered Offices: 80 Strand, London WC2R 0RL, England

www.penguin.com

First published 2008
1

Copyright © Denyse Woods, 2008

The moral right of the author has been asserted

All rights reserved
Without limiting the rights under copyright
reserved above, no part of this publication may be
reproduced, stored in or introduced into a retrieval system,
or transmitted, in any form or by any means (electronic, mechanical,
photocopying, recording or otherwise), without the prior
written permission of both the copyright owner and
the above publisher of this book

Set in Garamond MT
Typeset by Palimpsest Book Production Limited,
Grangemouth, Stirlingshire
Printed in Great Britain by Clays Ltd, St Ives plc

A CIP catalogue record for this book is available from the British Library

ISBN 978–1–844–88130–7

To Anne

# I

Onions and oranges, limes and lemons, tomatoes and dates . . . and people. People and dust. It was busy, and dusty, and hot. Marina wandered along the broad street, past the whitewashed shops with their elegant blue arches. No one was bothering her or pressing her to buy. Here, she could amble undisturbed. There was something about the chaos of it, the bustle, that made her feel calm. It was as if no one could see her, not even the guys offering fruit and veg with their gap-toothed smiles. Her clothes – a long cream cotton skirt and tan top – helped her to blend in. Sidestepping a cart piled high with mint, she saw one shopkeeper stretched out, sound asleep, across his vegetables, his head in the grapefruit and his feet in the lettuce, and turned into another street, narrower and more congested, where shoppers could be seen bobbing off into the distance. It seemed to go on into infinity, this funnel of commerce, so crowded that nobody paid heed to a woman on her own.

A feeling passed through her, briefly and suddenly, that she wasn't alone. She glanced over her shoulder, half expecting to see a familiar face. No one there, of course. Perhaps it was Aidan, she thought. She sometimes felt him nearby, as though he were in the same room. The same life.

This was the most difficult thing about being single – holidaying on her own – but she had learnt the hard way that feeling alone was worse than being alone. She had twice made the mistake of taking charter holidays to popular resorts where, surrounded by families with scrabbling children, and retired couples sailing into old age together, she had felt as conspicuous as a pyramid – and that was very lonely. Resorts were the safer option, but travelling alone, she hoped, would be more stimulating. It was certainly harder. In Marrakech, she had been so nervous and vigilant, she had despaired of ever daring to leave home again, but now, in Essaouira, with every shopkeeper who did *not* entreat her to come inside, she was relaxing, step by step, especially with this sense of a benign presence, somewhere behind her, tagging along.

She was determined to get the hang of this travelling-solo lark. There was a lot to be said for it. For one thing, it was sort of thrilling that no one knew exactly where she was, and for the first time in ages, nobody was looking for her or at her. She could explore without having to keep track of someone else in the crowd, without having to stop and browse where she didn't want to. Besides, being solitary, for her, was a kind of gesture. An act of love. If she had to make her way through the rest of her life on her own, like this, then it was because her love for Aidan had been so successful that she would never be able to replace him. Therefore she would be solitary with grace.

The medina of Essaouira, was a criss-cross of alleyways and passages, lined with narrow shops wearing their stock draped round their doors like women in shawls – beads, leathers, textiles, and lots of Moroccan slippers hanging like so many pairs of earrings. There was food too, and the real joy of the place was that there were more locals doing their household shopping than tourists buying trinkets.

Marina had her own trinkets to buy. Jacquie had given her a long shopping list, so she stopped outside a shoe shop to look at the leather slippers and clogs, in red and yellow, orange and blue, then went inside. When she asked to try a pair, the shopkeeper sat her on a stool, took off her sandal and placed her foot in a pointed yellow slipper.

'*Combien?*' she asked.

'*Mille euro!*'

A tourist who had strayed in smiled along with them.

'For that price,' Marina said in French, 'they should be encrusted with diamonds.'

The owner played his part: business had been slow that day, he said, so he would make a special price just for her. She held up her foot, and glanced inadvertently at the other customer.

'Very becoming,' he said quickly. 'I bought some for my mother. You can't leave Morocco without a pair of *baboushes*, by all accounts.'

'Oh,' she said, hearing a trace of her own accent. 'Irish?'

'Yes.'

'Me too.'

'Really?' He put his hands in his pockets. 'There aren't many of us round these parts.'

'No,' she said, 'most seem to go to Agadir. That's why I'm here, to be honest.'

'Oh. Should I leave?'

'Sorry?' Marina put on the other slipper.

'If you're avoiding the Irish . . .'

'Oh, God, no . . . I mean . . . I don't know what I mean.'

'I think I do,' he said, as awkwardly as if he had asked her for a date.

When Marina turned back, he had gone.

She bought the slippers and moved on, leaving the main drag to follow a narrow side-street, draped with carpets and rugs, that took her right and left. It was like walking through a blood-orange tunnel. On a corner, she came across a broad, cave-like shop. It wasn't packed tight with goods, like other places, but was cool and dim, with Tuareg and Berber crafts hanging on the walls. The owner was wearing the indigo Tuareg headscarf and a light blue kaftan, but it was his shiny eyes that made Marina go in. They twinkled warmly as he welcomed her, but then he stepped outside to chat to friends, leaving her to browse alone. Or even steal. She could have done either.

It was a smart tactic. Half on hour later, she was still there, kneeling on rugs at the back of the L-shaped shop. When the owner, Hamid, had strolled back in and heard that she was looking for jewellery, he had emptied coffers and chests of silver on to the floor, then opened boxes full of rings, and finally untied handkerchiefs to reveal a jumble of bracelets. Alternating between French and English, he told her about his home in the desert, near the Algerian border, and took out a photo album full of tantalizing shots of high sand dunes, oases, camels and tents. 'You should go,' he said. 'My family will look after you, take you round the desert a little bit.'

Marina was tempted. She wanted to test herself, get out of her comfort zone, do some of the things she and Aidan had long ago intended to do. 'I'll think about it.'

'*Wa-ha*,' he said, smiling. 'That means "okay". You like tea, yes?'

'Thank you. That would be lovely.'

He stepped over the jewellery spilt out across the rugs and went to make tea by the door. One particular necklace caught her attention – it was heavy, therefore expensive, but Marina had to try it. When she stood up to look in a mirror, she was startled to see the Irishman behind her.

She turned.

'Also very becoming,' he said. 'Rather more so than the slippers, in fact.' He had very deep-set eyes.

She looked again in the mirror, pulling back the collar of her blouse. 'Yeah, but it's going to be expensive,' she said casually, as if she knew him, fingering the long silver driblets that spread from her collarbone like splashed raindrops.

With an awkward smile, he turned his attention to an Arabic scroll on the wall.

Marina took off the necklace, acutely conscious of the man behind her, who, though slim and retiring, had the presence of a mammoth. She felt she should speak to him, make conversation as he had been trying to do, but no social nicety insisted that one should speak to another drifting customer when you coincided in the same place, even if you both happened to be Irish.

And yet he continued to make the effort. 'Are you, um, enjoying Morocco?'

'So far,' she said, hunkering back down among the silver. 'I've always wanted to come, but people kept telling me not to travel on my own, so . . .'

Well, that was really, really stupid, she thought. Why did she have to go and say that? Now he knew she was alone and would either come after her like a pest or – *worse* – think she was trying to chat him up. That was why she still wore her wedding and engagement rings – not that she had any intention of ever removing them. They were handy at times like these, when her mouth had severed contact with her brain. As her sentence withered into nothing, he turned away once again.

With perfect timing, Hamid stepped between them, over his treasure trove of goods, with a tray, three glasses and a small cream teapot. He poured an inch of tea to taste the brew, and then, deeming it ready, lifted the pot up and down as he poured them both a glass.

'Thank you,' said Marina, taking one and fingering more rings.

'Lovely, thank you.' The other customer sat near her on a pouffe. He might have been younger than her – early to mid-forties, perhaps, but then men aged better so there was no telling. They chatted with Hamid about the excellent tea

– not mint, like everywhere else, but a special Berber brew, and when Marina asked him how much the necklace would cost, he stood up to weigh it.

'Seven thousand dirhams,' he said, 'but I make you good price, all together.'

The Irishman removed himself tactfully from negotiations and feigned interest in some slim daggers on the wall.

'Sorry,' Marina said quietly to Hamid, 'that's beyond me, especially with so many other things, like that chair.' She pointed to a low African seat made of interlocked chunks of timber. 'Would you be able to ship that to Ireland? Because if I don't have to lug it home, I'd really love to get it for a friend who has a shop very like this.'

'Of course.' He made some calculations and told her what it would cost to ship.

'Oh, that's bearable. Great, I'll take it. Along with, umm, the six rings, four bracelets, these necklaces and six scarves.' Seeing the other guy glance over his shoulder at her stash, she laughed nervously. 'I have a large family.'

After putting the items into individual bags, Hamid said, 'One minute,' and burrowed in his coffers before pulling out a particular silver ring. Heavy, male. 'For someone special?'

'Oh . . . em, no, thank you.'

'No one special?'

Marina felt cornered. Had she been set up – the tourist behind her, the earnest Hamid in front? 'Just this lot,' she said firmly. 'They're all for someone special – I mean, special someones. There are a lot of special people in my life.'

The transaction complete, she left the shop with a nod at the Irishman, but just outside, to the right of the entrance, she bumped into a waist-high stuffed leather camel and stumbled over it.

'Go,' she heard Hamid say to the tourist.

There was no reply. Hamid spoke again, his voice low, and kind.

'I know,' the Irishman replied, 'I know that.'

Fifteen minutes later, after emerging from a carpet shop, Marina struggled along with a small rug under her arm, plastic bags banging against her calves, and her handbag slipping off her shoulder.

'Here,' an increasingly familiar voice said behind her, 'let me take that.'

The rolled-up mat slid seamlessly from under her arm to under his. 'Oh,' she said, disconcerted. 'Em . . . That's very kind, but are we going the same way?'

'I'm not going in any particular direction. Where are you staying?'

'A *riad* in the ramparts, over towards the beach. Riad Skala.'

'I know the place.' He steered her to the left, but walked on without speaking. Silence between strangers often asks to be broken, but in this instance it didn't seem to matter whether they spoke or not.

'You seem to know your way around,' Marina said, when he led her round another corner. 'Do you live here?'

'No, but I've been here before. You'll get used to this grid set-up pretty quickly.'

'I hope so.'

'When did you arrive?'

'Why?' she asked ruefully. 'Do I look like I stepped off the plane this morning?'

'Did you?'

She smiled. 'The day before yesterday.'

'Ah.'

'I'm Marina, by the way. Marina ffrench.'

He extracted his hand from under the roll. 'Luke Delahunt.'

Even names seemed to be an abstraction.

When they came through a small square, off the beaten track, they passed a café beside the old city wall. Luke hesitated. 'I don't suppose you'd fancy a quick coffee?'

It was kind of him to carry that damn mat, but that was not why Marina said, 'I would.'

She was breaking the rules. Marina's Rules. This one was somewhere in the top ten: *Don't accept the first invitation thrown at you willy-nilly or you'll look desperate*. For two years now she had mentally been composing a guide for single, mature, women on how to holiday alone. She liked to recite it to herself in vulnerable moments. Security, she would tell her imaginary readers, was paramount, of course, but beyond that they should maintain their dignity at all times and, if possible, give off an air of mystique. Accepting coffee from a stranger who offered to carry her carpet did neither.

Yet here she was, and here he was, ordering two coffees in a square below a bell-tower. A thick tree with a gnarled trunk shaded them. They watched the to and fro of locals – women with tightly veiled mouths, draped in great cream blankets; a boy pushing a cartload of firewood; and the man in the shop next door sweeping round the red and orange glass lampshades that were displayed on the pavement. Marina's day had gone well – she was happy with this town, with its sweep of beach, its manageable medina, and her beautiful boutique hotel, but she was still wary, and having coffee with a guy from home was nicer than doing so alone. She was taking advantage of him – doubly so: allowing him to carry her mat *and* using him as a stooge to allow her to relax in a café without fretting about someone trying to pick her up.

Unless, of course, *he* was.

'I'd love a little house in a place like this,' she said, in a chummier tone than she had intended.

'A bolt-hole?' he asked.

'A place of contemplation.'

He nodded.

There was an appealing diffidence about him, almost a lack of confidence, and he wasn't unattractive. Marina swung her eyes over him again. Actually, that was an understatement. He was very attractive: fair hair, pushed back, a good chin, and low eyebrows protecting those piercing eyes (roving around with a baffled expression). She liked good chins, and his clear-cut features wore his reticence – eyes that held back; a straight mouth with a brace of indents; and deep grooves dropping from his cheekbones.

The waiter brought his espresso, but her *café au lait* didn't come, so they sat, pretending not to mind. The shopkeeper next door was now sweeping away a kitten, gently. Every time it found its feet, he gave it another little shove and tossed it over again, with a smile, further confusing it. There were cats everywhere, scrappy things, curled up in corners and on doorsteps, but the locals cared for them, feeding them leftovers and bits of fish.

Luke had finished his coffee and Marina's had still not come. The waiter explained that they'd sent someone to fetch milk. Luke said no problem, but Marina felt awkward. The glut of silence was bearing down on her. 'Where are you from?' she asked.

Luke seemed startled, as if he had forgotten she was there. 'A little place in Tipperary, Skeheenarinky.'

'On the Cork–Dublin road?'

'You know it?'

'I've driven through it. I'm from Cork, but I lived in Dublin for years, so I went past it a lot, and I often wondered if people who came from there liked coming from somewhere with such a wonderful name.'

'I suppose I do. But I've lived in Italy for quite some time now.'

'Oh, wonderful.'

'You like Italy?' he asked.

'Doesn't everybody?'

'Yes,' he said. 'Yes.'

The waiter finally brought her coffee. There was another quiet interlude as Marina drank it, but she no longer felt uncomfortable. 'It's so much easier here than in Marrakech,' she said.

'Oh?'

She grimaced. 'I got myself into a bit of bother. When I went to the *souq* yesterday, I started off in a jewellery shop – my daughter does belly-dancing so I have orders from a whole troupe of women to buy jangly jewellery, but the guy refused to give me prices on anything until I'd decided what I would buy, so I left. And he followed me, haranguing me for walking out of his shop.'

'How unpleasant. That would intimidate *me*.'

'I went into another shop, and another, but came out each time to find him there. I nearly headed straight for the airport.'

'I'm glad you didn't.'

That almost threw her, but she went on, 'Anyway, a teenager rescued me, steered me through those warrens, and brought me to another jeweller's, where they gave me tea and made me sit down until they were sure the bloke had gone. I was pretty glad to get down here last night.'

'I can imagine.'

Beyond that, Luke had little to say. Marina knew she was prattling, confiding too much to a stranger, but she hadn't had a proper conversation in three days and, as she had discovered before, words, when left unspoken, begin to amass, like a crowd waiting to get into a football match: when the turnstiles open, they spew out in disorder. She would have to stem the flow. Her coffee finished, she said, 'That was lovely. I should get on.'

'Let me help with your things.'

They walked to her *riad*. Luke handed over her parcels, she thanked him, they said good evening, and he left.

He knew where she was staying.

Another rule broken: *Never reveal to solo persons of the opposite sex where you're staying.*

New rule: *Do as I say, not as I do.*

Marina had got lucky with the *riad*. Separated women and widows, her book would advise, ideally should travel independently. No charters. On charter holidays, you end up surrounded by the same people on the plane, in the bus, by the pool and everywhere you go. They move about in self-contained bubbles. If they're Irish, every single one will know at least three people you know back home. Far better to take a cheap flight and find little hotels like this one, central and near the beach, where you won't look like a spare toe trying to attach yourself to someone else's foot. Hang out in the neighbourhood. The locals will entertain and mind you, and have nothing to do with Moira O'Hanlon, who knows the sister of the friend of the woman who lived in the flat above you when you were in your first job and had that weird boyfriend.

Marina had once sought out people she knew, but it had been counter-productive. On her first holiday after Aidan had died, she ran into acquaintances from Dublin. She was glad of the company, until she found herself being dragged from one noisy bar to another, nights trailing into the small hours, far from the complex and reliant on them for a lift home. And nothing but hangovers poolside the next day – no one game for a walk or fit for conversation until, in the evenings, with a little fuel, their sociability returned. It happened again, another year, another couple, who bickered and bitched and tried to enlist her in their holiday groans. That was when she'd started writing her Rules: *Never, ever, elbow your way into other people's holidays. You'll never get out again.* And it was at that point she had decided to travel further afield, whatever the difficulties. She hoped she would hold out. Her book would never amount to much if it ended *When all else fails, return to resort.*

The *riad* was not as Moroccan in design as the dreamy place she had stayed at in Marrakech, but it was stylish, her room decorated in taupes and browns. The balcony, which looked on to a courtyard, had a white wall running round it, and Marina was pleased when a cat climbed up, sat on the wall and spent the evening watching her.

The couple who were staying in the next room intrigued her. (Rule Seven: *Man-watch, eavesdrop, snoop. Intrigue is a marvellous companion.*) They were English, and quite young, and there was something endearing about the socks and shorts drying on their balcony. They were like backpackers who had holed up in a nice hotel for a few days' comfort and hot showers. Marina could hear their voices, low and relaxed, and an occasional giggle. It made her wish there was someone in her own room, chatting to her, throwing a towel on the bed and interrupting her reading.

She pulled out a cream dress – she was a tan-and-cream type of person – which was fitted to the hips then broke out in unruly box pleats, and put it on, fussing over the creases, trying to distract herself from the one challenge that no amount of rules or tips ever seemed to make easier: dinner. The evening meal. Marina was tempted to stay in her room with bread and cheese, but there was no point in coming to Morocco if she was going to shy away from it. Besides, she had research to do for her future readers. She couldn't actually think of a single positive thing to say about going out for dinner on your own, every night of a holiday, when everyone else was socializing and bonding with their families, but she pulled a brush through her long, thick curls and headed out, determined to find the up-side.

Along the way she thought she glimpsed Luke, his white shirt zigzagging through the throng ahead, and even though it was unlikely to be him, her step quickened. There were many white shirts on the backs of tourists, but trying to catch up with that particular shirt showed her up as the hopeless solo traveller she really was. Instead of being independent-minded and looking forward to her own company over a nice meal, she was hoping to run into the only person in town she knew.

She chose a restaurant in one of the back-streets, with low seating, knee-high tables and red embroidered tapestries on the wall. All very Moroccan, except for the gap-toothed waiter in a Hawaiian shirt, tight jeans and baseball cap, with stringy wisps of hair sticking out from under its rim. He placed her along the wall beside the open doors, and since the seating faced out, Marina ate her chicken tagine watching the passing nightlife of Essaouira. There seemed to be a lot of ponytails out there – on men; middle-aged, beer-gutted, balding European men, with flaccid little ponytails hanging over their collars like some kind of emblem.

Luke appeared, in a navy shirt, when she was finishing her ice-cream. He caught her eye as he ambled by, hands in his pockets, alone. He stopped, as if trying to remember where he'd last seen her.

'Hello again,' she said, so close to the door that she could speak to him easily. 'Out for an evening constitutional?'

'Yes.' He looked down the street, then back at her. 'How was your, um, meal?'

'Lovely. Thanks for carrying my parcels, by the way. And for the coffee. Would you like to join me for another?' Inwardly, her jaw fell open. Being forward with strangers, especially slightly odd ones, was *not* conducive to personal safety. She might as well tear up the rule book and throw it away.

He stepped in. 'A quick tea,' he said, lowering himself to the stool at the side of her table.

The waiter gestured to her, his hand indicating tea-drinking. She nodded.

'So,' said Luke, 'your first day was a success?'

'A bit bewildering, but I'll feel more grounded tomorrow.'

'Do you always travel alone?'

Nothing like getting to the point.

'Er, no. Um, yes . . . well, I do now.'

'You look like an old hand.'

'Oh, that's practised, I'm afraid. If I looked as nervous as I sometimes feel, I could attract any number of . . .' they could both see where this was taking her '. . . um, kind souls wanting to help me out.'

'I'd imagine Morocco could be quite challenging for a woman on her own.'

'So people kept saying, but it's been absolutely fine. To tell the truth, the hassle factor is worse in Europe because you never know where that might lead. Anyway, I wanted a break from the usual resorts.'

'Yes,' he said, 'same food, same girls in tight clothes, same bodies on the beach lined up like biscuits on a tray.'

'Whereas this place,' Marina glanced out at the street, 'is like a colour-fest. The people, the clothes –'

'The old men.'

'Oh, the men! Their faces are so beautiful. I saw two old

blokes this evening, in the main square, both wearing green kaftans, you know, with the pointed hoods, sitting in a doorway, one in each corner, like mirror images of each other, watching the rest of us go by. They all seem so wise.'

'This must be a good place to be old.'

Marina talked on, loosely, freely. Never the biggest fan of her own company, she was gregarious by nature and liked to be with people, chattering away as she was now. She could see Luke taking everything in. His eyes were moving round her, from her silver-dashed hair, to her dangling white earrings, even to her mouth. It made her self-conscious. Was her lipstick subtle? Her dress flattering?

But he wasn't as preoccupied with her appearance as she fancied. He peered at his watch.

It annoyed her. 'Don't let me keep you,' she said tartly.

'I'm sorry, I do have to go, but it was lovely seeing you again.' He stood up, hesitated, said goodnight, and hurried off. He clearly had somewhere else to be.

Or someone else to be with.

Marina did not sleep well. 'The heat,' she kept whispering to herself, even though the cool sea breeze in Essaouira made it very bearable.

At night, optimism and courage always abandoned her, giving way to homesickness and a terrible sense of distance. She felt so far from her daughter and son, her bed, her mug, the smell of Ireland, that anxiety kicked in during the dark hours and sleep eluded her as she fretted over getting sick with no one to help, or even dying and nobody knowing. But here at least she could hear the sea, rumbling, purring beyond the ramparts, soothing and distracting her. Luke came in and out of her head in flushes, like an actor rushing on stage off-cue and jumping back into the wings. It made her blush to think of the things she'd said, her easy friendliness. It might have been misinterpreted as flirtatious, yet there was something safe about him, and compelling. She hoped she'd see him again.

In the early hours, the gulls began to squawk overhead, screeching like someone being strangled, which helped her to fall asleep, and when she got up later, she rejected the excellent hotel breakfast and managed to find her way back to Luke's café. She couldn't seem to stop herself, and wasn't in the least surprised to find him there, as if he was waiting for her.

'You haven't had breakfast, I hope?' he asked, standing to greet her.

'No. Just a cup of tea with my cat.'

He looked at her quizzically. 'You brought your cat on holiday?'

'No, no, he's a local and he sits on the balcony, staring in at me.'

'That's nice.'

'Yes, I must say I quite enjoy the . . .' Company? God, no. 'The, em, attention.'

'I meant for him. Nice for him.'

The waiter brought breakfast – two breakfasts. Olives, honey, Moroccan pancakes, croissants and butter were packed on to the tiny table. Marina looked at Luke. How had he known she would come?

'Did you sleep okay?' she asked, immediately regretting it. The question was slightly inappropriate, a little too personal. She'd sounded almost like a wife speaking groggily to her husband before they crawled out of bed.

'Not great. You?'

'I tossed and turned well into the small hours.' Marina blinked. He didn't need to know this! What had happened to distance and reserve? Her mystique, if she'd ever had any, had left home.

Luke looked off to the side, his fingers covering a smile, as if aware that she kept surprising herself. 'Too much mint tea, perhaps.'

She smiled.

He blinked, as if dazzled.

'Perhaps,' she said.

He was deeply, provocatively attractive, she realized with some relief. Thank God, she thought, there were still some men of her own vintage about who didn't sport ponytails and have T-shirts straining across their bellies. In fact, he dressed rather well, but it would probably be impossible to breach that diffidence. Women, many women, Marina was sure, must have thrown themselves at him, only to be forced to withdraw wounded, leaving him untouched. She guessed he was separated.

As if reading her mind, he said, 'So, you have a large family.'

'No,' she said, perplexed. 'Just three of us.'

'Ah. It's just you said . . . when you were buying all those gifts . . .'

'Oh, that was because of you. Didn't know what I was saying.' *Still don't, evidently*. Forget writing a book about this, she thought, with a hopeless sigh. She needed an entire film crew to follow her around, picking up her every gaffe and clumsy patois, for a television series entitled *How to Come Across as Needy, Pathetic and Desperate for a Man when Holidaying Alone*.'

'Yes, I'm sorry about that,' he said quickly. 'I'd been following you.'

Marina dipped a scrap of pancake into the honey. 'Oh?'

'I was right behind you when you were in the market, but I couldn't think what to say. I'm not very good at openers.'

Two whole sentences without a pause. 'You do all right,' she said.

'Just three of you, then?'

'Two children. Girl and a boy.'

His eyes fell to her wedding ring.

She liked the subtlety, the way he asked without asking. 'Widowed,' she said. 'Nearly four years ago.'

'I'm very sorry. Well, I'm sort of sorry.' He smiled for the first time.

She returned it. 'You?'

He made a low swoop with his hand – a gesture of dismissal. 'The usual amalgam: an ex-wife, some ex-partners, some kids.'

'Some?'

'Two boys. With my wife. I . . .' he sighed '. . . tend to accumulate people.'

This was something of a non-sequitur, but if it was meant as a warning, it served only to reel in Marina. 'Are they grown, your children?'

'Yes,' he said. 'We had them fairly young.'

'Me too. My eldest is nearly twenty-four.'

'Mine is twenty-seven!'

She laughed. 'What *were* we thinking?'

'Ah, but it pays off,' he said, 'at this end.'

'Maybe so, but at *that* end we gave ourselves no breathing space. An immediate family was not on the agenda when we got married.'

'Is that what happened?'

'On our wedding night,' she admitted, rolling her eyes. 'Or as good as. We were actually on a plane on our wedding night.' She popped some pancake into her mouth. 'Umm,' she said, chewing, 'we were both teachers, and we intended to explore one continent every summer, then start a family in our late twenties. We thought that was a pretty good plan.'

'Sounds like it.'

'Hmm, until we went to Nepal on our shoestring budget and found ourselves sharing a dormitory in a fleapit of a hostel in Kathmandu. The next night Aidan had food-poisoning. The third night, he wasn't much better. On the fourth, I pointed out that I could have our marriage annulled in view of the fact that . . .'

'Yes.'

She was on a roll now. 'That swiftly improved his health, so we checked into a more upmarket fleapit, where at least we had privacy, but then I got sick, which undermined . . .' This was getting way too personal, but there was no going back.

'Your precautions?' Luke said helpfully.

'Cue one daughter nine months later.'

He chuckled.

'It isn't funny,' she said, smiling. 'I mean, Jacquie was a delight, but I was barely twenty-three and all our plans got swallowed up. What's your excuse?'

'Yes, well,' he said, 'we were only twenty-two, but my wife couldn't entertain the idea of, um, precautions, being a devout Catholic. Still, we did well on it. My elder son lives near me in northern Italy, and his brother is volunteering for Oxfam in Peru. We don't see much of him.' He bit into an olive. 'Are both your children in Cork with you?'

It was as if he was determined to get the nuts and bolts out of the way, making sure neither of them had partners, small children or other dependants hanging out of them. She nodded. 'Dara's going into second year at UCC, and Jacquie's just starting a new job. This is her first week, actually.'

'Do you still teach?'

'Not full-time. I give French grinds to Leaving Cert students at home in the evenings. No colleagues or social life, but the money's okay.'

'I can imagine. Yes.'

Marina smiled at him. 'You use that word a lot. Yes.'

'It's a good word. Yoko Ono and John Lennon fell in love over that word.'

Across the way, a man was hanging his selection of carpets on the flaky pink town wall. Then he climbed up a ladder and hung a few more outside his shop. They watched him as they enjoyed their breakfast. Luke was fastidious, particular in how he addressed himself to tearing up the pancake, folding it, dipping it and popping it into his mouth without a drip of honey falling astray. He stirred his coffee like an Italian, as though he was stirring his thoughts, which somehow endeared him to her. They might have been having breakfast together for years, so familiar seemed each of these peculiarities.

There was no skirting it: she was attracted to him. Had been, she supposed, from the moment she had turned in Hamid's shop and seen his sunlit frame hovering behind her, like a partner waiting for her, as though they already had a life together somewhere else.

'You're very concerned about her,' Luke said, out of the blue.

'Who?'

'Your daughter.'

'Am I?'

'I think so.'

He was right. Marina felt guilty about coming away, just then, when Jacquie was starting her new job. 'She's had a few bumpy years,' she admitted, 'and is trying to settle in Cork without, so far, much success.'

'Settle in? Has she been away?'

'We all have. We lived in France until last year, and she had a boyfriend there. For, oh, four years or more, it was a very intense love affair. I couldn't quite understand it. I mean, why settle for such concentrated monogamy so young? But they were good together and he was very supportive when my husband was ill.

After she finished school – the kids boarded in Ireland – she took a year off to be with us in France, which was lovely for me, but it meant she burrowed deep into the relationship, as if she was hiding in it. Even when she went off to university in Dublin, they managed to keep it going. Obstinate, if you ask me. They gave each other a degree of freedom during term-time, but she didn't take advantage of it and never really got into college life, because she always had one eye on getting back to France to live with Didier, which she duly did. Of course, not long after they moved to Paris, it floundered.'

'Was she heartbroken?'

'Devastated, I'd say. She put on a brave face, but he hurt her very deeply, and it can't have been easy, either, coming home to live with Mum and starting from scratch somewhere new. She spent most of this year looking for work in Cork, so it's been a tough transition, and because of that long relationship, she has yet to make a life for herself. A life of her own – you know? It's all been about Didier since she was eighteen. I'd love to see her enjoying herself for a bit.'

Luke was, again, looking at his watch. He tried to do it discreetly, which made it worse, but with the sun beating down he had to squint to see the time. Marina was irritated, until he said, 'I was thinking that perhaps we could meet for lunch. A late lunch, if that suits you.'

Although that was exactly what she wanted, she dithered. She had yet to abide by a single one of her rules. What with Luke and the cat, she had hardly spent a moment alone since arriving. What kind of role model was she for single women of a certain age?

Her hesitation didn't spur him to say quickly, 'Oh, never mind, nice to see you, 'bye.' Instead he offered a protracted silence, his eyes lowered.

'I suppose . . . em, yes, that would be lovely,' she said.



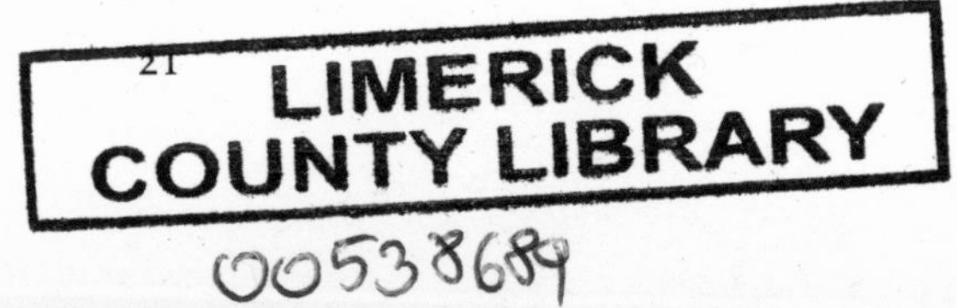
LIMERICK
COUNTY LIBRARY
00538689

'There's a place in the square, Taros. Blue and white building, with terraces on lots of levels going way up. Shall we meet on the top terrace at, say, two?'

'Okay.'

He stood up, saying, 'See you later, then,' and skittered off. Wherever he was going, he was late.

Good, she thought.

Odd, the way he kept taking off. And not what she expected, or wanted. It would have been so pleasant if he had stayed with her: they might have gone exploring together. But this was hopeless. Before she had run into this strange man, she'd been determined to manage alone. She must not become immediately reliant on someone else.

Even if he was good-looking.

Well-dressed.

Mannerly.

Soft-spoken.

Mysterious.

And gone.

Marina headed for the beach. On the promenade, a group of young people were standing in a circle singing and dancing. One drum, one tambourine, many hands clapping and the beat resounding up and down the shore. Pity, she thought, that our teenagers can't do that, just stand on a corner and get so much out of one small drum. She took off her sandals and walked by the sea. It was windy and bright. The old part of Essaouira, the low white medina surrounded by dusty pink walls, formed a hook at the end of the bay, where a fort rose out of the port. It looked like a sandcastle, especially with all the Moroccan flags sticking out of its towers.

A young local couple were paddling together. The girl put her arm on her husband's waist to steady herself and smiled at the water gurgling round her feet. Easy love, Marina thought, with a dash of regret. Easy love, as she might never have again.

She missed Jacquie, but it was just as well the new job had prevented her daughter coming, because if she'd been let loose in the medina, they would have needed a cargo ship to bring the stuff home. By quirk of telepathy, Marina's phone went off. 'Hello, sweetie.'

'Hi, Mum. How's . . . Jesus, how *do* you pronounce that word?'

'Essa-weir-ah. It's glorious. I love it. Much calmer than Marrakech, and the *riad* is divine – but listen, how's work?'

'A bit dull, to be honest. I'm out for lunch. It's a big open-plan office, with everyone sitting in front of screens. All I've done so far is send emails. I can't imagine that it's ever going to be riveting work. In fact, I can't quite remember how I ended up in the pharmaceutical industry.'

'Because you need the cash, remember? And it's a stop-gap to stop the gap on your CV.'

'Yeah, don't rub it in.'

'How's Dara behaving?'

'He's being good. Filling the dishwasher and everything. So you're *really* having a good time?'

'*Really* I am.' The nature of their lives these last few years had turned Jacquie into a worry-bug. 'In fact, I'm tempted to go out to the desert for a few days.'

'Cool! Wish I'd been able to come.'

'Me too.'

'But . . . you're not too lonely, are you?'

'Not a bit of it. Besides, I have company.'

'*Really?*'

'Yes, and he's *very* interested in me.'

'A he? What?'

'He's a bit scrawny, mind. Well, *very* scrawny and his eyes are gummy –'

'Eugh!'

'And he climbs up to my balcony, perches on the wall and peers in at me.'

'Mum! Sounds like a pervert!'

'Yeah. A perverted *cat*.'

Back in the *riad*, Marina showered and lay on her bed. She tried to be still, but her head was spinning. She was unprepared. Totally. Something was rising in her: not just attraction, but desire. It was like bumping into an old, lost friend on the street and hearing them say, 'Oh, my God, it's you! I thought I'd never see you again.'

Years before, coming away from grief and leaving it, like a mop outside the door, she had gone through a stage of wistfulness and longing. Soon afterwards, she went through another stage, more desperate, less wistful. It was a kind of panic – she was in her mid-forties and her life as a companion, as a sexual, romantic being, appeared to be over when she still had a long way to go. It wasn't that she needed a man – she had learnt that she could do perfecting well without – but she wanted one. She knew the joy of sharing, of companionship, and, fearing that each extra year would dim her chances of finding a mate, she fancied every decent-looking man she came across and got nowhere with any of them.

Fantasy had to fill in the gaps of longing: Al Pacino in a dark street; Liam Neeson on a yacht, for some reason; and she once imagined herself seducing Bob Dylan on the off-chance she might somehow suck those luscious words from his mouth. She had never been so consistently preoccupied with sex – not since her teenage years, anyway – and even though it was frustrating and fruitless, it was also, for a short while, invigorating. It cleared her mind of all those thoughts of illness and dying, of hopelessness and being alone, and when, finally, she passed beyond it, she arrived on the other side, where the loneliness was bearable and the hope contained. The longing for someone, *any*one, had gone away, unresolved and unsatisfied.

Marina mourned it, felt old and unattractive, but that, too, passed, and made way for the worst stage of all: resignation. The business of finding someone compatible, attractive, and attracted in return, was too hit-and-miss, altogether too difficult, so she had concentrated instead on the business of being alone. One successful love affair carried through to its natural (if premature) end was more of a privilege than many people enjoyed in a lifetime. Best not to be greedy in hoping for another. She would have admirers, no doubt, maybe even the occasional lover, but it seemed unlikely that she would again achieve that rare and extraordinary double: falling in love with someone who falls in love with you.

Now, just when she was about to graduate in the art of widowhood, she'd met a real flesh-and-blood man, a strange sort of stranger, who was making bits of her come back to life, and she hadn't a clue what to do about it.

She was tempted to call Suzanne, but reconsidered. Best not to overwork this. Far better to consult the cat.

'I think I've inadvertently picked up a man,' she told it quietly.

The cat closed its eyes, enjoying the sound of her voice.

'The thing is – is this lunch an actual date? Is that what I'm doing? Going on a date?'

It turned its head slightly to the side, as if to say, 'Apparently so.'

She had to wonder, though. Was Luke courting her or being friendly? He didn't exactly hang around for very long or even put much energy into entertaining her, but it wasn't so very unlikely that he might be interested. She remembered how, unabashed, he had admitted to envying the cat and being glad she was widowed . . . That seemed pretty incontrovertible.

So, if he was interested, she had to establish how she would handle it. What were the boundaries? Would she sleep with him? Was that, in fact, what he wanted from her? Was that, in fact, what she wanted from him? He lived in Italy. He'd be absolutely no good to her in the real world. Maybe that was the attraction. Maybe, she thought, I'm like those middle-aged women who go to the Gambia looking for boys on the beach.

Through narrowed eyes, the cat smiled. She scratched it between its ears.

There were such risks. She didn't know where he'd been, or with whom, or how he lived his life. It wasn't something you could bring up over lunch: 'So, do you, like, sleep around a lot?' And there was the more substantial risk to consider: that of becoming involved with someone she knew very little about, and finding at the end of it, when she returned home, that her heart ached and pulled at her. Then she would have to face the chore of getting over it. Alone.

What the hell. A rush of giddiness made her pump her fists. 'I'm going to go for it, pussycat!'

'Aw, isn't he lovely?' said a voice behind them.

Alarmed, the cat opened its eyes.

The young woman from the next room was standing at her own door, beaming.

'Oh, hello,' said Marina. Caught, totally and utterly caught, talking to a cat. 'I'm just,' she said quickly, 'having a word with the cat.'

'I know. He's ever such a good listener, isn't he?'

*Oh, God.* She'd heard.

Her neighbour had long dark hair, tied back, and a round, happy face. 'Isn't this strange? I was sitting near you this morning when you were having coffee with your husband near the bell-tower and here we are, neighbours.'

'Oh, he isn't my husband.'

The girl wrinkled her nose, nodding sagely. 'I thought he probably wasn't. Cute, though.'

Marina bit the side of her lip. 'Yes, you could say that.'

'And nothing like a bit of romance on holiday, I always say.'

'Oh, no, no, no, not at all. Nothing like that.'

The young woman glanced at the low wall. 'That's not what you were telling the cat.'

Only one of the many questions that were rolling over in her head was answered when she emerged breathless at the rooftop restaurant. All doubts about her own feelings were wiped out the moment she saw Luke. Her belly did a magnificent loop. She put her hand to it. It had been so long, yet the feeling was so familiar. And so *welcome*. Help, she thought, as she walked towards him, but a smile took her lips and her hands began to shake, and a few years fell off her.

He was sitting by the railing on the part of the vast and multi-layered terrace that gave directly on to the square, a straw parasol shading him. He looked bashful even while reading the menu that lay flat on the table. How such a reticent man had ever found the courage to invite her to lunch was baffling.

He stood up as she joined him, saying. 'I was just thinking how very much you would enjoy Lake Orta.'

Marina sat down, putting her bag on the ground. Of course she would enjoy Lake Orta, wherever the hell it was, but how could he presume to know this, or anything, about her?

And yet it wasn't presumption. He had an understanding of her, just as, somehow, she had an understanding of him.

'There's an island,' he went on, 'in the lake. You can see it from our place. There's rather an austere monastery over there, but in the mornings it catches the sun and glows on the water, and in the evenings . . .'

Marina was scarcely listening. He had a narrow mouth, and a slight smile that was powerful and positive. It spread across his face in creases and made his eyes brighten – those dark green eyes that seemed to be sucking in every thought in her head. He was no longer as monosyllabic as he had been. Nor was he afraid to seduce her. He did it every time his eyes stalled, got hooked on hers, not so much undressing her as telling her. She wasn't quite sure what exactly he was telling her, but she knew what she heard.

Yes, she thought, she would go to Lake Orta, though he had not, in so many words, asked her, and yes, she would be his lover there.

He rubbed his collarbone through his shirt. Marina wanted to do that for him. 'How did you come to live in Italy?' she asked, after they had ordered.

'By default.'

Enough of these two-word replies. A blank look provoked him to expand.

'A mad aunt,' he said, 'who married an Italian with a large house.'

He stopped again. Marina dipped her chin and almost made a face: *don't test me*.

'A house that,' he struggled on, 'when he died, she was completely unable to manage, financially or otherwise, so she roped me in to help. We sold off the upper floors, leaving her the ground and first floors to live in.'

'And you decided to stay on?'

'I married an Italian,' he said, 'but we lived in London until, um, we separated and my wife returned to Italy.'

'With your kids?'

'Yes. I followed as soon as I could. I wanted to be near

the boys and my mother was living with my aunt by then, so when the grand old dame died twelve years ago, she left what remained of the villa to my mother and me, which gave me an opportunity to make a living in Italy. I took a substantial risk and started buying back the apartments. The long-term tenants are now gone, and we've renovated the flats and turned them into holiday lets. It's quite profitable. All you need is a website, good-quality accommodation, and the bookings flood in.'

'Is that what you do?'

'In my spare time. Mostly I work with an *immobiliare* – estate agency – managing and selling properties.'

'Oh, you're an auctioneer?'

'Not by training, no. I have a law degree somewhere under my belt, which comes in handy, but I ended up in this line of work because of the villa and what I learnt managing it for my aunt.'

'How is somebody like you involved in property?' she teased.

'Oh . . . well . . . why not?'

'Property tycoons are tough and mean, aren't they?'

'I'm no tycoon, and I'm not mean.'

'That's for sure.' She laughed. 'I'd have had you for an academic or a poet. Something bookish. Anything but business, anyway.'

'I like poetry,' he said. 'I like reading a lovely poem, but I enjoy looking at lovely buildings more.' He glanced at the great sweep of beach beyond the ramparts. 'Morocco would be an interesting investment. They say it'll be the new Spain for Europeans, but . . .'

'But?'

'With global warming taking effect, this area could well become too dry in years to come and as northern Europe heats up, people will be less inclined to come south during the winter. On the other hand, some say that higher temperatures will prolong the tourist season in places like this.'

From where she sat, Marina could see a wind farm across the bay on a headland, hazy in the distance, its many windmills turning at a leisurely pace. 'Maybe you should invest in Ireland. They say we'll be growing vines in a year or two.'

'I'd love to, but it's expensive.' The waiter brought their meals – sardines for Luke, langoustines for Marina. 'I've no firm connection to Ireland any more,' he said, thoughtfully. 'I wish I had.'

'No family there?'

'I'm an only child. My father died when I was a year old. My mother's sister-in-law still lives in Skeheenarinky, but that's it. Shame, really. My sons have hardly any relationship with Ireland. We're terribly cut off from the place.'

'That's the way I felt when we were living in France, worried that we'd never get back home, especially when house prices started to rocket.'

'You didn't like France?'

'It was ok, but it was really Aidan's thing, having a go in rural France. And he loved it, so I'm glad we did it, because he got to live out the fantasy. But I always missed home, especially when the kids went off to school, and after Aidan died, I just couldn't contemplate getting old there, in someone else's dream.'

'Was he teaching in France?'

'No, he wrote textbooks. He had been a secondary-school teacher in Dublin, like me, but when the kids were small, he worked very hard during the summers on this idea he had for a revision book for Leaving Cert French. When it was finally published, it did really well, and the publishers asked Aidan to do another one for history, his other subject. So that was our chance to try something different. We moved to near Toulouse, where he wrote, and I taught English.'

They chatted on. Luke was more forthcoming than he had been – he did not always speak in monosyllables – until, having paid the bill, he put his wallet into his back pocket and said, 'I'm afraid I must go.'

Marina gritted her teeth – at least he hadn't looked at his watch – but then she smiled and waited. Dinner, surely. Breakfast and lunch were all very well, but should they not progress to the more sultry part of the day and its attendant possibilities?

'See you tomorrow?' he asked.

To hell with that, Marina thought. She didn't have days to mess around with. 'Actually,' she said, bolder than she had ever been but determined to test him, 'what about this evening? A walk and some dinner?'

It seemed to pain him to say, 'I'm sorry. That won't be possible.'

'Never mind.'

She watched him go, weaving through the tables and disappearing down the stairwell.

## 2

That evening, Luke was wandering the streets again, searching, when a voice called him. Hamid beckoned him into his shop and insisted that he sat down while he made tea. They sat together in the dim light.

'And the lady?' Hamid asked.

Luke sighed. 'A little more time, I think.'

'It has been a long time already.'

'A few days only.'

'More than few days,' said Hamid. 'Long, long time.' He waved his hand over his shoulder, behind him.

Luke frowned. 'How do you know that?'

'I will ask God this,' Hamid chortled, 'when I get to Paradise. I will ask God how I know such things!'

# 3

The phone rang as Jacquie was squeezing lemon juice into her green tea. She wasn't going to answer. It was late, her hot-water bottle was under her arm and, on this wet and miserable night, she was set for bed. A quick glance at the screen to make sure it wasn't her mother revealed an 001 number. America? Who would be calling from the States? Curiosity got the better of her. She lifted the phone, took her glass of tea and headed for the stairs. 'Hello?'

'Uh . . . hello?' A low, male voice.

'Yes?'

'Is that, ah, would that be the Enright household?'

'Used to be.'

'Right, never mind,' he said, 'it was a long shot, anyway. Sorry for disturbing you.'

'Who were you looking for?'

'Marina Enright. I'm an old friend and I've sort of lost track of her . . .'

'This is her number,' said Jacquie.

'Oh. Wow. She still lives there? That's great. Could I, ah, have a word with her?'

'I'm afraid she isn't here.'

'When do you expect her back?'

'Not for a few days. She's away.'

She heard him mutter, 'Damn.'

Jacquie didn't recognize the voice. Irish, though, with slight American intonation.

'That's, ahm, that's a real . . . shame.' He sounded more concerned than disappointed.

'I could take a message?' she suggested.

'Yeah, that would . . . ahm . . . No. That won't work. Look, who am I speaking with?'

'This is her daughter, Jacquie.'

He didn't say anything. The line could almost have gone dead.

'Hello?'

'I'm here. Jacquie, listen, this is Matthew McGonagle speaking. Your mom and I go way back.'

Jacquie's eyes widened. *Really? The* Matthew? The gorgeous tall one in the photos?

'And the thing is, I'm calling from Anchorage in the States, and I've got a problem. Do you . . . I wonder if your father might be there.'

Jacquie was at the door of her room. The hot-water bottle was too hot against her side and the glass was hot to hold. She felt affronted. How dare he say it like that, and not know, and phone like this, forcing her to say, as she had to, to a stranger at long distance, 'Dad died'?

A regretful gurgle bounced off the satellite. 'God, I'm so sorry,' he said. 'I hadn't heard. I'm really . . . that's really . . . I'm sorry to hear that.'

A pause. Come on, she thought. Get right out with it.

So he got right out with it. 'Jacquie, I need a favour. Urgently.'

She lifted her elbow to let the bottle drop on to her bed. Why had she picked up this damn call? 'A favour?'

'Dara? Where are you?'

'In the pub with the lads. Why?'

'Have you been drinking?'

'That's usually what people do in pubs.'

'Shit.'

'What's up?'

'I've just had this weird call from America. One of Mum's friends – remember that Matthew guy?'

'Hang on. Can't hear you.' Jacquie heard him step outside. 'Matthew who?'

'McGonagle.'

'Name doesn't ring a bell,' said Dara. 'What's he look like?'

'How would I know? We've never met him. Mum mutters about him sometimes.'

'Ohhhhh,' said Dara. 'You mean the guy who pissed off?'

'Yeah, him, and guess what – his daughter is stuck up in Cashel with no money and he wants us to go and get her. She was hitching from Dublin and got stranded at a petrol station. I was going to ring Mum, but there's not much she can do, and if you can't drive I'll have to go – in this bloody weather.'

'Christ.'

'I'm not even sure Mum would want us to do anything,' Jacquie went on. 'They fell out pretty badly.'

'So why'd he call *us*?'

'I don't think he had much option. He hasn't lived here for years, so maybe he doesn't know anyone else.'

'All the same – Cashel. Not exactly next door.'

'Maybe I should tell her to check into a bed-and-breakfast and I'll go for her in the morning.'

'Yeah, but, like, it's a bit late to be wandering around searching for a B-and-B, isn't it? What age is she?'

'No idea. And do I care? Not really. I mean, it isn't really my problem, is it?'

'It sort of is now,' said Dara. 'We can't leave her there. She might be attacked or God knows what.'

'*We* can't leave her there? You mean *I* can't. Feck it, Dara,

I'm not driving to bloody Cashel at midnight! It's wet and windy and I'm ready for bed.'

'Fine. Do what you want. All I'm saying is, you might land Mum in it if you leave the girl stranded. I mean, if something happened to her, like, it'd be pretty awkward.'

Jacquie bit her thumb nail.

'And if it was you out on a highway with no money,' Dara went on, 'I'll bet this guy, whoever he is, wouldn't just leave you there.'

'We don't know that. He and Mum are on really bad terms.'

'Yeah, so he's desperate. What'd he sound like?'

'He was very nice about it, to be fair. All apologetic and grovelling and . . . Oh, God, I'll have to go and get her, won't I?'

'Seems like it.'

'Will you be home later?'

'Probably not. Can't drive. I'll stay at Tom's.'

'*Ex*cellent.'

'My brother's had a few,' Jacquie told Matthew, when she called him back, 'so it looks like I'll have to go.'

'Jacquie, that would be fantastic. I'm real sorry to ask, but she sounded a bit panicky, and one of the lads she's with isn't too well –'

'She's with someone?'

'A couple of friends, I think.'

Jacquie sighed. If she was with friends, she wasn't going to be attacked, but it was too late to back out. 'Where are they exactly?'

'On the Dublin side of Cashel, a gas station on the left-hand side coming out of town. She's got wavy auburn hair, and she's slim and –'

'Yeah, I don't think it'll be that hard to pick her out.'

*

It was truly a filthy, black night, and it was going to be a long one. Rain pounded the windscreen and gusts kept throwing the car sideways. Leaves hurled round it, getting caught in the wipers. Cashel was two hours away, at Jacquie's speed. Every now and then, lorries came up behind her and nearly blew her off the road when overtaking, making her small car shudder and slide into the hard shoulder. She gripped the steering-wheel, leaning towards the windscreen as if that would make visibility any better. At times the rain was so heavy she could see only a few feet ahead and had to slow to a crawl, but she drove faster than usual, feeling sorry for this woman, any woman, stuck in such a downpour.

She saw the trio as she drove on to the forecourt of the petrol station. They were huddling outside the closed shop, sitting on luggage. Two stood up. This was no woman, Jacquie realized, as she pulled in. Kitt was a teenager.

'You're Jacquie, right?' she said, when Jacquie got out of the car.

'Yeah – Kitt?'

'At last!'

'Are we ever glad to see you,' said the guy, who looked about twenty.

The other was hunched on his rucksack, but he got to his feet and they loaded their stuff. As he leant over to get into the back of the car, Jacquie caught his eye. He was all black – black hair, eyeliner, clothes. 'Hi,' he said. 'I'm David. That's Bill.'

'Hi.'

Kitt got into the front seat and turned up the heating. She was shivering. 'I thought Dad said you lived near here. We'll have got hypothermia waiting,' she grumbled, sounding neither Irish nor American but English.

As she turned back for Cork, Jacquie tried to get a look

at her. 'Wavy auburn hair'? Hardly. Kitt's hair was jet black – dyed, obviously – and straight, and she wasn't particularly slim either. A lorry was bearing down on them. 'Damn.'

'Take your time,' a voice said behind her. 'Don't let him scare you.'

'He's right up my arse. God, I hate this road.'

'You should try sitting on the side of it in the rain,' said Kitt.

The truck hurtled past. 'Phew.'

'Sorry for dragging you out,' said the same voice in the back. 'Shit night for it.'

'Are you from Cork?' Jacquie asked, trying to see him in the mirror.

'Dublin.'

Kitt was so cold, she seemed to be shrinking. 'How did you end up there?' Jacquie asked her.

'We got a lift in a lorry, but he dropped us off. Said we'd have no problem hitching to Cork, but three isn't a great number. And the guys,' she glanced over her shoulder, 'wouldn't leave me there, which was really sweet.'

'You couldn't go to a bed-and-breakfast?'

'No money.'

'You should call your father and tell him I've got you.'

'You can call him when we get there,' the girl muttered.

Jacquie almost said, 'I beg your pardon?' But Kitt was beginning to sound even younger than she looked. 'Where are you going anyway?'

David leant forward. 'Bill and me, we're at college in Cork. CIT. We've been in the States for the summer. Just flew in this morning.'

'Yesterday morning,' said Bill.

'God, yeah, what a fucking long day.'

'And you, Kitt?'

'Oh, I'm just travelling. Decided to come and see where the old man was from.'

Jacquie couldn't resist asking, 'How old are you?'

'Eighteen.'

One of the boys grunted.

'How did you all hook up?'

'Hitching outside the airport,' said Bill.

They'd only just met. Jacquie had picked up two total strangers! Great. The heating was making her sleepy. She turned it down.

'Don't do that!' Kitt said. 'I'm freezing!'

When, finally, they came into the city, Jacquie asked the lads where she should drop them.

'Can't they stay with us?' asked Kitt. 'It's, like, four a.m.'

'The thing is,' said Bill, 'we can't move into our shared house until next week, so we were going to crash on a mate's floor but I haven't been able to get hold of him.'

Jacquie wanted her bed. No point collecting them from the side of the road only to dump them back on it. She headed for home, wishing the house wasn't empty.

Her grandfather's house, now their own, wasn't large but it was rambling. Jacquie let them in through a wooden gate in a high stone wall, then went along the short path to the front door on the left. In the hall there were two white doors, one on the right and one straight ahead, and an archway into another, darker, hall, with a staircase going up and a door leading into the kitchen.

The kitchen was more of a passageway than a room, with counter and cupboards aligned on the left, but this opened into a large room on the right with a long timber table and a stove.

'I suppose you'd like tea or something?' said Jacquie.

'That'd be excellent,' said Bill.

'Is there anything to eat?' Kitt asked. 'I'm famished.'

'You could have toast.' Jacquie put on the kettle and set out bread and butter. Tired and cold, they launched in. They seemed harmless enough, but she silently cursed Dara. Never bloody there when she needed him. 'Look, I want to get to bed. Can I show you where you're sleeping?'

They trooped up the stairs behind her. There were four bedrooms scattered around the first floor and, across a landing and through an annexe, the family room. Jacquie gave Kitt the spare room, then pulled bedding out of the hot press and led the boys up another staircase to the loft rooms, off a tiny landing on the top floor. 'This house is perverse,' said Bill.

'People get lost all the time.'

'Thanks for this,' he said. 'Really appreciate it.'

Downstairs, Kitt was standing outside her room with the duvet cover. 'What am I supposed to do with this?'

'Make the bed. You know, pull it on to the duvet.'

Jacquie went into her mother's room to check the phone. It wasn't blinking, so Matthew had not called again. She brought up the number of the last incoming call, hit redial and, when he answered, told him his daughter was fine, going to bed, and would call him in the morning. He spluttered gratitude, but she was too tired to hear it out and kept the call short. Before she rang off, he said, 'I suppose you'll be in touch with your mother?'

'Tomorrow, yeah.'

'I'd like to give her a call, explain myself a bit. Do you have a number for her?'

Jacquie hesitated. 'I don't have it handy.'

'Never mind,' he said, picking up on her reluctance.

'I'll tell her tomorrow,' said Jacquie, 'but I'm really tired now so . . .'

'Of course.'

Better not tell her mother about this yet, she thought. Marina always sounded slightly tense when she was away. It made Dara and Jacquie feel guilty about not going with her, but their mother always said she had to get used to it because she refused to be a burden to them. This time, though, she didn't sound quite so beleaguered. She'd even been quite chirpy when they'd spoken and Jacquie was not going to spoil it. A midnight dash to Cashel and three strangers in the house wouldn't exactly put Marina at ease. As for the Matthew connection . . . Jacquie was suddenly dead curious to know what the story was. He sounded nice. Careless, but nice. Besides, Kitt and company would be gone the next day; she could tell her mother all about it when she got back from Morocco.

She went across the hall. Kitt was struggling with the duvet and the cover was twisted round her feet. Jacquie took it from her, did it swiftly and threw it over the bed.

David was the first to appear the next morning. He thanked Jacquie again. 'It's okay,' she said. 'At least it was a Friday night so I got to sleep in.'

She showed him tea, coffee, but he didn't seem to know where to put himself, and she didn't know where to put him either. He was seriously hot. She cleared her throat. 'So which part of Dublin are you from?' she asked.

'Howth, but my parents have retired to Portugal.'

'We lived in Rathmines when we were kids,' she said.

'Oh, right. So you're not from Cork?'

'Mum is.' She was curt. Too welcoming and they might settle in. They might think they'd hit on a real opportunity here – big empty house, free accommodation. Jacquie wished her brother would get home and throw his weight around a bit, and sent him a text to that effect.

David was coughing. Jacquie didn't like the look of him . . . That wasn't true. She *loved* the look of him – dark, broody, moody – but he seemed unwell. 'Are you okay?'

'Just a cold,' he said, 'but I'd hate to think what it'd be like if you hadn't come for us last night. I'd probably be dead by now.'

'Don't be silly.' Her eyes kept drifting to him – that dark fringe hanging over his face. Small waist. Long, sinewy arms. He caught her eyeing him and stared right back. Then he came over to her. It was sudden. She stepped away, but bumped into the counter.

'Do you mind?' he said.

'Do *you*?'

'It's just . . .' he turned her head to the side '. . . you have amazing eyes.'

She would have melted there and then and dribbled on to the ground, had he not added, 'I'm a photographer. I'd love to take some shots of you.' He was examining her like she was some kind of fossil.

'Um . . . Tea? Coffee?'

David gathered up the Saturday-morning tangle that was her wavy brown hair and plonked it on top of her head, pulling out wisps and strands. 'Jeez,' he said, 'I could do stuff with you.'

*Likewise.*

Kitt ambled in.

'Morning,' said Jacquie, glad of the interruption. 'Sleep well?'

'Yeah.'

'So, the kettle's here, tea and coffee in the cupboard, bread there.'

'I'll have coffee.'

Jacquie started tidying up. David wandered over to the French windows and looked out at the garden. Kitt sat down. Jacquie couldn't work her out – she lived in Anchorage, but sounded English. She clearly hadn't been brought up in Alaska.

Kitt was staring at her. 'Like, hello? The coffee?'

In fact, Jacquie was beginning to wonder if she'd been brought up at all. 'Yeah, help yourself.'

Kitt sighed, but didn't get up. She was pretty in a rough sort of way. Her black hair, straight as a horse's mane, was laced with purple extensions, and she had a lovely blemish-free complexion that was coated with foundation. Her jeans were too tight, allowing a tube of flesh to hang over the waist, and her cropped top revealed the inevitable bellybutton ring. It looked forced, not her at all, as if she was wearing the wrong school uniform.

'You're to contact your father,' Jacquie told her.

'Why?'

'Because he wants to speak to you.'

'Yeah, later.'

The thank-you words had yet to cross her lips. 'Not later – now.' Jacquie caught a look from David, but couldn't tell whether it was approval or irritation. He had dark, thoughtful eyes. She handed Kitt the phone.

Without getting up, Kitt dialled. 'It's me,' she said, when her father picked up. 'Dad? I said it's me . . . Why? What time is it? . . . Anyway, I need money . . . I've spent it, haven't I? Paris was so cool . . . How would I know? I haven't seen her in three weeks.'

An angry murmur filtered into the kitchen, all the way from Alaska. Kitt was unmoved. 'Mum said to ask you if I needed money, so you'd better send some. Wotsit can give me some until it gets here.' She handed the phone to Jacquie.

'Hi,' she said, 'this is Wotsit.'

Matthew cleared his throat. 'Sorry about that.'

Jacquie didn't say anything.

'I'm a bit groggy,' he went on. 'It's the middle of the night. We're nine hours behind.'

'I realize that, but I told Kitt to ring. I thought you'd be worried.'

'No, yes, of course. Can I get your bank details and forward cash for her?'

'Yes, but, eh, where is she . . .' Jacquie tried to get it out: *Where is she going and when is she going there?*

He pre-empted her. 'And if she could hang on there for a few days, I mean, until I sort something out, I'd be so darned grateful. She's not as worldly as she looks . . . Have you spoken to your mother yet?'

'No. She's in Morocco. I'll fill her in when she gets back.'

Was that a sigh of relief over there in Anchorage?

'Okay. You've been amazing, Jacquie. An all-expenses-paid round-trip to Alaska is yours for the taking whenever it suits.'

Oh, she thought. Okay. Sounds good.

The three *guests* sat round the kitchen table for most of the day. Jacquie waited for Dara. She didn't know whether to entertain these people or get rid of them. Neither of the boys made any move to leave, but that was a mixed blessing. If they left, she would have to deal with Kitt single-handed.

But that wasn't the only reason she hesitated about kicking them out. The voices in the house, the kettle clicking on, boiling, clicking off, then boiling again, doors closing and loos flushing were all sounds reminiscent of the way things used to be a long time back. They had once, as a family, embraced visitors. Or, at least, they had before her father's accident, before the waiting began. Jacquie missed that life. Back then she never really knew, when she came through the door, who might be at their kitchen table: visitors from Dublin, neighbours, friends of hers or Dara's, and even sometimes strangers – backpackers and vagabonds that her mother picked up along the way. But then everything went quiet, and had been even quieter since they'd moved to Cork, where they knew hardly anyone and where, for a year, her mother had nursed their ailing grandfather. All in all, things had been pretty dull since they'd come back, and she missed their house in France. This one, where her mother had grown up, had been unkempt, sad, when they moved in, and although her mother had worked hard to make it feel like a home, it had yet to become one. Now Jacquie had picked up three strays of her own and there was noise and disorder about the place, which felt warm and familiar.

Dara finally came home before four. 'So where are the, um, visitors?'

'Oh, they tied me up, knocked me about and stole everything. They're gone, but don't worry, I was fine.'

'Yeah. Funny.'

'They're in the garden.'

'And, em, *who* are they?' he asked, looking out.

Dara was a rugby-player in search of a team. School rugby had thickened his neck, broken his nose and given him the build of a tank. University rugby eluded him. He was immediately selected, then rapidly deselected when he slept through every practice session. He was still well-toned and he wanted to play, but he also wanted to sleep. That was the joy of university living, he kept saying. He could sleep whenever he wanted to.

'The two lads are at CIT,' said Jacquie, 'and then there's the headcase. She's about ten years old and doing Europe and has no money so we're stuck with her.'

'Jesus, Mum's in for a shock.'

They wandered out to David and Bill, who were sitting on the low brick wall that rimmed the patio outside the kitchen.

Within minutes, Dara and Bill had connected on at least two mutual acquaintances.

'I like your garden,' David said to Jacquie.

'Thanks. Our grandparents were fanatical gardeners.'

It was very long, exquisitely landscaped, with small trees and shrubs strategically placed on either side of a zigzagging path, which led to a small expanse of lawn, behind which was a new timber shed.

He looked up at the house. 'Nice place.'

Jacquie smiled. He coughed. He was too pale, too thin, but she had never seen anything like him. Wiry. Cocky. Sweet.

No need to turf them out just yet.

# 4

Since Luke was always looking for her and she was now looking for him, they met again the following morning, as if it had been planned. Having broken so many of her rules, Marina had paid the price: the evening before had been lonely, mitigated only by intrigue and a delightful sense that something was brewing. Telling herself she was too weary to venture out, she had opted to eat at the *riad*, but it was the prospect of bumping into Luke with whoever was keeping him from her that had really kept her indoors.

In the bright daylight she felt more bullish, and when she came through the arch and into the square beneath the clock-tower, he was already there, reading outside the café, with one foot on a chair and a hand on the side of his sunglasses. He looked up, saw her and smiled. She gave a little wave, her own sunglasses pushed back into her hair, the heat making her glow, and joined him without being asked.

'How is your daughter getting on?' he said, after ordering for them both.

'So-so. Bit early to say.'

He nodded, encouraging her to go on. Like the cat, he seemed to enjoy listening to her prattle. There was something in his eyes when he looked at her – a smile, bordering on a smirk – and Marina suspected she looked back at him in the same smug way. They spoke to each other in a beguiling manner, as if they had had these conversations before; as if they were not at all surprised to have met, or to like one another. Acknowledgement sat between them, an invisible guest, but exactly what it was that they acknowledged, she could not quite say.

It was surprising, shocking even, to feel desire again, prickling her, coming up through the soles of her feet; she thought she should probably stamp it out, but even there, down in her feet, she could feel the benefits. A year or two had rolled off her already. In spite of her doubts and his elusiveness, her body-language was changing. From feeling frumpy, dumpy, past it, she felt already sexy and alluring. How quickly it was coming back (how close to the surface it had been . . .), the ability to move sensually. The subtle gestures of seduction were creeping out of her of their own accord. She moved more gracefully, used her hands more expressively, spread her fingers more widely, and smiled too often.

But feeling desire was quite different from acting on it, and still the questions taunted her: did she really want to go back into the realm of intimacy, and nudity, have her body exposed, its ravages revealed? Could she get that close, that bare, and share with someone else what had only ever been Aidan's and was still, in her mind, more Aidan's than her own? She had to think about these things, here and now over pancakes and honey, because if she was not ready to resume a physical, sexual life, she should stop this light banter, this sharing of stories, and the gentle, smiling eye contact. Otherwise she was being a flirt or, worse, a tease.

Luke was eating. He dressed like an Italian, smart and rigidly neat. She liked his hands, the lines on his face, that hint of grey in the hair peeking out from his open-necked shirt. She loved the way his eyes shone, the lines round them creasing out, like a web of happiness. Yes, she thought. I could be with him.

Perhaps he had no such intentions. Perhaps this was simply that most wondrous of things, the birth of a friendship, but it was certainly the beginning of something. Marina felt it, in the warmth that moved between them, in the way she spoke to him, as to someone she knew, someone she loved.

*Love.* What a thought! The word pounced on her, gave her a jolt so severe that Luke noticed. 'What is it?'

'Hmm? Oh, nothing.'

'Fancy a walk on the beach?'

They walked by the sea, her feet in the water. Marina had been longing to swim and was wearing her bikini beneath her dress, so she pulled off the dress and, skipping over a few waves, dipped into the sea, taking care not to get her hair wet and so allow him to see the frizzball it became when it made contact with water. She might be prepared to sleep with him, but letting him see her with her hair wet? They weren't ready for *that* kind of intimacy.

Luke did not join her. 'I live on a lake,' he said, handing over her towel when she got out, 'and I swim every day in the summer, but I'm not much of a one for the sea.'

'Why not?'

'It makes me feel out of control.'

Marina covered her smile with a bent forefinger. 'You really are an odd one.'

He grinned bashfully. He didn't do wit, or hadn't yet, but it was in his eyes, like a sitting tenant. It would come out. He *would* be fun. Something was holding him back, making him occasionally terse and distracted.

They were running out of time already. The watch-watching had started, discreetly, as they wandered back along the shore. Luke glanced at his wrist without taking his hand from his pocket. He was about to abscond. Marina braced herself. Her spirits sank as they reached her hotel. There would be no invitation to dinner. It would be another 'See you around.' The prospect prompted her to pre-empt him. 'Well,' she said, 'see you around.'

'Oh, right.'

'At least, I might. I'm thinking of heading south for a couple of days.'

'Really? When are you leaving?'

Playing hard to get was all very well if you knew how to do it. She gestured limply over her shoulder towards the *riad.* 'They're organizing something.'

'I see.'

Marina waited.

'I'll see you about, then,' he said.

'You might, I suppose.'

He clenched his teeth, was about to say something, then retreated along the lane, and was gone.

'Bugger!' She threw her bag on to the bed. 'Curse him, anyway!'

The cat licked its paw, then settled more comfortably on the wall to watch her. She went out to it. The English girl was sitting on a plastic chair next door, reading a thick novel. Without looking up, she said, 'Not going so well?'

'He keeps taking off!' said Marina, too frustrated to be discreet. 'I know I shouldn't care, but I've got used to him popping up during the day and I don't understand why he's never around in the evenings. He probably picks up other women!'

'Do you know where he's staying?'

It seemed Marina was the one providing the intrigue for the young couple, not the other way round. '*No.* He hasn't let slip any details about his hotel or who he's with. He just vanishes into the alleyways. Maybe he's a ghost, appearing and disappearing the way he does.'

'Do you have another date?'

'No. I mean, what's the point, really? And who is he anyway?

And I must be out of my small tree even to think about him twice, let alone get wound up about it!'

The girl smiled and got up. 'We're off out in a bit, but don't you worry. I bet he'll come looking for you.'

Marina heard the companionable grunt of a male, the tinkle of keys, the door closing, and felt a pull of envy. But at least the cat was still there. 'She's right. It's about time he came looking for me.'

The cat turned its face to her. He's always looking for you, it said.

And Marina thought, I know. I know that.

He found her the next afternoon as she came out of the *riad* on her way to the beach. They almost collided, but stopped dead, a step away from one another.

'Time for a cuppa?' he asked tentatively.

*Say no.* 'All right.'

He looked up at her building. 'I gather there's a nice terrace on the roof here.'

'Yeah, it's lovely. Come on up.'

Like many *riads*, there was a courtyard at the heart of the building, with fountain and tiling, and on the second floor Marina pointed Luke towards the steps that led to the roof, and told him she'd be up in a minute. She popped into her room to change out of her swimsuit and beach dress, and to catch her breath.

No cat on the wall, no girl next door. Calm. She must stay calm. He was here, had invited himself in. She'd got him off the streets. Time together, out of sight, away from pressing crowds. No one about, in the still afternoon. She put her hand to her chest. Aidan was all over her skin. This would be infidelity; she could see it is no other way. Aidan had left her life, yet still inhabited her, owned her . . .

But Luke was waiting.

Marina changed into a short denim skirt and peach top, then brushed her teeth again quickly. Everything had to be done quickly. It was as if the planet was spinning through space, out of control, and she was trying to hang on to it. If she thought too much – about Aidan, their marriage, the awkwardness of intimacy – she would lose her grasp on this mad galactic ride.

Luke was standing by the parapet, taking in the view. As she came up behind him, she almost put a hand on his shoulder. On the beach the bodies on the sand were fuzzy dark lines, like distant figures in a painting. The town lay subdued and reticent around them, as if it had turned down its own volume to lend quiet to their solitude. They retreated to the shade and sat on the broad, cushioned bench under an awning. Luke put his elbow on the back cushion, near her. Near enough to touch her shoulder. She wished he would, and knew he would. It was in every gesture they made, in the protracted eye contact and self-conscious smiles. They were ready to begin, and had found an opportunity – a lazy, silent afternoon.

A light breeze blew about them, the tarpaulin flapped discreetly, and Marina no longer believed that this had nowhere to go. It would go to Italy. And to Ireland.

The tea arrived, and they watched, not speaking, while the waiter went through the process of pouring and testing, then pouring from a height into two glasses. She took the glass and sat back, her legs crossed. Her shins were nicely tanned. A pity she hadn't painted her toenails. In reaching for his glass, Luke leant towards her and his arm slid further behind her shoulders.

Voices in the stairwell. Their idyll disturbed.

The young English couple came out, the girl in full flight, her beefy voice chattering to her boyfriend as they passed. 'Hello!' she said, when she saw Marina.

Marina blushed. 'Hello.'

They came over. 'I'm Becky, by the way, and this is Rob.' She shook their hands. 'Lovely to meet you at last. Properly.'

'Marina.'

'Luke Delahunt.' He took his arm from behind Marina to shake hands.

'We've been chatting,' Becky explained to Luke, 'across our balconies.'

'You and me and the cat.' Marina laughed, hoping Becky would move swiftly along.

'Well,' she said, doing just that and giving Rob a push, 'see you later.'

Marina drew a quiet sigh of relief.

Luke turned to her. 'When are you leaving?'

'Leaving?'

'You mentioned a trip?'

'I, em, haven't firmed up my plans.'

'Good. That's what I came to see you about. Some of us have hired a Land Cruiser and driver to take us to Ouarzazate tomorrow, and then we're going further west to do some camel-trekking. It'll be long – four days' travelling – but you're welcome to join us. All inclusive, it comes to about two hundred euro.' He didn't quite look at her.

'Camel-trekking? Are you serious?'

'And sleeping overnight in the desert.' He flashed a cheeky grin. 'Dare ya.'

Love had come. That funny little ingredient Marina had not expected to sprinkle over her days ever again drifted down. It simply came over them, like a veil settling.

It was disconcerting. Falling in love could never be like this, she thought. It came in a gradual slant, surely, climbing from normality to delight, through the hard graft of familiarization and capitulation, through the torments of 'Is he?' 'Isn't he?'

'Am I?' 'Are we?' It wouldn't be peaceful like this, nor so easily recognized, would it?

'Marina?' said Luke, and it was the first time he'd used her name.

'Oh, I don't know.'

'If *I* can get on a camel, anyone can.'

'It would certainly be . . . interesting.' And so much easier than going on her own.

'Excellent. I'll book you in. But it's an early start. We have to meet the driver at Bab Marrakech at six, if that's okay?'

'Don't I have to sign up with anyone?'

'I'll let them know there'll be another in the party.' He frowned, fidgeted. 'I'm afraid I have to go.'

'*Already?*'

Like laser beams, his eyes pierced hers, reading everything inside her head – that she had expected more, wanted more, that she didn't mind that he knew this. And she read, in that swift look, that although he might not have intended to wile away the afternoon in her bedroom, he wanted to.

He got up slowly, as if a great fist were pressing him down as he tried to stand.

'I'll see you out,' she said.

After waving him off from the steps, she sailed up to her room, closed the door, clenched her fists and whispered, '*Yes!*' He'd asked her away for a few days! How strange that it should go her way. Better than she could have planned or imagined it. She wanted to ring Suzanne to gush and tell her about it, but she was afraid that would jinx it.

Later, when her neighbours came back to their room, she heard Becky clearing her throat out on the balcony. Then she did it again, pointedly. Taking the hint, Marina stepped out. 'Hello.'

'Ooh, he's lovely!' said Becky, straight away.

'You think?'

'Nice voice too.'

'He's asked me to go away for a few days,' Marina blurted. 'To the desert.'

'How romantic!'

'Is it? I mean, maybe I'm reading too much into it.'

'Men don't go asking women out to the desert for the good of their health, though, do they?'

Marina looked doubtfully at the wall. 'What do you think the cat would say?'

'He'd say go for it. You mark my words.'

Much later Marina remembered what Luke had actually said. 'Some of us have hired a Land Cruiser . . .'

Some of whom?

# 5

Jacquie made tea and brought it up to the living room. David was taking photographs of the flames in the fireplace. He fiddled with his little camera and showed her the results: green flames in a spooky blue hue. 'Wow. That's weird.'

He twisted round and photographed her eye. Told her to look up, look down.

But my hair's a mess, she was thinking, and my skin's greasy and you're standing too close.

On the camera, he changed her eye from one colour to another until he found the mix he wanted. It was spectral. 'You're good,' she said.

'It's the software. Wait till you see what I can do to you on my laptop.'

'I can't wait.'

He spent ages on his laptop, loading and fiddling. The results were unsettling. He focused mostly on her right eye, set in negative, and after messing with it for a bit, said, 'Can I draw on you?'

'I'm sorry?'

He held up liquid eyeliner. 'On your face. Would you mind?'

'Em, suppose not.'

He took her chin in his hand. 'Look up.'

She blinked furiously and her eyes watered when he rimmed her eye with liner. His thumb was on her chin, his fingers on the side of her neck. She tried not to breathe. He drew a line across her cheekbone. She had become a mere canvas on which he would carry out his work. 'I must look like a cat,' she said.

'Cats don't wear eyeliner.'

He rubbed her cheek with his thumb, then took more photos. The session went on for hours: photos and eyeliner, and heavy breathing every time he leant into her face. 'Don't give me your virus,' she said at one point.

'Why not?'

# 6

The house was dark and chilly when Marina let herself in, but she could hear the television upstairs. *Home.* Always good to be home, she thought wearily, putting her keys on the hall table, but she couldn't help wondering. Wondering about everything – about Morocco, camels, being alone; about Luke, and Becky.

Her aching limbs demanded a bath. She'd been walking like a cowboy for two days, as if there was still a camel between her thighs, and even had a saddle sore. The flight home had been the most uncomfortable of her life. And all for what?

There was something odd about the house. She couldn't put her finger on it, but she recognized it – different sounds, movement, something stirring. She put down her bag, switched on the hall light and went into the kitchen. Chaos. The table was covered with food packets, plates, mugs. They weren't expecting her home till the next day. Interesting to see how things really were when she was away.

It was ten past seven. Marina headed upstairs to see if Jacquie was home yet. It wasn't the living-room television she could hear but the one in her own bedroom. 'Jacquie?' she said, going into the room. A fan of grey light spread from the television across the bed. Two people were lying there. Marina switched on the light. Neither of them was her daughter. 'Good God!'

A young couple lay stretched out with a rug over them. The girl, dragging her eyes from the screen, said, 'Hi.'

The boy scrambled off the bed. 'God, sorry. We didn't mean to –'

'Who the hell are you? And what are you doing in my room?' Marina stood over the girl, who was sitting up with unashamed reluctance. 'Do you mind?'

'So-*rreee*.'

Marina turned off the television. 'Are you friends of Dara's?'

'No,' said the lad.

'Jacquie's?'

'Em, no.'

Marina backed towards the door. Where were her children?

'See, Jacquie picked us up,' he said. 'We've been here a few days.'

'Picked you up?'

'Yeah. We couldn't get a lift.'

'You're *hitchhikers*?'

'Not really,' he said, glancing at the girl, but she didn't help him out. 'Well, I am, I suppose.' He stood forward, hand extended. 'David Roche. And this is Kitt.'

Marina did not shake his hand. 'Where is Jacquie?'

'Should be back soon,' he said.

Marina glanced at her bed. 'You haven't slept in it, have you?'

'God, no,' he said. 'Just watching telly. It was cold in the other room.'

They sidled past her and out, leaving Marina dumbstruck. As they went downstairs, the front door slammed. She stepped on to the landing. 'Jacquie?'

Her daughter came to the bottom of the stairs. 'Mum! What are you doing here?'

'I got back early. For heaven's sake, what's going on?'

Jacquie scurried up and gave her a hug. 'What happened? Why did you cut it short?'

Marina raised one hand. 'One thing at a time. Who are those people and what were they doing on my bed?'

'They were in your room?'

'The other room was too cold, apparently. Really, Jacquie –'

'I know, I know.' Jacquie hustled her back into the bedroom and closed the door. 'Right. Hi. Hope you had a lovely time, because you're in for a bit of a shock.'

'Oh, I've already had it, thanks. I don't mind you having friends to stay, but –'

'They're not my friends. Sit down.' They sat on the end of the bed. 'I was going to phone you, but I decided not to because I knew you'd worry and I wanted you to enjoy –'

'Jacquie!'

'All right. On Friday night, I got a call from an old friend of yours.'

'Who?'

'Guy by the name of Matthew.'

Marina's mouth opened. Her wide eyes stared back at Jacquie. '*Matthew?*'

'Yeah.'

'But I only know one Matthew and he –'

'Yeah, it's the same one,' Jacquie said quickly.

'How do you know?'

'He said so.'

'My God, what's brought *him* out of the woodwork?'

'Her.' Jacquie motioned towards the door. 'Madam. She's his daughter.'

For the second time, Marina gasped.

''Fraid so. She got herself into a spot of bother in Cashel. I had to go and get her – actually, there were three of them.'

'And where the hell is Matthew?'

'Anchorage, Alaska, like the song.'

'So that's where he ended up,' Marina muttered. 'No better place. I hope he freezes his –' She pulled herself back. 'What was his daughter doing in Cashel?'

Jacquie told her the full story. '. . . and between the jigs and the reels, I went to fetch them.'

Marina was shaking her head, eyes narrowed. 'How *dare* Matthew come out of nowhere and ask you to do that? You shouldn't have gone.'

'Like Dara said, if the tables were turned and it was me out on some Alaskan highway, you'd have called Matthew, wouldn't you?'

'Don't count on it.'

'It seemed like the right thing to do.'

'It was,' Marina conceded.

Jacquie gave her a squeeze. 'I'm so glad you're home.'

'Me, too. I think.'

'I suppose you want to call him? He's chomping at the bit to talk to you.'

'I'll bet he is.'

Jacquie reached for the phone.

'No, wait. I need a minute. I need a cuppa. Matthew can wait. What's she like, the girl?'

'Oh. My. God.' Jacquie said. 'She is *un*believable! Completely spoilt. She hasn't said thank you *once*. Not once! And she's been ensconced in front of the television since she arrived, eating biscuits and drinking gallons of milk. Bill's gone to a friend, but David hasn't been very well –'

'Oh, *great*. Get him out of here!'

'We tried, but their student house isn't ready and he has a filthy cough, so we said he could stay. He's in no fit state to sleep on someone's floor. But he's okay – he's nice. *She*'s the problem.'

Marina was shaking her head. 'I can't believe Matthew would do this after . . . twenty-six years.'

'What happened with you two, anyway?'

'Long story. Not now.'

They went down to the kitchen, where David was sitting at the table and Kitt was standing by the counter, fiddling with her split ends.

'This is my mum,' said Jacquie.

Marina extended her hand. 'Marina.'

'Yeah, I reckon,' said Kitt.

'Nice to meet you.' *Well, interesting, anyway.* 'So you're Matthew's daughter? What brings you to Ireland?'

'Just travelling.'

'I see. And how is Matthew? I haven't seen him for . . . oh, decades.'

'He's okay.'

'Jacquie tells me he lives in Alaska. That's a long way from home.' *Just not far enough.*

'Yeah.'

Marina crossed her arms. 'Have you been . . . travelling for long?'

'Whoa, twenty questions!' Kitt was on her way out of the room. 'Are you making tea?' she asked Jacquie over her shoulder. 'Bring me a cup, will you?'

'Wait,' said Marina. 'Where are you off to?'

'To watch the end of that programme.'

'Sorry, but you and your friend can tidy up the kitchen first.'

Kitt glanced at the table, confused. 'What?'

'This isn't a very pleasant sight to come home to after a holiday and Jacquie's been working all day, so it's only fair that you tidy up after yourselves.'

David immediately started clearing. Kitt watched him.

'Straight away, please, Kitt,' said Marina. 'I'm looking forward to a nice cup of tea in my nice tidy kitchen.'

Kitt picked up a plate and looked around to see where it might go.

Marina glared at Jacquie. *Is she for real?*

*Yes.* Jacquie nodded. *Welcome home.*

'Maybe I will talk to Matthew after all,' said Marina. 'Where's his number?'

In the study, she sat by her desk, heart racing and hands trembling, trying to compose herself. Everything comes back, she thought. Everything rebounds. Maybe that was good. Maybe it meant that one day even Gwen would reappear and there would be some kind of resolution. If Matthew could drop back into her life like this, landing on it like something thrown carelessly into the air that had not come down again, who knew what else might happen?

She took a deep breath. She had to sound calm and controlled, but the more she thought about it, the more nervous she became, so she picked up the phone, found his number and pressed redial before she could reconsider. This call could not be avoided.

The all-familiar voice was suddenly, inexplicably, in her ear. 'Hello?'

Marina didn't know what to say. There was so much to say, that was the problem. 'It's Marina.'

He, likewise, greeted her voice with a moment's silence, before saying, 'Hello, Marina. You're home?'

'Yeah. Got back just now to find *your* daughter watching television in my bed.'

'Oh, God.'

Marina was too bemused to know what to say next.

'Look,' he said. 'If I could explain . . .'

'Please do. Please tell me how your daughter ended up in my house with some hitchhiker she picked up off the side of the road.'

'I'm really sorry about the whole thing. I wish I hadn't had to call on you guys, but I didn't know what else to do. I couldn't leave Kitt on the roadside.'

'So *my* daughter had to go out in adverse conditions at midnight and drive for four hours?'

'What can I say?' he said quietly.

'What was she doing there?'

'I . . . Look, I don't know.'

'How old is she?'

'Seventeen.'

'*Seventeen?*'

'Um, actually, she will be seventeen next month.'

'She's only sixteen? Jesus, Matthew!'

'I know, but she's a bit of a free spirit. Kinda hard to tie down.'

'Why isn't she in school?'

'She left earlier this year. I tried to talk her out of it, but she was mad keen to travel.'

'Aren't they all? But, *generally speaking*, parents advise them to finish their education first. You're lucky she came to no harm.'

'Aw, she's pretty well able to look after herself.'

'Is that so? How is it, then, that she had to be bailed out by Jacquie?'

He sighed heavily.

'Who are the boys who were with her?'

'No idea.'

Marina rolled her eyes in frustration. Clearly Matthew wasn't much of a parent but, then, he hadn't been much of a boyfriend either. 'How can you have no idea who your teenage daughter is travelling with?'

'As I understand it, she met them that day so they headed to Cork together.'

The timbre of his voice hadn't changed, not one bit, but the American intonation was new. She imagined him, at the end of the line, in some swanky apartment, looking like the twenty-year-old she had once known. How did he visualize her? 'Where was she headed?' she asked.

'I'm not sure. Maybe she wanted to visit the oul' sod.'

'The old sod's in Anchorage, isn't he?'

He chuckled. 'Don't be like that.'

'Like what, Matthew? And why not, anyway? She can't just land in here without warning! What about your parents? Your brother?'

'They're in the States now. They live in San Francisco. Marina, please don't kick her out,' he said, suddenly sounding desperate. 'If you do, I won't be able to keep track of her.'

'Of course I won't throw her out, but I'm not running a boarding-house, you know.'

'Oh.'

*Oh?*

'Things have changed, then,' he said. 'I remember when your mother had that house full of people, and you were there, always at the heart of it, with coffee and biscuits.'

'You think I live my life like that? Serving tea and biscuits?'

'No, I just . . . Look, I'll get Kitt out of there as soon as possible.'

'Please do. I'm tired. I've had a long trip. You and –'

'Yeah, how was your holiday? Jacquie said you were in Morocco.'

Marina breathed angrily into the phone. 'You've used up as much of my goodwill as is due to you, Matthew. You and Kitt can let me know tomorrow what plans you've made.'

'I hear you. Meanwhile I've forwarded money. Jacquie has it. She's minding the purse-strings.'

Marina didn't like the way he talked about Jacquie. It was as if he'd taken something that belonged to her without asking. He had a foot inside the door already. Two feet, in fact.

'And by the way,' he went on, 'I was sorry to hear about your husband. That's rough. Who . . .'

'Aidan ffrench. We met in Dublin. I went there to teach. Goodbye, Matthew.'

Marina spent the rest of the evening in a stupor. Jacquie had warned her, but it was hard to grasp: Kitt really had no remorse, no manners, no gratitude. Only the most polished presumption. How could it be? Matthew had his faults, but he had always been mannerly. How had he managed to rear such a blob? Probably married some dolly-bird without a brain to her name, Marina thought wryly.

But Kitt had done her an enormous favour. The gut-churning homecoming she had dreaded had been wiped sideways by this unexpected arrival.

Sleep, at last. She fell into a near coma counting the nights since she'd slept well. When she woke the next morning, instead of scurrying downstairs for a cup of milky tea she lay in bed, pondering. She wanted to think about Luke, but Matthew McGonagle kept shunting him aside.

His daughter in her house. How had that happened? The past had been plonked at her feet. Rather than unfurling towards her, like a long carpet for her to step upon lightly, it was right there: a mat on the floor that tripped her up as she came in her own door. What kind of welcome had Matthew really expected Kitt to receive? She wished she'd been there to take that first call: she would have made him beg.

She wished, too, that Aidan was there, so they could look out at the trees with mugs of tea, talking in low voices about how other people messed up their lives. Aidan would be great with this. He'd let her rant and bitch and flush out all the residue of that time, which still lay, like grit, in her veins, but even he would be unable to stop her feeling it again.

When, at last, she managed to get up, she found Kitt in the kitchen on the phone. 'Yeah,' she was saying, 'here she is. I'll put her on.'

Marina took the phone outside.

'Hello, Marina,' Matthew said, his voice thick. 'You couldn't explain the time difference to that girl, could you?'

'Maybe *you* could explain to her about using other people's phones for long-distance calls without asking.'

'My God,' he said quietly, 'you really are pissed off.'

'That surprises you?'

'She's only a kid who doesn't know any better. It's not like she's a drug user.'

'That's not all I'm pissed off about.'

'I know that. I suppose I'm just . . .'

'What?'

'Surprised that after all this time you're still –'

'Not one word in twenty-six years, Matthew, and then this. What am I supposed to do? Greet her like my long-lost child?'

'What's wrong with asking for help from a friend when I need it?'

'Friend, did you say?'

'Even friends make mistakes, Marina. Please don't take that out on Kitt.'

Marina sat on the wall. What a thought. 'God, of course I won't. We're looking after her. You don't have to worry about that.'

She could hear Matthew move around – a couple of groans,

as if he was in pain. 'I only ever hear from her when she runs out of money, Reen.'

Something warm ran through Marina's body. It had been decades since anyone had called her 'Reen'. Truth be told, no one except Matthew had ever got away with it. To hear it slip out like that, so casual, sent her right back to leaving school and dances and UCC in the autumn. She wanted to say, 'Don't you "Reen" me!' but he sounded so bewildered. She drew back her shoulders. Her sniping had to stop. In his place, she would have done exactly the same thing. Moreover, she knew that had it been her daughter on the road, he would not have hesitated to look after her and would not have bitched about it either. This antagonism was counter-productive. It belonged to a different story. Now Matthew was trying to do his best for his child. Besides, they might never get rid of Kitt if Marina didn't keep him on side.

'Are you still there?' he asked.

'She's so young, Matthew. How did you and her mother let her go off without having places to stay? Anything could have happened to her.'

'Something great happened. You and I got back in touch.'

'Don't start with the charm,' she said.

'Hey, give me a break. I have a lot of ground to make up.'

Marina could tell he was smiling. The nerve of him, to be so cool. She bent over to clear some grit from between her toes. Her feet were tanned and had a white mark from her sandals. A whiff of Morocco, of Luke, washed over her.

'It's so amazing to hear your voice,' Matthew was saying.

'You could have heard it any time. You could have called years ago.'

'Yeah, but life gets in the way, doesn't it? Not that I haven't thought of you.'

'Have you been back to Ireland much?'

'The odd time. If I'd known you were still in Cork –'

'I wasn't. I've been living in France.'

'Well, there you are, then. Anyway, I never had time to look people up.'

'Right, until you needed a favour.'

He carried on, as if she hadn't spoken: 'I tell you what, Jacquie's a real credit to you. How many do you have? Kids, I mean.'

'Two.'

'Sensible number. One's more than enough for me.'

'That's fairly obvious.'

He chuckled.

'What arrangements have you made about getting Kitt home?'

'To tell the truth,' he said, 'I'm not sure what to do about that.'

'For God's sake, it isn't complicated. Book her on to a flight to New York out of Shannon and on from there. She needs to go home. Her mother must be beside herself.'

'Excuse me, who am I speaking to?' Matthew asked in that all-American tone.

'What?'

'Have you got harder over the years? This isn't the voice of the woman I remember.'

'You're right there.'

In the kitchen, Jacquie was making David toast. How nice for him, Marina thought sourly. Matthew was right – she was in a really foul mood. She had once had a reputation as a tireless hostess. Their house had been, as often as she could make it, full of people. But her hospitality had drained away. Perhaps the intervening years had wiped out her embracing qualities, or maybe she was just tired. Tired and disappointed.

David and Kitt were hardly ideal houseguests, but they fitted the ffrench tradition of spontaneous hospitality. The open door, the kettle on. Jacquie had, instinctively, done everything right. Marina would have to match that now, would have to work herself back into house-mother mode, so she offered to cook a fry for the youngsters, then flittered about putting bacon under the grill, milk into the jug and toast on the table. It didn't work. She was going through the motions. It wasn't what she wanted to be doing. What she wanted to be doing was living on an island with Luke, with no one to look after and no one to worry about.

Because David *was* a worry. He didn't eat much all day, and that afternoon fell asleep in the living room. A few hours later, when Jacquie was making him more tea, she told Marina she'd said to David he could hang on until the weekend.

'But I'm trying to get rid of these people, not hang on to them!' Marina screeched. 'The last thing I need is someone getting sick.'

'I think it might be too late. Whatever he's got, it's getting worse.'

Marina groaned.

'What *is* wrong? We can't put him out on the street!'

'I know, I know. It isn't really him. It's Kitt. She's so . . .' Marina clenched her fists '. . . *enervating*! You'd think she might know how to put a teabag into a mug and add water, but even these simple tasks confound her! And she's dumped a pile of dirty clothes outside her bedroom door. They must be wealthy,' she said, with a dismissive sniff. 'That child is clearly the offspring of privilege.'

'But if you and Matthew hadn't fallen out, wouldn't you feel differently? Wouldn't you be taking her on as one of your causes?'

'With the best will in the world,' Marina said regally, 'I would be defeated.'

Jacquie gave her a look. 'God, you're so crotchety. I thought you'd be all rested and chilled out after your holiday. David and Kitt think this is you – sour and snarly.'

'Yeah, well, it's a bit of a shock to come back and find that my skeletons have come out of the closet and are wandering around my home.'

'Fine. I just thought there might be something else,' Jacquie said, putting the teapot on the tray. 'I mean, you still haven't told me why you came back a day early.'

'It was nothing, really. There was an accident and –'

'An accident?'

'It's okay, I wasn't involved, but between one thing and another, I ended up in Marrakech a day early and it made sense to come back.'

'That's all?'

'That's all. Go on, take that up to David.'

'Okay, but we're going to the pub later, so Kitt's all yours. You two can bond!'

Marina groaned. 'At least I might get some information out of her.'

Had Jacquie stayed in the room another minute, Marina would have blurted. A huge part of her longed to tell her daughter about Luke. There wasn't much they didn't talk about; they were pretty tight. Since losing Aidan, they had been forever trying to protect one another, always looking on the bright side, one for the other; making the most of every little high that came their way. They weren't particularly alike – Jacquie was tougher, more guarded than Marina, and more intense – but they shared a sense of humour and a sense of tragedy, liked the same books, disagreed about movies, and enjoyed a healthy appreciation of the opposite sex. Jacquie's current obsession was the rugby player Donncha O'Callaghan, while Marina had always been hung up on Al Pacino, but telling her daughter about a real live man was another matter altogether. She might find it difficult to accept that her mother was distracted by thoughts of a man other than her father, and yet Marina wanted her to know that someone still found her attractive, that she still had romance buried in there somewhere . . . and hope.

She had been saving the story for Suzanne, but Matthew would now get in the way of all that. Suzanne would want every damn detail. They'd end up going over that whole territory again and Marina really didn't want to go back there, because when she did, whole compartments of baggage would tumble out in disarray. It would be stirred up, sniffed over, added to, taken from.

David didn't go to the pub. His throat was so sore he could barely swallow and his chest sounded like it was housing coal-fired steam engines. Marina sent him to bed, promising to take him to their GP the next morning, then went to make hot chocolate for herself and Kitt, and brought the mugs up to the living room. The girl didn't take her eyes off the television, so Marina turned it off.

'What did you do that for?'

'We should talk.'

'Talk?'

'That's right,' said Marina. 'It's when two people exchange information.'

'Huh?'

'If you're going to be staying with us for a bit, it'd be nice to know something about you.'

'Don't see why.'

'How is your dad doing? It's been so long since I've seen him.'

'Me too.'

'What do you mean?'

The girl widened her eyes as if she had stated the obvious.

Marina played dumb. 'You don't live with him?'

'I live with Mum.'

'Oh, your parents are no longer together?'

'Nope.'

'I presumed you all lived in Anchorage.'

'No way!' Kitt exclaimed. 'On the edge of the world? Not me, thank you.'

'Ah, so you *do* know those words!'

Kitt stared at her. 'What words?'

'"Thank you."'

Kitt reached for the remote control. Marina took it from her. 'Where does your mother live?'

'Málaga. She runs a hotel there.'

'But . . . when do you see your dad? Does he come over a lot?'

'Not really.'

Marina was beginning to boil. Matthew barely saw his own daughter, and yet had had the temerity to dump the girl on *her*! 'He doesn't come to visit?'

'Sometimes.' Kitt shrugged. 'I don't want to see him anyway.'

'Why not? Don't you get on with him?'

'He's all right. He's always telling me what to do.'

The barometer on which Matthew was travelling in Marina's head went back up again. So he *was* making an effort. 'Why aren't you in school?'

'Why are you so interested?' said Kitt. 'What I do is my own business.'

'Actually, while you're sleeping under my roof and eating

my food, what you do is *my* business, and it will be until your father gets you a flight to Anchorage.'

'I'm not going there!'

'Either that or you go back to your mother. Anyway, I thought you wanted to see the world.'

'I don't want to see *that* part. Mum hated it.' Kitt picked up a magazine and snapped through the pages in swift succession.

'Tell me how you got to Ireland . . . Kitt.' Marina put down her mug. 'You might as well answer these questions, because as soon as you do, I'll leave you to your programme. Your father says you've been on the road for three weeks.'

'Yeah. Went to Barcelona with my boyfriend, Jorge. It was great.' Kitt's face brightened and her dour features relaxed. 'We were there for ten days, then went to Nice, staying with friends of his. It was cool. We sunbathed all day and . . . and, you know, stuff.'

'What happened to Jorge?'

Kitt looked off to the side. 'See, we sort of got lost. He was supposed to meet me after I'd been shopping one day, but he never showed, and when I went back to his friends' place, turned out he'd taken off.'

The first smidgen of sympathy, of anything, that Marina had felt for the girl finally came to the surface. She was suddenly glad that Kitt was right there, safe in their living room. Abandoned by some shit after he'd no doubt taken as much as she could give, there were too many grim places in which she might have ended up. But sympathy would alienate Kitt, so she asked her simply, 'What did you do?'

'Couldn't stay, could I? They didn't want me hanging around, so I went to Paris. Have a friend there. I slept on her floor for a while, but her mother kicked me out. Sort of. Well, not really. They were going away, so I figured I'd come here and see Dad's relatives.'

'But they live in America, don't they?'

Kitt ran one nail under another. 'I forgot.'

Marina sighed and stood up. 'I'm going to call Matthew. Do you want to speak to him?'

'No.'

'"No, thank you" would work for me.'

'Yeah, whatever.'

Marina stood in front of her. 'Kitt, do you have *any* good manners that you can think of?'

'I have manners,' she mumbled.

'Are you sure? Because I haven't seen any. Maybe we could start with the simple things, like saying "please" and "thank you". That would go a long way.'

'Can I watch telly now?'

'Yes, but tidy up your things before you go to bed.'

As Marina left the room, Kitt muttered, 'This is like living with a terrorist.'

Marina turned. 'Sorry, that won't cut it, Kitt, unless of course you *want* to end up sleeping in the forecourt of that petrol station – because I'm very, very close to taking you back there.'

Curiosity needled Marina. For all the bubbling resentment deep inside her, she wanted to get into chat-mode with Matthew – find out how he'd ended up in Anchorage, what kind of a life he had there. She wondered what he looked like in his mid-forties. He had been handsome: dark-haired, bright-eyed, bulky and well-proportioned. Had he turned into a bloated, balding, middle-aged goon? And Kitt's mother was a source of fascination too. Between them, they didn't appear to have much in the way of parenting skills.

She settled herself against her pillows with the phone. 'You've told me nothing,' she said, when Matthew answered.

'I've just heard that you and Kitt's mother have separated.'

'There's so much to catch up on.'

'Apparently Kitt's been wandering around France, abandoned by her boyfriend, kicked out by friends . . . Why didn't you tell me?'

He said quietly, 'I didn't know any of that.'

'You *should* know. She's just a child!'

'It's all very well for you, Marina,' he snapped, 'with both your kids sorted and educated. Have you any idea what a nightmare it is when you can't keep track of your own daughter, who ducks every damn thing you try to do for her? Have you?'

'No. No, I haven't.'

'Look, I'm not expecting you to put her up for ever, but the thing is –'

'What *is* the thing, Matthew?'

'I told Kitt she should come out here, but she's not very keen.'

'Clearly, but what about your ex-wife? I haven't heard a word from her. I presume they're keeping in touch by mobile?'

'She isn't my ex. We were never married.'

'Oh . . . So has Kitt always lived in Málaga?

'No, they've moved around a lot, which hasn't been ideal.'

'Nor is it ideal that her mother has let her leave school and take off.'

'I know. She's soft on her. I mean, I send Kitt money and try to make her see sense, but what else, at this distance, can I do?'

Sympathy ran across Marina's chest, like a mouse across a kitchen floor. 'Don't *be* at that distance,' she urged him. 'If she won't go back to her mother, then you should come here.'

'I can't.'

'You can't be arsed, I suppose. And why bother anyway when you've got me to look after her?'

'That's not it, Reen.'

'So come over!'

'I *can't*.'

'What could possibly stand in the way of you coming to sort out this kid, who is desperate for *someone* to care about where she is and how she's doing? Anyone will do! She's not fussy. Nor I am. Why should I get stuck with this when you're sitting over there –'

'Up to my groin in plaster.'

'What?'

'I swear. Last week, before Kitt called me, I snapped my femur.'

'Ouch.'

'That's what I said . . . or words to that effect.'

'How'd you do that?'

'Parachuting. It was my first jump and I blew it. Landed badly.'

Marina couldn't help laughing. 'If you were anyone else, I'd assume you were joking, but the way this whole thing is going . . .'

He laughed, a quiet, self-deprecating laugh. 'I'm on my arse, as you said, for the next six weeks.'

'Oh, God, *don't* come, then. I've enough invalids on my hands!'

'I'd have to book three seats on the plane.'

'Is it painful?'

'They've given me strong stuff. I'm a bit out of my head.'

'What's new?' she said. 'Have you someone to look after you? Wife? Stepkids?' She wondered why she hadn't yet asked this.

'Kitt's it, I'm afraid.'

'You never married?'

'Nope.'

'Ever?'

'Nope.'

'You're a bachelor? Matthew McGonagle is a *bachelor*?'

'What can I tell you? I thought it was the only fair thing to do – leave myself available to the women of the world.'

'How thoughtful of you.'

'It is, isn't it?'

But Marina was thinking: What a blow. The only person he could call his own cared about no one but herself. 'Oh!' she said suddenly. 'Brainwave! I'll send Kitt over to look after you. That solves everything.'

'I wish you wouldn't.'

'Hmm? Oh, I suppose not. She wouldn't even be able to make you tea.'

'Is she still that bad?'

'Hopeless.'

'I did try, Marina, I really did, but that kid was born with attitude and we haven't been able to knock it out of her. To be fair to her mother, she tried too, in her own ineffectual way.'

'Fine, but you can't expect me to do it.'

'I'll come as soon as I can.'

'You won't be able to travel for weeks. No, I'm sorry, Matthew. Her mother will have to take responsibility. Kitt has to go back to Spain, and the sooner the better.'

Marina woke with a jolt from a deep sleep. Someone was shaking her. 'What? Who is it? What . . .'

'It's me,' said Kitt. 'You'd better come.'

Marina was already out of bed, pulling on her dressing-gown, shaking all over. 'Come where? What's happening?'

'David. I was going to the bathroom and I heard him.'

They hurried up to his room. He was wheezing, groaning

and tossing. Marina turned on the bedside light. 'Jesus, he's burning up. Quick, run downstairs and get a glass of water.'

Kitt zipped off, moving faster than she had in days, while Marina ran to the bathroom, soaked a facecloth, then grabbed the thermometer strip and Panadol from the medical chest.

'What's wrong?' said Kitt, coming back up. 'What's happening to him?'

Marina stuck the strip to his forehead and began to sponge him down. 'A hundred and four!'

'Shall I call an ambulance?'

'No, no, but we've got to get his temperature down.'

She sponged and sponged, with Kitt running in and out with bowls of cold water, until David calmed a bit, the wheezing eased and his temperature lowered. Marina sat back, wiping her forehead. They had avoided a night-time rush to Accident and Emergency. That would certainly have rounded off the ghastliness of her homecoming – hours spent in A and E. What *was* going on? Just when she had reason to believe that she had established a new order, everything went peculiar. A new man, an old man, a skittish teenager, a sick student, a snapped femur, concussion, bruised vertebrae . . . Was this the chaos theory in action, with her at its vortex?

'Are you all right?' Kitt asked.

'Fine. You go to bed. I'll mind him.'

David was delirious. He called her 'Mum', pushed her away and got the shivers. Marina gathered blankets and tucked them round him, all the while cursing Matthew. When, in a lull, David slept, she thought about Luke. She wished she could talk to him; soak up his still presence, his unflappability. But even if she had his phone number, he'd be asleep now, down in Morocco.

Matthew, on the other hand, would be awake. It was early evening in Anchorage, and since it was his fault this was happening, he could damn well keep her company during her vigil.

'Great!' he said cheerfully, when she explained why she'd phoned. 'I'm bored out of my head with this damn leg.'

'I *had* been hoping to inconvenience you hugely.'

'Just let me make a coffee and settle down.'

'How long will that take with a broken leg?'

'About fifteen minutes.'

She laughed, and wished she hadn't.

'The truth is,' Matthew admitted, when they had been talking for some time, 'Kitt is a stranger, and it's very weird to love, more than anyone else, someone you don't even know. She's a real worry to me. Natalie means well, but she's all for nurturing individuality. The smother-'em-with-love school of parenting. She didn't see the pitfalls.'

'Tell me about Natalie.'

Their initial affair had been brief, he said. He forgot where they'd met – Amsterdam or Brussels – but he did remember four days of energetic sex with a very beautiful, long-limbed woman, who had such a cool streak running through her that he found her unfathomable. She neither loved nor needed him, which suited them both, but when she conceived, they were in the soup. She'd contacted him from England, told him she was keeping the baby and that she'd be in touch. He thought he'd dreamt it. One two-minute call, followed by silence. One two-minute call telling him he was having a child with a woman he barely knew. But they'd handle it, he reckoned. They'd do whatever sensible people in their situation did, although he hoped he wouldn't have to leave Anchorage. He'd been in too much shock to take a number from her, and had no address, so when she didn't get back to him, he wasn't sure what to think. She might have got the paternity wrong or had a termination;

or perhaps she'd found a better bet, a bigger sucker, than the long-distance stooge father. He tried to let it go, but couldn't. Nine months after that fruitful European fling there was still no word, so eleven months after her call, tormented by the thought that he might now have a child he knew nothing about, he flew to London to find Natalie. It would be a wild-goose chase, he suspected, but he didn't want some stranger arriving on his doorstep twenty years later, saying, 'Hi, Dad!' He wasn't optimistic about finding her – there had to be more than one Natalie Swift in England, and she might have married, but for his own peace of mind he had to try.

Natalie was not only easy to find but impossible to avoid. She was all over the place. It was easy to remember those limpid green eyes and that flirtatious grin when they were staring down at him from giant billboards from Heathrow to Trafalgar Square. There was a silly caption on her fingertips for a chain of home stores. Matthew rang their head office, got the name of their advertising agency, from them her modelling agency, and had left a message for her within half an hour of reaching his hotel.

Within hours, she returned his call. She was apologetic about her silence, but told him they had a daughter, that she was the most beautiful thing in the world, and that her life would never be the same again. Matthew sat on his bed, eyes brimming.

He met his two-month-old daughter that afternoon, and she was indeed beautiful. Natalie had changed; she was warmer, softer, and had shed some of the scars of her uncaring upbringing. Her own parents had been cold, she told Matthew, and mostly absent, leaving their daughters to nannies and boarding-schools, but now, for the first time in her life she was loved and in love, and Matthew was moved by her happiness. She was amenable to co-parenting, except for the Alaskan inconvenience. She could not bear to be parted from their daughter, not for one day, so he agreed to pay maintenance and promised to visit Kitt whenever he could. He asked Natalie when exactly she had planned to let him know he was a father. 'Soon,' she'd said, 'but I wasn't ready to share her.'

He was drawn to those green eyes – two sets of them now, gazing up at him.

Three people arrived back in Anchorage.

It started well. He worked hard at the oil terminal, earned a lot, and had great sex. 'Natalie believed that being a mother was her true calling since she was so very good at it,' he told Marina. 'Only she wasn't very good at it. She was so bewitched by motherhood, so besotted with Kitt, that she completely indulged her.'

The rot had set in early. By the time Kitt was three, she was insufferable – filled to the gills with rubbish food, sucking sweet red cordials from her bottle and prone to gravity-defying tantrums. He tried to control her, but any time she whimpered, her mother gathered her up. Natalie never raised her voice, not even when the child behaved abominably in other people's homes, and Kitt was so catastrophically spoilt by the time she was four that his relationship with Natalie foundered. She hated everything about Anchorage – the small-town mentality, the weather, being cut off from the rest of the world – and returned to England. Matthew kept sending the cheques.

The last three weeks, he admitted to Marina, had been a nightmare. He didn't know where Kitt was, and her mother declared unhelpfully that their daughter was off finding herself. 'And will she still be finding herself when some sleaze molests her?' he'd asked.

'She's learning about life,' Natalie had replied. 'Just like I did when I was her age.'

He couldn't resist saying, 'And you think it worked for you?'

'Then came that call from Kitt,' he said. 'From Ireland, of all places. When I was expecting a call from Interpol, she calls from a gas station in Cashel, for God's sake.'

'Like a salmon,' said Marina quietly. 'Back to her father's birthplace.'

'I guess she doesn't quite hate me.'

You have a lovely voice, Marina thought.

'And what's more,' he went on, 'she landed sixty miles from the warmest and most welcoming person I've ever known.'

'Don't say that. I haven't been either.'

'Reen, Mother Teresa would have turned Kitt out. But you do sound a bit down. Is everything okay?'

'I'm a little unsettled,' she admitted, thinking, for a moment, that she might reveal herself, dump her thoughts in the distances that lay between them. She was holding Luke in her belly. He was there all the time, when she spooned tealeaves from the caddy, put the key in the front door, wiped down the counter . . . There had been so many distractions since she'd got home, when all she wanted – in her new teenage-like state – was to curl up, listen to Ray La Montagne and daydream about what might have happened. It had been mutual, she was sure, the attraction. Yet Luke had been simultaneously effusive and elusive, telling her nothing, taking her nowhere. He had been like water in a desert, disappearing into the sand – welcome, refreshing, clear, and as swiftly gone as he had appeared.

And then she'd done some vanishing of her own.

'What has you so unsettled?' Matthew asked.

The urge to blurt passed. 'Morocco, I suppose, made me restless. It made me realize that I'm ready to get my life back – to get past this parenting thing and, I don't know, do other stuff. When I was away, it was as if I'd never had a husband or family. It gave me a taste of the next stage. I got married way too young.'

'But it was good, wasn't it? The marriage.'

'It was fine. Great. But I had Jacquie when I was twenty-three, and you know why that happened.'

'You couldn't get contraception?' He snorted at his own awful quip.

'Why do you think I ran into marriage straight from college, Matthew?'

'You fell in love?' he asked, hoping to steer her away from where she was going.

'Because all my friends had taken off, just like my mother took off, and I was dead bloody lonely.'

He ducked this by saying, 'Don't wish it away. The family bit, I mean. I envy you the big family home and people coming and going.'

'David's getting hot again. I have to go.'

'Okay. Talk to you later, Florence.'

Odd, she thought, that they had talked through the night like close friends, but neither of them had been inclined to mention the foundering of their earlier relationship and had managed to evade it even when it came up of its own accord.

'Pneumonia,' said the GP. 'He won't be going anywhere for a while. Is he a lodger?'

Marina slumped on to the stairs. 'He is now.'

'He should improve when the antibiotics kick in. He's very ill, though. His parents should know.'

'He's not in danger, is he?'

'No, but if he'd been in student digs, he might be a lot worse now.'

Back in the bedroom, Jacquie was sponging David's arms and chest.

'How the hell am I supposed to contact his parents?' Marina asked her. 'Can you get in touch with his friend?'

'Bill? I'm not sure where he is.'

'Oh, Jacquie, I was hoping *he* could phone them.'

'Why don't we just ask David for their number?' she whispered.

'It might unsettle him. He got very agitated during the night – thought I was his mother and that I'd catch this from him.'

'We could get it from his phone.'

'I suppose. It is an emergency of sorts.'

When Jacquie went to work, Dara watched David so that Marina could get to bed. She slept for three hours, and when she got up, Dara and Kitt were holding David up, helping him to drink. It moved her, the sight of the three of them – even Kitt rowing in, trying to help. 'You've got to drink,' she was saying to him. 'You won't get better otherwise, the doctor says.'

In there somewhere, Marina thought, there's a good kid. If only someone cared enough to find her.

She called David's home from his mobile, doing her best not to give his mother heart failure. Mrs Roche had an initial panic, but when Marina reassured her that the worst was over, she expressed concern that he would be an imposition (unlike some mothers – Natalie had still not called). She was mortified that David had been picked up at a petrol station by strangers. 'I thought his accommodation was sorted.'

'It is, but he wasn't well enough to move,' said Marina, 'and I'm very glad he didn't.'

'Goodness, you've been so kind. We must make arrangements to get him home.'

'He's really in no condition to travel, but is there someone who could visit?'

'My daughter Bernie is in Dublin, but I don't want to land someone else on you.'

'She'd be very welcome. If that would set your mind at rest, tell her to come on down.'

Kitt had to move into Jacquie's room to make room for Bernie, who arrived that evening.

Three strangers and counting, Marina thought.

'Whose life,' she asked Jacquie, 'have I suddenly come to inhabit?'

'Your own, Mum. You just don't recognize it. The planets are finally realigning. Don't you remember how it always used to be like this? People everywhere? I think it's great.'

'You don't have to cook for them all.'

The next morning, Marina finally went to see Suzanne. It was such a lovely late-September day that when she got to the river she took a stroll alongside it. The tide was in, the water high, the seagulls gliding. Her hometown had changed since she'd left it in the eighties. New buildings filled in old gaps, with a hotchpotch of styles ranging from the quite attractive to the absolutely hideous; other buildings had been torn down, disappeared, spruced up and, in some cases, reborn. County Hall, still the tallest building in Ireland, had been unceremoniously stripped and left standing naked for several months while it was re-attired in gleaming, eco-friendly garb.

More than a year after returning Marina still felt a stranger to the new Cork. In the old days, she could scarcely have crossed Patrick Street without meeting someone she knew, whereas now she could wander the length of its gentle J-bend, from the river to Grand Parade, and back again, without seeing a single familiar face. And yet the city was still home in a way that Dublin and Toulouse had never been. It had history, *her* history, embedded in its streets, and for all the friends and families from her childhood who had gone abroad or merely vanished into the suburbs that crept like bramble over the Cork hills, she felt settled there, and content. Her feet were in the right place. So it was probably just as well that she had not become involved with someone who lived in Italy.

Even this passing thought of Luke caused an uncomfortable twist inside her. Marina wondered, sometimes, if she'd conjured him up, if the alleyways of Essaouira had created their own mystical romance and made her believe in it.

The door of Suzanne's shop tinkled when she went in. It was delightful, this incense-scented place, with its draped fabrics, hanging lanterns, Indian jewellery, cabinets with ivory chess sets and Chinese teasets. It was a small business, the trade mostly limited to yoga teachers, fortune-tellers and belly-dancers, but Marina loved coming to sit with Suzanne, and inhaling the smell of exotic places while having a good gossip.

Suzanne was behind the counter. 'Eventually, finally and at last!'

Marina meekly held up a bag. 'I brought Danish.'

'I'll make coffee.' She went out to an alcove. 'What *is* going on?'

Marina slowly lowered herself on to a pouffe in the corner. 'Ow, ow, ow!'

'What's wrong?'

'My thighs haven't recovered from having a camel between them. Sometimes I'd swear he's still there.'

'But that was days ago.'

'I *know*.'

'Forget your thighs. I've been on the edge of my seat.'

'Brace yourself,' said Marina, as Suzanne handed her a mug. 'You look great by the way.' Suzanne had hair a bit like Marina's, curly but blonder, and she always looked out of place in her own shop. Instead of funky gear that might have matched the décor, she fancied designer clothes that were more in keeping with her charmed lifestyle. She had an adoring husband, well-balanced kids, and a large, prim house outside the city.

'Brace myself? Oh, my God, you met someone in Morocco!'

'What . . . um, look, sit down, would you?'

Suzanne perched obediently on her stool. 'Tell me all! Who? How? When?'

'That's not it.'

'You didn't meet someone?'

'While I was away, Matthew phoned.'

'*Matthew?* McGonagle?'

'Yeah.'

'Is he home?' Suzanne made a face. 'Is he still *alive*?'

'No, and yes, and he has a daughter, Kitt, who *is* home and staying with us.'

'You're not *serious*?'

'And she's very much alive.'

'How . . . nice for you?' Suzanne asked tentatively.

'Not really, no.'

As she told the story, watching Suzanne pushing errant flakes of pastry from her lip and into her mouth with a finger, Marina wondered where she would be without her. Without this release. Suzanne had been a lifesaver. They hadn't been close in college, but they knew the same people, the same stories, and when they had run into each other in the English Market, Cork's vast indoor food market, not long after Marina had moved back, it felt as if they had always been indispensable to one another. Suzanne was certainly indispensable to Marina now.

'Does he know what became of Gwen?' she asked.

'I haven't asked. I'm not up for it yet. One resurrection at a time, thank you. But the point is, his daughter is impossible, and one of the lads she turned up with is now seriously ill and being nursed by his sister who came down from Dublin last night.'

Suzanne blinked at her, chewing. 'What a homecoming.'

'Exactly. And I'd far rather be telling you about my trip.'

'Fire away, but even Morocco might seem dull in comparison to Matthew McGonagle's prodigal reappearance.'

'Oh, I don't know about that . . .'

'How come?'

'As it happens, I *did* meet someone.'

'You!'

It took Marina an hour to get through those first three days of her acquaintance with Luke, allowing for several offshoots. In truth, she was putting off coming to the end of the story. To its sorry, rootless end.

'And so we went to the desert,' she said, feeling a great weight lift from her belly where the story had been sitting, undigested, for four days. 'We left at seven, in a sort of bland early light, the sky empty, the seagulls coasting. There are no cars in the medina, so these lads wheel your luggage out to one of the *babs* – gates – in carts, and even though I only had a small bag, a guy duly came to take it for me and showed me the way. There was hardly anyone around and walking through those waking streets made me feel like a character at the end of a film, leaving town, whereas I *wanted* to feel like someone at the beginning of the film, setting off on an adventure. I wondered if I should back out, stay put, but when we got to Bab Marrakech, the jeep was there, and Luke appeared, and, oh, Suz, it was . . . sort of devastating. Here was this divine-looking man, coming towards me with his overnight bags, and we were heading off to the Sahara together, and he threw me a smile, sort of intimate and close . . . That's when all was revealed: why he was never available for dinner and was always looking at his watch.'

Suzanne gaped. 'Don't tell me he was with another woman.'

'He was with another woman.'

'Shit! Not his wife?'

'No.'

'Please tell me it was his . . . niece?'

'He's an only child.'

'Who, then?'

'His mother. And that's not all.'

# 7

Love had come. There was no more doubt about it. When Luke appeared, following his cart under the archway, and threw Marina a coy grin, it sent a shot of tingles to her toes. Her stomach was in a jumble. Four days' travelling in close quarters – too much exposure, probably, on top of their truncated dates. It was a mad, stupid thing to do, but she was still going to do it. Her marriage had been safe, happy, but frequently humdrum, and there had been no time, before they got hitched, for significant youthful mistakes about which she could now squirm. Here at last was an opportunity, perhaps, to make a spectacular fool of herself and join the ranks of the Seriously Embarrassed in Love.

She had never felt her humanity, her own smallness, more than she did that day, standing outside Bab Marrakech. In this mingling of vulnerability and impudence, in the way she expected disappointment, but stood out right in front of it, she was so flawed and hopeful that it gave her comfort. This was surely better than giving up on herself, so she vowed never to allow herself one moment of regret about this excursion, not even if she had to carry crushing disappointment all the way back to Cork and face into the long winter with no hope of reprieve.

'Is this our guy?' Luke asked her.

'I gather so.'

He loaded his luggage and went back into the medina.

She glanced at his stuff. Four bags?

The driver started storing the luggage.

When Luke returned, his mother was tottering behind him, all big hat and big airy cotton dress, but the rest of her was slight, small. Sunglasses dangled from a ribbon round her neck and she was wearing white tennis shoes. Luke introduced them, but his mother, Bridget, almost immediately climbed into the front seat; Luke opened the back door for Marina. Perfect. They would be cosy in the back together, she was thinking, when she heard him say to Mouloud, the driver, '*Encore une.*'

'We can't go without her,' said Bridget.

Marina froze. So it wasn't only his mother . . .

'We're not going without her, Mother,' said Luke, climbing in next to Marina.

The final member of their party appeared, a dramatic-looking woman, probably Italian, probably late forties, with copper hair cropped into a bob, perfectly arched eyebrows, and large, red-rimmed sunglasses. Her tanned face was unblemished by sun or age, and she was ideally dressed, in taupe cotton trousers and jacket, and navy runners.

'Marina,' said Luke, 'this is Carlotta. Carlotta, Marina.'

'Ah,' said Carlotta, 'the lady from Ireland.'

Marina hadn't a rat's arse of an idea of who she was, but Carlotta climbed in, on Marina's side, which meant she had to slide into the awful middle seat. It was way too soon to be pressed up against Luke for a long journey, so she pulled in her knees and elbows, and tried not to be there as they made their way out of town. She felt *coincée*, braced, and all she could think was, Shit, shit, shit. So much for having no regrets. She had them already. This was a very bad idea. Who *were* these people?

When they reached the top of the hill, she looked back wistfully at twinkling Essaouira. She would be returning for her last two days, but right now she wished she wasn't leaving it.

Luke's mother kept turning to ask him fretful questions.

'Have you packed wipes?' 'Are you sure I don't have to go on a camel?' 'How long until we reach a lavatory?' Later, when they were driving through a stretch of desert on the Marrakech road, she asked a very odd one: 'Do you know what "gibbous" means?'

'Umm . . .' Luke nudged Marina, nodding towards two men travelling on a moped with a goat squashed between them. He wasn't to know she felt like the hapless goat. 'The moon,' he said to his mother. 'Isn't the moon gibbous when it isn't quite full?'

'Or it can mean humpbacked,' said Bridget, 'and I was wondering if you could say a camel is gibbous. What do you think?' She glanced back at him and her eye caught Marina's. 'Goodness. Who are you?'

'Ma, I introduced you earlier,' said Luke. 'This is Marina. I told you she was coming along for the ride.'

'What ride? I thought you said I didn't have to go on a camel.'

Luke sighed.

Oh dear, thought Marina. He has a mother. And this is she.

So much for taking off across the desert *à deux*. The disappointment made her chest tight. She should have expected it. Nothing was straightforward with Luke. What you saw was not necessarily what you got. She would have to proceed with caution.

'Heavens,' said Bridget. 'Did you see that? Goats standing in a tree?'

Mouloud laughed. 'Yes. These are argan trees. Goats like to eat the leaves.'

Bridget was breathless, bossy and talked a lot. No wonder Luke was shy. He'd been in this considerable shadow all his life and probably hadn't been able to get a word in since birth.

But Marina learnt more about him by eavesdropping on his mother than she could have gleaned in a month of dinner dates with him. The Carlotta person, meanwhile, was making phone calls, speaking very loudly and waving her hands, then snapping her phone shut and cursing like a man. She spoke to Luke in Italian, to his mother in English, and in no language at all to Marina, who, as they reached Marrakech, still didn't know exactly who she was.

The traffic was crazy as they skirted the pink city. 'Marrakech!' Mouloud exclaimed. 'Couscous for the head!'

It crossed Marina's mind that Luke might, in fact, be married to Carlotta, who kept leaning forward to talk to his mother, very much like a caring daughter-in-law.

It really was unbelievable. He had gone out of his way to meet Marina over and over again, had spoken of how she would love Lake Orta, and enticed her on this trip, only to deliver her into this awkward situation. She fumed. He had another woman with him, above and beyond his mother, which made her feel like the proverbial square peg. But she had only herself to blame. So desperate had she been to get away with him that she had asked no questions, had simply signed on the dotted line and agreed to travel off into the wilderness without having the faintest idea whom she was going with! The woman who was writing 'Marina's Rules' shook her head ominously at the woman who was not applying them.

Another horrible thought occurred – could Carlotta be Luke's ex-wife?

South of Marrakech, they headed into the Atlas mountains, turning loops and hoops and hairpin bends, with the deep gash of a valley on one side. On this perilous road, children in colourful clumps of five and six walked with their satchels to school. Berber villages, flat-roofed and grey, blended into the hills, with only their minarets standing out, but then the mountains got higher and less hospitable, and the only relief in the rocky landscape was a thin strip of green, far below, travelling hopefully through the gully.

It was a long, long morning. The landscape changed from pink to grey to tan, as they wove round the contours, sometimes painfully slowly, as when they got caught behind a truck with cattle in the back and sheep in a pen on the roof, and later when they were following the nervous progress of two Western women in a very small car. Every time they turned a bend, a new panorama spread out and in the distance snow twinkled on the High Atlas. When they finally stopped for lunch, the hills were pinker and the valley broader, and the restaurant's terrace overlooked a trough of green fields at the foot of an unforgiving mountain. Marina stood by the railing, taking photos. Her mood was improving. Perhaps she had done the right thing – it was cheaper, doing this with others, and wonderful to have their own transport, and four days wouldn't be such a long time with scenery like this to distract them.

Luke joined her. Carlotta and his mother had headed straight for the ladies' room. 'She loves to travel,' he said.

'Sorry?'

'My mother. She loves seeing new places. But it's a bit like *Travels With My Aunt*.'

'Your aunt?'

'The Graham Greene novel. You haven't read it?'

'No.'

'You must. I have it at home. I'll give it to you.'

'You never mentioned that you were . . . with people.'

'I never said I wasn't.'

Eye contact: hers said, Oh, come on; his said, All right, I should've said something.

'We're staying with friends who have a house in Essaouira,' he explained, 'but my mother likes to get out and about very



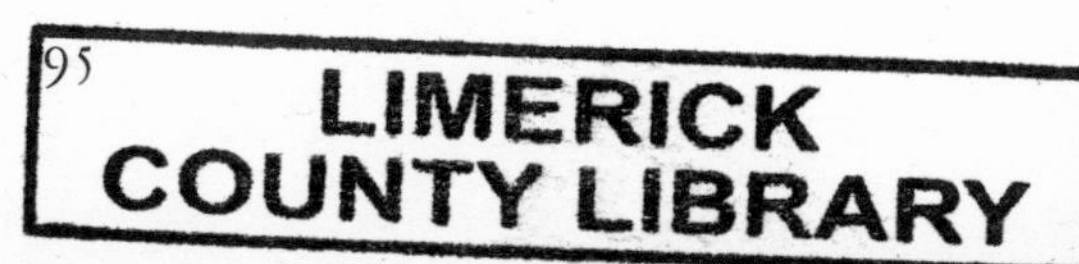
LIMERICK
COUNTY LIBRARY

early in the morning, then plants herself on the terrace with a book, and Carlotta's often busy with her work, so most of the time I'm effectively alone.'

'It's odd that I never ran into you all around the town.'

'I suppose, but Mother sleeps in the afternoons and we ate in most nights – there's a wonderful housekeeper, who cooks like a dream – so . . .'

He had not yet touched her, or even stood too close, or made any of those subtle moves that were the lowlands of seduction, but even in this vacuum of flirtation, he was moving steadily towards her.

Bridget sat beside Marina at lunch. She had dark beady eyes, and a sweep of lines, like an open fan, across her eyelids. Her greying black hair had tight curls. 'You do know, dear, don't you . . .'

Hoping for some unexpected confidence, Marina leant in.

'. . . that the dinosaurs aren't really extinct?'

Marina blinked. 'Em . . .' Luke and Carlotta were chatting to Mouloud. 'I . . . I think they are, aren't they? Wasn't there a bit of a problem with a meteor?'

'Nonsense!' Bridget said crossly. 'That's what everyone thinks! But palaeontologists know very well they never became extinct. It's the rest of the world can't accept it.'

'So, er, where are they?'

'Everywhere, dear. Everywhere! Even Antarctica and Siberia. Surbiton!' Bridget gripped Marina's wrist, her little eyes earnest. 'But not the desert. God knows, there's nothing much in the desert, is there?' She cackled. 'Except fossils from extinct species!'

Bridget then turned to her meal and didn't speak two words while she ate. Marina, in contrast, was off her food. She tried not to glance at Luke. She didn't want him to see the hot and thirsty look in her eyes. There could be no rushing this; no overtaking. It would happen or not on Luke's time.

Bridget chewed her last mouthful with sucking determination, and brushed crumbs off her lap. Then she was ready to speak again. 'They're everywhere, you see.'

'The dinosaurs?' Marina asked uncertainly, not sure if they were picking up where they'd left off, or starting on something else. 'Golly, I'd love to see one.'

The old woman's face dropped. 'A *dinosaur*? Don't be ridiculous!'

On their way out to the car, Luke came alongside her. 'Nice chat with Bridget?'

'Um,' said Marina. 'She was telling me about dinosaurs.'

'Not being extinct?'

She smiled. 'I wasn't sure what to say.'

'Nothing *to* say. She's right.'

*Great. Mad mother. Mad son.*

'She means the birds,' he explained.

Marina couldn't see his eyes through his shades. The lines beside his mouth were straight. 'Oh,' she said, as if that explained everything.

'They've evolved into birds. That's widely accepted now.'

'Is it?'

'Yes. She was making perfect sense.'

'I'll have to brush up on my palaeontology, so.'

'And every other subject as well,' he said ruefully. 'It's hard to follow her sometimes. She,' he rolled his hand around, 'rambles, but she has a very hungry mind. Lonely childhood, short marriage. All her life she's been waiting for . . .'

'What?'

'The Internet.'

They set off. Luke took the middle seat. Bridget's endless stream of loosely linked observations made an ongoing commentary: 'I wonder what that woman's thinking about while she's minding those goats?' 'Did you pack my white sweater, Carlotta? It's a little cool in these hills.' 'So many children. Children, children, everywhere.'

On the roadsides, packs of them proffered bunches of something green, men waved melons sliced in two, and at intervals pots and fossils were displayed outside flat little buildings, beleaguered on the hillsides. The mountains seemed to go on for ever – they could be seen way ahead, a peaked, and sometimes snowy, horizon. In the gully below, a grey river moved across gravel and women stood in the shade of trees, minding their flocks. Finally, mid-afternoon, they escaped the bends, the swaying and twisting, and emerged on to a red plain. Bridget dozed, snoring lightly, and Carlotta, too, closed her eyes.

'Aidan would have loved to see this,' Marina said. 'The way it keeps changing.'

'It must be tough,' said Luke, 'setting out alone, after all your plans.'

'It is, but I could sit at home and get crusty, or get off my arse and do it for the both of us. I can't hang out of my kids for the rest of my life.'

'How did Aidan die?' Luke asked suddenly.

She lifted her camera and took a shot of the looping river. 'Impatience.'

He waited.

'Impatience killed him,' she said. 'Someone coming along a road who couldn't be bothered to wait behind a slower car. A flicker of irritation, a flick of a switch – I often think about it, about that moment when the man's finger hit the indicator and ended Aidan's life.' Across the ravine, on the curve of a bare mountain, a lone, defiant tree stood out. 'It probably wasn't even a decision. More of an instinct – slower car therefore overtake, regardless of oncoming bend and whatever, whoever, might be beyond it . . . It's odd, really, how casually decisions like that are made every day, perhaps every minute, somewhere. Somewhere like here. They tumble into the abyss and it's all over.'

'You must have found today terrifying,' said Luke, aghast. 'Those bends. Had he been drinking, the other guy?'

'No, and he wasn't young and brazen. He just couldn't bear to get stuck behind a slower car, so he overtook it coming up to a bend and smashed right into us.'

'Jesus. You were in the car too?'

She nodded. 'I was unconscious for three days. Aidan was in a coma for longer.'

'How long?'

'For ever, you could say.'

His deep eyes watched her.

'Twenty-two months,' she said. 'They didn't think he'd last a week, so everyone rushed over to Toulouse from Ireland to say goodbye, and then we waited, and waited, and waited, watching him, already gone, but still there.'

'He must have been very strong.'

'He was in perfect health.'

'Did you think he'd come round?'

'Not for one minute. He'd already left, I knew that. It just took him a long time to die. He finally did so in the middle of the night when nobody was with him. The kids were in Ireland.' Marina's throat tightened. 'I'd gone back to the house. My father wasn't well.' Their surroundings were bleak, lunar, and she thought of Ireland's green hills and wished they were embracing her instead of this arid place. 'But those months left their mark,' she went on quietly. 'I aged by a lifetime. I can still feel the exhaustion of waiting to mourn, day after miserable day.'

'Brutal. Did the other driver survive?'

'No. He had small children, so for their sakes I wish he

hadn't died, but also for mine. At least then there'd be regret. Regret must be a terrible burden and I wish that burden on that killer – lifelong regret for flicking the switch on my husband's life. Nowadays Dara goes mad when people overtake only to end up a whole three metres in front of us at the next traffic-lights. And they go on, at home, about drink-driving and youths speeding, but so many accidents are caused by reckless overtaking, yet all they'll say on the radio is, "was in collision with . . ." What *is* that supposed to mean? "Was in collision with". They were on the wrong side of the road, that's what it means, but no one ever says that. They never say, "was using a mobile phone", "was fiddling with the radio" or "pulled out on a bend", so people keep on doing it, thinking they'll get round that slowcoach . . .'

Luke was looking grim. He moved his hand, as if he was about to take hers, but reconsidered. Marina was glad. She wanted him to touch her out of desire, not sympathy.

'Sorry,' she said. 'That was my rant. Ask how my husband died and you'll get my rant about "was in collision with".'

'How did you manage?' he asked. 'How *do* you manage?'

It was an odd kind of confessional, this Land Cruiser, with two snoozing women, strangers to her, beside them. They kept their voices very low.

'Badly at first,' she said. 'The world fell flat around me, and when the world is flat, there's no clear horizon. Nowhere to look. No gorges or shimmering mountains, no features in your own landscape – you know what I mean?'

'No, but go on.'

'You have to operate on the same dreary plain day after day. I didn't know which way to go. The children had their routines of school, college, friends, but I was so disoriented. Losing Aidan was like losing my motor, the thing that drove me. When I woke up every morning, he was no longer there, behind me in the bed. Never there when I stood in front of the wardrobe dressing for work. He used to watch me dress. I liked to be watched. We might discuss which earrings I should wear, which cardigan in case there was a chill later, what comb to put in my hair . . . I'd lost my audience. I didn't know which way to face.'

Some miles before Ouarzazate, they turned off the main road to get to their hotel in Tamdaght, and stopped on a ridge to take photos of one of Morocco's star performers, a well-known character actor: the Kasbah, or fortified town, of Aït Benhaddou. Immediately recognizable from films and post-cards, its buildings – squat, rust-coloured boxes and stumpy towers – ringed one side of a hill, which rose out of a broad riverbed.

'Used in *Gladiator*,' said Mouloud. 'And *Hidalgo*. *Lawrence of Arabia*.'

It was windy. Marina's skirt was blowing round her so she hunkered down to take photos. A little boy appeared out of nowhere – as they were wont to do in these desolate places – holding a large lizardy thing with a string round its neck. A pet, a money-earning pet. He put it on the ground, but it didn't move.

'Just a baby,' said Mouloud. 'He doesn't like the wind.'

Luke gave the boy some coins and wandered over to Marina.

'Did you ever see Bertolucci's *Sheltering Sky*?' she asked.

'Yes,' he said.

'It keeps coming back to me.'

'Because of the landscapes, I hope?'

'What else?'

'Don't you remember the highly irritating mother-and-son travelling duo?'

Marina laughed. 'I'd forgotten them.' She shielded her eyes to gaze across the valley. The river was almost dry. A woman was crossing it with a donkey. 'No, it's the mood of it that keeps creeping up on me. The feeling of being so far away from everything that you'll never get home.'

'And yet,' he said, 'this time next week you'll be back in Cork with your family.'

'And I'll be wondering if I was ever really here.'

'So will I.' He said it wistfully. Marina caught his eye.

They said these things as though they were together. It was as if she had acquired a lover without having to reveal herself to him, but their inadequate phrases were as personal and giving as a kiss. Words had, of necessity, become gestures of affection, private but powerful.

When they got back into the car, Carlotta talked away to Luke in Italian, and Marina wasn't surprised when he finally snapped, '*Basta. Parla inglese!*'

They had reached their Kasbah in Tamdaght, a rust-coloured adobe village behind a crumbling fort, where they were greeted in the courtyard by the owner. The hotel was like a small fort itself, with its arches and low towers, and they were shown along an open passage to rooms on the first floor. Bridget and Carlotta shared, and Luke was taken to a room on the roof in one of the square terracotta towers that braced the building.

Marina's room had deep pink walls and a good, hard bed, but she didn't waste time settling in. Even more than a shower, she wanted tea and went to find it. A passageway led over to the maze-like terrace, which offered a selection of seating areas on different levels. On the left, there was a boxed rectangle of seats where a few German tourists were having aperitifs, and beyond, a walkway led to a squat, square tower with an arched opening inside which a woman sat writing among cushions. How much she would have to write about, Marina thought, as she stepped up to a longer stretch of rooftop terrace, shaded by bamboo awning and perfectly pitched above the lush gorge that lay between the village and the flat heap of a mountain opposite. Leaning against a timber balustrade, she didn't know which way to look: at the tall, pockmarked blood-red towers of the abandoned fort, with stork nests sticking out of them like tufts of hair, or along the valley to the brown hills in the distance that gave a hint of the dryness beyond, or just below her at a group of women coming out of the dense grove across the street, carrying huge baskets piled high with green shoots. When a donkey got in their way, one of the older women gave it a slap and sent it running, yelling such abuse after it that the others cracked up, laughing so much that they had to put down their loads to double over.

Determined not to allow her attraction to Luke to blunt her appreciation of their surroundings, Marina rooted herself in the moment. The sun was going down, turning the earthen buildings a deeper red and sharpening the already mesmerizing contrast between the rusty mountain and the gushing green of the oasis, while the chortle of the women and the bray of donkeys stole the silence.

'Can't see my mother lugging a load like that in from the field.'

Luke was right behind her. 'Jesus! Don't creep up on me like that!'

He put his hand on her forearm. Pleasure flooded through her. His thumb and fingers moved up to her elbow, and with a light grip of her upper arm, he brought her closer. Her hand touched his shirt, she felt his belt against her side.

'*Eccoti!*'

Too late.

Carlotta swept towards them, but stopped in her tracks when her eye caught the splendid expanse of almond groves and palm trees. '*Che meraviglia!*'

With a slight squeeze, Luke let go of Marina's arm.

'I have ordered tea,' Carlotta said imperiously, coming over to them, as if it was at her behest and not the first thing that happened whenever you crossed any Moroccan threshold.

Bridget soon followed, stopping to look over a railing, then joining them at the low table under the awning. 'There are camels down there,' she said to Luke.

'Well, there would be, Ma. This is Morocco, after all.'

'Yes, but why aren't they in the car park?'

Marina sucked in her lips. Bridget was frequently disconcerted, and always disconcerting. It was, as Luke said, hard to follow her train of thought, her direction. You had to concentrate fully to stay with her, because she was often perfectly lucid, but you could lose her, suddenly, and not know where you'd ended up, which was probably how Bridget felt. Marina wasn't inclined to put in the effort. She'd minded her own father for years and simply hadn't the energy, or inclination, to take Bridget on, even for a few days. Her patience had grown thin. Far better, she decided, to be subdued, like Luke, and absolve herself of conversational responsibilities where his mother was concerned.

A tall angular man in a fez and white *jellabah* brought their tea, introduced himself as Ahmed and sat down. While he poured, tasted, and poured, Marina sat back, enjoying the pink evening, the soft voices around the roof, and the thrill of anticipation. They had been foiled, but not for long. It was now only a question of opportunity. In this beautiful place, with Luke sitting across from her in a deep rattan chair, she felt a surge of happiness such as she had not experienced for years.

Ahmed was telling them that there were ninety-nine different words for 'God'.

'Indeed,' said Bridget, 'and I'll tell you another one – *Dia*. God, in Irish!'

Luke caught Marina's eye. Neither of them looked away until Carlotta squeezed his knee, then left her hand resting on his thigh while asking, 'And, Marina, what business are you in?'

'Teaching. I give grinds – private tuition – to secondary-school students.'

'Ah, you mean a part-time position? How lucky for you that you don't have to work! I suppose you received some considerable insurance when your husband died?'

'Carlotta!' said Luke. 'That's hardly our business!'

She had been eavesdropping in the car, had heard Marina speak of her raw loneliness. 'As it happens,' she said, trying to pass beyond an acute feeling of nakedness, 'I work very hard. I see students four nights a week, which requires a lot of preparation. These are important exams for them, and tough ones too.'

'Are the teachers in Irish schools not good enough?'

'They're excellent. They're also very overworked.'

'But there is no such thing as too much work,' Carlotta declared.

Marina could think of no reply, which was exactly, she suspected, as Carlotta liked it. She was formidable – successful, multilingual, confident – and deeply intimidating.

Bridget's endless perambulations round a subject made dinner in the blue-tiled dining room a tedious affair, but Luke, rightly, showed no sign of being embarrassed by his mother. He let her be who she was; it wasn't up to him to apologize for an elderly woman's irritating foibles. But he did fiddle with his food, glancing reproachfully at Marina, as if it was she who had taken his appetite. Her mind wasn't on food either. She could think only of darkness, of being alone with him, of how it might be.

The others opted to have coffee in the sitting room by the

courtyard, but Marina retired early. Luke was unlikely to come to her room and yet she waited. Luke, after all, did not behave like anyone else and it wasn't inconceivable that he might knock on her door and get this under way, quickly and sharply. It wouldn't be hard to escape his mother, if he wanted to, so she didn't undress. All she had to sleep in was an over-large T-shirt – hardly alluring; instead, she sat in her jeans, captive to the sounds from the courtyard, tormented by that furtive grasp of her elbow, that almost kiss.

It was half past ten when she heard them come up, Bridget saying to Carlotta, 'Really, dear, I don't know what I'd do without you,' as they walked past her window.

'Well, you don't have to worry about that, *cara*,' Carlotta replied, in her throaty Italian accent. 'I will always be here for you.'

Luke called goodnight. Doors closed. Marina sat rigidly on her bed, missing the cat and Becky. When, half an hour later, he had not come, she pulled on her T-shirt, wondering what on earth she'd been thinking. Of course he hadn't come! What kind of a bloke would go to a woman's room before he'd even kissed her, and with his mother in the next room? It would have been completely inappropriate, as well as unattractive. Where, along the way, had she left her common sense?

In the middle of the night, she woke, and lay listening to the quiet. The sheets were laundered to a crisp and she was tucked into the blankets as tightly as a baby. Here, a long, long way from home, in a mud village on the edge of the desert, she did not feel anxious or homesick, and that, she suspected, was because Luke was upstairs in his tower.

The next morning, he was first down, Marina second. They met like lovers, carefully timing their arrival in the dining room, he standing as she sat down, Marina not quite looking at him, her hand elegantly swiping along the back of her skirt as she pulled it in to sit.

'Breakfast as usual,' he said.

She helped herself to a pancake.

'Ready for another long day?'

'It's the long night I'm worried about,' she said. 'And the trek.'

'It'll be fine. It's only short. We meet the guy in a place called M'Hamid, right at the end of the road, and he'll take us into the dunes. But if you're not up to it, you could stay here with Ma. We're coming back for her tomorrow.'

'I'm not chickening out! It's exciting.'

'Yes, it is,' he said, holding her eye. 'I'm very excited.'

Before they left, Marina went to the terrace to take in once more that extraordinary view, this time in brisk, early-morning sunlight. Across the street, at the foot of a huge and magnificent palm tree, a woman was rinsing clothes under a tap with a washboard. Further along, kids were feeding a young white camel. Behind her, Carlotta and Bridget came from their room and went down the steps. Marina was apprehensive about closing herself into a jeep with Luke and Carlotta and, in some strange way, was already missing Bridget's neutralizing presence.

She could see her own shadow on the greenery across the street and, as she looked out, Luke's shadow appeared beside hers as he came up behind her. He took her elbow again, turned her, threw a glance across the almond grove, and kissed her.

Twenty years fell away.

Bridget waved them off, reassuring Luke that she would probably snooze until they came back the next day. Carlotta took the front seat. She was a family friend, Luke had said, and Marina wanted to like her, but Carlotta kept a gully of indifference firmly lodged between them. By speaking Italian to Luke, she made it impossible for Marina to take part in their conversations, which was fine. Marina's mind was on other things.

Bliss, it was, in the back seat. They had loads of space when they no longer wanted it, but Luke was restrained and Marina concurred. She didn't really know Carlotta or, so far, much like her. Their fledgling relationship was none of her business.

They reached Ouarzazate – Hollywood in the desert – early on, and Mouloud took them to a hill from which they could look down on sound stages, trailers, fake Ancient Egyptian monuments and a fake Chinese yard. 'It's because of the light,' Mouloud explained, 'and because this can look like many different places. *Alexander*, *Babel* – all made here.'

The Drâa valley, a curve of green, several hundred miles long, crammed with trees and gardens, fields and forts, mud villages and modern towns, was far more captivating. Its palm trees looked like pineapples wedged into a box, and when Mouloud took them off-road, they bumped along a track through busy villages deep in the oasis. Carlotta scarcely put down her camera, while Marina barely noticed the screaming children running alongside or the coy smiles of the working women. Luke had his arm on the back of the seat. He touched her shirt collar, fingered her hair. Her knees fell towards his, though she looked away from him, gazing out, seeing nothing, aware only of his hand on the nape of her neck. She bit her knuckle, remembering the grove that morning, the swift kiss, the quick flick of a tongue before they had to pull apart and carry their luggage downstairs. Quietly she took a deep breath, resisting the temptation to lean into his hand. Perhaps Bridget and Carlotta's presence was a good thing. Had they not been with him in Morocco, it might have been a hot, breathless affair, all sultry nights and physical delight, instead of this discreet, and thrilling, courtship.

The winding Drâa valley went on and on, juicy and lush, aridity pressing in on both sides. It had the effect on the eyes of a gumdrop on a dry mouth. The day, like the valley, was long, with tea here, photographs there, and lunch by a swimming-pool in a hotel shaded by clumps of palms. When they were waiting for the food to come, Luke and Marina cooled their feet in the water, listening to a group of musicians clapping and singing in the bar.

Carlotta was tapping away on her laptop at their table in the garden. 'What does she do?' Marina asked Luke.

'She's worked in shipping most of her life.'

'Shipping?'

'Yes. You'd expect it to be the arts, or Milanese fashion, but she's made her living sending cargo ships round the world. She made some shrewd investments, which allowed her to retire early to Orta, which was what she thought she wanted, but she couldn't stick it, of course, so now she works from home as a consultant.'

'Doesn't she ever stop?'

'She can't. It's the air she breathes.'

It got hotter, much hotter. They came across their first large dune late that afternoon, not long after seeing a herd of camels grazing on a stony plain, but it was nearly five when they reached the end of the road in the dust-blown town of M'Hamid and fell out of the car into the belly of a still scorching day.

Marina sent a text to her kids: 'Have found the end of the road, and it's in Morocco.'

'I'd rather see it as the beginning of the road,' Luke said to her.

Mouloud introduced them to Hachim, who in turn introduced them to their camels. There was no delaying. It was out of the car and on to the camel. Marina got a leg over and was made to sit right back, behind the hump, before being jolted forward when the camel stood up. She nearly went over its head. Carlotta was led out first and Luke took up the rear, which meant Marina could not laugh at him as he could at her when they set off, heading out from under clumps of greenery across a grey plain, Tuareg scarves wrapped round their heads and faces to protect them from the heat.

The camel's gait made for a pleasant, rolling ride, but without saddle or stirrups, her legs hung limply over the coarse blanket, which was as uncomfortable as it was ungainly. She made mental notes for her book: *How to get rid of an unwanted suitor: take him on a camel trek. Your face will go puce, your posture will be compromised, your legs will dangle, you'll giggle like a child, and every time the camel goes down the tiniest slope, you'll lurch forward like a sack of potatoes being thrown into a truck.* Marina-of-the-Rules had clearly dissociated herself from the real one. They were no longer the same person. In fact, Marina didn't much like her alter ego. Such a priss.

As for herself, she preferred a more positive perspective: seeing the sun set in the desert, enjoying the rolling motion and the quiet. Riding a camel was a very quiet experience, as its spongy feet spread out across the sand – until it had something to say. At one point, the rope yoking her camel to Carlotta's became detached, and he whined and whimpered and took off to the right. Without a rope pulling him forward, he didn't seem to realize that all he had to do was follow the arse in front of him. (Or, indeed, Marina thought, the arses in front of him.) Hachim responded to its distress by catching the camel and soothing it with endearments, as if it was a child who had dropped its toy.

With dusk well established, they saw in the distance a huddle of low, brown tents – not a moment too soon: the coarse blanket was chafing Marina's legs. But when they came into the camp, she didn't want to get off. The camel had other ideas and knelt down, almost propelling her over its cute little ears. Stiff and sore, she hobbled away, smiling at Carlotta, who was none the worse for the exertion. She wasn't even a tiny bit pink, but stood with her hands on her lower back, well satisfied. Her cream cottons betrayed no sign of nearly two hours on a camel and nine on the road. There probably wouldn't be a single bloody grain of sand on her, Marina thought ruefully, pulling off her headscarf and feeling her own dried-out hair, which was already providing housing for enough Saharan particles to make a sand dune.

They were shown to a large tent with red carpets laid out, but no cushions. Marina lowered her weary limbs and sore bottom on to the hard ground. The smaller tents were unexpected. Luke had said bedding would be provided, but she had imagined them lying round a fire, staring at the stars all night. Instead, Hachim explained that there was one tent for the women and one for Luke. Marina had to share with Carlotta. Luke would, once again, be kept from her.

'And we have modern toilet.' Hachim pointed to a small white cubicle, nestling in a dip between ridges of sand.

'I think I'd prefer to pee behind a dune,' said Marina, relieved to see one of the lads coming over with a tea-tray. 'Mind you, I once read about a girl on a trip like this, further south, who went out to pee at night and got lost. No amount of shouting roused anyone from her camp.'

'Could easily happen.' Luke stretched his legs out on the rug. He also looked dead cool and uncrushed.

How did they do it, these Italians? Marina wondered wearily.

'What happened to her?' Carlotta asked.

Marina blinked. It was the first thing Carlotta had said directly to her all day. 'A Tuareg found her at dawn,' she replied, 'and brought her back to the camp. Oh – Carlotta, you should maybe get up, there's a large spider –'

Carlotta leapt so swiftly to her feet that she lost her balance and fell back, right into Luke's arms – he was getting up beside her. He caught her as the ugly white spider crawled past them on the carpet. Marina also stood up. It wasn't so much the way he had caught her as the way he held her, his arms clasped below her breasts, her hands gripping his forearms. There wasn't a trace of self-consciousness. Luke took his time, putting Carlotta back on her feet, and she took her time letting go of him.

He had held her before. They had held one another.

Later, they sat round a large fire, enjoying a tagine made in a kitchen tent further along the ridge. A thin sliver of moon, shadowed by Saturn, dangled in the sky, while Hachim told them how things had changed since the rains had stopped coming. Fifteen years before, a family would have had a hundred or more camels, he said, and they would go out to the sands for long stretches, and come back into the oasis when they needed to, living a rich, simple life. But since the rains had stopped – Marina had seen dying palm trees at the edge of the oasis – the animals had gone hungry and the people had left. Tourism, he said, was now allowing some of them to stay in their homes by their desert.

'That makes me feel better about my carbon emissions coming here,' Marina said.

'How strange,' said Carlotta. She was even more beautiful in the glow of a campfire. 'The desert was once in its rightful place, but now it is spreading like a disease where it should not go, and we are to blame.'

Hachim invited them over to the other, smaller fire, near the kitchen tent, to watch the cook bake bread in the sand. They sat round a clump of burning twigs, and when the dough was ready, the cook pushed aside a pile of embers, making a dent beneath them in the sand, and put the dough down, covering it with hot embers. They watched it rise.

'I know about this,' said Carlotta. 'It is thousands of years old, this method.'

Marina could feel Luke's knee against her back. She was like the bread – smothered in glowing heat, burning, rising – but would they have any opportunity to be together? She could hardly go to his tent, and they'd get lost if they strayed from the camp, so how were they to make this most memorable night even more perfect?

The cook scraped away the embers and pulled out a crunchy ring of hot, delicious, bread, which they munched while Hachim and his friends sang, using empty plastic containers for drums. Marina clapped along, feeling Luke's hand come beneath her shirt, his thumb massaging her lower spine, his fingers on her hip, just inside the waistband of her loose cotton trousers. But by the time the twigs had burnt out, so had she. Exhaustion had outpaced desire. She was too whacked to think of anything except sleep, but Luke and Hachim coerced her into climbing a high dune to get a perfect view of the night sky. Carlotta turned in, but following Hachim into total darkness, they lumbered up the side of the dune, where they sat on the crest, talking dreams and constellations. Luke found Marina's hand in the cold sand and squeezed her fingers. Her heart contracted.

'Marina!'

Jolted awake, she opened her eyes and saw, beyond the flaps of the tent, the overly adorned sky. It was wearing too many stars. Too much bling, she thought groggily, pulling up her blankets. A sprinkle of sand showered her face. There was a fine layer of particles on her neck. She had become a piece of sandpaper in her sleep.

Again, the whispered call. 'Marina!'

Luke, coming to squirrel her away to his tent?

No – Carlotta, needing to pee. 'Will you come with me?'

'Of course. The torch is outside.'

They crawled from their bedding, bumped into each other, and felt their way out. Someone in the camp was snoring. Mouloud was asleep on the roof of the jeep. Marina felt for the torch, found it and switched it on, just as she tripped over a guy rope. She sniggered, and Carlotta laughed too, as they linked arms. They followed the beam until Carlotta also tripped, this time on Luke's tent, and stumbled on towards the 'modern' toilet – a canvas box over a hole in the ground some way beyond the nearest dune. Their legs began to sink into the sand as they skirted the dune and when Marina's disappeared knee-deep, Carlotta had to pull her out, while she gripped her sandal with her toes so as not to lose it in the belly of the Sahara. It made them laugh more, and they struggled on, giggling like schoolgirls and falling over each other, saying, 'Shush! Shush!'

It was lovely. Fun. The start of a friendship, Marina thought.

# 8

Two days later, after an arduous journey back across the plain, along the valley, through the mountains and with a stopover in Marrakech, they arrived in Essaouira. As they unloaded outside the medina walls, Marina no longer knew where she stood. One kiss in four days did not amount to the romantic adventure she had anticipated; she felt dispirited, and lonely again. Declining the offer of a cart, she watched Carlotta and Bridget walk off together without saying goodbye. Exhausted as she was, it cut her to the core.

Luke caught her expression. 'They probably think you're going the same way.'

'Well, I'm not. Look, thanks for everything. Great trip. See you.' She turned on her heel so as not to appear to be waiting for another invitation.

'Marina?' he called. 'Tomorrow? Usual place?'

*Always tomorrow. Never tonight.* She could play that game too. 'Maybe.'

Back in the same room in the *riad*, nothing could take from the pleasure of a shower. Her thighs ached and her coccyx was bruised, but she'd done it, and she had Luke to thank for that. Standing under the flow of water, she sighed and wondered. Luke provoked a lot of wondering. In the end of it all, their desert trek had not been conducive to intimacy, but had been hard-going and draining, resulting only in a sore body and a sore heart. After her shower, she pulled on a kaftan and started to pack, so that she could spend all the next day, her last, with

Luke, should he wish to spend it with her. He had one more chance to show decisiveness, intent.

As she folded her things, she heard a voice.

'Marina?' Low and quiet. She stepped out on to the balcony and looked into the courtyard. No one.

'Marina?'

'Becky?' She leant towards their window.

'Can you come in here?' Becky's voice was faint.

Alarmed, Marina hurried next door. She knocked lightly and went in. Their room was in darkness.

'Thank God you're back,' Becky said. The bedside lamp went on. She and Rob were lying on their bed.

'Good God. What happened?'

Becky's face was swollen, bruised, and she had plasters on her chin and over an eyebrow. Her wrist was bandaged. Rob was flat on his back, asleep, his arm in a cast. 'Car accident. This morning. Our fault, I think.'

'You poor things!' Marina sat beside her. 'Are you okay?'

'They said we were fine to leave hospital and fly home tomorrow, but I feel so faint. Every time I try to get up, I want to pass out.'

'What about Rob?'

'He's broken his wrist and hurt his back. The painkillers knocked him out. How are we going to get home? I can barely stand, but we have to pack and order a taxi and –'

'You can't possibly travel tomorrow!'

'We have to, and if you could help us pack, we'll manage.'

'But what about the journey to Marrakech?'

'I know. It'll be ever so hard. I'm not sure how Rob'll manage, he was in such pain, and, God, I just wish we were home right now! We can't afford to stay – our insurance won't cover it, not when the hospital cleared us to travel. Will you help me pack? I've got such a bad headache.'

‘Of course, but you need to calm down. Let me get you some tea.’

‘Can you help me to the bathroom? Every time I try, I get woozy.’

‘Okay, take my arm, sit up slowly . . . Good girl. Here, lean on me.’ They hobbled across the floor. ‘Are you sure they cleared you to travel? You’re probably concussed.’

‘If I am, I want to be concussed in England.’

Marina gave her water, tea and painkillers, and heard about the skid they’d taken on the Safi road, hitting another car side on. Becky talked about police and ambulances, and cried a lot. She was in shock, completely unfit to move, but the more Marina tried to persuade her to stay, the more desperate she became to get home. When at last she fell asleep, Marina tried to pack their stuff into as few items of luggage as possible. How could they do it? Three hours in a taxi, then the airport, the flight . . .

Her own exhaustion didn’t help. She had slept little in the tent, and hardly at all in Marrakech where, again, she had waited pointlessly for Luke to come to her. It was catching up, her little adventure, bringing with it a gloomy self-pity. And now this: a car accident. A ruddy car accident. She could hear the horns, the skids, the impact . . .

Rob stirred. ‘Oh,’ he said, when he saw her.

‘I came in to help Becky,’ she whispered. ‘She asked me to do your packing.’

‘*Fuck*. My back. I can’t move.’

‘What?’

‘I can’t . . .’

She hurried over to him. ‘You’re probably just stiff. You haven’t moved for hours. Roll on to your side and try to get up from there.’

Even turning caused him to groan, but at least he was moving.

'You should never have been released from hospital.'

'We're okay. We got off lightly, considering. I'm really sorry – but I need to pee.'

Marina helped him to his feet, through lots of cursing, and walked him to the bathroom. When he emerged, he shuffled back to the bed unaided, but watching him lie down made Marina wince. 'Did they say what you've done to your back?'

'They said it's just bruised. But, fuck, the pain.'

'Do you really have to travel tomorrow?'

'God, yes. At least at home our families can look after us. And I want someone to check my back. Feels like more than bruising to me.'

'But how will you sit in a bouncing taxi for three hours, let alone a plane for another four?'

'Dunno, but I'm not lying here for the next three days either.'

'Look,' said Marina, 'I'll bunk down on your couch in case you need me. And I'll come to Marrakech with you.' Words flowed out. She was so deeply tired; their fretful homesickness was catching and the crash had made her jittery. Just like them, she wanted to be home. 'In fact, I'll fly back with you. I'm due to travel the next day anyway, so they can bump someone off your flight on to mine.'

Rob still hadn't interrupted to protest and say, no, no they'd be fine, not at all, wouldn't hear of it. Instead he said, 'Jesus, thanks, that'd be great,' and fell asleep.

Back in the shop, in Cork, Suzanne's eyes were wide with amazement. 'And Luke?'

Marina bit her lip. 'Yeah. And Luke. We were gone by seven the next morning. He probably assumed we'd missed each other on that last day.'

'But that last day was his chance to get your number, your address! Did you leave a message?'

'Yes.'

'And?'

'Nothing. I told them at Reception that if anyone asked for me to explain what happened and give them my number. That's as much as I could do.' She sighed heavily.

'And all because you chose to help two strangers who, if you don't mind my saying, would have found their way home perfectly well without you. How much did this little escapade cost you?'

'A few hundred euro. I had to pay the full price to get a seat on the Cork flight, but I really didn't care. It's my worst nightmare, you know, when I'm away – getting sick or hurt when I'm on my own, and the car accident . . . freaked me out.'

'Oh, sweetie, of course it did,' said Suzanne, gently. 'I wasn't thinking.'

'Besides, Becky and Rob were in a state. Getting to Marrakech was desperate – he was stretched out in the back and she kept keeling over, and when we got to the airport, we had to bully the airline into accommodating us. Rob couldn't take the painkillers until he was actually on the plane or I would have had to carry him through the airport. There were no damn seats on the flight, but he persuaded a couple to stay another night at his expense to make room for me. Then we had to change the tickets and names – it was a fiasco. They're hoping to claim it all back.'

'But what about Luke?'

'Luke's gone. We thought we'd have another day. We didn't. I don't know where he lives; he doesn't know where I live. If he did get my number, he hasn't called, and if he didn't, he thinks I took off without saying goodbye.' With difficulty, Marina got to her feet and went to the window. 'And there was me, thinking of romantic assignations on the shores of Lake Orta.'

The largest bouquet she had ever seen was waiting in the hall when she got home. 'Could barely get it through the front door,' Kitt grumbled, as if it had been sent to annoy her.

Marina stood staring at it, everything inside her going jingly-jangly. How had he found her address? She pursed her lips to discourage a smug smile. Her hand was shaking when she took the card.

'Wow,' said Jacquie, coming in behind her. 'Who are those from?'

Marina was staring at the card.

'Well?'

'Becky and Rob. "Forever grateful to our guardian angel."'

'Good on them. You earned it.'

'You're popular,' Kitt said, when Marina came in the next afternoon to the sight of another bouquet. She was more cautious this time, but could not stop her heart flittering about when she picked up the card. 'For your astonishing generosity, love always, Matthew.'

'Love, indeed,' she said out loud, considering the flowers. They were from the wrong man, but they were beautiful, especially with another bouquet next to them in the bay window of the living room.

Get over it, get over it, get over it, she told herself. It was a holiday thing, a mild flirtation. He wasn't going to come looking for her.

On the third day, more flowers. Dreading another disappointment, she tried to guess who could have sent this wonderful presentation before opening the card. She couldn't think of anyone, and although there was no reason for Luke to do so either, that first bouquet had sparked her expectations and with every new Interflora delivery, those expectations would not be smothered. 'Warmest gratitude', from David's parents.

David was over the worst. His lungs sounded like those of someone shovelling coal, and his raucous coughing made every other chest in the house ache in sympathy, but he was improving. His sister, Bernie, was unobtrusive. When David slept, she went for walks, or into town, trying to make something of her unexpected week off.

Kitt wouldn't shift. As much as she didn't want to leave, Marina didn't want her to stay. It was the principle of it, and the infuriating presumption. She refused to be taken for granted by these two useless parents. Matthew, perhaps, could be forgiven in his current state of immobility, but Natalie was chancing it. Her voice, the one time Marina had spoken to her, was vague, wishy-washy. She probably had a limp handshake. Limp, like the way she mothered. In many respects, it would have been easier to allow Kitt to stay until Matthew came for her – plant her in front of the television, Marina thought, for the next six weeks and no one would notice. Let her eat biscuits.

But that would be condoning neglect. The parents had to take account of their daughter.

'I've asked your father to make arrangements for you to go home to Málaga,' she told Kitt one evening.

Kitt was aghast. 'But I don't want to leave yet!'

'You can't stay here indefinitely.'

'But you've loads of room. God.'

'You should be with your mother.'

'Why?'

'Why not?'

'I don't like her boyfriend.'

'What's wrong with him?'

'I just don't like him.'

'You're not avoiding him, are you?'

'You mean did he try to touch me up? As if I'd let that prick anywhere near me. Can't I stay a bit longer?' she whined.

'Kitt, since you don't care about us, why should we care about you?'

Kitt ran her fingertips over grains of sugar on the table. No smartarse reply was forthcoming. Progress, perhaps, but Marina didn't like her tone. Her own tone. She was being so unrelentingly sour to the girl that it shouldn't surprise her that Kitt was being sour to her. And she wasn't being fair either. Kitt's unfortunate presence, her lumbering ingratitude, was the most obvious target upon which to take out her frustration about Morocco. Every time she opened her mouth to be kind to Kitt, bitterness seeped out. 'Have you even phoned your dad to see how he's managing with his broken leg?'

'Why should I?' said Kitt. 'There's nothing I can do about it.'

'He's in a lot of pain. Wouldn't it be nice to see him? He's all on his own.'

'If you're that worried about him, you go.'

'I'd love to,' said Marina, 'but I have to look after you.'

'I don't need looking after.'

'Fine. If that's the way you want to live – dirty clothes and fast food – you know where the door is.'

For a moment she thought she'd got through to her. Then Kitt wrinkled her nose. 'Yeah, how come my clothes haven't been washed yet?'

Suzanne turned up later that evening, curiosity hanging off her like an ill-fitting skirt. Kitt was, as ever, slouched in front of the television with biscuits, *sans* plate, and milk.

‘It’s quite endearing, really,’ Marina whispered, when they went down to the kitchen. ‘Under all that foundation, there’s a little girl who just wants a glass of milk.’

Suzanne sat down. ‘You’re not becoming attached, are you?’

‘No chance. Especially at the moment when I’m . . .’

‘Sore and in love?’

‘Well, I’m certainly still sore – from my desert campaign – and as for being in love, it’s not much use to me, is it?’

‘I can’t believe you let this happen, Marina. Don’t get me wrong – I feel for the English couple, but for heaven’s sake, good men are hard to come by and you’ve walked away from one of them. What are the chances of meeting someone else you like this much?’

‘Nil, but what am I supposed to do about it? Anyway, he was probably just in it for the sex.’

‘What sex? There wasn’t any!’

‘You know what I mean,’ said Marina.

‘No, I don’t. He was extraordinarily restrained, which means he took you seriously. Please don’t give up on him. He sounds like a real dote.’

‘Yes, and with a doting mother too.’

‘Have you looked him up online?’

Marina gazed towards the window. ‘Yes.’

‘Excellent. Correct answer.’

‘There’s nothing there.’

‘That’s odd, if he’s renting holiday lets.’

‘There are loads of villas and apartments up for grabs near Lake Orta, but not one website makes reference to a Luke Delahunt. Maybe he gave me a pseudonym.’

‘What did his mother call him?’

‘“Dorrling.”’ They laughed.

‘With an Irish *orr*,’ said Suzanne. ‘Where is it exactly, this lake?’

'Near Maggiore. Much smaller, though. Looks divine.' Marina propped her cheeks on her fists. 'What am I going to do, Suz? I feel sick all the time and I'm crotchety with the kids. When I think of the hoops and loops I put myself through and all the *angst* about whether to risk getting involved again, only for it all to go out with a tiny *pfff* . . . It's soul-destroying. All this stuff – David and Kitt and the house filling up again – it's like a new start, and I should be getting a real buzz out of it, but I'm not, because it can't compare to the buzz I was getting this time last week. I came too close,' she said, 'that's the problem. It was right there, but I just couldn't grasp it.'

'Look, if you can't find him, he'll find you. He can look you up in the phone book. Doesn't take a genius.'

'The number's still under my father's name, remember?'

'Oh, shit.'

Marina had six students that term, who came across the week, for an hour each, Monday to Thursday, after dinner. It was a welcome distraction, when they settled into the groove that October, and she was usually done by nine, when she made herself hot chocolate and went to her bedroom with the phone.

Although she could scarcely admit it, she had come to enjoy – no, to *love* – her conversations with Matthew at the end of the day, when she sat up in bed and he lay on some couch, relying on his Filipina maid to bring him food. 'How are you washing yourself?' she asked one evening.

'Let's not go there!'

'Is there no woman in your life at all? Even an ex, who could help you out?'

'An ex-girlfriend, yeah, but I'd rather put myself in the care of a piranha.'

Marina chuckled.

'I'm okay,' he said. 'I've got good mates and lovely colleagues. My secretary, Pearl has been with me for fifteen years, but I don't think I'll ask her to help me wash.'

'I haven't even asked what you do in Anchorage. Or how you got there.'

'I came up to see bear. I was living in San Francisco, and came up with some mates for an all-boys adventure. Bears, sea-planes, cabins in the wilderness. And it's spectacular, you know, up north. It really blew me away, but Anchorage . . . man. From downtown you can see live volcanoes, mountain ranges, even Mount McKinley, tallest peak on the continent, and in the winter the snow turns a beautiful pinky-orange, so that you're, like, surrounded by this glowing ridge. It's breath-taking any day of the year.'

Marina smiled at his enthusiasm.

'San Francisco, when I went back, seemed rather limited in comparison, and Anchorage was on a real drive to get people up here, so I gave it a shot. I thought six months tops before the isolation would get to me, but the place has developed a lot in the last twenty years. The work is good, and the money's excellent.'

'What do you do?'

'Supply and transport for one of the oil companies. Kind of a desk job, but the conditions are great and it's, you know, home now.'

'Isn't it cold?'

'Cold enough, but the city's pretty mild. Loads of snow, but it rarely goes below minus ten, and in the summer it's a lot like Ireland – mild and wet and everyone talking about the weather.'

'Minus ten – *mild*? You really have acclimatized!'

'S'pose.'

Through all this chat, they touched again on the closeness

they had once known, and it was as comforting as chocolate to her mildly broken heart. Although he had hurt her, although she was still angry with him, Matthew was making her feel good when no one else could, which was just as it had always been. Nothing could have persuaded her to ask the one question she should have asked on their very first call: 'Why?'

Natalie was delighted that Kitt was spending time in her father's hometown and told her to stay as long as she liked. There was no need for her to rush back to Málaga, she said, and then she went quiet. There were no calls, no text messages. Kitt wasn't bothered; her mother had gone off the radar – what of it? But Marina was furious. She kept haranguing Kitt to see if she'd heard from Natalie, then came very swiftly to a decision.

'This is what we're going to do,' she told Matthew, the next time he called.

'About what?'

'About your daughter! Jesus, get a grip, would you? You think it's all dandy, don't you? That we're playing happy families, but it's no picnic over here, Matthew. Your daughter leaves a disaster zone everywhere she goes, I've got a sick boy upstairs – thanks to you – who's still spiking a temperature and whose sister sometimes sleeps on the floor beside his bed, and I have students coming in four days a week, cramming for their Leaving Cert. I can't keep this up. I'm not the Old Woman Who Lived in a Shoe, you know.'

'Whoa! Down, boy, down!'

'There is only one solution. I'm taking Kitt back to her mother.'

He didn't say anything. That was a good start, she thought.

'And I do mean *taking* her. Physically, personally, myself. If someone doesn't go with her, she'll abscond and end up back here again. We're going to fly to Málaga next weekend.'

'I'll pay,' he said quickly. 'For everything.'

'Thanks. I was afraid I'd have to ask. And if I were you, I'd head for Spain as soon as you're able, and put some manners on those women.'

'I had been hoping to come to Ireland.'

'Don't be ridiculous. You need to go over there, throw some weight around and get your daughter back into school.'

'Yes, ma'am. Whatever you say, ma'am.'

Although she hadn't tried very hard, Marina was nonetheless disappointed she'd made no impact on Kitt. Matthew must think her pretty useless. But why would that matter? Why should she care what Matthew thought? He was the cause of this miscreant. Had he not casually slept with her mother in Amsterdam, this young lady would not have found herself tossing around in Marina's life, like a T-shirt in an otherwise empty washing-machine, trying to make sense of her parents. It bothered Marina that she was being uncharitable, but it bothered her more that they were taking advantage of her. Oprah once said that turning forty meant learning to say no. Marina was forty-seven and had yet to say it. This would be her first big 'no'. A mega-no.

Meanwhile, she needed textbooks, so she drove into town a few days before they were due to leave, parked in a multistorey, and hurried across to Oliver Plunkett Street. She used Aidan's book for her French students. It was still the best, and it was still bringing in some royalties. Had he had the foresight to stay alive, they would have made a lot more money from his books, but since they could not be updated, or the series expanded, the publishers kept the bare minimum of copies in print.

She was running late. It was already three and one of her students was coming at four, but just as she reached Liam Russell's, a hand gripped her elbow from behind and a low voice said, 'Just keep walking, woman, and no harm will come to you.'

She swung round.

Luke!

He was panting. 'You're fit,' he said, and before she could formulate a word or even gasp, he kissed her full-on, right there, in the doorway of Cork's oldest bookshop.

A low wave of embarrassment washed over her – they weren't teenagers: this was not the way middle-aged people behaved in public – but then she felt his hand on her waist, and the unshaven feel of his upper lip on hers, and she didn't even care that a customer who was trying to get out of the shop had to wait.

Luke relaxed his grasp. 'I drove up to your house when you were pulling out, and I've been waving and flashing at you all the way into town. I even called out to you in the car park.' He looked to the side. 'I had to park fairly imaginatively to keep up with you.'

'Excuse me,' said the customer.

They stepped out of his way and into the shop.

'Let's get a coffee,' said Luke.

'I don't have time.'

He pulled back, as if rejected.

'What are you doing here?' she asked.

Again his eyes slipped to the side. She loved the way he did that. 'I thought I'd just made that fairly obvious.'

'But how did you find me?'

'Our friend in the shop. Hamid.'

'He's clairvoyant now?'

'Probably,' said Luke, 'in fact, almost certainly, but he also had a receipt for the stool he was sending you . . . I would've called first, but I don't have your number, do I?'

'I left it for you – at Reception in the *riad*.'

'Ah.'

'They didn't give it to you?'

More customers pressed past them.

'They just said you'd left. You'd been a bit frosty at the end of our trip, so I thought you'd had second thoughts.' He looked over her shoulder at the rows of books on their deep green shelves, then back at her. 'But when I got home I realized I had to find out, one way or another. Just in case.' He moved his chin sideways. '*Have* you reconsidered?'

'Luke, I have a class. I'm going to be late.'

He put his hands into the pockets of his overcoat, nodding. 'Right.'

'But what is it, exactly, that I'm supposed to have reconsidered?'

'You. Me. This.'

Marina tilted her head. 'You didn't give me much to go on, though, did you? In the reconsidering department.'

'It, um, proved a little difficult – especially with you vaporizing like that. I thought I'd imagined you.'

'I know *that* feeling.'

'Yes,' he conceded, 'I suppose you do.'

'But as it happens, I haven't reconsidered . . . you, me, this.'

They walked back to the car park. 'I really didn't know,' he said, 'if I should come or not, but I figured that, either way, I'd be chancing my neck.'

'I'm glad you did.'

'You've no idea how good it is to hear you say that,' he said, with a sigh of relief. 'But why did you take off ?'

'That young couple in my *riad* had an accident. She was concussed and he'd hurt his back, so I had to travel with them. Didn't the manager tell you?'

'No, but then I didn't really ask. I presumed you'd thought better of things and decided to slip away gracefully. I suspected my mother had frightened you off.'

'That wasn't it at all. Those two weren't fit to travel alone.'

'You should have come for me,' he said. 'I could've helped, gone with you to Marrakech.'

'I didn't know where you were staying, remember? I didn't know anything, Luke.'

'That's what Hamid said. When I went to drown my sorrows in his tea, he wasn't a bit impressed that I'd let you get away. He muttered and grumbled, then rooted out your address. I said, no, no, you'd made yourself clear. He said nothing was clear.'

'Bit of a nerve, giving you my address.' *Best thing he ever did.*

'So I told him I'd think about it.' Luke sidestepped a schoolgirl as they got into the lift. 'And he told me not to think, just to do.'

'Sound advice.'

'Yes. I'm afraid I'm guilty of thinking way too much a few weeks ago.'

'Whereas I didn't know what to think.' When they reached her car, she said, 'How long can you stay?'

'Till tomorrow. I didn't want to hang around if I was going to get short shrift, so I've booked myself out tomorrow lunchtime.'

Marina squirmed a little. 'I'm afraid my house is crammed to the rafters at the moment. I won't be able to –'

'I wouldn't expect you to. I'll check into a hotel. But dinner later?'

'About time you took me to dinner,' she teased.

He kissed her again, pressing her against her car. Then they smiled at one another as if they'd cracked some secret code. 'I'll pick you up at half seven,' he said.

Marina drove away, skittish, leaving him standing among the

cars, watching her go. From sunrise by the almond groves in Tamdaght to a multistorey car park in Cork – love, the second time round, was proving to be a jolting thing, but the spurts of pleasure were worth the baffling uncertainties.

Dazed and delighted, she walked up her gravel path twenty minutes later, taking her keys from her bag, but as she lifted them to the keyhole, the front door swept open.

'Hi!' said a woman she'd never seen before. 'I saw you coming!'

Marina looked back at her garden door. Had she come to the right house?

'Come on in,' said the woman. There was something familiar about her. She had a gorgeous smile, shoulder-length blonde hair and vivid green eyes, and her slender figure was lost in a long cotton skirt and a baggy sweater. Marina felt she should know who she was, and on any other day might have done so, but Luke's sudden appearance had apparently nullified her memory card.

Kitt was leaning against the archway when Marina stepped into the hall. 'This is my mum,' she said. 'And this is Marina. She wants to get rid of me. I'm not welcome here any more.'

'It isn't quite like that.' Marina extended her hand. 'Pleased to meet you, Natalie,' she said over Kitt, who was saying, 'Yes, it is.'

Natalie fiddled with the end of a long scarf thrown over her shoulders. 'Sorry about landing on you like this, but I wanted to see Kitt. I hope that's all right?' She widened her eyes as if it was a jolly idea for all of them.

The doorbell rang. Marina's four o'clock appointment. She directed the student towards the study, then led Natalie and Kitt to the kitchen. 'I'm glad you've come,' she said to Natalie. 'It's high time Kitt went home and got on with her school work. Will you be leaving straight away?'

'Leaving?' said Kitt.

'Oh, ahm . . .' Natalie sat down, her hands tightly clasped in her lap. 'I wonder if Kitt could stay for another few days. Give me time to –'

'Look, Natalie,' said Marina, firmly, 'I have a student waiting, and with all due respect, I have fed and housed your daughter –'

'Dad's been paying her,' Kitt interrupted.

'– for several weeks now and I'm not doing it any more.'

'Told you,' Kitt said to her mother. 'She doesn't want me around.'

Natalie looked up at Marina. 'You don't?'

'Nope.'

'Why not?'

Marina nearly laughed. 'I could ask you the same question!'

'I beg your pardon?'

'Look, you have dumped your underage daughter on people who are strangers to you, and to her, without a blind bit of regard for the consequences. We could be a family of child-molesters, for all you know. Nor have you given any consideration to our circumstances. I have concerns of my own, a family of my own, and I'm not going to look after your daughter just because you and Matthew can't be bothered.'

Natalie's lip trembled.

Oh, no, thought Marina. Not tears.

'I'm terribly sorry.' Natalie had a clipped English accent. 'I thought you and Matthew had an understanding. Isn't that what you told me, Kitt?' she asked, without looking at her daughter.

Kitt muttered something about Matthew saying it was okay.

'It *was* okay,' said Marina, 'for a while, but you can't live with us indefinitely.'

'But I really like it here.'

'What you like,' said Marina, 'is hanging around with no one telling you what to do, no school, no job . . . I'm sorry, Natalie, but you'll have to take her home. She needs to be with you.'

'But I have nowhere to go either!'

Kitt and Marina stared at her. Natalie's eyes dropped. 'I've left my job. Or . . . well, it didn't work out. Sandro was fired, so I had to go too.'

'I thought you ran a hotel?'

'I didn't, *he* did. And the apartment came with the job. Anyway, I'd had enough of Spain and I wanted to see Kitt so I came here.'

Marina crossed her arms, rolled her eyes, and wondered if she had 'Salvation Army' printed on her forehead.

But Natalie was clearly down on herself. She looked frail. Done in, somehow. 'What about your father, Kitt?' she asked quietly. 'Can't you stay with him?'

'I'm *not* going to bloody Alaska.'

'Maybe you could, darling, for a little while. I'm a bit stuck at the moment.'

Marina couldn't believe it. They were as helpless as each other. 'I have to teach,' she said, 'and then I'm going out. You can stay here tonight, Natalie, and we'll sort this out tomorrow. Feel free to get yourselves something to eat.'

'She's unemployed *and* homeless?'

'That's about the sum of it.'

'Excellent,' said Matthew. 'Just great.'

Marina had gone out to the garden to call him as soon as her student had left. It was cold, but she didn't feel it. 'You're going to have to do something,' she said, glancing into the kitchen where Natalie was preparing a meal. Not as useless as her daughter, then. 'She strikes me as deflated, empty. Does she have any relatives?'

‘A sister in London.’

‘Oh, good,’ said Marina.

‘Not good.’

‘Don’t tell me, they don’t get on?’

‘They don’t get on.’

‘Marvellous.’

‘I’ll never persuade Natalie to come back here, Marina,’ said Matthew. ‘She hates it. She left without even telling me, you know. I came home one day and the house was empty. The two of them gone. Just like that.’

Marina stopped pacing.

‘Marina?’

‘Just like that, eh?’ she said. ‘That must have been karma.’

She heard him sigh, move around, wince a little. ‘Oh, shit. At last it comes out. The big ugly toad.’

Marina hadn’t seen it coming either, and she was in no mood for it. Not today. But this time Matthew didn’t duck so she couldn’t either.

‘I didn’t know what to say, Reen. I’d sacrificed you for Gwen because I thought she was *it*, and then I discovered she wasn’t. I was so cut up, I took off.’

‘All you had to do was come over and let me know you were leaving,’ she said. ‘At least then we might have cleared the air. I thought you hated me too.’

‘I’ve never hated you. Not ever.’

‘Funny way of showing it. When you fell for Gwen, I became invisible to you. It didn’t matter what she dished out – what she said or did to me – you just let her at it, you hung back, out of sight, and then you fucked off.’

‘I didn’t think you’d want me to see me after all that stuff. But if it’s any consolation, leaving without saying goodbye . . . well, it didn’t feel good.’

‘Oh, my heart bleeds. I found out in Patrick Street, Matthew.

Outside Roches Stores. Ran into Adam. "Oh, and by the way," he said, "Matthew's good – arrived safely." I had to ask where it was that you had so safely arrived!'

'All right, all right, I should have called, but I was out of my head, Reen. I was so in love with her, I thought I was dead already.'

She paced, he sighed, they said nothing, but kept each other company, holding the phones to their ears. 'Is she the reason you never married?'

'Could be. She was a big wound, anyway.' After a moment, he added, 'So I might as well ask, I've been putting it off, but, well, how's she doing?'

Marina stared into the darkness, where her garden lay beyond the glow of light from the kitchen. '*Gwen?* I haven't set eyes on her since college.'

'Huh?'

'You didn't seriously think we'd kiss and make up, did you,' Marina asked, 'after all she put me through?'

'But a friendship like that . . .'

'Yeah, right, but taking things out of the rubbish is usually a bad idea.'

'And all my fault, of course,' he said.

'Not entirely . . . Anyway, I have no idea where she is, or if she is.'

'Last I heard,' he said, 'she'd married a musician in London.'

'Good. I've been dreading running into her in Easons.'

'I'm sorry, Reen, about everything. More sorry than I'll ever be able to say.'

# 9

Marina couldn't think straight. Luke was there, his mother wasn't, and they had a date. As for her children, she lied to them. Told them she and Suzanne were going out and that she might stay at her house for the night. Then she had a long bath, did legs, armpits, and went rooting for lingerie. It was a sorry haul. She'd had no call for good underwear in far too long, and she wasn't touching her honeymoon silks, which she still kept, wrapped in tissue paper, in a drawer. If she'd known he was coming, she would have hit the lingerie shops; instead, she had to settle for sporty cottons – at least they were sort of flattering and her stomach was sort of flat. She pulled on a low-cut top, a fitted skirt and a broad leather belt. Casual, but sexy. She felt neat and slim, and couldn't remember when last she'd been so nervous, or so optimistic. Everything was pumping on the inside, her blood racing round her limbs in hot anticipation, and apprehension.

To keep things simple, she had told Luke to park at the end of the street. Standing by the window, she called Suzanne. 'You and I are having dinner tonight.'

'Oh, Jesus, are we? I completely forgot!'

Marina went on, 'And, with any luck, I'm going to feel *very* tired and stay at your place for the night.'

'Are you? Why?'

Marina waited.

'Oh, my God!' said Suzanne. 'He's here.'

'Uh-huh.'

'Fan*tas*tic! How did he do it? How'd he trace you?'

'A Tuareg showed him the way.'

'Huh?'

'Never mind.'

'I *knew* he'd come. What happened?'

'Enough.'

'Oh, Marina, this is excellent!'

'Not sure, though.'

'*What?*' Suzanne snapped, making it a tiny, tiny word, so sharp it was bordering on vicious. 'What do you mean, not sure?'

'I'm not sure I'm ready.'

'You've been celibate for five years! How much more ready do you need to be?'

'I've probably forgotten how it's done.'

'Marina – take my word for it – you'll remember.'

'And what about contraception?'

'He's probably brought something.'

'You think? That's a bit presumptuous.'

'Oh, for crying out loud! You're not to go all nunny on me, d'you hear?'

Marina's mobile phone beeped on the table. Her heart rammed itself at high speed against her chest, like a car hitting a wall. 'That's him. 'Bye!' She grabbed her phone and coat and ran downstairs, calling goodbye to her bewildered children, who were trying to come to terms with the strange Englishwoman who was wafting round their kitchen, cooking their dinner like she was the new nanny.

Luke had parked near the corner. Marina hopped in and they fell into each other, the hire car offering more privacy than they had ever been allowed. It was delicious, cosy, and Marina was right – she *had* forgotten, forgotten it all: the taste of someone else, the smell, the rough smoothness of a freshly shaved face. She'd forgotten that when you kissed someone you loved, you wanted to swallow them, ingest them into your being.

'You look absolutely stunning,' he said. 'When you came skipping along the street, I couldn't believe such a beautiful woman was going to get into my car.'

'Where are you taking me?'

'I booked a table at Jacques'.'

'Lovely.'

'But . . .'

She tensed. 'What? Don't tell me your mother's turned up?'

His fingers were on her neck, his other hand on her hip. 'Would it be too forward to suggest we default on dinner?'

He had taken a room at the Clarion. They made their way through the smart, functional lobby and stepped into the lift. There was resolve in everything about him, determination in every move he made. All that reserve and brevity had got them nowhere. There wasn't time, now, for holding back. In this one night, they intended to plant their future, which made them additionally nervous. Any degree of awkwardness or failure would make one or both recoil. It had to go well.

In the hushed corridor, their feet made only the slightest shuffle on the carpet, as if the hotel was holding its breath, so that the click of the card in the door sounded loud and slightly criminal. Marina went in. It seemed odd that it should start in a hotel room, during a night stolen from their families and responsibilities, like lovers slinking out to have an extra-marital affair. A genteel country guesthouse would have been more apt, but after the dust and difficulties of Morocco, this room, with its earthy colours, fresh white bedding and little luxuries – fluffy white robes, slippers, and chocolates laid out on the bed – seemed hard-earned. Balancing lust and reluctance, and slightly embarrassed now by this rush for sex, instead of romancing one another over a slow dinner, Marina opened the dinky little box of chocolates and took one. Luke threw down his trench-coat and took her jacket from her shoulders. She offered him a chocolate. He shook his head, holding her like a dancer, his hands on her hips. Oh, God, she thought, blushing. Now he can't kiss me because my mouth's full of chocolate . . .

He kissed her neck while she chewed and sucked, but the rich chocolate lingered on her teeth as if resolved not to give her up. The back of her hand was pressed against his shirt; she could feel his heartbeat through her fingernails. She leant into his shoulder and for a moment they stood still, because they could.

They lay down. Marina had not forgotten the satisfying, and promising, sensation of half a man's weight lying along one side of her body. She'd missed it, and welcomed it now. The rest followed seamlessly: the fumble with buttons, the slide of straps and zips, the co-operation of limbs and skins. But when Marina slid her hand across his belly and under his waistband, her rings got caught on his belt. She should probably have taken them off, but they were so much part of her that she hadn't even thought about it. Her other arm was wrapped round his back, under his shirt. Aware of her dilemma, Luke had also stalled. Aidan had managed to come between them.

Marina took out her hand, reached round him, took off her engagement ring and put it on the bedside table. It tinkled on the glass. But when she pulled gently on her wedding ring, it jammed against her knuckle. It wouldn't come, or maybe she didn't have the heart to pull hard enough. Twenty-five years it had been there. Through pregnancies and heatwaves and arguments, it had never come off. She had twiddled it, fiddled with it, got soap caught on it, stared at it by that hospital bed – the ring of eternity when eternity had let her down.

Lying there, neither breathed while she tugged. It would not come.

'You don't have to,' Luke whispered.

'I do.'

So he took her hand and put her finger into his mouth to

wet it. She tried again and let out a whimper as she felt the ring go. It, too, tinkled on the glass.

The streetlights threw a blue hue across the room. Marina stretched against the crisp sheets. Everything felt clean, starched, perfect.

'I can't believe I almost let you go,' Luke said.

'Pretty careless, if you ask me.'

'It won't happen again.'

'Glad to hear it.'

'Can you stay?' he asked.

'Yes.'

'What about the family?'

'I lied to my children.'

'Oh, good.'

She tapped his chest. 'Still, the things you'll do to get out of buying me dinner.'

'Let's try Room Service.'

They ate in bed – Peking duck wrap for her, roasted pepper for him, and shoestring fries – while she told him about the long-lost friend, the daughter, the student, the sister and the mother. But mostly the daughter.

'You seem very concerned about her,' Luke said.

'Not as concerned as I should be. Kitt comes from such an unfortunate part of my life that I haven't even been particularly hospitable. She reminds me of a whole string of events that I'd sooner forget.' Her thumb went to where her wedding ring used to be. Spreading her naked fingers on the sheet, she caught Luke's expression – apprehensive, as if he was waiting for a backlash, a reaction to the way they had unmarried her. She scrunched up her hand. 'And now her mother has turned up. I should have seen *that* coming.'

'Who is this Matthew, anyway?'

'Oh, Matthew. Now, *there*'s a tale.' She raised her chin. He would have to work harder for that story.

Luke gave her the full force of his eyes, knowing she was toying with him. 'Someone special obviously.'

'Very. He was a big part of the landscape right through my teens and early twenties – the intense years. God, it's such an intense age, isn't it? You feel everything so absolutely. That's what Jacquie's missing out on. The focus. The density of experience. Even the self-absorption . . . She spends too much time worrying about me and trying to make things right for us all. I wish she'd be a bit selfish for a change.'

'We were talking about Matthew.'

'We met through friends,' she said, putting her plate aside, 'when I was sixteen. I targeted him because I fancied his mate. Didn't work out with the mate, but it worked for Matthew and me. We just got on so well, and when he started coming round to the house a lot, we became very close. I adored him, really loved him. I thought he was my soul-mate and that nothing could happen to either of us that the other wouldn't feel almost as deeply. He went all the way down to my foundations.' She drew circles on the sheet with her finger. 'In fact, he *was* my foundation, but when we were in college, he hurt me, badly, and then he left, so we never got to sort it out.'

'Was it a love thing? Unrequited?'

'God, no. Nothing like that. No, he stood by when someone very close to both of us dismantled me. Dismantled the life I had. I'll tell you about it some time.'

'Have you patched things up?'

She shook her head. 'We're sidestepping it. I want this to be about Kitt, to sort her out and move on. I don't want to go backwards. Not just now.'

'But you already have,' said Luke.

'I suppose.'

He put the tray on the floor and reached for his jacket. 'I have something for you.'

'Oh?'

'I couldn't help it.' He took a pink paper bag out of his pocket and gave it to her.

She frowned. It was heavy.

'I know you're going to get cross,' he said, 'but I wish you wouldn't.'

Inside the bag, she saw a jumble of dark silver. Emptying it on to her palm, she recognized immediately the necklace from Hamid's shop she had been unable to afford.

'After you left that first day,' Luke said, replying to the question in her eyes, 'I just bought it. I had to. I didn't know when or where I'd give it to you, and it would've seemed presumptuous before now. I mean, it might still seem presumptuous, but it looked so great on you, it was already yours.'

'You've no idea how I hated leaving it.' She spread the heavy necklace across her hand. 'Or maybe you did.'

He took the necklace and put it round her neck. 'So you don't mind?'

'I love it too much to mind. Thank you.' Marina lay back, fingering it. 'And while we're on the subject, what did Hamid say to you that day after I left? Because I heard him say something, and you replied, "I know."'

Luke lay back beside her. 'He said, "Go. Or you will lose her again."'

'"Again"? What did he mean?'

'Maybe he was reading my mind.'

'Why? What were you thinking?'

'I was thinking . . . that you would be a blessing in anyone's life, and that if I didn't let you out of my sight again, I might be the one to be so blessed.'

'If you'd only said so at the time . . .' she teased.

'I know. I was a prat in Morocco.'

'You courted me. I liked that.'

'Didn't get me anywhere, though. A bit of hand-holding in the sand and you coming home not knowing what to make of it.'

'What should I make of it?'

Luke pulled her further down the bed and lay over her. He seemed to be wondering how much he could say, or how he should say it. 'I seem to be falling rather deeply in love with you, that's all.'

'That's enough.'

When he'd turned out the light, Marina found it strange to head into sleep with someone by her side once again, but she touched his thigh, his hip, his back, and listened as his breathing grew level, then deepened. They knew so little of each other, and so much.

The next morning, she stepped on to the small balcony, pulling the robe round her ears against the chill. The south channel of the Lee was a cranky brown in the grey October morning, but it curved round the island on which she stood with the confident elegance of a city river, drifting past the silver-grey College of Commerce and the orange façade of Moore's Hotel, behind which the steeple of Holy Trinity seemed brittle against the dull sky. Down to her left, a green ship was being unloaded and stacks of timber stood on the quayside. Marina inhaled, her senses on high alert. She had never seen her city from this perspective – City Hall to the right, with its green cupola, buses crossing the nearest of three bridges, and the boardwalk below, busy with hurried pedestrians.

Luke was on the phone, slipping from English to Italian with such fluidity that he seemed to be switching language in the middle of words, let alone sentences. The call ended on a laugh. 'Sorry,' he said to Marina. 'That was Nico.'

'Your eldest?'

'Yeah. We're working together on a dilapidated farmhouse up in the hills. His firm specializes in restoring old buildings.'

'I love the way you vacillate between the two languages.'

'Oh, I just blather whatever comes out. Nico had two first languages. Even though his mother always spoke Italian with him, English was his first language during his formative years because we were living in England. When they moved to Italy, bit by bit Italian became his first language to the point where he now speaks English with an accent. Francesco – Frankie – isn't as fluent, so I always speak English to him, to keep it up.' He chuckled. 'Nico tends to speak Italian when he's pissed off with me and English when he's being nice to me.'

'You obviously get on really well.'

'Yeah, he's great. Smart. Gets it from his mother. Frankie isn't much like me either. He's the creative, compassionate one.'

Marina's gaze drifted back to the window. 'Dara will never have that – what you have with your boys. An adult father-son friendship.'

'We're very blessed, I know.'

'And I suppose,' she said, 'unlike *my* children, Nico knows where you are.'

Luke looked sheepish. 'Not only that, he played a large part in persuading me to come. He'd love to see me settle down, but, then, he's had the same girlfriend since he was about nine.'

They ordered breakfast and had it at the table by their bedroom window. 'Did you really think it was about your mother?' Marina asked. 'My leaving.'

Luke put down his coffee. 'Wouldn't be the first time.'

'Really? Women have left you because of Bridget?'

He threw his head to the side. 'It's not like she makes for

an easy package. I'm an only child with an ageing parent. It's fairly ironic – just when we think we're in the clear and have our lives back, kids grown up, careers secure, we look round and realize we've accumulated all this stuff, and that anyone who takes *us* on will have to take *it* on too. And Bridget's hard-going. She's strong and well, and has long-life genes on both sides. She'll be around for a while.'

'You're very good to her.'

He raised his eyes. 'Why wouldn't I be? In other cultures, it's the very least I'd be expected to do. There'd be fewer people lingering in miserable retirement homes if more children were prepared to look after their parents as diligently as their parents looked after them.'

'All I'm saying is that, generally speaking, men who haven't hit fifty don't have to plan their lives round their mothers.'

'Plenty of Italians do.'

'And their wives and sisters do all the work.'

'True,' he conceded. 'Anyway, this is the hand I've been dealt. Only child. Dead father. You make of it what you can.'

'How did you lose your father?'

'Pancreatic cancer at thirty-one. He was a GP, building up his practice. My mother didn't know what hit her. They had nothing – they were just starting out – so we had to live on a farm with his sister until I'd finished school. When I'd graduated and emigrated, Ma went to Italy to live with her own sister. The fact is, she never had a home of her own until her sixties, when her sister died.'

'Golly. Poor thing.'

'So I won't be throwing her into an old folks' home any time soon.'

'If it's any consolation, I know what it's like – being primary care-giver.'

'Your mother?'

'Oh, no, she's hale and hearty. No, Dad had a stroke before Aidan died, and he came to live with us.'

'But you already had your hands full. What about your siblings?'

'My brother is a failed priest, maybe gay, living alone in a flat in Roscommon, where he manages a supermarket, and my sister never got on with Dad. She's high-maintenance, high-pitch, so when he became incapacitated he wanted to be with me in France. He wasn't seriously affected – he'd lost the use of one arm and the side of his face was wonky, but he could walk, with a hobble, so he came for a few weeks to recuperate and just stayed on. It suited me. When I was out at the hospital so much, it was nice to get back to a house with the lights on and a friendly face waiting with a cup of cocoa. But after Aidan died, Dad had another stroke and, this time, he was much worse. He wanted to come home, which was okay, because I did too. That's how I ended up in the family home. I'm still paying off my brother and sister for it. Dad was very poorly for the last year of his life. He died in March.'

'So you lost your husband and your father within a matter of years?'

She shrugged. 'It happens.'

When Luke dropped her back to the house before going to the airport, he turned in his seat to look at her. 'Fancy a bit of shunting back and forth?'

'I beg your pardon?'

'Between Italy and Ireland.'

'Oh.'

'Marina, all I've been able to think about since Morocco is seeing you sitting in my lakeside garden. Come to Orta. Soon. We'll have time and space there.'

'You come back here first. I need to get used to this and . . . you know, prepare the ground with Dara and Jacquie.'

Luke closed one eye in a lazy wink. 'So, we're going to give this a proper go?'

'Hamid will be cross if we don't.'

'He's a very weird guy, you know,' said Luke. 'He can only be in his twenties, what with the jeans and Adidas under his kaftan, but he knows stuff he shouldn't know.'

'Like what?'

'Like the fact that the first time I saw you *wasn't* at Marrakech airport.'

'You saw me at the airport?'

He nodded. 'Taking your luggage off the conveyor-belt. Speaking of which, I'd better go.' He leant across to open the car door for her.

'Wait. And that wasn't the first time?'

'No. Go on, shoo. I'll miss my flight.'

She got out and looked back in. 'Really? So when Hamid said you'd lose me "again" you *did* know what he meant?'

Luke threw her a sly smile.

'Don't try to be enigmatic. You look ridiculous. When did you first see me?'

'Guess.'

'I don't know. Were we on the same flight?'

'Nah, it was ages ago.'

'*When?*'

'Work it out in your own good time,' he said, pulling the door over.

'Mutual friends? A dinner party?' she persisted, through the half-open window.

'Nope.'

'In a bar? A supermarket?'

'No.'

'You're trying to tell me that we've already met but I've forgotten?'

'You *have* forgotten.' Luke started up the engine. 'And it was so much more than just a meeting.'

Back in the real world, Kitt McGonagle and her mother were sitting at the table in an unusually tidy kitchen.

'So!' said Marina, unable to dampen her good mood. 'What's the plan?'

'Plan?' said Kitt. 'There isn't one.'

Natalie gathered her hair at the nape of her neck, avoiding eye contact.

'There is now,' said Marina. 'For one thing, *you*'re going to Anchorage.'

'You can't make me go anywhere.' Kitt glanced at her mother.

'I can't look after you, darling,' said Natalie. 'I have nowhere to live.'

'I don't care. I'm not going!'

'You know what?' said Marina. 'You absolutely *are*. Most people go through life doing stuff they don't want to do and it's about time you did likewise.'

'But what about Mum? What's she going to do?'

'Your mother will be fine.'

'Because, see, we were thinking . . .' Kitt said quickly.

Oh, God, thought Marina. What have they been thinking?

'Are you out of your tiny mind?' Matthew bellowed.

Marina sighed happily.

'Hell, Marina, I asked you to help Kitt in a crisis, not martyr yourself to my mistakes!'

'It's fine, really.'

'But it'll all go wrong and you'll blame me, and you're

holding quite enough of a grudge against me as it is!'

Pleasantly weary and quietly delirious, Marina let him rant. Instead of offloading one waif, she had indeed acquired another, but she didn't mind. She didn't mind about anything. The madness of love. The Luke effect. Who cared?

Besides, now the itch had been scratched, she might revert to her old self and actually be good for Kitt. And her mother.

Natalie, at least, had some qualities in her favour – she was tidy, grateful and not afraid to express it, and, unlike her daughter, she was quite good company. They had spent a couple of hours chatting over tea, and Marina was amazed to find that she liked her. In fact, she would have liked anyone that morning, but she said to Matthew, 'Natalie just needs a bit of nurturing, like we all do sometimes.'

'What if they won't move on?'

'We have a deal. Natalie is going to get a job and Kitt has agreed to do a computer course or something. They've got one month to sort themselves out.'

'I don't know what to say.'

'I don't suppose my children will either.'

The front door slammed – Jacquie, in from work. Marina was standing by the stove, stirring a sauce. She had told them on the phone, but now braced herself for their reaction.

Dara was sitting at the table, reading the paper. Jacquie gave Marina a hug. 'So they're *both* staying with us now? Dara, get your foot off my sweater!'

He moved his foot.

'This is something of a turnaround,' she said to her mother.

'I know, but when it came to it, I couldn't throw them out. It's a huge imposition on you two, but –'

'It's fine,' said Jacquie, filling the kettle. 'The more the merrier, I say.'

'But I thought you hated . . .' Marina lowered her voice '. . . the cookie monster?'

'Ach, I don't mind. This house is too big for three people.'

'Bloody hell,' said Dara.

'What?' said Jacquie.

'This article – churning out the old argument about rugby being the exclusive preserve of the middle classes. It's such bullshit.'

'No, it isn't.'

'Dara, do you mind?' Marina asked.

'Of course I bloody mind.'

'But it *is* only played by people who go to expensive private schools,' Jacquie argued.

'I mean about Natalie and Kitt,' said Marina.

'Yeah, yeah, fine,' he said.

'Good, because if it works out I might ask them to stay on. I have to rent those rooms and I'd rather have women, preferably not students.'

Dara got up. 'Yeah, great. I'm off. I'll be late.'

Marina was stunned. Was this the sum of their reaction?

'Mum.' Jacquie had gone white.

'What is it?'

'Your rings . . .'

'Oh!' She lifted her hand. 'That's okay. I took them off.'

'Phew. But why?'

Tell her, Marina thought. Tell her *now*. 'I just . . . Time had come.'

'Oh, Mum. That must be huge.'

'Mm, huge.'

'But you're right. In fact, I've moved on myself.'

Marina looked at her more closely. 'Have you . . . What have you been up to?'

Jacquie pursed her lips as if she'd been caught doing something naughty but fun.

'*Who?*'

'Shush! He's in the other room.'

Marina's jaw dropped. '*David?* You didn't!'

'I *so* did. Have you seen the guy?'

Marina raised her chin. 'Yes, well, I take your point.'

Jacquie was pouring steaming water into the little teapot she used for green tea.

'Is it serious?'

'God, no,' said Jacquie. 'Dead casual. He's younger than me for a start.'

'Goodness. You're taking this in your stride.'

'I know, it's the new me. I'm in a shit job, but I'm not going to let that drag me down. You keep saying I should get out there and enjoy myself, and at long last I'm enjoying myself.'

Marina bit her lip. Me too, she wanted to say.

'Speaking of which,' her daughter went on, 'I take it, what with Natalie moving in and all, that you and Matthew have kissed and made up – albeit transatlantically?'

'Not entirely, no.'

Jacquie sat down. 'When are you going to tell me what happened with you two?'

'Not now, that's for sure. I'm in *far* too good a mood to go there.'

'So give me the gist of it.'

Marina stopped stirring, and thought about it. 'Because of Matthew,' she said at last, 'I betrayed my best friend, and because of Matthew, she found out.'

The next day Marina enrolled Kitt on a computer course and dropped Natalie into town with a list of employment agencies. Natalie had no desire to return to England. 'I escaped it once,' she said. 'Why would I go back?' She was fixed on the idea that she should consider childcare as a career option. Marina dissuaded her. Someone else's spoilt kids, who eat rubbish, have no manners, discipline or sense of anyone else's boundaries?

Natalie frowned. 'You're right. That would be horrendous.'

They agreed she would start looking for jobs in restaurants and shops.

Kitt was a nightmare to get out of bed every morning, but finally, Marina was on a mission. She wanted to get these two set up, give something back, show a little generosity when the cosmos had been so generous to her. Her grumpy resentment at Kitt's appearance had made way for compassion – a state of mind that was far more familiar to her. Where Matthew's compliments and expectations had failed to change her attitude, Natalie had succeeded. Here was a woman who, at almost the same age as Marina, had found herself with no home, no work and no partner – as a result of her own bad decisions, perhaps, but it was a stiff price to pay for poor judgement. The last thing she deserved was to be disdained by some snotty middle-class widow.

Besides, Kitt and Matthew had depicted very different people in their accounts of Natalie, and both were wrong. She was certainly gorgeous, splendid, but she was also a harmless type, not very good at life, and she had not messed up her daughter through wilful means; she had simply not known how to do otherwise. Losing her job and her man in Málaga had left her teetering on the edge of collapse, and Marina could not let her sink. She was far more vulnerable than Matthew understood, so Marina coached her in the art of selling herself and encouraged her to play up her experience of running the holiday complex.

'But I didn't run it! I stood around greeting people.'

'So that's what you're good at. Tell them so.'

By the end of the week, Natalie had a job in a large department store. She had probably been bred for far better things, but she was so relieved that she came running through the door to tell Marina like a kid who'd got picked for the hockey team. And working, it quickly transpired, agreed with her. She came back to life like a parched houseplant and her eyes lost their vagueness.

Matthew's gratitude knew no bounds. He phoned regularly, but his attempts to ingratiate himself with Kitt were fruitless. She usually handed the phone to Marina, who took it up to her room to chat. By unspoken agreement, they did not return to Gwen. Marina had been close to Matthew for much longer than Gwen had; she was entitled to claim him back for herself.

Everything was lovely. She wafted through her days, delighted with her busy household and enchanted by her new relationship. One night did not, perhaps, amount to a relationship, but their curious courtship did. Physical intimacy was not the only marker for the beginning of an affair and, in Marina's view, they had been a couple-designate since that lunch in Essaouira when he had said how much she would enjoy Orta. She sighed whenever she thought of the delicious manner in which they had moved towards one another, using a private language they somehow knew how to speak without ever having learnt it. Not only was this a true relationship, it was also one of the three most significant love affairs of her life.

Jacquie and Dara didn't need to know just yet. It might ruffle the calm they were all enjoying. Jacquie, in particular, was more upbeat than she had been for some time, and David was playing a large part in her rehabilitation, with his fringe falling over his eyes whenever they sat at the kitchen table, talking and flirting. He had little energy still, but he was always sketching, and he loved Jacquie to pose for him. It had been a while since Marina had seen her daughter so unfettered.

She wasn't sure when Luke would make it to Cork again, but she knew he wouldn't leave it too long, and he did not disappoint. One Thursday afternoon in mid-November, she answered the front door and found him standing there in his grey raincoat. He didn't say anything; she didn't leap. They simply smiled, happy to be in the same space again, until Marina put her hand to her head. 'Oh, God, I look like a total bleeding disaster!'

'Those aren't words that spring to mind.' He came in.

She put her arms round his neck. 'You, on the other hand, look absolutely wonderful.'

'Anyone home?'

'A few bodies upstairs, I'm afraid.'

'Shucks.'

She led him into the kitchen. 'Thanks for not letting on. I like surprises.'

'Well, couldn't afford to leave it too long, could I, and risk someone else moving in on you? But do I need to, ahm, check in somewhere?'

Once again, Marina squirmed. 'Would you mind? There's a guesthouse down the road, if that's okay. It's pathetic of me, I know, but I haven't told the children yet.'

His hand caught hers. 'Not pathetic. Not anything.'

'It's just that I haven't gone out with anyone since their father died. I'm not sure how to handle it. Your children, I suppose, are well used to it?'

'Well, there have been a few . . .'

'Hmm. I have a lot to live up to, then?'

He shook his head. 'You've left them all in the shade.'

*

Jacquie came bounding into the kitchen a couple of hours later, all lively and quick, with a block of cold air coming in behind her. There was a man peeling carrots into the sink and no one else in the room. 'Oh. Hello.'

'Hello.' He put down the carrot, wiped his hands, and reached out to shake hers.

She looked at him oddly. '*Matthew?*'

'Ah. Um, no. Luke. Luke Delahunt.'

'God, *sorry*. Of course you're not Matthew. He's tall and dark and has a broken leg.' Whereas this man was fair, slight, and had the most penetrating eyes Jacquie had ever seen.

Her mother came in behind her. 'Hi, sweetie. Good day?'

'Yeah, umm . . .'

'Oh, this is Luke. We met in Morocco. Luke, this is my daughter, Jacquie.'

'Yes, we've –'

'When I went trekking, I shared a lift with Luke and his mother,' Marina explained to Jacquie. 'We've hardly had a chance to talk about it, have we, with everything that's been going on, but it was an amazing trip, wasn't it, Luke? And . . .' She chattered on.

Jacquie watched. Her mother was babbling.

Luke turned back to the carrots, as if taking refuge.

Jacquie had seen the photos – figures standing by a jeep and sitting on camels, obscured by sunglasses and scarves. A party from Italy, her mother had said, but Luke was clearly not Italian, and what was he doing peeling carrots in their kitchen?

The clan filtered in for dinner – David and Natalie, Kitt, Dara and Bernie, who had come down from Dublin again to see her brother. Average attendance at the evening meal these days seemed like a party. As she moved round the kitchen, Marina could feel Luke's eyes moving with her, like a warm beam on her back.

'I don't know how you do it,' said Natalie, when Marina put a large chicken casserole on the table. 'Feeding so many of us so well.'

'When Mum was away,' said Dara, 'we had tuna. Every night. Tuna on toast, tuna on rice, tuna on . . . a plate.'

Everyone laughed, but Jacquie thought, How odd. That was only weeks before. How much bigger the house had seemed then, and darker, and lonelier.

'You'd think, after all those years in France, one of you would have learnt to cook,' said Marina, sitting down.

'You used to live in France?' Bernie asked.

'For a few years, yes.'

'Why did you come back?' said Natalie.

Marina pushed her hand through her hair, then rested her chin on her knuckles. 'It had been coming since my husband died. It just took me a little while to make it happen.'

'One should never make rash decisions after a bereavement,' said Luke.

'Oh.' Natalie raised her eyebrows. 'Have you . . .'

'No, no,' he said. 'I've been fortunate in that regard. I lost my father when I'd barely arrived, but all my significant others are alive and kicking. Not least my mother.'

'Oh, she's kicking all right,' said Marina.

They smiled at one another, and since they were sitting at opposite ends of the table, everyone in between got caught in it, as if they'd been forced into a room where people were making love with the lights on.

They opened more wine, had second helpings. No one was keen to decamp, but Marina was delighted with her gathered crew. They were bathing in the beams of gentle light emanating from her elation. A shot of codeine could not have made her see the world from a more favourable perspective, but she wondered what Luke would make of it.

He glanced around with a hint of mischief in his eyes. 'So, this is a bit like a boarding-house, is it?'

Marina scowled at him. Stop it.

'That'd be about right,' Dara muttered.

'A boarding-house?' said Jacquie. '*No.*'

Marina started to clear the dishes. 'Natalie and her daughter . . . and David and his sister are just passing through.'

'Oh, I see,' said Luke. 'You're all on holidays?'

'We're not on holidays,' said Kitt.

'You're always on holidays,' said Dara.

'We live here,' Kitt said to Luke.

'Just for a while, darling,' said Natalie.

'I'll be shifting soon,' said David, his eyes lowered.

'And I'm only here to make sure he does shift,' Bernie explained. 'Once he gets comfortable, it can be quite hard to get him to go anywhere.'

'If it's any help,' Dara said to Luke, '*I* live here. I don't take off on holidays like she does,' he waved at his mother, 'and I didn't feck off back to France like she did,' jerking a thumb towards Jacquie. 'I am the only true Corkonian at this table.'

'Excuse me,' said Marina. 'You were born in Dublin!'

'I'm a Munster man by choice.'

'That's only because of the rugby team,' said Jacquie.

'What about you, Luke?' said Natalie. 'Are you permanently based in Italy?'

'Yes.'

They waited for him to elaborate.

Sensing their expectation, he added, 'I am.'

'He has a gorgeous place on Lake Orta,' Marina said wistfully, as if she'd been there.

Jacquie and Dara glanced at one another. There was something . . .

'What do you do there?' Natalie asked.

'Property.'

'Ooh, property on the Italian lakes!' She made eyes at Marina. 'Sounds divine.'

'I'm originally from Skeheenarinky,' he said, as if at a loss.

'So what brings you to Cork?' Jacquie asked him.

The man with the deep-set eyes turned to her. 'Your mother.'

'That was subtle,' Marina said, when they were walking to Mrs Norris's guesthouse at the end of the street.

'It slipped out,' said Luke.

'It did not. You did it deliberately.'

'Jacquie asked a full-on question. I thought she deserved a full-on reply. Have I landed you in it?'

'Probably, but it saves me bringing it up.'

Luke looked up at the guesthouse. 'I don't suppose you'd like to come in and help me turn down my bed?'

'And shock poor Mrs Norris?'

He ran his knuckle along her chin. 'We're not doing very well in this regard, are we?'

'We could go away tomorrow, if you like?'

'I like.'

Marina let herself back into the house. They'd been standing in the street talking for half an hour. The kitchen was cleared. Natalie was wiping the clean table, Jacquie sweeping the floor. It looked staged, as if they were parents waiting for their child to come in long after curfew.

'Have trouble finding the end of the street?' Jacquie asked.

Marina unbuttoned her coat.

'I have to say,' she stopped sweeping and put her palm on

the top of the broom, 'you've collected some strange things from your travels, but this is the first time you've brought home a man.'

'I didn't mean to.' Marina hung her coat in the passageway. 'Honest.'

'But what about Matthew?'

Marina's eyes widened, then jumped to Natalie, who raised her hands, saying, 'Don't look at me. Matthew Grizzly-Bear McGonagle is not for me, thanks. Not with his . . .' her fingers fluttered towards her chest '. . . fleecy plaid shirts and earmuffs and mosquitoes buzzing around him.'

'Mosquitoes?' said Marina.

'Oh, please! The rugged outdoor life. Not one bit my style.'

'Rugged? Outdoor? He was never like that!'

'Alaska does things to people,' said Natalie. 'If it isn't the bears, it's the salmon; if it isn't the salmon, it's cross-country skiing. Do you know that sometimes moose actually come into your garden and pull at your laundry? And people refer to the rest of the country as "outside" – that'll give you some idea of the mindset.'

'You *really* didn't like it, did you?' Marina laughed.

'You could say that. So you're welcome to Matthew. Help yourself.'

'*I* don't want him!' Marina turned to Jacquie. 'What on earth are you suggesting?'

'I thought . . . maybe . . . I mean, you're always on the phone and you took off your rings recently, and he's quite cute, or he was, once, but if he's gone all lumberjack . . .'

'There is *nothing* between me and Matthew!' Marina said. 'There never has been.'

'Really? I thought you'd had a big bust-up.'

'We did, but only as friends. That's all we've ever been.'

Jacquie stuck out her chin. 'Oh. Right. But you and Luke, on the other hand . . .'

'We're very good friends, yes.'

'Mum, don't give me that! Spill.'

Natalie smiled at Marina. It was supportive, encouraging. Marina was glad she was there. 'I'm not one of your girlfriends, you know,' she said to Jacquie. 'As your mother, I have to retain a certain degree of mystery.'

'But where did you get him? He's like Ralph Fiennes with a few years added!'

'And those eyes,' said Natalie.

'Aw, they'd bore a hole right into your soul, they would,' said Jacquie.

Natalie nodded at Marina. 'I think maybe they already have.'

'Why didn't you say anything?' Jacquie asked Marina. 'It happened in Morocco, right?'

'I'm not going to give *you* the juicy details!'

'Why not?'

'Would you tell me?'

'Jesus, no.'

'Right. Anyway, I wouldn't want to embarrass you,' Marina said primly.

'Oh. My. God. You just have.' Jacquie dropped the broom. 'It's for real. My mother is having an affair . . . Dara!' She hurried out of the room.

Natalie took two glasses down from the wooden cabinet and poured wine.

Marina took several gulps. 'Do you think that's it? She seemed fine about it.'

'Why wouldn't she be?'

'Their father . . . The whole bit.'

'Nonsense,' said Natalie. 'It might seem odd to them at first, but they'll get used to it. They don't want you being on your own in the long-term, do they? So don't worry. It's lovely. And, by the way,' she cleared her throat, '*he*'s lovely too.'

Marina smiled. 'It feels so strange. Like trying to fit into a dress that's too small.'

'No harm trying to get back into a size ten once in a while!'

'So, where are you taking me?' Luke asked, when he sat into the car the next morning.

'Away from that house to where I can take advantage of you.'

'Sounds picturesque.'

'Actually,' said Marina, 'we're going to a rock.'

'A rock?'

'Yes, on a hill. Somewhere near Kenmare.'

'A rock on a hill somewhere near Kenmare,' said Luke. 'I *am* blessed.'

When the landscape changed on the Cork-Kerry border, becoming hillier and wilder, they chatted less and looked out more, but whenever Luke caught Marina's eye, her heart raced. Take those eyes off me, she thought, take them *off*.

Beyond Kenmare they soon found the turn on to the road that curved round the brow of Knockatee. It twisted between the hills, climbed and dipped, until they came over another hump and Kilmackillogue harbour spread out below, glittering like an interactive painting. Locating her landmark, Marina pulled on to the verge. 'Out you get.'

The narrow road continued without them, slipping down the hill in loops until it disappeared into a wooded valley. Luke stood beside the car, silenced. The view was dazzling – the headland below, Kenmare Bay beyond, and the mountains, distant enough to be mysterious but close enough to dazzle.

Beams of sunlight shone through tufts of cloud, like spotlights over a stage, as if God wanted to highlight His best work: a silver river making its way through a yellow bog, the unassuming blue of the inlet sneaking behind the headland, and the perfect smile-like U of a valley carved out of the mountain opposite, its deep green flanks as smooth as moss.

'It's like . . . Paradise,' he said. 'Or the way I imagine such a place would look if it existed. All blue and green and empty. Where's this rock of yours?'

'About three minutes up.' Marina pointed, but the grey mountain was rimmed with rocky layers, so it was hard to pick out her platform. They set off across sludgy bog, sinking into the spongy tufts of grass, and stepping on rocks where possible. 'I thought it'd be dryer,' she said, 'after such a dry summer.'

'Surely the whole point about bog is that it never dries.' Luke was humping the picnic box up ahead. 'Is this the one?' he called, reaching a rock on a knuckle of the hill.

'Yeah.'

When he pulled her alongside him, Marina stared at their clasped hands. 'What's wrong?'

'The opposite of *déjà vu*, I suppose,' she said. 'Like a reel going backwards.'

'How so?'

'For months after Aidan died, when I went for a walk over rocks or up a hill, I sometimes found myself putting my hand out . . . when there was no one there.'

Luke kissed her wrist. 'There's someone here now.'

'This isn't going to blow up on me, is it?'

'Absolutely and categorically not.'

'But you've always had lots of women. Why stop now?'

'Because I've found someone to help me get over the rocks and up the hills.'

Marina's rock was the size of a small swimming-pool, smooth but not flat, sloping downwards, but level enough for a rug. The raised end was like the prow of a boat, sticking out over a drop. Luke stood there, gazing at the great sweep of bay. 'What an unbelievable spot.'

Marina breathed in her own sense of satisfaction. The hills were rounded or sharp and linear; the unremarkable ocean reached out to its horizon; and the headland below was spotted with clumps of woodland and flat green fields. The grey mountain they stood on was striated with green all the way down to the flecked water, and below them, on the left, the stretch of bog with its tufts of grass looked like an army of trolls having their hair blow-dried. On the deep green side of the mountain opposite, a line of rocks glittered like a waterfall, as if they were cascading down the crevasse. 'You can almost hear the ice age,' said Luke, 'the glaciers scraping out those valleys.'

Marina wanted to say, 'I love you,' but wouldn't interrupt this rare communion.

'You know,' he said, 'I'd forgotten what a spectacular country Ireland is.'

'Why did you leave? The usual thing – work?'

'Yeah, there wasn't much to keep anyone here, career-wise, and Bridget would have smothered me if I'd stayed. As it was, she smothered every girl I ever went out with.' He motioned towards the horizon. 'That's where I wanted to go. America. New York, New Orleans. I ended up in Wandsworth.'

Marina had raided the English Market – cheeses, cold meats, couscous salad, olives, chocolate and a bottle of white wine. She set it all out. The sun was unusually warm for November. 'How's Bridget managing without you this weekend?'

'Carlotta's looking out for her.'

'God bless Carlotta.'

'How did you find it?' he asked. 'This rock?'

'It found me.'

Luke sat next to her, his legs stretched out. 'Go on.'

'After we moved back last year,' she said, 'things were pretty bleak, especially before Dara started college. I'd promised the kids it'd be great, living here, but the reality was rather different. Dad was cantankerous and a lot of the people I'd known had left Cork, so we were really isolated. There were days, late last summer, awful days, when the house was in chaos and the skies were heavy, and Jacquie and Dara were going, "And we're here because . . . ?" So one morning I forced them into the car as if they were restless toddlers and we went exploring. I'd had good times in Kerry with Matthew and Gwen, my best friend, and I thought the kids and I could find some nice spots.' Marina wrapped her arms round her knees. 'And we did.' She looked at the silvery hill behind her. 'We found Knockatee. We stopped down on the road to take in the view, and Dara set off, up the hill, and found this rock . . . That was a good day. It made us realize that, even without Aidan, we were still a family. So after Dad died, we came back again, just the three of us.'

'So this is a very special place for you?'

She smiled. 'We love our rock.'

Luke laid his plate on his legs and muttered about eating with the smell of sheep shit in his nose. Clumps of droppings were dotted around in what looked like carefully constructed miniature pyramids. 'Tell me about those trips you made with your friends.'

She squinted at him. 'You're very interested in Matthew.'

'Of course I am. Why didn't it work out between him and Natalie?'

'She left him. And now she has forsaken men, she tells me. She reckons they were her downfall with Kitt. There was always a man distracting her, apparently.'

'So. Those college trips?'

'If you're trying to find out if I ever slept with Matthew, I didn't.'

'Not even nearly?'

'Oh, nearly . . . who knows about nearly? I suppose it almost happened once or twice, when we were both lonely, but it wasn't worth risking our friendship. No, for much of the time I was the gooseberry. He was with Gwen in college, and whenever he had his brother's car, we'd take off, the three of us. Once we drove round the coast from Cork to Killarney,' Marina spooned couscous on to her plate. 'That was the best time. We kept playing Neil Young. You know that song "Peace Of Mind"? I can't listen to it any more because it brings all that back so exactly – the curving roads in this wreck of a Fiat, drinking milk, music playing, everyone happy.'

Luke balanced their plastic cups in tufts of gorse to pour the wine.

A light wind whistled between the hills, causing the grass below to rustle. A sheep bleated in the distance, and another, high on a ridge, replied. 'They're so white and fluffy,' said Marina, 'you'd think they'd been through a woollen cycle in the washing-machine.'

'They have. It's called the Irish-weather cycle. Another reason I left this country.'

When November stole the midday warmth, they headed round the coast and checked into a quiet, upmarket hotel near Ballylickey. The bay window in their bedroom overlooked a landscaped garden, now sinking into dusk. Luke put down the bags, Marina snooped around; they talked about whether to stay in for dinner or go to Bantry. Without really noticing, they had slipped into coupledom, their banter light and mundane: 'What a view.' 'Firm mattress.' 'Let's find some tea.'

In the bar, over scones and shortbread, Marina couldn't quite get a handle on how this had happened to her. An unusual joy filled her, but it was an elusive thing, flitting about like a fairy. There, but not supposed to be there.

'You look confused,' said Luke.

'I am. This – you and me. It can't be so easy, can it?'

'Ooh, I do love a good pessimist!'

'But think of the impediments,' she said. 'Your family, mine, Italy, Ireland . . . We've both got so much excess baggage.'

'Inevitably, but we've also shed a lot. We've done the marriages, the child-rearing. Our time is our own again, and it's up to us to make the most of the next stage, whatever the complications, so don't give me your Irish Catholic guilt, thinking you don't deserve to enjoy yourself.'

'Maybe that's it. I've always paid a high price for the good things. Now I expect the worst.'

'Whereas you should be thinking, I've paid my dues. Because you have, Marina.'

They went back to their room. Luke put on the bedside light, saying, 'Would you like a bath, my love?' But she was behind him. She put her arms round his waist and opened his belt. 'Ah. Maybe later.'

Afterwards, she watched him walk across to the bathroom. He was fit. Lithe as a blade of grass. His body wasn't ageing yet, like hers, with her no-longer-quite-so-firm belly and gathering creases.

As he got back under the covers, she said, 'Maybe I don't want this after all – this monogamy lark. I mean, if there are lots of nice taut bodies like yours out there, I really ought to make the most of them.'

'Sleeping around isn't all it's cracked up to be, you know.'

She laughed. 'That's my very point! You've had lots of lovers. After a long monogamous marriage, don't you think I should play the field a little?'

'Certainly not. God, I've just made love to you like you're the only woman in the universe and this is what I get for it!'

Marina ran her finger along his chin. 'So you reckon we met before Morocco?'

'I know we did.'

'Where?'

'Ah. That's for me to know and for you to remember.'

'Was it in Ireland?'

No reply.

'At UCC?' she asked.

'I didn't go to UCC.'

'But you might have come down to . . . I don't know – take part in a debate?'

'Me? Debate? That would be the shortest debate in history.'

'Seriously, were we actually introduced?'

'I'll run that bath for you now.' And he did – with bubbles and all. Marina couldn't remember the last time someone had done that for her.

The scream came from deep below her. She had to call on it, force it up from the depths, so that it would wake her and save her from . . . Brown water. Aidan diving in. Jacquie disappearing into thick, murky sea. It was too much. Unendurable. In the horror of it, she knew she had to scream and push for the surface. Push up. She felt herself doing it. Up. Up. Get up there, away from this. A coarse uneven cry came from her body. It worked. She woke. In silence.

The room was brightening. Marina swept her legs out of the bed. She needed to move, to reconnect with real surroundings.

Luke turned sleepily. 'You okay?'

'Yeah. Horrible dream, that's all.'

'Huh?' He made himself wake. 'What was it?'

Marina stared towards the window. 'Just imagine the worst possible . . . and one of your kids.'

Luke sat up and pulled her back against him. 'God. One of those.'

'But I've never had one like it before. Never anything like that. It was Jacquie. Why would I have such a dream during such a perfect night?'

'Because you're happy and secure, but you think you don't deserve it, so your mind drags out the worst possible thing that could ever happen to make sure you spoil it good and proper. We're hopeless beings, really. Interesting, but hopeless.'

'But I never have nightmares. And why Jacquie?'

'Maybe you're afraid of her disapproval?'

'But it was too severe. And the depth of it, the weight – it felt like a warning.' She motioned towards the window. 'Lovely day. You. The smell of breakfast . . . I'm awake now. But it still feels like a warning. It meant something, Luke. Something to do with you and me, and Jacquie drowning.'

# 10

'What time of the night do you call this?' David squinted against the light from the bedside lamp.

'I call it seven o'clock in the morning,' said Jacquie, pulling on a slip. The dark, miserable November mornings were disgusting.

'I don't have to get up, do I?'

'No, but try not to let Mum catch you in my bed.'

'Why don't you get back in?' He pulled back the duvet. 'Go on. Pull a sickie.'

'I can't. And I really can't do these late-night parties either, David. I've had two hours' sleep. I'm barely functioning at work as it is.'

'Yeah, you were, like, *sooooo* much fun last night.' He pulled the duvet over him again, and said, as she went to the door, 'Can I photograph you naked?'

'Why? So you can make me glow bright orange?'

'Royal blue, I was thinking.'

She smiled. 'Dream on.'

Downstairs, Dara was up – a rare sight at that time of the morning, but he needed the car so had to drive her to work. 'I'm beginning to understand why Mum asked Natalie to live here,' he said, slurping his coffee. 'I mean, look at this place. It's like a fucking operating theatre. I can't even find stuff in my own kitchen, she's so neat.'

'Maybe that explains why Kitt is so pathologically untidy.'

'Yeah, because her mother's anally retentive. You look wrecked. Good party?'

'A drag. Everyone getting drunk for the sake of it, and smoking their brains out.'

Dara gave her a look. 'Don't go getting middle-aged before your time, sis.'

'I already *am* middle-aged – surely that's the problem? I mean, I'm twenty-three and working for a bloody multinational, for Christ's sake, because of the great pay and the excellent health plan, and I spend my days with a load of people whose idea of fun is going to the fitness centre! If I mention an interesting film I've seen at the Kino, they won't have heard of the cinema, let alone the film, just because it isn't a multiplex!'

'So why don't you quit if it's so bad?'

'Because I have a student loan, remember? And a loan-loan, and until they're paid off, I can't afford to move. While you're out partying, I'm living like a nun.'

'Oh, so that's what you get up to with David. You *pray* together!'

'Hurry up. I'll be late.'

When they were in the car, Dara asked, 'How bad are these debts, anyway?'

'Worse than Mum knows.'

'How come?'

'Paris. Cost me a fortune. And all that flying back and forth to Cork with practically no earnings . . . I lost my first job within two weeks. The *patron* was a *salot*.'

'It must have been tough,' said Dara, 'with no money and the relationship going arseways.' He glanced at her. 'Sorry I never thought to ask.'

It wasn't tough, she thought. Not tough at all. 'Anyway, the good news is that the loan is finally losing weight, and when it's paid off, I'm going to do something spectacular. I'm going to be spontaneous, throw caution to the wind, and take a chance on . . . something yet to be determined.'

'Great,' said Dara, warmly. 'You've been way too sensible way too long. Even Mum thinks so. I mean, there's been a lot going on, but it's time to break out.'

'Don't worry. I'm ready for the next big thing – and it had better be good!'

'Hmm, looks like Mum's already found the next big thing. What's going on with this Luke guy?'

'I wish I knew,' said Jacquie.

'Doesn't she talk to you about it?'

'She hasn't mentioned him since he went back. Maybe it's off.'

'With her bounding around like a giddy puppy? I don't think so. She alternates between being very silly and incredibly vague.'

Jacquie chuckled. 'I know. Sometimes you have to jump around and wave flags to get her attention! But at least she isn't looking dragged down like she used to.'

'That's for sure. No doubt people are saying she's "glowing". And we all know why.'

'Dara!'

'What? Aren't you curious about it?'

'Of course I am, but she clearly doesn't want to talk about it.'

'Maybe she's too embarrassed,' he said, 'or afraid we would be. You should bring it up.'

'*Me?* I don't want to embarrass her any more than she wants to be embarrassed!'

'Yeah, but, fuck it, we have to know what's going on.'

'You ask her so.'

'All right, I will.'

But Marina had her own discussion planned. That evening, when the three of them were getting dinner together, she said to Jacquie, 'You know, I'm really *not* okay with seeing David coming out of your room in his boxer shorts first thing in the morning.'

Jacquie bristled; she wasn't okay with it either.

'This is a family home, Jacquie, not a student house, and I don't think it gives a very good example to Kitt if your sometimes-there-sometimes-not-sort-of-boyfriend-cum-toyboy is staying in your room.'

'Quite a few little prejudices seeping out there, Mum,' said Jacquie. 'You sound as if you don't like it being casual and you don't like him being younger than me. You're not going all conservative on us, are you?'

'Jacquie, this relationship –'

'It isn't a relationship.'

'But that's crass – sleeping with him for the sake of it.'

'It isn't for the sake of it. I like him. I just don't want any complications.'

'But he's besotted with you,' said Marina. 'You're not being fair. You're using him to make you feel better about Didier.'

Jacquie huffed. 'What has any of this got to do with Kitt?'

'Simply that we should be sensitive to what Natalie's trying to do, which is get Kitt back on the straight and narrow, and your example is frankly –'

'But she's *failing*,' Jacquie whispered, raising her hands. 'Her mild-mannered approach has *no* effect on that child!'

'Personally,' said Dara, in a deep voice, 'I think babies must have been switched at the hospital. There is *no* way that woman can be that girl's mother.'

'Look,' Marina said to Jacquie, 'Kitt has very skewed ideas about boys and relationships, and I wish you'd bear that in mind.'

'Speaking of relationships,' said Dara, somewhat off the point, 'how's the Italian connection going, *Mother*?'

'Hmm?'

'You know – Luke? The man with the lake?'

Marina was ladling rice on to plates. 'I haven't quite made enough.'

'I mean, is he, like, your boyfriend or what?'

'Oh, I don't think we'd use that terminology at our age,' Marina said, looking up gratefully when Natalie came in with a cheery hello and pulled off her coat. 'Good day?'

Dara wasn't about to be put off. 'But you're together, right? I mean, you're *having a relationship*, yeah? Or was it just a fling?'

Marina put plates on the table. 'Sit down, everyone, it'll get cold.'

They sat. Dara poured glasses of water, Jacquie passed the butter to Marina, Natalie sprinkled pepper, and Kitt appeared, took a plate and said, 'I'll eat in front of the telly.'

Before the conversation died a total death, Jacquie said to Natalie, 'We were just talking about this Luke guy.'

'Ooh, isn't he yummy? Do you think you'll move to Italy, Marina?'

Marina shot her a look. It said, 'Not helpful.'

But Natalie's eyes flashed with mischief. 'Or even get married again?'

'*Married*?' said Jacquie. 'They only met two months ago!'

'I know, but when you get to our age, there isn't much point hanging about.'

'All right, you guys,' said Marina. 'Enough.'

Jacquie's hands went out. 'What? We can't say anything about it? Mum, we haven't a clue what's going on. Was it a holiday thing, with a weekend thrown in, or are you . . . is this . . .'

Marina looked up. 'If it were, would you . . .'

'I don't know. Probably not, but . . .'

'Gosh,' said Natalie, 'doesn't anyone in this family ever finish a sentence?'

'I never really thought about it,' said Jacquie.

'Me neither,' Marina said frankly. 'I never expected anything like this, but I never expected to end up on my own either. It isn't actually much fun.'

'You used to say you'd never get over Dad,' Dara said. 'That no one else would . . .'

'And I never will and no one else ever will. But you two'll be gone soon – off into your lives. It'll be easier for you if I'm not . . . alone.'

Dara and Jacquie exchanged a glance. Oh, so she's doing it for *us*.

'But he lives in Italy,' said Jacquie. 'You'd have to move there, like Natalie said.'

'Don't be silly. It's too soon for that kind of talk.' She cleared her throat. 'Although Luke *would* like me to spend some time there, and I'd really like to, if it's all right with you two. Opportunities like this don't come along very often. Not at our stage.'

'You don't need our permission,' Dara said grudgingly.

'Nonetheless, I'd like you to be happy about it.'

Natalie beamed at them. 'Think of the holidays in Italy!'

'Well, yes,' Marina said hopefully.

'It isn't about holidays,' Jacquie said to her. 'It's about having some kind of family life for a change. All of us together. I mean, we moved to Cork because *you* wanted to. I thought that was the whole point – that we'd all be in the same place for a bit.'

Her mother put down her fork. 'When you went to France last year, Jacquie, you weren't that bothered about family life. You'd still be there if it had worked out.'

'Ouch,' said Dara, but the blow was much, much lower than anyone knew.

'Anyway, I thought you liked Luke,' said Marina.

'He seemed nice enough,' said Jacquie.

'Nice?' said Natalie. 'He's drop-dead *gorgeous*.'

Marina brightened. 'We're not planning to drop dead just yet, thank you.'

'In fact, when you're done with him,' Natalie went on, 'pass him on to me, would you?'

'Oh,' Marina said, blushing. 'I don't think I'll ever be done with him.'

Dara and Jacquie exchanged another glance. So that was it, then: their mother was in love.

Marina's knees were up against her breasts. 'I wish you'd get something decent to sit on. This pouffe is so uncomfortable.'

'I don't want people to be comfortable,' said Suzanne. 'I want them to buy stuff and leave.'

'*I*'ll leave if you don't find me a proper seat.'

Suzanne sipped her coffee. 'So, heard from himself today?'

'Many times. This texting lark's great.'

'How are the kids handling it?'

'Fine, so long as I don't gush too much. It's great having Natalie there – who'd have thought it? She defuses things. I can't help feeling that if she and Kitt weren't there, Dara and Jacquie would be more uptight about it.'

'How's Natalie getting on in the job?'

'Loves it. Says it's great to be earning. It's all beginning to make sense, you know. She told me a few weeks ago that, in her view, it's too late to do anything about Kitt, so I said that that was a cop-out, that she can't expect to be treated like a parent until she behaves like one. But the trouble is, she has nothing to go on. Her own parents were almost completely absent from her childhood, apparently, and she and her sister were raised by a string of ineffectual au-pairs in a large house in the country. The only discipline and good sense she learnt came from boarding-school.'

'So you're probably the first mothering role model she's ever come across?'

'Probably, yeah. So I'm giving her my hard-earned gems of wisdom and she's teaching me yoga. Turns out she's a qualified yoga teacher.'

'That should help you limber up. No doubt you'd like to improve your flexibility.'

'Sod off!'

'Come on, don't be so coy. It must be amazing . . . getting back into the water, so to speak?'

Marina grinned. 'It's pretty much amazing, all right. Different, though. I keep expecting him to do things the way Aidan did, but he doesn't, so every move he makes is . . . sort of startling.'

Suzanne huffed. 'God, that sounds good. I don't think there's *anything* left that Ronan could do to surprise me, short of introducing a third party!'

When Marina got off the phone to Matthew that night, she joined Natalie and Jacquie in the sitting room, where they were having tea by the fire.

'How's his leg?' Natalie asked.

'He's going mad with it, poor thing.'

'For two people who fell out,' said Jacquie, 'you don't half spend a lot of time gassing on the phone. Have you forgiven him his major misdemeanour?'

'I try to block it out.' Marina sat down and poured herself tea.

'Oh, that's a terrible idea,' said Jacquie, 'isn't it, Natalie?

Blocking things. Far better to get it out there. Talk about it. To *us*, for instance. What the hell happened?'

Marina tapped a teaspoon against the mug and sat back. 'In short, a very important relationship was wiped out by a few ill-chosen words. In this case, seven words. Ill-spoken, ill-timed, damage done.'

'What did he say?' Jacquie asked.

'Oh, it wasn't Matthew who said it, it was me.'

'What were the seven words?' said Natalie.

'"You're not the only one, you know."'

'It's an odd kind of a story,' she began, when they had assured her they had no interest in the short version. 'Undramatic, in many ways, but it was dramatic for me, and there was such a curious . . . shade to it. Throughout my teens, Gwen was my best friend. She lived in Dublin, near my aunt's place, and whenever I went to stay with my cousins, I ended up in her house, and we became really close, until during the summers we were both going back and forth to Dublin and Cork all the time. We even had holidays together – I went to Donegal with her family, she came to France with mine, so when it came to third level, we were determined to go to the same college and both got into UCC.

'But first year was a tough one for me,' Marina explained to Natalie. 'My mother left home, my brother was in the seminary, and my sister had skittered off to Dublin, leaving me with my heartbroken father. Great fun. But I had good friends, not least Matthew, who was like part of the furniture around here – we'd been friends for two or three years by then – and he and Gwen looked out for me. They made quite a team when it came to cheering me up, and Gwen often stayed here, which helped a lot. Her voice took the place of Mum's and her cooking gave me and Dad something to laugh about. She was a Godsend.

'In second year, we managed to get five people together to share a house. I was mad keen to leave home and my brother had moved back for a bit, and he told me to go off and enjoy myself. We rented a red-brick terrace up the road from college and shared with two guys and another girl, so there were lots of late nights and parties and, you know, a typical student scene . . . Matthew was two years ahead of us, doing engineering, so he wasn't always around, but he and Gwen had grown closer through my crisis, and towards the end of that year they got together. It was fairly casual, but I was delighted – my two best friends et cetera – and we had some *craic* that summer, the three of us.

'We also worked our guts out to make money, because Gwen and I wanted to go on a charter holiday that September, which we duly did. It was great – at first. We lay on the beach all day and danced all night, and it was going really well . . . until I caught Gwen with one of the Turkish waiters she'd been flirting with. Selim. I was furious on Matthew's behalf, and then on my own behalf, because before I knew it she'd as good as disappeared. She spent the days sitting around his restaurant, so I was alone on the beach all day and pretty much left to my own devices at night, because I wouldn't trail round nightclubs with them. Instead I festered in our hotel, brooding about her cheating on Matthew and ruining my holiday. Inevitably, it all poured out and we had a huge fight on the last day, but on the flight home, we sorted it out. She said she was feeling ambivalent about Matthew anyway and was going to break it off with him. I said fair enough.

'As soon as I got home – here, to spend a few days with Dad – Matthew called down with a friend of ours, George. They gave me huge hugs, chastised me for not taking them with us, and when we went into the kitchen to have tea, they larked about, you know, being lads, but they were pretty giddy even by Matthew's standards. I didn't think too much about why he'd come to see me and not Gwen, but their carry-on started to grate. They clearly had some agenda going on. George kept ribbing Matthew about a gorgeous girl we knew, Aisling, whom Gwen loathed, but I wouldn't take the bait. I was tidying up, trying to ignore them, but they wanted me to pay attention, so the nudging and winking went on until finally it came out. Matthew had been with Aisling while we were away. I couldn't believe it. I was so mad, I *boiled.* I'd fallen out with Gwen and spoiled my holiday on *his* account, while he'd been cheating back home – and then had the nerve to brag about it! To me! But what was really despicable was that they expected me to join in. To joke about it behind Gwen's back. Matthew almost expected me to congratulate him for scoring with this woman. I still can't quite get my head round it, but he absolutely presumed I would take his part. Instead, I turned around, eyeballed him and said, "You're not the only one, you know."'

Jacquie and Natalie winced.

'And that did it for me. That was why I lost both of them.'

'What did he say?' Jacquie asked.

'He *froze*. He knew exactly what I meant – that Gwen had been fooling around.' Marina put her mug on the hearth. 'The gadding-about stopped. Oh, it was okay for him to be unfaithful, but he didn't like it one bit that Gwen had been, and I, meanwhile, was in deep trouble. I realized that if Gwen found out what I'd said, I wouldn't be able to explain the circumstances without telling her about Aisling. The only saving grace was that Matthew couldn't say anything either, for exactly the same reason, and anyway, at one level I wasn't too worried because she was about to break it off with him.

'But inevitably, and unfortunately for me, the opposite happened. Gwen and Matthew soon afterwards fell passionately in love. And men in love are very, very possessive. That was when things went sour for me. About a month after they became the golden couple, a freeze descended between Gwen and me, as sudden as an ice-storm. I didn't twig at first. I trusted Matthew not to drop me in it, just as he could be sure I wouldn't do likewise to him. But things with Gwen went from bad to worse. We'd be out with friends and she'd snipe and cut me down, belittling my opinions, heaping scorn whenever possible, yet always in a way that was just above reproach. If I complained or answered back, she accused me of being over-sensitive. She always kept it at a level that was hurtful to me, but not obviously offensive to anyone else. She was never available for coffee or a chat any more because she was always with one or other of her "super" pals, and when we did coincide, I had to endure hearing how wonderful Sarah was, or Mary, or June. In the house, she was scathing. "God, who made this mess?" Or "We don't all have a room as big as yours, Marina." It got to the point where she hardly spoke to me. I'd hear third-hand about things they were doing – parties, concerts – but somehow I was never invited. I had other friends, but I was comprehensively ostracized by my own group, the people I lived with, because Gwen kept me out of the loop.

'When I confronted Matthew, he owned up. Unable to contain his jealousy about the Turk, he had challenged her, and there was only one way he could have known about it: me. So she cut me off like a gangrenous limb, and I had no defence to make.

'Matthew, of course, couldn't tell her exactly how it had come out without letting on to her about Aisling, and he was so much in love with Gwen by then, I couldn't ask him to. It would have spoilt their lovely romance. So I was collateral damage. As long as Matthew wouldn't come clean, I looked like a spiteful snitch. I lost my best friend over seven ill-timed words. I know it was my fault. I couldn't blame Gwen for backing off, but the way she did it was brutal.

'Living in the house was miserable: trying to avoid her and her friends, never getting to chat with Matthew, relentless digs about every bloody thing . . . until I came home one day that February and Gwen asked me to leave. We couldn't go on like this, she said, the atmosphere was terrible, everyone was feeling it, and she implied that since it was my fault anyway, I should be the one to decamp. So I moved back home.

'Months later, after our finals, Gwen dumped Matthew. Finally I had my chance to tell her how it came about – I didn't expect forgiveness, I just wanted her to know that I'd blurted it out of loyalty, not disloyalty, that my spikes came out because they were scorning her. I hoped Matthew would back me up, but Matthew, it transpired, had skipped the country and, not long afterwards, Gwen did too, so I never got to speak to either of them.'

'Wait a minute,' said Jacquie. 'They cheated on each other. It had nothing to do with you.'

'That's the unbearable irony. They did the cheating, I paid the price. And Matthew,' Marina stuck out her finger, 'let that happen.'

# 11

Lake Orta, the infant of the great Italian lakes, appeared as a pitch-dark gap between the trees on the near shore and the lights on the other side. Marina's impression of northern Italy, so far, was of motorways, winding roads, tail-lights weaving ahead and, finally, this flat black floor to their left. A hole in her vision.

They turned into a gravelled entrance and stopped in front of a huge door with a light shining over it. When she stepped out, a large house rose above her, four or five storeys high. Luke took her bag. There was a sharp chill in the air, on this cold December night, refreshing after Cork's muggy autumn evenings.

'Come on in.' Luke led her up the steps to the front door. She was tense. She had been excited about spending time with him without having to deal with any of the many people who wandered daily through her railway-station life, but now that she'd arrived, she was as rigid as a steel girder. Discovering how Luke lived and how she might find a way to fit into this place – his place – was daunting from any perspective. She would have to meet his friends and family, a whole web of people, learn to handle Bridget, and stand about while everybody jabbered in Italian. She would probably meet Luke's son, the one who lived nearby, and what would he make of her?

The house was quiet when they stepped into a large hall, which had a grey marble floor and doors going off in all directions. Luke led her into the drawing room, which was spacious and bright, with pale yellow walls, a high ceiling and French windows. He took her coat. She gazed around. It didn't smack of wealth. Luke was only marginally better off than she was (although on paper probably significantly so) and the baroque cream silk furniture was slightly jaded, the décor a little dull. There was an open fireplace with a huge gilt-edged mirror over the marble mantelpiece, but Marina was drawn to the windows. Lake Orta was out there, invisible, but waiting.

'It seems like an age since you first told me about this place,' she said.

Luke stood by the fireplace, smiling at her. 'You've no idea how often I've wished I could see you right there, where you are now.' He came over and kissed the nape of her neck. 'We have the house to ourselves. Ma's been taken out for the evening. We'll have supper here by the fire.'

'Lovely.'

'But first let me show you your . . .' He hesitated.

'My what?'

'Room.'

'Oh.'

'Carlotta had the guest room made up,' he said, his eyes shifting away from her. 'She thought you'd want your own space.'

'Whatever suits,' she said. All his talk about how they could be together in Orta without impediment – and here she was being shunted into the guest room.

'What would suit me is to sleep in the same bed as you every night for the rest of my life,' said Luke, 'but just as you have issues with your children, I have to take the softly-softly approach with Ma and,' he waved his hand about, 'some of the other people drifting around here.'

'Your son?'

'Oh, no. He's well used to it. Call it . . . logistics.'

Logistics, she thought. Indeed. She was in no position to

argue. She had not even offered him a room, let alone her bed, when he was in Cork.

He showed her around the two-floor apartment: a large, stainless-steel kitchen at the back, a cheerful morning room with faded tapestries hanging on the walls, a neat study and his mother's bedroom on the ground floor. Upstairs, a sort of old-fashioned dressing room, with a small desk and an armchair, led into Luke's modest bedroom. The guest room was lovely: two huge windows, a cream shaggy rug on a parquet floor, a vast double bed and a roomy bathroom. On reflection, Marina decided, Carlotta was right. This would be very pleasant; best not to leap into cohabitation too soon . . . but what the hell did Carlotta have to do with it?

The bed linen was neatly turned back and there were roses on the bedside table. 'Did you do all this?'

'God, no,' said Luke. 'I have help. Maria does the housework and much of the cooking. I need someone here for when I'm at work.'

'Can your mother never be left alone?'

'Not every day, no.'

'But she's so feisty.'

'Feisty, but frequently confused. It's best to have someone around.'

'And the rest of the building is apartments?'

'Yes. Two per floor, but they're not all done up yet. I'll show you tomorrow. Come on, let's eat.'

They had dinner, *osso bucco*, by the fire. Marina sipped her wine, glancing around the room and at the man opposite her. Gorgeous, gorgeous, gorgeous.

'Here's to Hamid,' he said, raising his glass.

When Marina woke the next morning, pale light was filtering round her curtains and the house was as quiet as a chapel, but it was such a big old house, with those thick walls, that there might have been a political conference going on downstairs and she wouldn't have heard a sound. She rolled over in the warm, cosy bed. Luke was gone, vanished in the night. He'd been there, when she'd drifted off to sleep curled up with her back to him, his arm round her thigh.

She wondered if he might bring her breakfast and hop in for a cuddle before they faced his mother, but he didn't come. Some time later she heard his voice, but it faded into the walls. She would have to get up. It was ten to ten already.

The house was completely still when, showered and dressed, she made her way downstairs. She was cross with Luke for leaving her like this, wandering round a strange house on her first morning. Her heels made a clip-clop racket as she crossed the hall, so she tiptoed to maintain the chapel-like silence. There was no one in the drawing room; Luke's study was empty, and so was the morning room. Still, it was set for breakfast, so she went in and stood by the window, her head full of dark thoughts. What did she know about Luke? Would he take to vanishing in his own house as he had vanished in the lanes of Essaouira?

After the night they'd spent, intense and emotional, the morning was isolating and nerve-racking. Where *was* he? The lake, surrounded by green hills, was glowing in the early light, and on the street below the villa an old man was walking past with two dogs. The only cars allowed in Orta belonged to residents, Luke said, so the little street that ran along the shore was as eerily quiet as the house.

The door opened behind her and a stocky woman in a blue housecoat came in. '*Buon giorno, signora. Caffè? Tè?*'

'Oh, thank you. Tea would be lovely.'

'*Prego.*' Maria withdrew.

Phew. At least she'd get a cuppa. She turned back to the

window, thinking that she really must learn Italian, but shook her head even as the thought went through it. *Must learn Italian? Like, for why?* Where was her certainty about the longevity of this relationship coming from?

Hands came on to her shoulders.

She spun round. 'Jesus! Sneaking up on me again!'

Luke smiled. 'Not my fault you were miles away.'

'But where have you been? I didn't know where to go.'

'I thought I'd let you sleep. What do you think of my lake?'

She had scarcely taken it in. 'Stunning.'

'There's a better view from your room, but you can just see the tip of the island over there to the right – see?'

Over tea and coffee, they sat in the sunlit room, delighting in one another's company and in the peaceful quiet that had earlier unsettled her.

But there, in that inauspicious way in the morning room, Marina's short idyll ended.

The voice intruded first – a low, familiar growl that seemed to be issuing instructions as it came across the hall – before the door burst open and Carlotta appeared, chin over her shoulder, as she remonstrated with Maria behind her. She turned then, and came fully into the room. 'Marina, how lovely to see you again!'

They embraced. 'You, too,' Marina said warmly.

'Sit down, sit down. Don't let me disturb you. Eat, eat.'

Marina did as she was told.

'*Allora*,' Carlotta said to Luke, and proceeded to prattle in Italian. Her hair was pinned into a chignon and her slim figure was emphasized by a tailored skirt and brown cashmere jumper. Her wrist jangled with bangles.

'I'm afraid that's impossible,' Luke said in English. 'I'm taking Marina to Stresa.'

A number of charming, gurgly words came from Carlotta, who then switched to English, throwing a small smile in Marina's direction. 'Very well. But you must all have dinner with me this evening. You can't keep Marina to yourself, darling. Ah! Ma-*reen*-na,' she said, stretching the middle syllable. 'What a sympathetic name! Like the sea.'

*Reen*. It made Marina think of Matthew. It made her wish he was there. She felt like a schoolgirl on an exchange, staying with a glamorous family and not understanding much of what was going on around her.

'Where is Stresa?' she asked Luke.

'A town on Lake Maggiore. Over the hill. But let me show you Orta first.'

The neatly cobbled road that led into the village had two cement tracks running down the middle for cars 'and for a tourist train that tootles along here in the summer,' Luke said. Marina walked on the smooth bits, trying to take it all in – the lake on one side, ochre and yellow villas on the other, and then the road narrowing, as they neared the town, and dipping between tall houses that threw everything into shade. There were arches, stone steps slipping under houses, cast-iron gates protecting villas, and exquisitely decorated shop windows, but when they reached the square, she came to a halt. 'Oh, wow.'

'Yes,' said Luke.

One side of the rectangular piazza was open to the lake. Straight across, about five hundred metres away, the island of San Giulio, with its huge L-shaped seminary rising behind a ring of outfacing houses, beamed out serenity. Marina felt as if she should genuflect. Old hotels cornered the square at either end and, on the right, an arcade of shops and cafés, quiet and restrained, hummed with summer potential. 'No wonder you don't come home very often,' she said.

They walked across the square, towards the ochre town hall, which stood on stilts at one end, and stopped at the foot of a broad, stepped street that led up to a yellow church at the top of the rise. 'And down that way,' said Luke, waving towards the tight little street that continued on out of town, 'more shops and restaurants, and then it turns into a bumpy path that goes the whole way round the edge of the peninsula – it's shaped like a head – and brings you back to where we started. We'll walk it some time, but we'd better get back if we're going to make lunch in Stresa.'

They left soon afterwards, with Bridget. Marina sat in the back, trying to catch the views and wondering why on earth his mother had had to come. The prospect had been so delightful – a late romantic lunch on Lake Maggiore – and here they were, together with Mother. They had yet to spend twenty-four hours alone without being forced to incorporate other people into the frame. She tried to zone out, which was easy enough: Bridget chatted to Luke as if no one else was in the car.

This had not quite dawned on Marina: the reality that was Luke's mother. Her pre-eminence in his life, the responsibility he had, the very nature of her, all had to be taken into account. Bridget appeared to be very dependent. She had never learnt Italian – not in twenty-five years, on and off, in Orta – and although physically strong, her personality would have confounded Freud. But Marina would have to learn to deal with her because she could not allow Bridget to interfere with this relationship. Perhaps Luke simply needed retraining. Taking your mother along on an early date was a no-no; it might be helpful to point this out to him.

Marina's spirits rose when they got to Stresa and drove along the shore, past grand hotels left over from another era, with majestic façades and magnificent gardens. A pink promenade offered jaw-dropping views of blue mountains tipped with white, like tables draped in linen tablecloths, and a trio of islands sat pert in the water.

'The Borromean Islands,' Luke said to her. 'Bella, Madre, and Pescatori.'

'It must get packed here in the summer.'

'And the winter, with skiers from surrounding resorts.'

'Who's skiing?' Bridget asked.

'No one, Ma. I'm explaining to Marina about the resorts.'

'Resort to what?'

'The ski resorts,' he said patiently.

They parked and took a walk along the promenade. Marina inhaled the brittle air. Bridget grasped Luke's arm, more or less ignoring Marina, but they had walked for barely ten minutes when she said, 'I'd like to sit down now.'

'There's a place over there,' said Luke, 'where we can get lunch.'

'Do you mind if I walk a little longer?' Marina asked.

'I'll catch up,' said Luke, and did so after he had settled his mother with a cappuccino in the little café. They walked up and down, within her sight. Marina was quiet; Luke asked where her thoughts had gone.

'Can I ask you something?' she said in reply.

'*Certo.*'

'Why couldn't we have lunch alone when I'm only here for a bare three days?'

He raised his eyebrows.

'It's a fair question,' she said, 'especially with all your talk of wanting to get me here so we could have a little privacy.'

'It's a long day for her. We'll be out for the best part of it. Maria takes the afternoons off, and Ma doesn't see much of me during the week.'

Marina nodded, walked on, looking not at the lake or its islands, with their red roofs cluttered together like pedestrians on overcrowded ferries, but at her feet. She liked her new boots. Low heel, sharp toe. Italian, of course. 'It's the way she blots me out. It's hard to know how to handle it.'

Luke shifted awkwardly, his collar round his chin. 'She does that when she's uncertain of her ground. Humour her and she'll be fine.'

'I'm afraid I'm not very good at the humouring thing. I did it for years with Dad. My patience isn't what it used to be.'

Luke inhaled, his eyes narrowing to minimize the harsh sunlight. 'I don't expect you to become her carer, you know. We have that covered.'

'Good. Because I don't want to do it again. Not yet. This is my time off. *You*'re my time off.'

He walked on, his elbow against hers. 'What do you mean "Not yet"?'

'I mean that I'll probably have to do it for my own mother at some point, and I'd appreciate a bit of a window between her and Dad.'

'You hardly ever mention your mother.'

Marina veered over to the railing. The water looked so cold. Blue with cold. 'I hate this bit,' she said. 'Telling each other things. Dragging up the past, so that we know where we've come from and what it's done to us.' She looked at him. 'Is it really necessary? Couldn't we be together without having to know absolutely everything about each other? Shouldn't we keep a bit of mystique?'

'I only need to know the bits that matter,' said Luke.

'What matters is that I'm a well-rounded, middle-aged woman from a normal background, who had a normal childhood and has a perfectly normal dysfunctional relationship with her mother. Like so many women of my age.'

'Whenever you're ready, then,' he said, turning back.

Their flimsy weekend could not be spoiled. She scurried alongside him, and hooked her arm through his. 'Mum's fine, really. She was a lovely mother when we were kids. The house was always full of people because she loved our friends and they loved her, and we all had a lovely time.'

'Until?'

'Until . . . I was nineteen and she sort of . . . evaporated. She became vague, never heard what anyone said, spent the day listening to sloppy music and went out a lot. Dad asked me if I thought she might be going through "the change". I was mortified, but muttered that, yeah, probably, that was it. As time went on, she was no longer the warm, bubbly person we'd been used to. She'd become . . .'

'What?'

'Cold. She went through the motions of looking after us, but didn't seem to care much any more. And then all was explained. She ran away with her first cousin.'

Luke stopped.

'It was quite a scandal in Cork at the time. He was a well-known dentist with a family of his own, so the gossip spread well beyond our family. Rumours abounded about how long it had been going on . . . You can imagine. They'd spent a lot of time together in their grandmother's house as kids, so people speculated. Dad was wretched, of course, but Mum was just fine. She went off to live in England and there she has lived happily ever since with her cousin. They play golf, live by the sea, and enjoy rude health.'

'In many cultures, first cousins marry.'

'Oh, don't give me that! Not in *our* culture, they don't. The whole bloody community was tut-tutting, everyone getting themselves into such a heap about the scandal that it detracted from what Dad was going through. Whether the guy was her cousin or not was irrelevant to him. He'd still been left. And so had we.'

'That must have been a tough call at nineteen.'

'It was awful, and . . . bewildering trying to deal with my own hurt, and Dad's, *and* the shame, which I know was completely irrational but I still felt it. My brother and sister had left home, so I had to cope with Dad alone. He was a very unassuming man, polite, and it was humiliating for him to have a whole community talking about him. He hated having to endure their pity.'

'Sympathy, surely?'

'No, he was pretty clear that it was pity, and even disdain. He never got over it. These days a guy would go out and find someone else, but Dad felt he had to maintain what he perceived to be a moral position to save us kids from further disgrace. He wouldn't dream of remarrying, so the rest of his life was lonely, and I watched that loneliness, day in, day out, until he died.'

'Do you see much of your mother now?'

'Christmas cards and the occasional phone-call. I don't kill myself. She made her choice. But no doubt she'll land back on my doorstep one day and expect to be cared for.'

'Maybe she'll stay in the UK and –'

'Do the decent thing and die there? I wouldn't count on it.'

Luke guided her across the road, frowning. They had hit a bump, some kind of bump, that was clear, but neither of them could quite put a shape to it.

Carlotta lived in a waterfront cottage down the road from the villa, so she was a neighbour as well as friend, shipping magnate, and very probably ex-lover. Reached by steps coming down from the street, the house was covered with climbing tomatoes and vines, so close to the water you could rinse your lettuce in the lake, Marina thought, without leaving the kitchen. The rooms were small, but there was a dreamy terrace, with its own slipway, and a weeping willow falling over one end of it.

'Our family had a property near Corconio,' Carlotta told her over drinks. 'We came here every summer, and when we sold it, I couldn't bear to be parted from the lake so I bought this little place.'

'It's beautiful,' said Marina. 'I envy you.'

'Of course you do, *cara*. Everyone who comes here says the same thing.'

'Marina has a lovely house too,' said Luke. 'You'd love her garden, Carlotta. It –'

'Oh, gardens, I don't know. I hardly have the time to sit in a garden. *Allora, mangiamo!*'

They moved into the tight, dim dining room, where Carlotta ladled pasta into their bowls. Luke's mother shovelled it in. She never spoke when she was eating.

'Luke very much enjoyed his weekend in Ireland,' Carlotta said to Marina, as if she was a mother speaking for her teenage son. 'But, *cara mia*, who are all these people who live with you?'

Marina glanced at Luke. He winked, with a sideways grin, and was instantly forgiven. 'Well,' she said, 'my children, for a start.'

'Children should never stay at home beyond eighteen. It isn't good for them. Eat your capers, darling,' Carlotta said to Bridget. 'Don't leave them on the side of the plate.'

Bridget pushed the rejected capers further out with her knife, so they were lined up along the flat rim of the bowl.

'Marina is a bit of a magnet for people in trouble,' said Luke. 'In the short time I've known her, she has rescued five people, one of whom might have died.'

'Yes, yes, you told me about that,' said Carlotta, curtly.

Oh, did he? Marina thought. *Good.*

Another caper was fished out of the sauce and driven round the bowl to join the others. There were aspects of Bridget to which Marina was quite drawn.

Dinner at Carlotta's had been pleasant; breakfast with her the previous morning had been interesting, but when she burst in on their breakfast again the next day, Marina felt tension clench her lower spine.

'Good morning!' Carlotta bent to kiss her, but when she put her hand on the back of Luke's neck and kissed him three times also, Marina began to wonder what exactly she was dealing with.

Pouring herself coffee at the sideboard, Carlotta again spoke Italian to Luke, who persisted in responding in English and translating every word for Marina. His eyes were always on her – Carlotta was merely the noise in his ears to which he was responding – and she enjoyed being the axis of his attention, especially now, when their situation was seeming . . . rather less straightforward.

But as soon as breakfast was over, Marina found herself in Carlotta's debt when she offered to stay with Bridget, so that Luke could take Marina up to the mountains. They set off for Forno, a health resort way up behind Omegna. It was a long drive that got steeper and windier, but Marina sat with her hand on Luke's thigh, absorbing the views and the calm they always enjoyed on the rare occasions when they were alone. The road climbed, passing hamlets with higgledy-piggledy stone houses straight out of a fairytale, and when they reached Forno, they stood for a while by a gushing river, its waters hurling themselves over rocks and into shafts with such momentum that Marina could barely hear her own voice above the roar. 'Fill me in on Carlotta,' she said loudly to Luke.

'Just an old friend, like I said.'

'See, that's kind of vague, and the vagueness makes me wonder why you'd be so vague. Is she a Matthew type of friend or a significant type of friend?'

'Isn't Matthew significant?' They turned to walk away from the noise.

'Not in romantic terms.'

'There's an impressive church here, recently restored.'

'Luke.'

'You're the one who wanted to hold back on our murky pasts.'

'This isn't the past. I meet her every day.'

He sighed. 'Let's get a coffee.'

They found a café and sat by the window. Luke took his time about stirring sugar into his espresso. 'We were involved,' he said, 'years ago, when I first came here. She was my aunt's secretary and we had a . . . thing.'

'A fling thing or a love thing?'

He was struggling. 'A love affair first, and then a fling. Or two . . . Or maybe three.'

'It went on and on, you mean?'

'More like on and off.' He rubbed his collarbone. 'The truth is, we were lovers for years. In between husbands and wives.'

'Jesus, you could have warned me.'

'About what? It's as over as it can be.'

'Still, it would have been helpful to know there was a previous incumbent hanging out of you.'

'I told you my life was crowded.'

'You didn't say your home was. In Morocco I thought she was a friend, one of the party, whereas in fact I was squashed up against one of your exes in that jeep! She must have been watching my every move.'

LIMERICK
COUNTY LIBRARY

'I doubt it. She was on the phone most of the time.'

'How often was she married?'

'Twice. It didn't suit her.'

'So when you and I are done, you'll likely end up back with her?'

Luke squeezed her fingers and said, without looking at her, 'It's becoming a little tedious, you know, your pessimism.'

'I'm sorry, but it's also a little *tedious* that this ex of yours has such a firm foothold in your life.'

'I love you.' He had a way of dissolving tension with a flip of a gesture or a snap of words.

'I know.'

He looked up. 'Do you, though?'

For her last night, they had a candlelit four-course dinner at the villa – with Carlotta and Bridget. 'And when will we be seeing you again, Marina?' Carlotta asked, over the starter.

'Christmas,' said Luke, turning to Marina. 'You must come for Christmas. The three of you.'

'Em, oh. God. Don't know that I'm ready to miss Christmas at home.' She loathed having this conversation in front of the others. 'Don't suppose you'd come to us, Luke?'

'Oh, that's impossible,' said Carlotta. 'Our children will be here.'

Marina coughed, almost choked. They had children together? She put down her glass and frowned at Luke. 'Your children?'

'My son and Carlotta's daughter,' he explained. 'They've been together for years, so we usually spend Christmas together.'

'I see.' Another damn knot, she thought, binding him to Carlotta. Untangling this lot would be near impossible.

'How about New Year?' he said.

Marina smiled. 'I'll ask the kids.'

For the rest of the evening, she watched Luke and Carlotta with different eyes. It was clearly a sturdy friendship, one that had survived the rocks and knocks of long acquaintance, but it was undeniably underpinned by an attraction that had not yet, and perhaps never would, wane. Since his divorce, Luke had had a number of companions, often, by his own admission, at the same time, but Carlotta appeared to be a constant. The chemistry between them was terribly elegant, like something out of a languid novel. She moved gracefully, slowly. Her neck was long, her fingers too. Luke seemed to blend into her when they sat close together, and yet Marina didn't feel threatened. It was something else that Carlotta brought out in her, something oddly familiar that she couldn't put her finger on.

Surveying the scene in Orta, she had only one thought that night: What a lot of housekeeping.

# 12

That time of year, Marina thought, as Christmas bolted towards her, that time of year which is such a challenge to those for whom somebody is missing, gone, and cannot be retrieved. Whatever her feelings for Luke, it was too soon to incorporate him into their family Christmas, when they missed Aidan most acutely. It wasn't only his absence that was hard to endure, it was the reminders of everything that went with it – the bitter sight of Dara gamely attempting to carve a turkey when he was only fifteen, and the excruciating loneliness of just three people sitting down to Christmas dinner. It was such an effort every year, cranking herself up, feigning the spirit, and trying to carry the family along in false anticipation, but they often laughed at themselves for missing Aidan so much, when he had been one of those curmudgeons who loathed Christmas and everything about it. But that was the thing – he had made such a performance of hating it that he had put his stamp on it, so that every December when she faced into the shops, Marina could hear his voice moaning about consumerism and money, as if he was standing right behind her.

This year would be different. She would miss Aidan no less, but that deep crevasse would no longer stand before her, as it always had during the dark months: an aimless future, emotional emptiness, sexual deprivation. This time, there would be loving texts from Luke the moment she woke, phone calls later, and a special gift, which he had already given her, had been stashed away. There would be a different kind of missing, but the sweet pain of distance was much more tolerable than the loneliness of for ever. Every pang of longing for Luke's company could be greeted with relief. In time, no doubt, being with Luke would be more important than being without Aidan, but Aidan's almost corporeal absence on Christmas Day could not yet be set aside.

As for New Year, her children were unenthusiastic about going to Orta. 'Oh, Gawd,' Jacquie groaned, 'we don't have to start playing happy families, do we?'

'Of course not,' said Marina. They were sitting round the fire after dinner.

'I'm not going,' Dara said. Jacquie glared at him. 'I can't! I'll have practice. I'm not taking off just when I've got back on a team.'

'And what about *my* plans for New Year?' said Jacquie.

'You don't have any. Especially not since you dumped David.'

'*Did* you?' said their mother. 'Why?'

'He's too intense,' Jacquie mumbled. 'Too young, and don't say, "I told you so."'

'Wouldn't dream of it.'

Natalie was still stuck on New Year. 'Wait. You'd turn down a chance to spend time in Italy? Really?'

'Exactly,' said Marina. 'You'd think I wanted to bury you both in a pit of slurry.'

'I just think it's a bit soon to be throwing us all into the mix,' said Jacquie. 'Making us feel like we have to get on. I refuse to be pressurized into liking Luke's children.'

'You don't have to like them,' said Marina. 'I'm not even sure they'll be there, but it would be nice for me to have some of *my* family with me.'

'I'll think about it,' said Jacquie. 'Come on, Dara, take your sis to the pictures.'

'Umm, about Christmas,' Natalie said, after they'd left. 'Kitt and I, well, we could go to my sister in England, but that's a little expensive and Kitt isn't very keen, and if I stay here, I could get work in the sales, so I was wondering if –'

'Of course you can spend Christmas with us.'

'Oh, Marina, are you sure? It's so much to ask. You'll want to be with your family and –'

'Natalie, we'd welcome it. My brother's going to my sister, so it'll be horribly quiet if you don't. And while we're on the subject, about the rooms – I'd like you to stay on.'

'What? Are you sure?'

'Absolutely. I'm lucky to have such good tenants. I mean, *sometimes* Kitt even puts her mug in the dishwasher!'

Natalie didn't laugh. Keeping her eyes on the fire and straining to sound casual, she said, 'You saved my life, you know.'

'I've done nothing of the sort!'

'I was so much lower than I let on. That's why I let Kitt go. Didn't think I had anything to give her when I had so little for myself, and I knew she'd end up with Matthew eventually. That's how I kidded myself that her trip was a good idea – Matthew would sort her out. And he did. But I never expected he'd sort me out too.'

'Natalie –'

'No, really, you've no idea what it's like for us, being part of a family. I see you and Jacquie, how you get on together, and I wish I could be like that with Kitt. I know she's hopeless and I know I'm not the right person to fix it, but when we're all here and everyone's having fun and mucking in, well, it *has* to make some impression, doesn't it? Somewhere in there she must be learning something.'

'She's mostly benefiting from having your undivided attention.'

'I just hope you know how grateful we are.' Natalie stood up. 'I'll let you get some peace and quiet.'

After she left, Marina stared into the flames. 'And now we are five.'

Christmas was a good day. Carried out along the lines of ffrench yuletide traditions, it also incorporated some of Natalie and Kitt's customs, and when they sat down to a cooked breakfast, Marina could see that, in spite of their occasional weariness with Kitt, her children were getting a kick out of having more faces round the table. Kitt was excited too; her face glowed with good health and happiness, which felt like a kind of a gift to Marina.

'You'd better make sure Luke comes next year, Mum,' Dara grumbled, 'because I'm beginning to feel like the stripper at a hen party.'

Their numbers expanded that afternoon when friends of Dara's called in and Suzanne came with her family for tea and mince pies. There was music in one room, chat in another, streamers and poppers, bangers going off in the garden, and people ambling about. Marina loved it. The house was breathing again, exhaling a good mood, a warm and convivial atmosphere that her mother would have been proud of.

'Things really have changed round here, haven't they?' said Suzanne, when she and Marina were coming down from the living room.

'Totally. I think you could say that this place has finally reacquired its old clothes, and you know what? I put that down to Kitt.'

'*Kitt?*'

'The way she just installed herself.' Marina stopped at the foot of the stairs. 'I mean, she slouched in and made the house her home, and therefore it became a home – hers – so it started to feel like one, and everyone else responded to it as such, by staying in, spreading out, having people over, so there's more warmth and fewer empty corners and –'

The doorbell rang.

'And here's someone else!' said Suzanne, going into the kitchen.

When Marina opened the front door, all she could see was an enormous bouquet of flowers. Luke had come to surprise her!

It was certainly a surprise. When the bouquet dropped sideways, Marina nearly fell backwards. The face was older, but easily recognizable. 'Matthew!'

'Happy Christmas, Reen.'

'Good God! Where did you spring from?'

'The airport, and before that another airport, and before that another airport.'

'But it's Christmas Day!'

'Flew into Shannon last night. Called round earlier, but there was no one here, so had to go to a horrible hotel and watch all the detritus of life who've nowhere else to go having their tea and fruit cake.'

'We went for a walk. You should have phoned. We'd have come to get you.'

'Would've been a bit stupid to blow the surprise at the last fence.'

The shock was not diminishing but growing while they stood there, and the shakes were spreading through Marina so fast that he probably noticed.

'My God,' he said, 'you look fantastic.'

She covered her mouth with her hand. Flesh-and-blood Matthew. Right there. Her heart was pounding.

He glanced into the house. 'Can I come in?'

She reached out to stop him. 'Just one minute, you. I have something I want to say. Something I've been waiting to say for quite some time.'

'Oh, man. Here it comes.'

'How *dare* you disappear like that? Sneaking away like a miserable rat, without the basic decency to tell the people who cared about you where you were going! And as for *staying* away, without so much as a Christmas card, a phone call –'

'Marina, it's dark and damp, and with all my misdemeanours, we could be here all night.'

'That's all right – I have all night! Why? Are you pushed for time?'

'Reen –'

'Don't you "Reen" me!' But then she smiled and stepped back to let him in. 'You look . . .'

'Completely jaded?'

'No, you look really well.' It wasn't that he hadn't changed. He had. He managed to appear boyish, but mature. His hair had hints of grey. As she was considering this – the lines on his face, the eyes so well remembered – he dipped forward to kiss her cheek, but sort of deliberately missed and hit her mouth. 'Missed you, Reen.'

'Right.'

'I hope you don't mind me turning up like this.'

'Whether I mind or not seems a bit academic at this point, but I'm sure we can find an old chicken wing for you.'

'You're a hard woman.' He looked around. 'It's like no time has passed.'

Still reluctant to move in, they stood in the hall where, long ago, they had often stayed chatting for hours into the night when he was supposed to be hopping on his bike to cycle home. They wanted to be back there again, just for a moment.

'Where's Kitt?' he asked, breaking the spell.

'In front of the telly, I'm afraid.' He followed her to the foot of the stairs. 'Kitt! Got something for you!'

They heard the door open. Matthew looked round Marina's

shoulder and up the stairwell. When Kitt appeared, she stared down at them. 'Oh. Dad. Hi.'

'Hello, sweetie. Happy Christmas.'

'What are you doing here?'

'Thought I'd surprise you.'

Nothing. There was nothing in her face for him, not even any pretence of surprise.

'Cool,' she said, and went back to the living room.

Marina felt wounded for Matthew. He thrust the flowers at her. 'For you.'

'Where did you get them?'

'Airport, poor things.' He bent his knees, flexing his legs.

'Oh! Your leg! How did it cope?'

'Didn't much appreciate being cramped for nigh on fifteen hours.'

'Come into the kitchen. You're going to cause quite a stir. I like your timing, by the way – we'll be eating in half an hour.'

Jacquie was stirring the bread sauce and Natalie folding napkins into swan-like shapes, but it was Suzanne, leaning against the stove, who looked up first, and said, 'I don't believe it! Matthew McGonagle!'

'Matthew!' Natalie swept over to him. 'Goodness, darling! What a surprise!' He hugged her, grinning at Marina over her shoulder. Natalie was right: he was wearing a red check shirt, jeans and heavy boots.

'Kitt will be so excited!' said Natalie, drawing back. 'Where is she, Marina?'

'Where she always is when she isn't in bed.'

'She knows I'm here,' he said. 'She's quite overcome.'

Suzanne came over to kiss her old college friend. 'You haven't changed a bit.'

'So, this is Dara,' said Marina. 'And you sort of know Jacquie.'

Matthew's face softened. 'Jacquie, at last. I hope you haven't forgotten that trip to Anchorage.'

'All I did was drive a few miles.'

'Nonsense,' said Natalie. 'You've been wonderful to Kitt.'

'I'll see if I can get her to come down,' said Marina, but she scurried upstairs and slipped into her bedroom, where she sat on her bed, overcome in a way that Kitt was not. The smell of those years was in her nose, the feel of their friendship on her fingertips. Whoever said memory was abstract? It was more physical than pain.

Suzanne tapped her nails on the door and let herself in. 'My.'

'Hmm.'

'Good surprise or bad surprise?'

'Too much of a surprise.' She leant over her knees. 'Oh, God, Suz, why didn't I see this coming? That he'd turn up for Christmas. Blinking obvious! And it's going to be so awkward. Kitt has *nothing* to say to him, he and Natalie haven't been under the same roof for years, and then there's our stuff.'

'Yeah, but that's not what has you up here, though, is it? Awkwardness?'

'It's lots of things – great memories, awful memories. Anger.'

Suzanne, glimpsing herself in the mirror, fiddled with her hair. 'He looks good.'

Marina groaned. '*So* good!'

'I like a man with nice bone structure. Do you like this hair colour? Or is it a bit, you know, thrushy?'

'Trashy?'

'*Thrushy* – you know, like the bird. I mean, is it all a bit too flecked and multicoloured, like a thrush's breast? I think I need something more discreet.'

'And I think *I* need to slip out to the local for a stiff drink!'

'It's closed and, besides, avoidance will get you nowhere. You're to come downstairs at once and entertain your blast from the past.' She reached for the door. 'But stay clear of those memory-thingies. They could land you God knows where.'

Marina stood up. 'You're right, you know. All those tones are a bit trashy.'

Natalie had given Matthew a whiskey. He was bending his knees, trying to loosen his leg.

'If Natalie and Kitt double up,' said Marina, 'I can put you in the back room.'

'No, no,' he said quickly, 'I'll find a hotel.'

'I'm not turning you out on Christmas night.'

'Well, thanks. That'd be great.'

Marina poked the resting turkey with a carving fork. 'And now we are six.'

'Huh?' said Matthew.

'Every now and then I do a head count. Otherwise, I might lose someone.'

'So what are the ffrench traditions for Boxing Day?' Natalie asked, when she came down the next morning.

'Playing Scrabble, watching telly, and eating mince pies by the fire,' said Marina. 'This is one day of the year when we pride ourselves on doing nothing.'

'I should drag Kitt out for some air. She watches quite enough television.'

Matthew appeared, tousled and pale, craving coffee, so the three of them sat chatting, while their respective doses of caffeine took effect. Marina looked for lingering chemistry between Matthew and Natalie, but neither seemed to be smouldering with their passionate past. For her own part, she could not get used to hearing, right there in her kitchen, the voice that for months had been at the end of the line. It brought back Gwen's voice, and her mother's, as if they were standing behind her, as they often had been, all together. To avoid them, and other ghosts from other times, Marina started preparing breakfast. Busy was better.

Matthew was watching her, as curious to see the embodiment of those phone calls as she was. Occasionally he caught her eye, and it struck her as intimate, conspiratorial.

After breakfast, when Natalie went to entice Kitt into a 'family' walk, they took their mugs to the living room.

'That's one Christmas I won't forget in a hurry,' Matthew said, reviving the fire from the night before. 'It's really nice to feel like a family again.'

'Who do you mean?'

'Me and Kitt and Natalie.'

'But you aren't a family,' said Marina, 'and don't you dare let Kitt fall for some kind of fairytale scenario that you and Natalie can't provide.'

He stared sadly into the fire. Such bad luck, Marina thought, that his one chance at family life had been messed up.

'I can't believe you took them in,' he said, sitting down opposite her. 'It's a bit overwhelming.'

'Natalie pays rent. There's nothing grand in it.'

'Yeah, there is, and I'll never be able to make it up to you. But what's new, right?' He eyeballed her.

'You're not in my debt, Matthew. You never have been.'

'Still, I want to mend things. Undo the damage, if I can.'

'It isn't me you have to mend things with. It's Kitt. And you'll have plenty of opportunity because Jacquie and I are going to Italy for New Year, so you'll have the house to yourselves. Dara will be here, but you won't see much of him.'

'Italy? Whereabouts?'

'The lakes.'

'Nice,' he said. 'And would this have anything to do with all those messages you've been getting? The long phone call last night?'

'Could do.'

'You didn't mention you were involved with anyone.'

She sighed. 'So much to catch up on . . .'

He smiled. '*Touché*. Do I get to meet him?'

'No, he lives over there.'

'Oh.' He reached for his mug on the hearth. 'Is it serious?'

'Seems to be.'

Matthew stirred his coffee. Marina was tempted to potter, to look at the books she'd got for Christmas, tidy up the wrapping paper, but they had to get through this conversation. It wouldn't go away until they did.

'Funny, we had no trouble talking on the phone,' he said. 'Now I'm not sure what to say.'

Marina crossed her legs and bounced her foot up and down.

'You try to hide it,' he said, 'but the antagonism keeps coming through.'

'It isn't antagonism, Matthew. It's hurt.'

'So, here I am. Go for it.'

Given such a platform for a speech so often rehearsed, Marina felt as if she was standing on stage preparing to recite a piece for the judges in her speech-and-drama *feis cheol*. The space around her felt huge, empty, and there were so many words waiting to be gathered up and delivered that she suspected she'd get them mixed up. She did. 'You left me twice,' she said, which wasn't really where she had ever planned to begin. 'When she cut me off, you did too. You looked the other way. I was ostracized because I was protecting *you*, but you hadn't the balls to stick up for me, and, Jesus, Matthew, after what I'd been through with Mum leaving . . . How could you help me deal with all that and then a year later look right past me? You and Gwen were my support structure, but you pulled it away without a second thought. What happened to loyalty? Integrity? How could you allow mine to be called into question, when you were demonstrating about as much integrity as a gnat?'

Shamefaced, Matthew stared at his coffee.

'You knew,' she said, her voice low, 'better than anyone, how raw I felt. Fathers leave all the time, and that's bad enough, but when a mother goes . . .'

'I know,' he said. 'I know you were really cut up about that, but I thought you were getting over it.'

'Getting over it? My mother left and hardly ever contacted me – that's the worst rejection there is! And do you know what the *second* worst rejection is for most women? Being dumped by their best friend. And I got dealt both in one year, and all I've ever wanted to ask you is *why*? Why did you tell Gwen you knew about the Turk? Didn't you see what would happen to *me*?'

'I couldn't see beyond the jealousy, Reen. The green mist.'

'Not even when she was taking me apart?'

'Look, I got my priorities wrong, okay? But I was twenty-one and so crazy in love I didn't know which end was up. I felt bad about what she put you through, but the fact is, you *did* squeal on her, and I was afraid that if I looked at her sideways she'd find out about Aisling. I was afraid to move. Bastard, yeah. Covering my own arse. What can I tell you, except that I'm really deeply, terribly sorry?'

'Great. Lovely. But if it weren't for Kitt, would you ever have made an effort to get in touch with me?'

'Probably not, but only because I didn't think I was fit to cross your threshold. I'm ashamed, all right? But I want to make it up to you, Marina. I've done a lot of thinking recently, and I've realized what I dropped along the way. That year of my life is a very black one – not because I lost Gwen but because I lost you.'

Marina's mouth was dry. The heat from the fire was burning her shins. 'I thought you'd want her to know I wasn't a bad person. You allowed her to believe that I was.'

'As Dylan once said, you can't be wise and in love at the same time.'

That evening, the house was full again. Party-time. In the main room, furniture had been shoved aside, and everyone from Kitt to the stiff-legged Matthew was bopping about and singing along to Bell X1's marshmallow song, as Natalie called it.

Suzanne watched while Marina carved cold turkey, the knife sliding through the flesh like a hand through air. 'Help.' Marina held it up. 'Dara must have sharpened this.'

'Be careful,' said Suzanne, quietly.

'Yeah, it's lethal.'

'I didn't mean the knife. I meant Matthew.'

Marina looked up.

'He can't take his eyes off you.'

'Ach, that's just the weirdness of it all. I can't stop looking at him either. It's really peculiar. It feels as if no time has passed, as if there was nothing in between.'

'You're not attracted to him, then?'

'I have no more interest in Matthew now than I ever did.'

'But that was always open to question, wasn't it? You and Matthew.'

Marina stopped carving. 'Was it?'

'Before I met you,' said Suzanne, 'when I saw you around the campus, I thought you were a couple. When I discovered you weren't, I figured it was only a matter of time. Now I'm beginning to wonder if it's still only a matter of time.'

'Don't be stupid. It's completely platonic!'

'You know what they say about platonic relationships – they're only ever platonic on one side.'

'Yeah, well, I never did give that theory much credence.'

'Me neither, until I saw Matthew gazing at you over the mince pies.'

'Did you like them? New recipe.'

'Excellent mince pies. Excellent recipe. But be careful, Marina.'

Marina dismissed this, but she knew exactly what Suzanne was talking about. Matthew was looking at her far more often than he should have been.

# 13

The fireworks were best seen from the terrace off Jacquie's bedroom, so Luke made them troop up there just before midnight – Marina, Bridget and assorted guests. It was cold. Over to the right, on the island, the former seminary and the basilica's bell-tower were floodlit and their reflections glowed on the water. The fireworks were also mirrored in the lake, so it was like having double vision whenever they exploded. Jacquie didn't know whether to look up at the sky or down at the shimmering colours on the inky expanse between the house and the island.

She had come to Orta without further quibble. A cheap holiday and nothing else to do anyway were reasons enough to face up to these new people. The Step-people, she and Dara called them. But apprehension had tailed her during the long day's travelling, not helped by too many hours spent in a seasonally heaving Gatwick airport, as she tried to anticipate what it would be like to be exposed, at close quarters, to her mother's romance, to Luke, whom she barely knew, and to his family. Yet she could not ignore how much it meant to Marina that she had come along.

The villa lived up to her mother's superlatives. Luke had put her at the very top in a gorgeous, newly decorated apartment, which was so pleasant that Jacquie began to chill as soon as she stepped into it. She relaxed further over a lively dinner, enthralled by the house-party atmosphere, and was finally and comprehensively seduced by an elaborate meringue dessert, several layers high, bloated with cream and dripping with hot chocolate sauce. Her mother had done well. Luke was a keeper.

There had been about fifteen for dinner, mostly nattering away in Italian, which allowed Jacquie to sit back and observe. She loved their clothes, their gestures, the enthusiasm with which they ate and debated. After the meal, they had moved into a large room, with high ceilings and vaulted doors, to have coffee and mint chocolates.

'This house belonged to my aunt,' Luke explained, when she asked about it.

'Mum mentioned that.'

'Yes.'

'And, eh, how did your mother . . .' Luke looked at her earnestly '. . . come to be living here?'

'She moved over from Tipp to be with her sister.' He nodded as if this explained everything.

Jacquie wanted to like Luke, she really did, but he rarely delivered more than one sentence at a time. She looked to her mother for help.

'Luke's aunt married an Italian,' Marina explained, 'and the two sisters lived here after he died, and then when Luke's aunt died, she left the house to him and Bridget.'

'I didn't want it,' he said.

'Oh?'

'Not really, no.'

Jacquie's eyes roamed round the room – there was beautiful cornicing round the ceiling – but Luke didn't go on, so she had to enlist her mother again. 'Why wouldn't anyone want a place like this?'

'Shouldering the costs,' said Marina, 'and Luke was working in London at the time, but he moved over here and set about saving it.'

'As you've seen,' said Luke, referring to the wiring and

plastering that was being carried out on the middle floors. 'But it'll be worth it.' He glanced at Marina. 'It'll make a handy retirement fund for us.'

She gave him an admonishing look. He said little, yet managed to say too much.

Jacquie wondered if she should dislike him, as an act of loyalty to her father, but apart from his appreciation of short sentences, Luke was okay. It was uncomfortable, seeing another man dance attention on her mother, but it was impossible to ignore the attraction between them, or to overlook the little gestures that showed the struggle they were having in containing it.

On the terrace after midnight, she watched them again: their profiles, side by side, turning red and blue with the skyward colours. Even on her father's behalf she could not resent their happiness.

Her mother squeezed her arm. This was going to be a good year, she seemed to be saying, for both of them, and as the final display exploded in bangs and flares over their heads, Jacquie found herself agreeing.

The next morning winter light was squeezing through the shutters into her room. Impatient to see the view her mother had been raving about, Jacquie leapt up and went through to the other room – a kitchen-cum-sitting-room that opened on to a large terrace – and stopped in her tracks. 'Whoa.' Her first sight of the island was literally dazzling; it lured her across the warm tiles to the vast window. The milky-white one-time seminary and the villas that stood around it, like sentinels, laid their creamy reflections across the still water. The grey-yellow lake looked icy and beautiful, and on the far shore wooded hills were sprinkled with snow. Jacquie turned. The view behind her was pretty good too. She loved the modern décor of this apartment – its purple plastic kitchen chairs, glass dining-table, lampshades shaped like buckets and moulded blue door handles. It had two bathrooms, a sparse white bedroom, and two window balconies as well as the terrace. Her mother had indeed done well.

She showered, pulled on jeans and a jumper, brushed her hair and meandered down the stone staircase, which seemed to go on and on. They'd probably put her way up near the roof, she was thinking, to keep her well away from whatever high jinks they were getting up to downstairs. On the ground floor she crossed into the morning room.

Only one of the other guests was there and he was behind a newspaper. She hoped she would recognize him from the night before and maybe even come up with a name. With a bit of luck, he'd speak English.

His bespectacled eyes appeared over the top of his newspaper, his fingers clasping a small cup of coffee.

'Morning,' she said.

'Good morning.'

Jacquie slipped into the embroidered high-backed chair. The table was laid with jams, butter, silver, white china, buns and breads, but there was no sign of a pot of tea or a teabag or . . . her mother. She couldn't go looking for her – heaven alone knew where she might find her – but how was she to get some tea? She wished Dara had come. Surely the only point of younger brothers was that they eased awkward situations by being brash and gung-ho, joyfully unaware of their impact on the surroundings? Why was he never around when she needed him?

The man behind the paper said, 'Ring the bell.'

'What? No. What bell? I couldn't.'

So he reached forward towards a copper bell on the table and shook it.

A woman in a blue dress materialized behind her. '*Buon giorno, signorina. Tè*?'

'Umm, yes, please.' The housekeeper withdrew.

The bloke was back inside his newspaper. Good. At least he wasn't trying to make conversation. Jacquie helped herself to a croissant and cut it open. Apricot purée spilled out. *Oh, God. Not for buttering, then.* She glanced up. He peeped round the side of his broadsheet, grinned mildly, then held it between them again, allowing her to extricate herself without an audience. She licked the goo off her fingers, closed the croissant, and bit into it. This time, purée oozed all over the side of her mouth. She wished whoever-he-was would go away and allow her to suffer humiliation undisturbed.

Instead he said, without revealing his face, 'Did you enjoy the fireworks?'

'Umm, yeah. Amazing.'

At last he put down the paper, folding it with precision. Rimless spectacles perched on his nose, with almond-green eyes behind them. He had short dark hair and a wiry build. He wasn't as old as she had at first presumed. Probably not in his thirties yet.

'Would you like to come out tonight?' he asked.

'Excuse me?'

'Some of us are going to a nightclub. You should come.'

'That would be lovely, but . . .' *Who are you?*

'Yes?'

'I wouldn't know anyone.' *You, for instance.*

'It's just me and some friends. You'll be very welcome. I'll pick you up at eight.' He got up and was gone before Jacquie had formulated a polite way of saying no.

'Nico!' she heard her mother say, as they crossed paths in the hall. 'Happy new year.' Marina's happy face came round the door. 'Good morning, love.'

'So who the hell is Nico when he's at home?' Jacquie hissed at her.

'You met him last night, didn't you?'

'I met loads of people last night, most of them speaking a foreign language. Which one was he?'

'He arrived quite late, with his fiancée. They didn't stay long.'

'Fiancée?'

'A pretty dark-haired girl. Elegant.'

'That's odd. He just asked me out. We haven't even been introduced.'

Maria brought in pots of tea and coffee. 'Thank you, Maria. I only met him briefly the last time. He's an architect.' Marina poured them both tea. 'In fact, he's responsible for most of the redesigning of this building. Did you say you'd go?'

'I didn't get the chance. You didn't put him up to it, did you?'

'Certainly not. Why would I do that?'

'Finding me friends and so on . . .'

'I'm sure you're well able to find your own friends.'

'Or maybe Luke told him to take me out and show me a good time?'

Marina's eyes widened. 'I wouldn't thank him if he did!'

Nico instantly became more interesting. 'Why not?'

'He's Luke's son!'

'Oh. Whoops.'

'He wasn't asking you on a date, he's just being friendly.'

'God, yeah. No, not a date. There's a load of them going. Is he really an architect? He looks like an academic. An eternal student.'

'You haven't seen his car.'

And more interesting again . . .

'Good morning, *darlings*!'

Carlotta. Jacquie had not forgotten *her* from the night before. She was loud, lively and Italian. She seemed to be in the room without having come through the door.

'So what are you going to do today?' she asked, in her big voice, pouring herself coffee. 'I suggest a walk up to Sacro Monte. There are twenty chapels up there in the forest, each dedicated to an event in the life of St Francis. It is a very spiritual place.'

'That's a good idea,' said Marina. 'I'll have a word with Luke.'

'Ah, *mia cara*! I'm afraid he is busy working this morning.'

'It's New Year's Day,' said Jacquie.

'Even on holidays there is much to do for those who work.' Carlotta rang the bell. 'Maria,' she said, when the housekeeper appeared, then spoke in Italian, finishing off with 'English Breakfast Tea.' She turned back to the table. 'I'm so sorry we have none of your Irish soda bread.'

'But this is lovely,' said Marina. 'It's always nice to –'

'Luke brings it back sometimes,' Carlotta interrupted. 'He likes it, I think, in a sentimental way. I myself find it very heavy. Now, for the walk – turn right outside the gate and follow the road until you see steps going up the hill. That will lead you to the shrines.'

When she had left the room, in much the same manner as she had come into it, Jacquie whispered, 'Who is she again?'

'Friend of the family. She has a cottage across the road.'

'You'd think she owned the place, the way she goes on.'

Marina nodded. A firm little knot had formed in her stomach. They'd only just arrived, but she couldn't help feeling as if she'd been well and truly gazumped.

Luke came in, wished them both good morning, and asked Jacquie if she was comfortable in the apartment.

'It's fantastic,' she gushed.

'I hoped you'd like it,' he said, as Maria handed him an espresso. 'So, you two only have a week – what are we going to do with it?'

'Oh, I'm sure we can keep ourselves entertained,' Marina said curtly. 'I understand you're busy.'

Clearly surprised by her tone, Jacquie gave her a look that seemed to say, 'Mum! He's here, he's being nice.'

'Not really,' Luke said vaguely. 'I have to take Ma for her morning constitutional, but after that I'm free. Why don't you show Jacquie the village?'

'Aren't you going to sit down?' Marina asked, still dead frosty.

'I'll get on, if that's all right. Meet you back here at, say, two?'

Marina's eyebrows went up. *Two?* 'Fine.'

'I know Bridget's slow,' Jacquie whispered after he'd left, 'but that's going to be a very long walk!'

The villa hugged the hill behind it, and a high green gate led on to the lakeside road that ran into Orta. Marina and Jacquie dipped their noses into their scarves and strolled into the village, the road tapering as they neared the square. Just beyond an inhabited arch that spanned the street, they came across a domestic crisis – a man and woman were standing at the foot of a ladder that was leaning against a windowsill. Necks craned, they were calling upwards in silly voices, 'Pish-pish-pish,' and 'Zozo, Zozo!' A distressed cry came from beyond the window. A cat. Its nose peeked over the sill, prompting more frenzied encouragement from below, but it rejected their entreaties, jumped back inside and continued howling.

'Must have got locked in over the holiday,' said Marina.

When they reached the main square, Jacquie stopped, as her mother had done before her. '*Class!*'

'Isn't it stunning?'

They wandered along the arcade and turned up the cobblestoned rise that led to the church. 'This has to be one of the most beautiful streets in the world,' Marina said, as they made their way up the steps, past peeling cream and grey houses, each of its own era, from medieval to recent. Wisteria twisted its way up to balconies, fading frescos decorated a wall here, a curve there, and empty cloisters seemed to be waiting for a cast of players.

'I feel like I'm on a Shakespearean set,' said Jacquie. 'You could forget what century this is.'

'I know,' her mother said happily. 'It's just glorious.'

'Not a bad place to spend time. Will you be coming over a lot?'

'Only when it's convenient for you two.'

'Mother – it's convenient. We're well able to look after ourselves and we don't want you ending up a lonely old crone, do we?' She turned on the steps of the church. Between the houses she could see stripes of lake and slivers of island. 'What a view. Imagine getting married here.'

They walked back down and across the square to the benches beneath the trees by the quayside. Boats were tethered at moorings and the stumps of the timber jetties stood stiff as soldiers in the cold water, which slapped against the hulls of boats. A frosty glare came off the seminary.

'Your dad would have loved it here,' said Marina. 'He'd like Luke too.'

'Don't bring Dad into it.'

'Why not? How can I not think about him when I know how much he'd love to be with us?'

'He wouldn't like the reason we're here, though, would he? Is there anywhere we can get a coffee?'

'Dad and I talked about this, you know. About the proverbial bus. One of us going under it. We both hoped the other would marry again, given the chance.'

'Is that place open?'

Lunch was another New Year celebration, with a whole different set of guests. Marina and Jacquie came upon it unprepared. When Luke steered Marina about the room, his hand lightly on her forearm, introducing her to friends, she smiled sweetly and cursed inwardly. They had not had one minute alone since she'd arrived, and it was exasperating to have to make small-talk to another bunch of strangers, with a serious language difficulty thrown in.

Carlotta welcomed people effusively and showed them to the buffet lunch. She also fussed over Bridget, who called her 'dear' and kept asking her for things. Carlotta's patience was admirable. 'Yes, darling,' they kept hearing. 'Just one tiny little minute, darling.'

Jacquie sidled up to Marina. 'Who *is* that woman? She's behaving like his wife!'

'Don't I know it? Excuse me while I go and ingratiate myself with his mother.' She took her plate across the room and sat next to Bridget. 'How are you doing, Bridget?'

The beady brown eyes seemed confused. 'Why would I be doing anything?'

'No, I mean – how are you? How is that pain you had in your wrist in Morocco?'

Bridget looked at her oddly. 'Were you in Morocco?'

'Yes. We travelled together. Don't you remember?'

'I remember everything, thank you very much.'

'Oh, well, lucky you. My memory's like a sieve.'

Bridget looked at her, her eyes scrunched up. 'That's right. Luke said you were coming. Is that your girl there?'

'Jacquie, yes.'

'Pretty, isn't she?'

'It's kind of you to say so.'

'To say what?'

'That Jacquie . . . Never mind. Can I get you anything? Dessert? I remember how you loved your dessert when we were away.'

'Away where?'

'Um, profiteroles, perhaps?'

'Carlotta will see to it.'

Luke came over with his lunch and sat on the couch beside Marina. 'At last,' he said, 'a break from looking after everyone.'

'Is this an annual thing, the New Year's lunch?'

'Not really. Carlotta thought it'd be a good idea, that's all.' He was as dainty with his food as his mother was not. 'She felt it was time we had some of this lot in.'

*We?* 'She didn't mention it this morning. Nor did you.'

'I didn't know about it,' he said, 'until after you'd gone out.'

'It's just, we would have liked to change, be a bit smarter when we meet your friends.'

'They're not really my friends. Mostly Carlotta's and Ma's.'

'But why have you had them all to lunch, then?'

He raised his eyebrows. 'Search me. I just do as I'm told.'

'I hate it when men say that. It's such a neat way of blaming women for everything.'

'Do you think Jacquie's enjoying herself?'

'She's fine,' said Marina. 'Actually, Nico has asked her to join him and his friends tonight.'

'Excellent. Much better for her than getting stuck with us oldies.'

'So maybe we could go out tonight or . . .' Her stomach tightened. She was speaking to him as if he were a stranger she was trying to pick up in a bar.

'They're expecting us for dinner, I'm afraid,' he said.

'Who? Have we been invited out?'

'No, no, at home. Carlotta and Maria have dinner organized.'

'Oh.'

'Is that all right?'

'I suppose so. It's just – are we going to get *any* time together?'

'Private time is a bit hard to come by round here.'

'But –'

'Much as it is at your place,' he added, catching her eye.

Nico picked Jacquie up on the dot of eight in a very swish car. Half the cars on the roads seemed to be cousins of the Porsche. This was something blue and low, and getting in was like falling into a barrel. Nico matched it perfectly. His navy jacket, blue shirt and jeans somehow looked totally different from any blue blazer and jeans she'd ever seen on guys at home, or maybe it was the way he wore them. He told her they were meeting his friends in Omegna, and whizzed off.

Jacquie felt uneasy. Whatever about his parentage, she knew little about this person on whom she must rely for the rest of the evening. 'So, you're Luke's eldest?' she asked, starting with what she did know.

'Yes.' He turned his head towards her, then back to the road.

Oh, God. Not another Luke? 'But you grew up in Italy?'

'Mostly.' Another sideways glance, his eyes catching hers in the dark. 'My mother is from Omegna. We lived in England for a while, but when they divorced, she came back home.'

'Do you know Ireland at all?'

'Not enough.' It seemed strange that this guy with a

pronounced Italian accent, but perfect English, was in fact half Irish. 'We used to go when we were small sometimes, from London, but after we all moved here, there was very little opportunity.'

'Do you feel in any way Irish?'

'Of course.' The Italians had a way, she noted, of making English words sound short and stiff. 'You can't explain it. There's something,' he gathered his fingers and hit his chest lightly, 'inside that you can't define. I am in some way different from my friends, but I can't say how.'

Jacquie relaxed. It was okay. He talked more than his father. 'You must come to Ireland again. If you feel it in your blood, you should know it better.'

'*Certo*. You are absolutely right. That will be my resolution.'

They met his friends in a restaurant somewhere. There were six of them, men and women, and they seemed nice, but they greeted her in a mildly disinterested way, as if Nico was always turning up with new faces. His fiancée did not appear to be among them – at least, none of the girls made any special claim to him. Over dinner, Nico made an effort to translate the conversation that criss-crossed the table, but he couldn't keep up with the high-speed delivery, since his friends talked over one another, and Jacquie again wished Dara was there. For all Nico's efforts, she felt like a spare wheel.

One of his friends was talking about her.

'What's he saying?' she asked Nico.

'That I should take you skiing. It's very good, up at Mottarone. And very beautiful. You can see Lake Maggiore and Lake Orta at the same time.'

'Thanks, but I can't ski.'

'You will,' he said.

'Maybe I don't want to.'

'I will teach you, and then you will want to.'

Jacquie couldn't work out whether he was incredibly arrogant or well-meaning.

They went on to the nightclub. It was easier than the restaurant – too noisy for anyone to hear what anyone was saying – and Nico was kind enough to dance with her. By the time they were driving home, following the curving road round the lake, they were bantering quite easily.

'You had a good time?' he asked, when he stopped outside the house.

'I did, thanks. You have lovely friends.'

He nodded. 'I'll see you again.'

'Duty done,' she muttered, as he drove off. 'For both of us.'

An uneven peal of bells woke Marina the next morning, as it did every day. It sounded as if the bell-ringers hadn't a clue – two peals together, then one, then maybe three or just one. It was haphazard, yet somehow paced, and the lack of an obvious rhythm was satisfying. She visualized nuns flying up and down on the ends of ropes in the bell-tower. Before going downstairs, she stepped on to her narrow balcony and watched the police launch heading towards Orta, a tail of shifting water fanning out in its wake. The morning was fresh and had a whiff of the Alpine about it, and the lake was like a polished screen between the dark green hills. Sparrows skidded on to the tiles and slid towards her, hoping for crumbs.

'How'd it go?' she asked Jacquie, when they coincided in the morning room.

'Fine. He's sweet. Very polite.'

'Gets that from his father.'

'Give his mother some credit. She brought him up.'

'True. Nice friends?'

'Yes, but they're all so well-dressed! I felt like a grubby student. And what I don't get is, how can they afford it?'

'The Italians live for their clothes, you know that.'

'I'm going to be Italian, then.'

'Actually, we must go shopping,' said Marina. 'Hit some of the local boutiques.'

'Yes, *please*. I need to keep up. Did I miss anything here?'

Her mother's shoulders slumped. 'Just more of the same. Carlotta and Bridget, Bridget and Carlotta, and even Luke's ex-wife, Francesca.'

*'No!'*

'Swear to God. These are the joys of a mid-life relationship. Spending New Year with your partner and his mother and his ex-wife and his girlfriend and . . .'

Jacquie cleared her throat.

'. . . every damn person he ever went out with.'

'Morning, Luke,' said Jacquie, looking over her mother's head.

'Morning, Jacquie. Sleep well?'

'Great, yeah.' She stood up. 'I'll just see if I can find the kitchen to make some toast.'

'There is a toaster in there somewhere,' he said.

'Morning,' Marina said lightly.

He sat sideways in the chair next to her. 'Is that how you feel? Submerged by my past women?'

'You have to admit . . .'

He didn't take up the sentence.

'. . . there *are* rather a lot of them around.'

'But it's that time of year,' he said.

'I know, but so far we've been out for one coffee on our own.'

'You're right. We've been bulldozed. What would Jacquie like to do today?'

'Jacquie will be fine. *I*'m the one who needs attention.'

‘Okay, look. Why don’t we go for a long walk, have lunch somewhere, then,’ he leant towards her until he was less than an inch from her face, ‘we’ll sneak back here for a shower and I’ll take you out to –’

‘*Buon giorno*!’

Luke pulled back. Marina closed her eyes. Carlotta stood over them, beaming, her hands clasped below her breasts like a frightfully pleased matron. ‘*Mio caro*,’ she said, all sweetness, ‘I absolutely must have you today. You must look over this contract –’

‘I’m afraid I can’t,’ said Luke. ‘We have plans.’

Carlotta’s eyes fell on Marina with unmistakable chilliness. ‘But this is important. Marina can find something to do. Shopping – you and Jacquie should go to Milan and . . .’ Her hand went up and down, indicating Marina’s frame.

‘Sorry,’ said Luke, ‘you’ll have to do without me.’

Carlotta broke into Italian.

‘It’s New Year,’ he said firmly. ‘Nothing is that urgent.’

More Italian. Marina was glad she didn’t understand. It put a distance between herself and Carlotta that she relished as much as Carlotta did, but for entirely different reasons.

Nico kept turning up. Jacquie never had time to think or dissimulate. He simply swooped, and it was impossible to say no, because he never asked. Issuing commands was more his style. It didn’t seem to bother him that she might not want to spend time with him; he clearly felt it was incumbent on him to entertain her while his father romanced her mother. It was the kind of mannerly behaviour one would expect from someone like him, and in spite of herself, she quite enjoyed the evenings with his friends. It was certainly more entertaining than sitting around with Carlotta’s booming presumptions, Bridget’s singularities, and Luke dancing attention on her moon-eyed mother, so for three nights in a row she put on her new Italian clothes, purchased during a somewhat uncontrolled spree with her mother, bade everyone goodnight and went out with Nico.

His friends made an attractive bunch. It was a pleasure to be surrounded by well-to-do guys who dressed well, had flashy cars, and spoke the most beautiful language in Europe. They were charming to her, teased her because she didn't understand them, and, had she had her pick, any one of them would have done. She was in the mood for a fling. In fact, fling, flirtation, all-out affair or full-on relationship – anything would do. She'd done her time in the wilderness, and here in Orta the longing for romance was stronger than ever. But she couldn't shake off Nico, who attended to her with care and consideration, paid for everything, and behaved as if she was his responsibility. Or his date. Sometimes she felt like his date. There had been no sign of his fiancée since New Year's Eve, and no one, as far as Jacquie could understand, mentioned her. Apparently she lived and worked in Rome, but in her absence, Jacquie had to keep reminding herself that Nico was simply being fraternally attentive.

She found herself becoming fond of him, which wasn't a bad thing, since he might well become a permanent fixture in her life. It was impossible not to think about this when they were together, and when he leant sideways in a restaurant, one elbow on the table, his shoulder bunched up under his chin, to fill her in on what was going on, it wasn't difficult to see him as an older-brother type: someone she could rely on, who would smooth her passage through the Italian way of things. And she, in turn, would look after him in Ireland and show him the best of his own country. She was already looking forward to it and teased him about the things she would make him do there.

One night, leaning towards her in that way he had, he said, 'You look a little lost. Next time we won't go out with all these people.'

*

A strange light was ducking into Jacquie's room when she woke the next morning. She got up and pushed back her bedroom shutters. It had snowed. Her mouth hanging open, she walked across to the window for her wake-up view of Isola di San Giulio. There was snow from the lakeside to the hilltops, on the branches of the trees that ran along the shore, and on the posts at the end of the jetty across the road. Snow-covered roofs on the island glittered, and on her terrace, bird prints were like a swirling pattern on a thick carpet. Jacquie pulled her coat round her, put on slippers and slid back the door, adding her footprints to the birds'. It was very cold, but she stood for several minutes, alone and happy, until a horrible thought occurred: *Oh, God. Now he'll want to take me skiing!*

When Nico turned up that evening, he suggested they walk into the village and have dinner in the square. No friends. She was more pleased than she should have been, and dressed more carefully than seemed appropriate, but this would be their first opportunity to talk properly, and listen, to one another, without a crowd babbling around them. As she skipped down the steps to the hall, she realized that, without her really noticing, Nico had become a good friend.

In a hotel right by the water, at a table beside the window, he told her about Orta. 'There is a legend that San Giulio sent the snakes and reptiles away from the island.'

'Really? Was he related to St Patrick?'

'I'm sorry?'

'St Patrick did the same for Ireland – got rid of the snakes. The reptilian ones, anyway.'

'In fact, he . . .' Nico gesticulated '. . . sailed across the lake on his cloak.' He made a face, a quirky, endearing expression. Attractive too.

Something inside her skidded to a halt. God, no, she thought. Not *him*.

'Now,' he said, 'there is the basilica and a convent over there.'

'It looks so eerie,' she said, gazing across the water, 'like something emerging out of the fog in a ghost story.'

'Yes, but in the summer it is very beautiful. I will take you there then.'

She raised her eyebrows. 'That's assuming a lot. Who's to say Mum and Luke will still be together?'

He made a clucking sound. 'You will be here in the summer. For sure.' He poured more wine.

'So,' she said, fiddling with an earring, 'I understand your fiancée works in Rome?'

Nico looked up. 'Fiancée?'

'Yes, Mum was telling me you've been engaged for some time.'

'Engaged . . . not really, but probably I will marry Cristina. Our families are friends.'

'You mean an arranged marriage?'

'Not at all.' He laughed. 'If we marry, it will be because we want to. And because we are well matched. We have many similar aims and plans. We've known each other since we were small.'

He made it sound like a business plan. 'So you've always been together?'

He threw his head to the side. 'A long time, anyway.'

'But don't you want to have lots of lovers – lots of loves?' she corrected herself quickly, suspecting that he did not deny himself the lovers.

Nico shifted uneasily. 'I have found the one I would like to be my wife. We are working towards our future.'

It was an opaque reply. Jacquie was too intrigued to let it go, though he clearly wanted her to. 'But are you attracted to each other?'

He held his glass near his face, looking at her. 'Love does not always make good marriages, you know.'

'I didn't mention love. Only attraction.'

'Ah. That comes. Like love, that comes.'

'You can't be serious,' she said. 'That's so old-fashioned!'

'Perhaps,' he conceded, 'but marriages have been made this way for centuries, in many different cultures. With the help of families. It has a good success.'

'But what about falling in love?'

'You want to fall in love?' he asked.

'Of course.'

'Yes. Me too.'

'But . . .' Jacquie gave up. She couldn't make head or tail of him, but this absurd point of view made him more interesting. More interesting and more attractive. It was probably a mistake, then, that they went on to a nightclub, just the two of them, because it was too early to go home and they felt like dancing. Or so they kept saying. They took a booth in the dark club, and talked, shouting over the music, about where they'd been and what they'd done and where they hoped they were headed. Every now and then, Nico's dark eyes caught hers in the flashing lights. When he left her to go to the gents', Jacquie's eyes scarcely left the door until he came back through it, and they followed him as he came round the dance-floor, his white shirt turned blue by the lights, his slender frame neat and straight.

This isn't good, she thought. This really isn't good.

As he reached the table, a slow set started. He put out his hand in a way that meant he expected no argument and, without argument, she took it, and they joined the writhing couples under the blue light, while some Italian crooner sang as if he was dying of love. If this is death by love, Jacquie thought, with that voice, in that language, I want some of it.

It could have been awkward, this close dance, so they

maintained a thin, comfortable slice of distance. But being comfortable with Nico, with her hand in his and his arm round her back, had nothing to do with the slight gap between them. They were easy because they'd arrived in the same place at exactly the same time.

Nico ran his knuckle along her chin without letting go of her hand. 'We must be careful.'

'I know.'

Out in the freezing night, they walked to the car without speaking and drove home in silence. Jacquie looked despondently at the mounds of snow pushed to the side of the roads, feeling cross and hard-done-by. She hadn't felt this good with anyone since she'd been with Didier, but Nico was as good as married. Typical.

He pulled into the driveway, turned off the engine, and dipped his head to look up at the house. 'Our parents are still up,' he said. 'I'll come in.'

He got out of the car. Jacquie sat, stunned. *Our parents.*

Marina was sitting on one of the couches as stiffly as if there were a ramrod down the back of her dress, which wasn't surprising since Carlotta was perched on the arm of Luke's chair, saying darling this and darling that. It was too much.

She came at them with kisses, greeting first Jacquie, '*Ciao, bella*,' then Nico.

Really too much, Jacquie thought. *Mwah, mwah, mwah.* She liked Carlotta less every time she saw her.

'Did you have a pleasant evening?' Carlotta asked them. 'You're so late. What time is it? One o'clock?' She raised her eyebrows at Nico.

'We went to a club,' he said. 'Pa, I have a rattle.'

Jacquie reached for the arm of the nearest chair and sat. *Pa.* Christ. *Our parents.* Jesus. It had bothered her outside, but it came at her now like a cricket bat aimed straight at her head. *Pa.*

'What do you mean, a rattle?' Luke asked. 'The car?'

The blood in Jacquie's head was making a dash for the ground. *Fuck*. She was attracted to Luke's *son*. She knew it because she was so very conscious of him, just behind her. It wasn't that she had forgotten who he was, but with a few drinks and general bonhomie, with loud music and a fiancée keeping things simple, she hadn't given any thought to the possibility that such a thing could happen. It *really* didn't suit her. What she wanted was to fall for some nice lad who lived down the road in Cork and didn't have a girlfriend. That was what she needed: something simple. And yet an attraction had slipped into her head, like a cat zipping into a room before the door closed. Her mother was in love with this man's father, and his father was stone-crazy about her mother. She fancied her mother's potential stepson. Her own potential stepbrother.

A strange little though went through her head: So what?

How, she wondered, had it not occurred to her when her mother brought home a good-looking man that he might have a good-looking son?

Marina was staring at her. Jacquie smiled, trying to conceal the blanching that had, no doubt, swept across her face. 'I think I'll turn in,' she said, making eyes at her mother to follow her, and said goodnight.

They went up to the first floor and sat on the steps. 'You look like you've had a horrible night,' Jacquie said.

A groan gurgled deep in Marina's throat. 'Lousy. One little dig after another. How *do* I manage all these *wild* curls? And my son is studying *arts*? Goodness. What kind of a career can a young man make out of an arts degree? And "*Best* not to let Bridget know you don't attend Mass. She has a very deep faith, you know." As if it could have escaped me!'

Jacquie smiled at the neat take-off of Carlotta. 'Why doesn't Luke say something?'

'You know what men are like. They've so little grasp on innuendo. They don't pick up vibes, and if I try to point them out, I'll just end up looking petty.'

'Sounds like you should have come out with us.'

Marina shook her head. 'Oh, it was fine. It's just all these other people. We can't seem to get away from them. And who am I to complain, in view of our crew back home?'

'Still, I don't like Carlotta's tone,' said Jacquie. 'The way she speaks to you. You shouldn't take it.'

'Like I have any choice.'

'You *do* have a choice. Why should you be nice to her when she's incredibly rude?'

'I can't alienate Carlotta, Jacquie. She's like the core of this damn family, without even being part of it!'

'Yeah, how does she get away with that?'

'I don't know,' said Marina. 'Guile?'

'Does she have some kind of hold over Luke?'

'Yes. His mother. She takes her to Mass every day and looks after her. They're good friends.'

'But what about Luke? Should I take it that she's some kind of ex?'

'Of sorts,' said Marina. 'Anyway, you go to bed and get a good night's sleep.'

'You should turn in too. Why are you up so late, anyway?'

'On the *off* chance I might get an opportunity to talk to Luke.'

Jacquie stood up, smirking. 'To "talk" to him, is it? Do you think I was born yesterday?'

'I know exactly when you were born, young lady.'

Her daughter skipped on up the stairs. 'Don't stay up too late, Mummy.'

Marina went back downstairs and let herself out the front door. She pulled her cardigan round her and leant over the stone balustrade beside the steps. She would have to toughen up to see her way through this, which was unfortunate, because having Luke, enjoying his care and attention, had allowed her to cede a little. It was refreshing, for a change, not always having to be tough and on top of everything, and yet she could not relinquish her strength now when it was being so coarsely challenged. Jacquie was right. She had to stop floundering every time Carlotta appeared, but how was she to handle it without coming across like a jealous teenager?

A hand swept along her back. Luke. 'How are you, my love?'

'A little lonely for you, to tell the truth.'

He gave her a squeeze. The tension fell off her. 'Let's go up,' he said.

They went to his room. He usually came to hers. In the dressing room, he didn't turn on the light. Her cardigan came off, his shirt, shoes, her dress. Cold, they hurried to the bed, where he bundled her under the thick duvet. She heard his belt tinkle, felt the heave and bounce of clothes coming off, until he shuffled across to her, his body warm and bare.

She woke the next morning in his bed for the first time. He was gone, had left for work already. Marina pondered. The signs had been there on her first visit but she had paid no heed, because when they were together everything else seemed irrelevant. Being with Luke was always better than being without him, and yet, in Orta, she felt increasingly resentful of his commitments. It was silly. She could hardly expect him to stop the world and get off it whenever she turned up – and besides, whenever they had time alone Luke made her feel as if she was the centre of his universe. But she was not the centre of his universe, and could not be, no matter how much he wished it.

Her expectations had been unrealistic. Luke's talk of Lake

Orta had made her imagine a quiet place, somewhere that she could think and consider, take a break from her responsibilities and keep him company while he managed his. Certainly, she was well looked after, the surroundings were everything he'd described, and when she walked by the lake, it brought her a kind of stillness. The difficulties were all inside the villa. To be a good partner to Luke, she should be kind to Bridget, become involved with her, suggest things, but she had no will or desire to do so. His mother was wearying at every level, and the Carlotta Factor made that even harder. *Her* devotion to Bridget made Marina look worse.

She was losing heart. Every morning she felt more reluctant to go downstairs and face Bridget and Carlotta over breakfast. Like now – lying there, slow to get up, like a schoolgirl who didn't want to leave home because she was dreading the bully at school.

The word rebounded off the walls.

Marina sat up.

Surely not. Surely she wasn't being bullied. No, it was her fault. She was allowing Carlotta to call the shots, because she had a much bigger personality and had known Luke for ever. Besides, good manners and courtesy determined her own behaviour and would continue to do so, whatever the provocation.

From Luke's bed, she texted Jacquie to see if she was ready to go down to breakfast. She had done this the previous morning – like a schoolgirl again, texting her pal to make sure they could walk to school together. An alarming thought: was she using her daughter to protect her? No, that wasn't it. *Couldn't* be. No, they enjoyed having tea and brioches together, their whispered chats, after the others had finished. Bridget, to Jacquie, was a joke, not a problem, and Jacquie was right about Carlotta – she should not be allowed to be rude, and that was all it was, Marina told herself. Carlotta was rude and condescending. That did not make her a bully.

Jacquie was already at the table when she got downstairs. Marina poured herself tea. 'You're up early.'

'That's because I'm going skiing. Against my better judgement, I should add. Nico's a force to be reckoned with when he makes up his mind about something.'

'Should be lovely.'

'Yeah, Luke says the views are spectacular.' Jacquie lowered her voice. 'Why don't you come? Get out of here for a bit.'

'Jacquie, about Nico – be careful, won't you?'

Her daughter's eyes shot open. 'What *are* you suggesting?'

'It's just that you look lovely at the moment – yes, I *would* say that, I *am* your mother, but you could create an . . . impression without meaning to.'

'He's engaged, for God's sake. I do know where the boundaries are, you know.'

'But do you know that the girl he's engaged to is Carlotta's daughter?'

Jacquie's trim china cup came slamming down on its neat china saucer. '*What?*'

'Ah. You didn't know.'

'Why didn't you tell me?'

'I am telling you.'

Jacquie let out a low moan. 'Oh. My. God.'

Her mother looked up, alarmed. 'What's wrong? You haven't . . . he hasn't . . . there isn't . . .'

'That poor pet! Marrying *her* daughter? Can you imagine? A mini-Carlotta? And then having Carlotta for a mother-in-law?'

Marina giggled. 'Shush.'

'What a *nightmare*! Why didn't Luke stop them?'

'Why on earth would he do that?' Jacquie raised an eyebrow, which made Marina laugh more. 'I'll have you know Luke is very fond of Carlotta.'

'No, he isn't,' Jacquie hissed. 'He's just so tightly wrapped round her finger that he can't untangle himself! God, maybe I should save Nico from this dreadful fate.'

'Don't you dare! You're to behave yourself, do you hear me? Don't be gorgeous or funny. I've seen what it does to men. You close it down right now, Jacquie ffrench.'

'Yeah, yeah, whatever.'

'Carlotta was looking at her watch last night when you were out. She's on guard, so don't make things difficult. Can you imagine the uproar if . . . Well, it's proving hard enough for me as it is, so be careful. There are a lot of people to consider.'

'As if I'd go for a guy who's spoken for! Honestly, Mum, what has got into you? And with you and Luke involved? That'd be a bit too cosy for me, thanks.'

Unmistakable relief crossed Marina's face. 'Sorry. I'm losing it a bit. It's just . . . I don't know, I thought this was going to be so straightforward, and it just isn't.'

'You and Luke, you mean?'

'Hmm. There seem to be considerable obstacles barring the way.'

'Carlotta-shaped obstacles?'

'And Bridget-shaped ones.'

'They really are a pair, those two. But nothing my mummy can't handle.'

'What are you waiting for, dear?'

Marina was sitting in the hall when Bridget came pottering across in her slippers and housecoat. She could have been in a farmyard, going to get the eggs, rather than trundling across this polished marble hall. 'Luke,' Marina said. 'We're going for a drive.'

'Are we?' said Bridget.

'No, *we* are.'

'But I prefer to walk.'

'Me too,' said Marina. There were times when Bridget's lack

of concentration had its advantages. Marina was learning to follow the confused flow of things.

'He falls in love so easily, that's the thing,' Bridget muttered, as she shuffled past.

'I'm sorry?'

'Always in and out of love. Always the next grand love affair. Sure, what would I be doing with him?'

A chill went down Marina's back.

'Like he can't breathe,' Bridget went on. 'Like this is the love of his life. Always the same, so Carlotta says.'

'Is that so? And what else does Carlotta say?'

Bridget frowned, as if trying to remember. 'Fickle, she says. Easily blinded and more easily bored, that's our Luke, isn't it, dear? Sure, isn't he always the same?'

How neat. Carlotta was now drip-feeding Bridget, in the hope she would repeat this mantra in Marina's presence. How well it had worked.

Bridget went on along the corridor. 'I said that, I did, to his teacher. "He's always like this," I said.'

Luke made the most of Marina's last day. They drove to Armeno for lunch and sat for hours eating, talking, being alone. She teased him about being fickle. 'Always in and out of love, that's what your mother says.'

'I've been in love twice, thank you very much,' he protested. 'Ask my kids.' On cue, Francesco, or Frankie, as Luke called him, phoned just then from Peru. Watching Luke's face as they talked, Marina realized how much he missed his younger son, even though he was saying, 'Of course you must stay on. It's fine, Frankie, really. You're doing good work.'

Marina squeezed his wrist when they were done.

'It's just so bloody far away,' he said, 'and now he wants to stay till Christmas. Another year!'

'Maybe we should visit him.'

'Yeah, Ma's keen to do that, but I'm not sure she's up to the journey.'

Marina let it pass. 'You must be very proud of him. Of both of them. Nico is being so sweet to Jacquie. He really doesn't have to take her out so much. You didn't ask him to, did you?'

'Even if I had, Nico only does what Nico bloody well feels like doing. No, he must enjoy her company or he wouldn't do it – which is pretty handy for us.'

She smiled.

'And she's making his Irish roots wiggle, which is great.' He summoned the waiter. 'Where has this week gone? You're barely here and you're leaving again.'

'That's going to be the way of it, though, isn't it?'

'Come again soon,' he said. 'Come next weekend.'

'You come to me.'

'I'll try, but . . .'

'I know, I know. Your mother.'

'Maybe I could bring her with me and dump her on her sister-in-law in Tipp for a week.'

'A week? That would be brilliant.'

'I'll try, but when you get home, book yourself over here for as soon as you can.'

'I will if you will.'

Nico had it all – boots her size, skis her size, even a white ski-suit.

'Who does this lot belong to?' she asked, as he took his car up the winding hairpin bends to the top of the mountain behind Orta. 'A former girlfriend you took skiing who died in an avalanche, I suppose.'

'Of course not,' he said, dismissively. 'She went over a crevasse.'

She laughed. 'Yeah, right.'

'The gear belongs to a friend. A girlfriend.'

'Your fiancée?'

He smiled. 'No, not my fiancée.'

'Poor Cristina. Have you no conscience?'

'She is having a good time, believe me. She also is sometimes with someone else.'

'Following your example, no doubt,' said Jacquie. 'If she has any sense, she'll leave you for him.'

'She won't. When she comes back from Rome, we won't leave each other. We'll make a good couple.' He pulled the car round a tight corner. It was sexy, the way the blue bonnet hugged the roads, slinked round the bends, with snow on either side interlaced between the pine trees.

'Will you be faithful then?' Jacquie asked.

'I hope. That is why, now, it is okay. We are not properly together yet.' He glanced at her. 'But don't tell my family that.'

'A nod towards the future, but live for today? I suppose that's not a bad way to go about things.'

'As long as you don't fall in love,' he said, 'it's okay.'

'And how do you stop that happening?'

'I . . .' he said, drawing out the word so that it sounded like a pained 'aiiee' '. . . have no idea at all.'

When they reached a car park near the top of the mountain, he helped her get into the gear. She lost her balance putting on the suit, and that was before she'd even touched the skis. To their right, the hill rose to a humpy peak. There were a few low buildings, ski hire and ski schools, a shop and a bar, but Nico refused to let her have a drink until she'd made some effort to ski.

'We'll go to the top, where the view is best. It's easy skiing down from there.'

'I'm not going up in that thing,' she said, pointing at the ski lift.

'How else should we get there?'

'Walk?'

He laughed. They were laughing a lot.

'I'd never keep my balance! I've been on skis for all of two minutes.'

'It's easy, really.'

It wasn't a bit easy, especially with a pair of planks attached to her feet that kept going where she didn't tell them to. They stood in line and when their T-bar came round, Nico grabbed it and grabbed her and somehow they were travelling up the mountain with a bar beneath their bums and their feet sliding along the ground. 'See?' he said. 'Easy.'

Jacquie gripped the bar. 'But how do we get off?'

He looked at her deadpan. 'Ski. Ski off.'

'See, there's a problem right there.' The top of the hill was coming ever closer.

'What is it?'

'I can't ski, can I?'

The T-bar was about to swing round and go back down. Nico yelled at her to let go and gave her a shove. She slid off to the right and saw with terror that the hill dropped away. It took her with it. Slithering down the slope she went, her speed increasing. In an attempt to stop herself, she fell back on her bum, but carried on down, screeching, hands and sticks in the snow behind her. It seemed as if *she* was going to be the one to go over the crevasse, not Nico's imaginary dead girlfriend, but she couldn't stop laughing. It seemed an age before he swooped in front of her, put his skis under hers, which didn't work, so he tried to bring her to a halt by throwing himself on top of her. For a few moments they kept on sliding, until they came to a gentle stop.

'I couldn't catch you!' he said.

'Yeah, I'm a real whiz.'

When they'd stopped laughing, he was right there, on top of her. He took off his goggles and lay panting into her face. They considered it. Only one of them had to move, minimally, and it would happen. Jacquie came close. His lovely mouth was just there, with the same thoughts on his lips as she had on hers. Had they been a couple, it would have been a moment of deep affection. An urge to dispel that affection – so much more dangerous than lust – propelled Jacquie into a sitting position. Their skis criss-crossed on the snow like the fingers of two hands. From where they were sitting, they could see Lake Maggiore, winking down in the valley, wedged into its snowy contours. From further up behind them, Nico said, they would be able see Lake Orta too, but Jacquie's mind was not on alpine lakes. This was the moment to *clarify*. To make sure that he was clear that this was about nothing at all, that she wasn't about to incur Carlotta's wrath, or emulate her mother by taking a lover on Lake Orta, engaged or otherwise.

Just in time, she caught herself. Held back from saying something stupid. Nico didn't need to be told how things stood! He was Italian, for Christ's sake. This was probably no more than a fun flirtation for him. With his fiancée out of sight, he probably handled all women like this. He stood up, put out his hand, and helped her to her feet.

It was nothing to him.

There was no need to spell out that it was nothing to her either.

# 14

Matthew greeted them at the door with a friendly hug for Jacquie and a warm hug for Marina, who sank into it, her cheek against his soft shirt. Picking up on this, he held her for a moment.

'Do come in,' he said. 'You're very welcome.'

'To my own home?'

'I'll get you girls a cup of coffee.'

'Tea,' said Marina, following him to the kitchen. 'This isn't America, remember?'

'Where is everyone?' Jacquie asked.

'Natalie and Kitt are having some quality time with a wad of cash I gave them, so I said I'd hold the fort.'

He made a pot of tea. Jacquie stood by the French windows, looking out at the garden, while Marina sat at the table, feeling home seep into her bones. Matthew put out the mugs and milk and sat opposite her.

'I'll take this upstairs,' said Jacquie, 'if that's okay.'

'Sure.' Matthew turned to Marina. 'So? All well in paradise?'

'All well. How about you? Any progress with Kitt?'

'You know, there has been progress. I've managed to persuade her to go back to school.'

'*What?* But that's brilliant! Where?'

'Somewhere local, if that's okay?'

'Of course it's okay. But how did you persuade her?'

'Blackmail. Either she comes to Anchorage or she goes to school. She's a child who needs school. She has to see it through or God knows where she'll end up.'

'Oh, Matthew, that's such good news. How about Natalie? You two didn't succumb to old passions, did you?'

'No.'

'Admirable restraint.'

'Yes, I thought so,' he said, nodding, 'but let's face it, my heart wouldn't have been in it.'

Marina didn't want to think about what that was supposed to mean.

'Anyway, I'm going to help them with a deposit for a flat. Natalie said she'd start looking.' He shook his head. 'I should have sorted them out years ago.'

'You couldn't turn Natalie into something she wasn't. There was always a man.'

'Yeah, but I shouldn't have let her wander around with my daughter, either. I can't believe she's working as a shop assistant. She has so much more to offer.'

'Give her time. She likes the *craic* in there and when she's ready to move on to something more challenging, she will. Suzanne wants her to give yoga classes.'

'How about you? Planning to move on anywhere? Like Italy, maybe?'

'Not immediately. I've got to get my students through their Leaving Certs, for one thing. Three have the same unbelievably bad teacher. She can't even pronounce certain words and she's teaching honours French!'

'You'll sort them.'

'I will. I'll get them A1s and she'll get the credit.'

'Not from them.'

She smiled. 'When are you leaving?'

'Day after tomorrow, but I was wondering if I could come back at Easter. Kitt still hates me, but if we see more of each other, we might get there.'

'You come any time you like. This was your second home

once. It can be again.' Marina turned to the window and looked at the reflection of the two of them sitting there. The heating came on, the pipes vibrating and grumbling as their work started. The fridge hummed diffidently. 'Do you remember,' she said quietly, 'that weekend you and Gwen and the others went off to Valentia Island?'

'Don't remind me.'

'You were all tumbling out of the house with your sleeping-bags and food, and Gwen was saying, "I didn't think you'd want to come anyway . . ." I remember the door slamming behind you, and coming back here and sitting exactly like this with Dad, feeling like the kid who wasn't asked to the party.'

'I tell you what,' said Matthew, 'being here again, this last week, it's all been coming back – like the time your dad and I went up to the loft to fix that leak and spent all day there in a heat-wave, remember?' He gestured towards the garden. 'And there's a shrub out there – I watched your mother planting it, and now, man, it's huge . . . Things were certainly different after she took off. Your dad always in his study and the place so quiet.'

Marina wasn't interested in his strategic reminiscences. 'I wish I'd known back then,' she said.

'Known what?'

'That I was being bullied.'

*'Bullied?'*

She was still looking at their reflections. 'I didn't see it at the time. I thought it only happened in the playground, but now I realize that's what was happening to me – exclusion, ridicule, decisions being made for me . . .'

'Bullied by whom?'

She turned to him. 'Gwen, of course. And you, because you stood by.'

His eyes didn't even flicker. 'That's hard.'

'Yeah, it was hard.'

'What do you want me to say, Reen? I didn't get it. I thought it was two women having a spat. But bullying – I don't know about that.'

'I do. I didn't, but I do now.'

He sighed and put his mug down. 'I'm sorry if my being here is bringing all that shit back.'

'It isn't you who's brought it back.'

# 15

Marina arrived again in Orta on a Tuesday at the beginning of February. It was a crisp, cold day; the sky was bright blue, and the lake, when they came alongside it, shone like a polished floor. The snow-covered hill tops and mountains looked smug and beautiful. It was worth every minute of the dreaded Carlotta, Marina resolved, as they got out of the car.

'*Ciao, bella!*' Carlotta exclaimed, as they stepped into the hall, coming towards her with arms outstretched and embracing her as if they were long-lost sisters. 'Come in, come in. Tea, yes? You like your tea.' She blabbered at Maria. Luke took Marina's suitcase upstairs – to his room, she hoped.

Bridget was sitting in her chair by the fireplace. 'Ah, there you are, dear. Did you have a good walk?'

Progress, thought Marina. Bridget remembered her. 'Not bad, thanks, Bridget,' she said, bending to kiss her. 'How are you?'

'How am I what?'

'How are you keeping?'

'Keeping what?'

'Sit, sit.' Carlotta waved at the couch beside Bridget. Marina was only now noticing that Carlotta often said everything twice.

'Thank you.' She sat down, then cursed herself. No need to thank another guest.

Bridget leant forward. 'Do you know what a Blue Moon is?'

'Em, now you mention it,' said Marina, 'I don't think I do.'

'A Blue Moon is two moons.'

'Really?'

Carlotta rested her elbow on the armrest, cupped her hands, crossed her ankles, and looked for all the world like the hostess. 'It must be lovely for you, Marina, to be able to take two weeks' holiday whenever you like.'

'Oh, I'll have to make up for it, believe me, with extra hours next –'

'I should have done something like that, shouldn't I, Bridget, when I tried to retire? Got a little job that didn't involve long hours and late nights. Something completely different from international trade. No stress or strain or concerns about corporate law.' She turned back to Marina. 'But what could I do? Everyone came after me, wanting this and that and every other thing! None of my clients would let me go.'

*I am indispensable.* Now that Marina could see them for what they were, Carlotta's tactics were unimaginatively standard – undermine by bragging, by setting yourself so far above your victim that they will cower at your magnificence. But recognizing it made it no easier to handle. Marina remembered how, when she was teaching in Dublin, she had counselled girls who were being targeted by others to stand firm and let the barbed comments wash over their heads. It was no easier for them then than it was for her now.

'Do you work in a shop?' Bridget asked suddenly.

'No,' said Marina. 'I teach.'

'Teach what?'

'French and sometimes English.'

'But everyone in Ireland speaks English.'

'Not any more. Many immigrants need help with their studies.'

'Everyone does everything on the Internet, these days,' said Bridget. 'Why can't they learn it that way?'

'I think that might be quite difficult, with a language.'

'I taught myself English, you know,' said Carlotta. 'Three months, from books and the radio.'

'Goodness,' Marina said tonelessly, 'and you speak it so well.'

Luke, thankfully, reappeared. It was good to see him, and there were other aspects of being back in this house that were pleasant, like Maria bringing tea and a delicious fruit cake, laced with chocolate.

Carlotta held out a cup to Marina. 'And how is your busy household? Are you still saving lives?'

This was quite an onslaught. She had upped the ante. The subtlety had gone, which suggested that it had not worked to her satisfaction. Perhaps she had not expected Marina to keep coming back, which was exactly why she had returned so soon – on Suzanne's orders. 'You have to strategize,' Suzanne had declared when, after New Year, Marina had despaired of handling an ex-lover who wouldn't decamp and an extremely bizarre mother. 'If Carlotta's trying to get you off her patch, then you must let her know you won't be intimidated.'

'But I am intimidated!' Marina had said, and now she sat there wondering if this was worth the effort. Strategizing. Playing the game. Trying to go one better than this creature, when all she wanted was to be with the man with whom she had fallen in love on holidays.

Because she had not answered the question, Carlotta went on, 'Do you still have, how do you say . . . *eccentrici* . . . eccentrics – would that be the word? – living with you?'

'That would not be the word, no.' Carlotta had inadvertently left herself open to correction. 'But if you mean Natalie and Kitt, they are friends who live with us, just as you live with Bridget and Luke. Except you don't, really, do you? But they are very well, thank you, and so are my children.'

Luke looked at Marina with either shock or admiration.

Carlotta, poised to pour another cup, looked at him, then back at Marina.

Bridget leant towards Luke. 'Does Carlotta not live here?'

'Of course I do, darling. I am always here for you.'

Luke cleared the air by clearing his throat. 'So Jacquie's joining us on Friday?'

'Yes,' said Marina.

Carlotta resumed pouring. 'How lovely. Just for the weekend?'

'No, she'll be here for a week.' Marina glanced at Luke. 'I hope that's okay?'

'Absolutely. Delighted to have her.'

'Doesn't she work either?' Carlotta asked, more imperiously than ever.

'You know she does, Carlotta,' said Marina. 'She's taking time off. It's rather a long journey for a weekend, when we have to go through London or Dublin.'

'Is Jacquie the pretty one?' Bridget asked.

'The other pretty one,' said Luke.

Back in Cork, Dara and Jacquie were arguing about the same trip.

'I wouldn't mind if you were going for the skiing,' Dara was saying, 'but going over to hold Mum's hand is a really bad idea. She's well able to deal with this Carlotta character.'

'*You* haven't met her!'

'And she has Luke.'

'He's working and walking his mother like she's a dog, and he doesn't hear the jibes. Carlotta is charm personified whenever he's around, but she gets these digs in. She even does it to me – labouring the point that I'm not *really* qualified for anything, unlike her daughter, who works in international finance, and how my relationship didn't come to anything, whereas *her* daughter is going to marry Luke's talented architect son . . . It's relentless, and if Mum is left at her mercy, she might back out of this whole thing.'

'But she has to learn to handle it. You're not always going to be there.'

'Fair enough, but why shouldn't she have a bit of back-up from time to time? Luke's surrounded by people. She's alone. And if I was in a tricky relationship, Mum'd do everything to support me, so I should do the same for her.'

'Jacquie, if this isn't going to work, there's nothing you can do about it.'

'Oh, so it's just, like, to hell with it, is it? Dara! Can't you see how happy she's been? I mean, do you recognize her? She's had six years of grief and looking after other people – don't you think she's earned a break? Or is it, "Oh, gee, tough," if this doesn't work out? No relationship exists in a vacuum, you know.'

'You've been reading too many self-help books.'

'Don't be so bloody condescending. We owe Mum, and if that means flying to Italy when, *frankly*, I have better things to do, then I'm bloody well going to do it.'

Nico picked her up at the airport. She wished he hadn't. She had hoped not to see him at all. 'Thanks for collecting me. I was expecting Luke.'

'I offered to come,' he said. 'I thought you'd prefer my car.'

'Why?'

'It goes faster. You like that.'

'I do not. It's bad for the environment.'

'If you're so worried about carbon emissions, why did you fly instead of taking the train?'

'Because I would have had to leave as soon as I arrived, *obviously*.'

'You're here for a week, Dad says.'

'Yeah, escaping my job if the truth be told,' she said, lest he suspected she had hurried back to see him.

They crossed over to the car park and found his car. 'It's good to see you,' Nico said, when they sat in.

'It's good to see your car.'

He pulled out.

'So how's my mother doing?'

'Very well. She is having a very good time.'

Marina was not having a good time. She greeted Jacquie as if she hadn't seen her for six weeks, and hurried her upstairs to the top-floor apartment.

'But we are about to have cocktails,' Carlotta called after them.

'You go ahead,' Marina replied.

'How's it been?' Jacquie asked, when they let themselves into the flat and turned on some lights.

'*Awful*.' Marina's eyes filled.

'Oh, Mum, no.'

'Don't mind me,' Marina said, taking out a tissue, 'I'm being silly, but at this stage I just want to get out of here.'

'What? It can't be that bad! What about Luke?'

'He has to work all day and I'm left at the mercy of those two dragons. Carlotta's overwhelming hospitality will drive me away, I swear, which is *exactly* as she intends it.'

'But have you had any time with Luke?'

'We've managed to get out for dinner twice, but not without Carlotta whining about how she had to sit with his mother, and we've had some nice walks, but then we come back and I have to grin and bear the side-swipes and put-downs.'

'Can't you throw in some of your own?'

'I could and I'd like to, but it's too petty. I'm not even sure Carlotta means it personally. Maybe she's just an inveterate snob who treats everyone like this.'

'Or maybe she's still in love with him.'

'I don't think that's it. If anything, it's territorial. Anyway, we'd better go down.'

'Why? Because you're afraid she'll get cross if we don't? *Mum.*'

'Because it isn't worth the hassle. We'd never hear the end of how dinner was delayed, and how the meat got dried out, and how Bridget can't eat too late.'

'Have you spoken to Luke about it?'

'No. The last thing I want is him rapping Carlotta on the knuckles and forcing her to be nice to me. Besides, I'd come across like a jealous, possessive hag if I said anything. I've got to handle this quietly and stick it out until Carlotta accepts that I'm not going anywhere.'

'A minute ago you said you wanted to leave.'

'That's why it's so great you're here,' said Marina. 'You and Suzanne have to keep me focused. Don't let me run. Two years down the road I'd never forgive myself for letting that witch spoil things for us.'

'If only she'd slip up in front of Luke.'

'Come on, you must be hungry.' They set off down the stairs. 'I'm sorry about not coming to the airport. I hope you didn't mind about Nico?'

'No, I didn't mind.' *God, no.*

On the way down, Jacquie sent Dara a text: 'Good thing I came. Mum miz.'

Nico had stayed on for dinner. Marina's difficulty was obvious as soon as they went into the dining room. Carlotta planted herself at the top of the table and told everyone else where to sit, placing Marina at the far end from Luke. Jacquie began to boil. The only reason Carlotta got away with this diva stuff was because Luke allowed it. He seemed to be blind to the fact that her overbearing presence made it difficult for Marina. Jacquie watched carefully all evening, and got a sense of how Carlotta operated.

She was very sweet to the women in Luke's life. That was how she did it. She annihilated them by flooding them with hugs and hospitality and insincerities. Jacquie remembered her fawning over Nico's mother at New Year. Her confidence in her own role would crush anyone hoping to usurp her, but Jacquie and Dara, and Nico, could not allow her to crush Marina.

Tricky, though. Carlotta was close to Luke's children in a way Marina could never be. She had watched them grow up, had always been there, and she used endearments for Nico in French, English and Italian. Possibly, probably, she loved Luke's sons.

But Carlotta did not hold all the cards. Jacquie also noted that Luke changed in her mother's presence. He seemed to become taller when she came into the room and he was relaxed whenever she was near him, as if she made him more at ease in his own space. It was quite endearing, the extent to which he was besotted, and the way Marina glowed, as she absorbed his affectionate gaze. Luke could be intense, considered, while Marina was more laid-back, but she could be distant in her own way, and her abstraction seemed to suit Luke, just as his efficiency and reticence suited her. Rarely overtly physical, they exuded good chemistry, and it was because of this, Jacquie was sure, that Carlotta did not have as much power over him as she pretended.

Nico caught Jacquie's eye during dinner and tilted his head as if to ask, 'What are you so curious about?' She had been watching his father. She raised her eyebrows in response and sipped her wine. He might be useful. He might be able to tell her the true nature of Luke's relationship with Carlotta. There had to be more to it than any of them knew.

Luke made his own statement at the end of the meal. When Carlotta called for coffee, he said, 'Not for us, thanks. We're having an early night,' and put his napkin to his mouth, with a furtive glance at Jacquie, as if in apology for making this oblique reference to his and Marina's intimate life.

'But we must have coffee,' said Carlotta.

'Not for us,' he said again, opening the door for Marina. 'Night, Ma. Don't stay up too late on the computer. You know it makes you crabby.'

Yay, Jacquie thought. *One to Luke!* Subtle, but firm. Perhaps he was sensitive to the situation. A few more statements like that and Carlotta would have to give up.

When Jacquie went down the next morning, Nico was at the breakfast table, reading a newspaper, as he had been the first day they'd met, but so too were Bridget, Marina and Luke, who said, 'I'm afraid there isn't enough snow on Mottarone for skiing, Jacquie.'

'*Typical*,' she said. 'Just my luck!'

Nico gave her a wry look over the top of his newspaper, then folded it and said, 'I could take you shopping in Milan instead, if you like?'

'Ooh, Jacquie, that would be lovely,' said Marina. 'The shops are fantastic.'

'But what about you, Mum. What do *you* want to do?'

'We were never allowed to use the "want" word when we were growing up,' said Bridget. 'You must always say "like". "What would you *like* to do?"'

'Don't worry about me,' Marina said to her daughter. 'I'll keep myself busy.'

'Maybe you should come with us?'

'I have plans for today,' said Luke, chasing a prune round his bowl with his spoon.

Marina's face fell.

'Then you *must* come with us,' Jacquie said. 'I'll squeeze into the back seat.'

Luke looked up. 'I mean I have plans for your mother and me. For both of us.'

'Oh,' said Jacquie. 'Good. I will come shopping then, Nico. If you're sure?'

'It's my pleasure.'

She smiled. 'Thanks. It'll make up for the disappointment about skiing.'

Bridget gathered breadcrumbs on to the tip of her finger. 'The White Cliffs of Dover should really be called the Ivory Coast.'

Nico lay staring at the ceiling, his fingers interlaced on his lower abdomen.

'That was amazing,' said Jacquie. He had not taken her into Milan – too busy on a Saturday, he said – but to warehouse stores on the outskirts that sold off designer clothes, items with tiny flaws, at cut prices. Jacquie had shopped with abandon, putting an unthinkable overload on her credit card.

They had been lying on her bed since they'd got back. Exhausted, Jacquie had gone into her room and crashed out, unaware that Nico had followed her up the stairs. He also followed her into her bedroom, uninvited, and crashed out with her.

'Did you buy enough?' he asked.

They glanced at the row of shopping bags along the wall. 'More than. I hope it wasn't a bore for you?'

'Not at all. I did well also.'

'Too right. We spent more time looking at men's clothes than women's!'

'One of my weaknesses,' he admitted.

'A good thing you have style, then.'

'A gift from my father, I think.'

'Yeah, he scrubs up pretty well. I'm so glad he's taken Mum away. I wonder where they've gone?'

They had come home to a note saying their parents would not be home that night.

'There are many impressive places near here,' said Nico. 'Romantic places.'

'I can imagine. I wouldn't mind a night in one of those grand old hotels in Stresa.'

'I'll arrange that some time.'

'Yeah, right.' Jacquie elbowed him playfully, but he was closer than she thought.

'*Haia! Che cazzo fai!*' He rubbed his arm.

'"*Haia?*" Hey, you're Irish, remember? When you hurt yourself you say, "Ow."'

'I didn't hurt myself. *You* hurt me.'

'Or, "Fucking hell, that hurt!"'

'That is what I said,' he leant up, 'or something like it.'

'Why, what does "*cazzo*" mean?'

'Cock, I suppose.' He swung his legs off the bed. 'I must go home and change.'

'Thanks for a lovely day.'

'I'll come at eight.'

'Sorry?'

'We will have dinner.'

'Nico, it really would be nice if you would *ask* me sometimes, instead of presuming. I might have other plans.'

'You are already going out?'

'No, but –'

'So we will go out, yes?'

'Well, all right, but . . .'

He pushed on his knees and stood up. 'So. No need to ask.'

It went on like that. Nico kept turning up as before and, as before, Jacquie kept failing to turn him down. His decisiveness and confidence, for all that she railed against both, were alluring, as was his cool professionalism and, after she'd seen a couple of the buildings he was restoring, his obvious talent. She liked the way his car was pristine, not full of sweet wrappers and discarded socks like other men's. Nico was neat: he always placed his sunglasses on the dashboard, his house keys in the glove compartment, and left his jacket hanging on the back of his seat. When he took off his glasses to wipe them, his intelligence shone out, even while the deep red groove on the bridge of his nose made him seem vulnerable. Above all, he was great company. Neither of them chose to correct the notion held in the villa that they were going out with his friends. They went out alone, and over pizza and espresso, over music in bars and clubs, they talked and laughed. It was cheerful stuff, until one night, in a restaurant beyond the square, the conversation turned to heavier things.

Nico watched her from behind his spectacles, his hand on his glass, as Jacquie told him about her father dying.

'I was relieved,' she said, 'when he died. He was never going to get better, and watching Mum being worn down, month by month, was unbearable. She'd get so tired sometimes she didn't know what day it was. She planned her days round the hospital visit, so that she could sit there, talking to . . . this body in the bed. Dad, but not Dad. The accident was worse, though. We thought we'd lost both of them. Dara was only fourteen. We'd always fought like terriers, but when I realized

I might be the only person left to look after him, I felt such a surge of adoration for him that I've never got over it.'

She looked out. Their table was on the second floor, next to a tiny balcony that was engulfed in wisteria, its contorted trunk twisting about the iron railing. The greenery drooped round the window like a poorly hung curtain. 'It was pretty strange, having both of them unconscious. I've never been so scared. I mean, the family rushed in, arriving from Ireland, fussing over us, but I was so relieved when Mum came round. I cried and cried. She didn't know what to say to me, and then my aunt had to tell her about Dad. For a while we thought that because Mum had woken up Dad would too, but when reality dawned, aunts and uncles had to get back to their jobs, their own families, and we were left, the three of us. Actually, Mum was glad when they decamped – she was out of hospital by then – but the awful thing was that Dara and I had to go too. Back to school. You've no idea what that was like, leaving her there, once, twice, three times . . . The first time I did it, I was still in school; the last time, I was in college. My Leaving Cert results were pretty dire –'

'Understandably,' said Nico.

'Yeah, but . . . I might have studied law or something if I'd done better. Instead I took a year off after finishing school to stay with Mum and to be with Didier, my boyfriend, then I applied to do an arts degree the following year, which meant leaving Mum, again, in that abnormal bubble, to go to college in Dublin.' Jacquie fiddled with her dessert fork. 'It does things to your head, stuff like that.'

'It must.'

'Twenty-two months we endured it, the three of us, and if that wasn't bad enough, as if to punish us or something, her dad went and had a stroke.'

Nico swore quietly, and discreetly motioned to the waiter.

'I was pretty selfish about that. I told her to put him in a home. I couldn't believe this had been dumped on us, but apparently disaster does strike twice. Double whammies. Triple whammies. If there is a God, He has no sense of fair play – either that or He can't count. Granddad moved to France, which meant Mum wasn't on her own so much, but it was full-time, full-on, for her until Dad died and it was over. No hospital visits, no false hope, and Mum coming round, again, like she'd been in her own coma all that time.'

They walked very slowly back to the square, her ankles wobbling sometimes on uneven cobbles and Nico's arm firmly through hers.

'And then Granddad started worrying about his house in Cork getting damp,' she went on, 'and Mum couldn't cope with his fretting, so she decided to sell up and move home. She had her own reasons, I think.'

'And you?'

'I was . . . pissed off. I'd done the sensible thing – gone away to college and got a degree, like my mother wanted me to, but as soon I could be with Didier full-time, lo and behold, we didn't live there any more! It wasn't a big deal for Dara – he'd only just finished school in Ireland, so for him it wasn't like moving anywhere, but Didier and I had managed to keep something going all the time I was in Dublin, and we were looking forward to *not* being a long-distance couple for a change.'

'You could have stayed, no?'

'Not really. Didier was living with his parents over the summer, so I'd have had nowhere to live. Besides, I wanted to help Mum settle in, so I spent a miserable summer in Cork and finally moved to Paris, where Didier was studying. It was . . .' she paused, hoping to find a word that would adequately describe those four months, but came up only with an emphatic '. . . *blissful*. We got on better than ever. We were like a pair of lovers on a French postcard. He even smoked Gitanes. I got waitressing jobs – couldn't find anything else, but even that didn't matter, because everything was falling into place. We figured we'd earned it. We'd been patient, done all the right things, and could at last be together.'

'So what went wrong?'

Her foot wobbled on a cobble. Nico's grip tightened on her arm. 'What went wrong was that whenever I went over to Cork they were struggling. Dara wasn't driving yet so Mum had to drive him everywhere, as well as look after my grandfather, and the house was dank and messy, a real old man's place, and I felt like such a heel.'

Nico veered towards a little gate opposite the villa and led her down the iron steps to Luke's waterside terrace, where they sat on a low wall in the dark.

'Things were tough for them, but I, meanwhile, was having a dreamlike existence in Paris, and there came a point when the guilt outweighed the happiness. It was there when I woke up and there when I went to bed. Every night, I wondered how Mum had coped with Granddad that day, and whether Dara was making friends. Mum had no life. She'd become a nurse in a town she used to call home. I suppose I was worried that she'd crumble . . . When I went back to France after Christmas, it didn't feel right or good. It felt like this was a time when family had to come first. And Didier agreed.' It surprised Jacquie that her eyes had blurred. 'He was wonderful. He said he'd wait, but I'd made him wait for three years through college and I couldn't do it to him again. It wouldn't have been fair, so I ended it, and went home, and broke both our hearts in the process.'

Nico put his thumb to her cheek. 'Are you sure that was the right decision?'

'Yes. We've been a bit battered as a family, but being together, this last year, has helped all of us. And it meant I was there for Mum when Granddad died.'

'But we have to live our own lives, regardless of our parents.'

She smiled at him in the dark. 'Says he who has allowed himself to be railroaded into an engagement that keeps "the families" happy.'

With a shrug, he took the point. 'That's because I don't want to be like my father.'

'Why? How is he?'

Nico shrugged again, his shoulders bulky in his thick coat. 'He's a very . . . You know, he's a lonely person. Someone like him should have had a long, happy marriage, a big family. That was what he wanted, because his childhood was so solitary. Women – there have always been women, but when we were kids, after the divorce, I remember him always doing things alone, cycling, walking, listening to music, and at family occasions, he was always off to the side, thinking. I mean, he made some mistakes, big ones, for sure, but –'

'Like what?'

He dismissed the question with a shake of the head. 'But I have learnt from him that it's easy to end up where you don't want to be. The big love affair doesn't always come, doesn't always work, and if it doesn't, you're basically fucked.'

'But it did. It *has* come, for him.'

'*Certo*, a bit late, but, sure. And if it comes for me, I'll take it. No mistakes. But if it doesn't –'

'You'll marry Cristina. You have all the bases covered. Poor Cristina.'

He stood up. 'Don't feel bad for her.'

Jacquie sat still. Filaments of information fluttered before her. He'd told her things, about himself as well as his father, but she couldn't make sense of any of it because of all the things he had left unsaid.

'Come on,' he said. 'I have a new toy I want to play with on your terrace.'

A telescope. 'Perfect night,' he said, going outside. 'Just a slice of moon. If there's too much, the sky is no good.'

Jacquie stepped out after him, but he spent so long fidgeting and fiddling that she went back in again. He seemed not to notice. She turned out the main light and sat on the couch watching his dark outline, turning the telescope this way and that.

'Come here,' he called. 'I've got something special for you.'

'You should try this in Ireland,' she said, joining him. 'There's too much light pollution here.'

'I'd love to. Next time Dad goes for a visit, we'll go too.' He patted his telescope. 'Look in there.'

'This is a bit of an old trick, isn't it? Showing a girl the stars?'

'Hey, I'm looking at the stars because it's a clear night and this is the best place to do it.' He gave her waist an affectionate squeeze.

She had to bend over to look into the eyepiece, but it was hard to see much with her eyelashes getting in the way and Nico standing behind her, his hands on her hips, holding her in position. She was about to straighten up to get him off her when she saw it. 'Oh, my God! Wow. That is . . .'

'Beautiful, no?'

'What is it? Saturn?'

'Yes. You are looking at the rings of Saturn.'

'It's so . . .' Between her blinking eyelashes, she could see the rings, glowing a bright creamy white, perched round their planet like a hula-hoop round a waist.

‘The guy who sold me the telescope said Saturn would blow my mind the first time I saw it,’ said Nico.

‘He was right! My mind is totally blown! I thought the rings’d be all pinky red, like in the pictures.’ She straightened up. ‘Thank you. It’s like swimming with dolphins or boating with whales.’ She bent over the eyepiece again.

‘Here, have a look at the rim of the moon.’ He moved the telescope, peered through it, stood back and made way for her.

‘Why is it all bubbly round the edge?’

‘Those are craters.’

‘God, yeah. Cool.’ She let him have another look. He took off his glasses, rubbed his eyes and bent over, swivelling the telescope away from the moon. Jacquie leant against the railing, watching him. Feeling the cold for the first time, she shivered.

Without moving from the telescope, Nico reached out and rubbed her arm. ‘You’re cold. Go to bed. I won’t disturb you.’

‘How long are you planning on staying out here?’

‘Until I find a new planet.’

‘Yeah? Who’ll you name it after? Your fiancée?’

‘She isn’t my fiancée yet.’

‘Everyone else thinks so.’

‘I told you, we have a very loose arrangement.’

‘Carlotta doesn’t give that impression. In fact, why don’t you call the planet “Carlotta”? What greater compliment could a man make to his future mother-in-law?’

‘I can tell you one thing,’ he said. ‘I won’t be calling it Jacquie.’

It was rather abrupt. ‘Oh. Why not?’

‘Stupid name for a planet. And it would only alert people.’

‘Alert them to what?’

Nico lifted his head to look at her. She glanced over her shoulder, towards the reassuring sight of the island and its floodlights.

'Alert them,' he said, 'to what we are trying to ignore.'

He came over and leant against the railing beside her, his arms crossed. Neither of them spoke until, with another shiver, Jacquie said quietly, 'Maybe you should take your telescope to one of the other terraces.'

His voice was low, deep. 'You're worried about Cristina?'

She gave him a look. 'Do you really think I'm the kind of person who'd mess about with someone else's fiancé?'

'Why not?' he said lightly. 'I do it all the time.'

'Don't be facetious.'

'So does she,' he said. 'Sleep with others, I mean. We are not tied in yet.'

'But it isn't just her, is it?'

'You mean our parents?'

Jacquie shivered again. 'I cannot believe I'm hearing that. *Our* parents.'

'Jacquie.' Nico swivelled round and put one hand on either side of her on the railing. 'We must be careful –'

'I know, you said so already. That's what I'm trying to do.'

'Careful not to miss an opportunity.'

'There *is* no opportunity, Nico. Can you imagine the uproar if we . . .' She trailed off, unable to be specific.

'I'm not sure that's enough.'

'Enough?' He wasn't even touching her, but she was surrounded by him.

'Enough reason to stop something that might be good for us.'

'It wouldn't be good for *any* of us. Not for Cristina, or Carlotta, and my mother has a lot at stake here. If I became a factor in your engagement, *she*'ll pay the price. So please,' she pulled his arm off the railing and released herself, 'take the rings of Saturn somewhere else.'

'Are you really depriving me –'

'Yes, I am.'

'– of such a sky?'

'Oh. Sorry. Of course not. Stay as long as you want.'

He went back to his stars. Jacquie went into the main bathroom and sat on the edge of the bath, quivering. Nico was so comprehensively off-limits for so many different reasons that she would have laughed had she had the heart for it. 'Okay,' she whispered to herself, 'he's out there, I'm in here, and it's bedtime. Do I get undressed? Would that look like seduction?' Her fleecy pyjamas, with the blue and grey penguins' feet imprint, were hanging from a hook on the back of the door. 'Probably not.' She got changed and went quickly through the kitchen, calling, 'Night!'

'Good night, Jacquie.'

Unable to sleep, she lay still, waiting for him to leave and trying to hear every slight move he made. Whatever had just happened – or not happened – she knew she wasn't up for it. Nothing must come of it. She could just imagine the scenario if it did: the hysterical Italian girlfriend; Carlotta screeching betrayal; Bridget asking, 'What creatures survive at twenty thousand feet below sea level?' And Luke going, 'Hmm?'

Her chin under the duvet, Jacquie giggled. It would be riotous. Weird. Hopeless.

Probably twenty minutes later, she heard the glass door being slid across and clicking shut. Her heart rate increased, her breathing decreased. She waited, listening. The bedroom door handle dropped, and Nico came in. He sat on the side of her bed, with his back to her. Jacquie reached out and put her hand on his knee; he took it, and held it between his knees, their fingers interlaced. Then he got up and left.

*

Marina stopped in front of a shop window in the narrow road beyond the square, and gazed at a display of jars of honey, bottles of oil, packets of multicoloured pasta, and different kinds of mushrooms. 'They do like their mushrooms,' she said.

'I really seriously totally hate my job.'

'Jacquie!' Marina turned. 'You never said.'

'I've only just this minute realized how much. The thought of going back did it.'

'Then you must look for something else.'

'What, though? I want to use my languages, like I was supposed to be doing in this job, but I don't want to go back to France and I don't fancy Spain. Here's nice. I wish I'd studied Italian instead of Spanish.'

'Maybe you could ask Carlotta for a job? She's *so* busy!'

'God, I wish they'd stop asking us to go to Mass. They're desperately holy, the two of them.'

'Don't knock them for being devout. Come on, we'd better head back.'

'Mum, stop. You're doing it again, letting them shunt you around. We're out for a walk. We don't have a curfew. We don't *have* to be back for tea at five.'

'Of course we do. We're Bridget's guests and she's expecting us. It would be rude not to show up. Besides, when I was ten minutes late the other day, it was, like, "Oh, my, but the tea's cold." I said, "No problem, I'll make more," only to be told that that would not be necessary. Maria could make the tea.'

'But I want to walk further out and see where this leads.'

'It goes round the peninsula and ends up back at our place. It takes an hour. Come on, let's not upset the apple cart.' They headed back towards the square. 'Are you seeing Nico's friends tonight?'

'Maybe. Why?'

'I'm planning an escape.'

'Excellent. We'll create a diversion.'

Luke and Marina went out that night when no one was looking. Jacquie was pleased for them, but had to sit through dinner with Bridget and Carlotta on her own. Her mother's allergy to Bridget was not entirely justified. Luke's mother was certainly challenging, but Jacquie quite liked the old bat. Talking to her was oddly stimulating, because you thought you were having one conversation, then found you were having quite another.

Carlotta was rabbiting on about her daughter's glittering career, when Bridget said to Jacquie, 'Did you know, dear, that if you go to Confession just once, God will forgive you for all the times you didn't go?'

'Sorry, Bridget, I don't really believe in Confession.'

'But you must ask forgiveness for your sins.'

'Must I?'

'We must all ask God's forgiveness,' Carlotta said, more quietly than usual, turning her knife repeatedly on the tablecloth.

'Did you know,' Bridget went on, quite on her own route, 'that an oak tree Hitler gave to a long-distance runner in 1936 is still flourishing at a school in New Zealand?'

'I had no idea.'

'Don't you think it should be chopped down?'

'Umm, not really,' said Jacquie. 'It's hardly the tree's fault, what Hitler did.'

'But it's a terrible reminder of his sins,' said Bridget.

'Isn't it good to be reminded?'

Bridget stared at her. 'About what?'

Nico arrived in time to save her, and when they were moving

into the other room, he said, 'I have to put away my telescope. Give me a hand, would you, Jacquie?'

She loved her terrace. Dawn, morning, night-time, and most of all when Nico was on it. 'You could live off this view,' she said, when he was dismantling the telescope. She wished he would hurry up and go, and she wished he would never leave. It was becoming difficult, trying to put a cap on the tumult inside her when he was there, and when he wasn't, on the naughty determination to act on it the next time she saw him. Only a few more days and there would be distance between them, which was a good thing, because all the reasons for keeping herself from him became less defined every day. Being with him aroused her, and there was something else, indistinct but certain, about being with Nico. He made her feel as if she was in the past and the present and the future all at once.

The telescope packed away, he leant against the railing with his back to the lake, while she faced it.

'Please go,' she said quietly.

He reached out languidly, and slid her along the railing to him. He smelt good. He put his mouth to her wrist, her hand, her fingers.

'I won't sleep with you,' she said.

'I know.'

And he knew what he was doing; he knew so well what he was doing when he kissed her.

Not so many miles away, in a four-star hotel on Lake Maggiore, Marina and Luke were also kissing, lying across a huge bed, but unlike their children, they were well satisfied.

'Were you a check-out boy in my local supermarket?'

'No.'

'A petrol pump attendant?'

'No'

'Did we speak?'

'Yes.'

'Make eye contact?'

'Oh, yes.'

# 16

Marina was looking forward to Easter. Time with Luke on her own patch. She even welcomed the opportunity, while not exactly relishing the prospect, to spend time with Bridget. With Carlotta circling like a queen wasp in Orta, it had proved impossible to form any kind of relationship with the woman, but maybe here, with her own family around her, she would find it easier to relate to her lover's mother. This time they would be doing things *her* way, which would give her confidence, which in turn would make her more relaxed, which would make her kinder. She hoped. She and Bridget might even establish some kind of rapport that could be built on back in Orta. But, best of all, she would have Luke under her own roof, and in her own bed.

Nico had been invited, but Jacquie heard, with a mixture of relief and disappointment, that he would be spending Easter in Rome. He was giving her no end of trouble. Every time she retreated into her thoughts, she found him there. It was hardly surprising that they got along so well. She was quite like her mother, and he was, he said, *au fond*, quite like his father, so the genes and general dispositions were compatible and in place, which was all very sweet – and totally unworkable. If only she could stop thinking about him. If only his engagement were more secure, and heartfelt. Had that been the case, he would dutifully have taken her out to dinner in January and nothing would have come of it. Instead, they had been drawn to one another, seen each other again and again, until they had been together too much. She felt close to him; he made her laugh, he made her warm. It was worse than disappointing: it was devastating. So it was good he wasn't coming for Easter, and completely miserable too.

Dara collected Luke and Bridget from the airport on Easter Thursday so that Marina could bake scones and serve them hot from the oven. She would always have done this for visitors, yet felt herself competing with Maria. The house was pristine, and Natalie was also working in the kitchen, tidying around her. When they heard the car pull up, she squeezed Marina's arm. 'Sock it to her, sweetie.'

Bridget walked into the house as if she were visiting an interesting chapel, looking up at the ceilings and taking big steps, like someone deciding which pew to sit in. They followed, waiting to see where she would sit. Marina patted a few cushions on the couch, told Dara to bring the suitcases upstairs, and asked Jacquie to put on the kettle, though the water had already boiled three times. She was so busy issuing instructions that she was unaware of a figure hovering behind her, and when she turned to rush to the kitchen, she bumped into him.

'Well, hello, you,' said Luke.

'I almost forgot you were coming,' she said, laughing.

He tried to hustle her into the study, but got short shrift. 'Later. I've got to get your mother her tea!'

In the kitchen, Kitt was sitting at the table, leafing through a magazine.

'Kitt, what are you doing?' Marina asked, exasperated.

'Waiting for tea.'

'So stop waiting and do something! Take one of these trays inside. Jacquie, bring the cake.'

The four women filed into the sitting-room, each carrying something.

'Goodness. What a procession,' said Bridget. 'And so much food. One shouldn't make a fuss on Holy Thursday. This is the day of Christ's Agony in the Garden, the day of His Betrayal. We should be fasting.'

Marina glanced at Natalie. *I am calm. I am centred. I am reasonable.*

'Also the day of the Last Supper,' said Luke. 'Let's eat.'

Bridget, eyeing the sponge cake, made no further protest.

Kitt put down the tray, poured herself a cup of tea and sat down. Thankfully, she did not put her feet on the table, but she did not escape those sharp eyes. 'My,' said Bridget, 'you must be the rude one.'

Marina almost melted into the ground.

Natalie turned on her. 'Is that what you call her?'

Marina glared at Luke. *Is that what you called her?*

'You shouldn't take the first cup,' Bridget went on. 'You should take the last. You're the youngest. You wait the longest. Didn't your mother teach you that?'

'Ma,' said Luke, 'nose back in place. Sorry, Natalie.'

'Actually,' said Marina, 'when *we* were growing up, the youngest always went first.'

Kitt and Natalie gaped at her.

'That must have been a very peculiar household,' said Bridget, as if she wouldn't expect otherwise. Marina felt Carlotta in the room, *somewhere*, looking down on this.

Luke moved to the bay window, where, with cup and saucer in one hand, he leafed through a glossy book about the English Market. Marina still admired his detachment; the way his mother's fluctuating sanity didn't bother him.

'What nice scones,' Bridget said unexpectedly. 'Do you have a Maria too?'

'I make them myself, Bridget,' said Marina. 'It's a lovely recipe, with wheatgerm. It gives them extra crunch.'

'Maria makes the *best* scones. And she's Italian. She didn't know what I meant when I first tried to explain. If it weren't for Carlotta, we'd still be eating rock buns.'

'Can I have one?' Kitt asked warily.

Marina did a double-take. Poor child. Bridget had been in the house all of twenty minutes and she'd already brought about a change in Kitt. The old bag probably terrified her. 'Of course you can, pet,' she said. 'Help yourself.'

Kitt stared. 'Did you call me "pet"?'

Marina lifted her teacup. 'Mmm, think so.'

Flashing her big wide eyes, Kitt took a scone and set about buttering it.

'Thank you,' Bridget said to her.

Kitt looked up, knife in hand. 'You're welcome,' she said cautiously, with a confused glance at Marina.

'No, no, dear. That is what *you* should say. To Marina. "Thank you for the scone."'

'It's fine, Kitt,' said Marina. 'Just enjoy it.'

'She'll never learn, you know, with that attitude,' said Bridget. 'You must be firm with youngsters.'

*Oh, sweet Jesus,* Marina thought. It felt like they'd been in there for a week. All of them. In that room. Having scones and tea. Like in the parlour at school. Maybe they'd be there for ever, getting lessons in etiquette. She looked to the man she loved, standing in the bay window with his book, in his gorgeous linen jacket and pale green trousers, his deliciously long fingers turning the pages with a kind of reverence. He might have been in another country such was his apparent ignorance of the tension in the room behind him.

Kitt was trying to be invisible, her shoulders rounded so much that she'd become concave, but Bridget wouldn't let her off. 'I know just what you need,' she said regally. '*You* need Carlotta. She'll knock you into shape in no time, just like she knocked Maria into shape. By Monday, she'll have put manners on you, young lady.'

Four sets of eyes widened. Four heads looked up. Even Natalie ignored this slight to her daughter and stared at

Marina, who turned to Luke and said, 'By Monday? What's this, Luke?'

'Hmm?'

'Carlotta . . . Monday?'

'Oh, yes, she can only stay until Monday night, I'm afraid.'

'Stay . . . where?'

He looked up. 'Here. She's arriving on a later flight this evening.'

Marina stood up abruptly, then didn't know what to do with herself, so she went to the kitchen, where she paced, rubbing her forehead, thinking, How? How? What had she missed?

Luke came looking for her. His eyes brightened as he approached her, but she stopped him in his tracks. 'Carlotta is coming here?'

He frowned. 'You didn't know?'

'I had no idea! In fact, I'm not even aware that I invited her. Sorry – correction: I know very well that I did *not* invite her!'

'But . . . you said all of us.'

'Yes – all of you. *Your* family. You and Nico and your mother. I've nowhere to put Carlotta!'

'But where were you going to put Nico?'

'On a camp bed in the sitting-room. Carlotta will need a room. And I have Matthew coming. I'll have to put him on a floor somewhere.'

'God, I'm sorry. I misunderstood. When Carlotta heard the plans, she sort of assumed she was included. So did I. I didn't realize it would be difficult.'

'You *should* have realized! Why would anyone assume she'd be coming? I mean, is she related to you? Is she attached to you – is that it? Is there some invisible cord running between the two of you that I can't see?'

'Marina, calm down. I thought we'd discussed it. It made sense.'

'It doesn't make any sense!' she hissed, speaking so quickly the words ran one into the other. 'She has a daughter, hasn't she? And a beautiful home! She isn't destitute!' It came out in such a screech that Luke jumped back. 'I mean, come on! I was hoping to have some time with you and Bridget and my kids. Proper family time.'

'Natalie and Kitt aren't family.'

'They *live* here.'

'Nor is Matthew.'

'That's low, Luke. Matthew is coming to see his daughter.'

'All right, I'm sorry. But I genuinely thought it was an amalgamation of both our households. Like a house party.'

Marina flapped her arms. 'She *isn't* a member of your household!'

He recoiled. 'She may not live with us, but –'

'I just wanted to have some time with you without her breathing down my neck. Is that too much to ask?'

'I thought you liked her well enough.'

'Well, I don't! In fact, I don't like her at all!'

'Really? Marina, I had no idea you felt this way.'

'If you'd been paying attention, you *would* have. Luke, she's always there when I'm in Italy. We can't get away from her. And now she's going to be *here*. Am I not entitled to spend time with my partner without his appendage coming along?' She was snapping and shouting and it felt great. 'I'll have to get into a whole different gear. She has such ruddy high expectations.'

'But she's so excited about seeing you.'

'Bull*shit*! She's delighted she's not letting *you* out of her sight!'

Everything was coming out now. The green-eyed monster, and all her other demons. Her current hormone levels were not conducive to a more measured reaction, and she didn't give a damn. This was the kind of release she needed.

Luke sat at the table, evidently confused. Marina closed her eyes, her fists clenched. Damn that woman! She was causing havoc and she hadn't even arrived yet!

'Why didn't you tell me?' he asked.

'Tell you what – how to run your home? That she should be removed when I come over? I hoped you'd notice. I hoped you'd handle it in your own way.'

'Perhaps I could ask her to stay in a hotel. Or that guest-house down the road.'

'Don't be stupid, that would be horrible for her. We'll fit her in somewhere. I just wish you hadn't presumed upon me.' She made her way to the door. 'In fact, you know what, Luke? I wish you hadn't wanted her to come.'

'Maybe I didn't,' he said, when she had left the room.

Carlotta arrived at seven, greeting Marina as though she were the only other sentient being on earth. She seemed genuinely excited about being in Ireland again. She had been there before. With Luke. They had toured the west together ten years back. Everything was 'sweet' – the house, the fireplace, the stove in the kitchen.

Marina managed to rise above her anger. She had to be forthright, and insanely welcoming. Carlotta's own methods were, after all, the most effective. But Natalie and Jacquie, and even Kitt, were sullen. 'Be nice to her,' Marina whispered to them in the kitchen, 'or it'll make me look bad. And, to be fair, she doesn't know she isn't welcome here. That's Luke's fault, so don't take it out on her.'

As they moved into the dining room, Marina took pleasure in telling everyone where to sit, putting Carlotta between Kitt and Dara. 'Bridget, are you warm enough there?'

'Don't fret, *carina*,' Carlotta said. 'Bridget is fine, aren't you, darling?'

'I'm not fretting, Carlotta, I'm simply looking after my guest, same as I look after all my guests.'

'Oh, do you entertain a lot?'

'*Loads*,' said Jacquie.

'I can see why,' said Luke. 'This house lends itself to it, don't you think, Carlotta?'

'I suppose that depends on whom you are entertaining,' she replied, with a low chuckle, trying to make a joke. She sounded like a man.

With Natalie tight on her heels, Marina stomped out to the kitchen. '"Don't fret", indeed!' She pointed towards the dining room. 'Can you see now? Can you? Can you see what I've been dealing with?'

'We are calm,' Natalie said. 'We are centred.' She took the vegetable dishes from the oven: potato gratin, baked fennel, and parsnips with mustard and honey glaze.

Marina looked at them disconsolately. 'I'm trying too hard, amn't I? We should be having bangers and mash.'

'That woman!' Jacquie came through, carrying plates. 'Now the smoked salmon is "sweet", and our plates are sweet. She's so frigging condescending!'

'And we know what that's about, don't we?' said Natalie, in her yoga-teaching voice. 'People who are condescending are only trying to make themselves feel better about their own inadequacies. We should feel sorry for her.'

Jacquie glanced at her mother and back at Natalie. 'I give you two days, Nat. We'll see then how you're fixed on the feeling-sorry front.'

Natalie giggled. 'Next thing she'll be bunking down on your bedroom floor, Marina, beside you and Luke.'

'Why would she be on the floor,' Marina asked, flatly, 'when she could be in the bed with us? Here,' she handed Jacquie a plate. 'This one's for Madam Melodrama.'

'Melanoma, more like.'

As the evening went on, the three became giddier every time they coincided in the kitchen. When Natalie was dishing out the dessert – a failed soufflé – Marina sighed. 'If I must have airs and graces and attempt to show off my culinary prowess, things are bound to go wrong and lemon soufflés are bound to flop.'

'It's fine,' said Jacquie, 'it's just a little shy.' They went through to the dining room.

'Ah,' said Carlotta, 'dessert before cheese?'

Bridget dropped her chin towards her bowl. 'Did you . . .'

Marina rolled her eyes. Undercook it? Overcook it? Forget the lemons?

'. . . know that the longest corridor in Europe is in Cork?'

'Did this collapse?' Kitt asked, scowling at her pudding.

Natalie and Marina said, 'No,' and 'Yes,' simultaneously.

'Soufflé is, of course, rather difficult,' said Carlotta.

Marina gestured discreetly at Natalie, holding her thumb and forefinger half a centimetre apart to indicate how small she'd been made to feel, but instead of eliciting sympathy, it made Natalie snort, which set Jacquie off. She covered her mouth with her napkin and seemed to cough. Marina's eyes watered.

'What's with you guys?' Dara asked.

Luke's jaw was set.

'Darling, do eat up,' Carlotta said to Bridget. 'We're waiting for the cheese.'

'In the mental hospital,' said Bridget.

'We're waiting for cheese in the mental hospital,' said Kitt. 'Huh?'

'It's beginning to feel like it,' Jacquie muttered.

Dara, who alone had managed to keep up with Bridget, said, 'Yeah, that's right. The longest corridor in Europe is in the old mental hospital, but it's being converted into apartments now. It's a huge building.'

'I imagine you must have a lot of mental problems in this country,' Carlotta said.

'I'm sorry?' said Marina.

'Being an island,' Carlotta explained, 'with such a small population, there must have been a lot of, you know, inbreeding.'

This time Dara snorted, and Jacquie had to bite every part of her mouth to stop herself laughing out loud, but Marina was stung. Luke caught her eye, as if to say, No, I have not told her about your mother and her cousin. 'Oh, absolutely,' she said suddenly. 'We're all half mad in this country, but we do *so* enjoy our inbreeding!'

'Marina,' Luke said reproachfully.

Carlotta blushed.

'I don't like poured cream,' said Kitt. 'Why isn't it whipped?'

'*I*'m not half mad,' said Bridget.

Marina was almost asleep when Luke got into bed behind her. He'd had to get his mother a drink and a hot-water bottle, which took longer than usual because she and Carlotta said the rosary together before going to bed.

He pulled her against him, kissing her shoulder. 'Don't you see,' he said quietly, 'that she knows, this time, there's no going back for me?'

'Who? What?'

'Carlotta.'

She turned to face him. He got it. Had he always got it?

'It's panicking her,' he said. 'That's why she's a little overbearing.'

'A little? Tonight was mild, Luke. When you're at work in Orta and she's in full flight – I flounder.'

'You'd never flounder.'

'I do. It's been so difficult, and overbearing is *not* the word. Bullying, more like.'

'Hardly.'

'People always say that about the bullying word. "Oh, hardly." Just because she isn't beating me up doesn't mean it isn't bullying. I know all the tricks – over-enthusiastic and completely insincere admiration, while simultaneously undercutting me. Sorry to sound like a teacher, but disrespect is bullying, and she has never given me the least respect.'

'So she can be a bit sharp, but put yourself in her place. I mean, you have to think – we can look forward to growing old together, to looking after each other's disabilities, counting each other's pills, feeding each other mush . . .'

She chuckled. 'Is that what this is about? A relationship in geriatrics?'

'No, but that's when it'll be important to have someone. My mother will be long gone and you and I'll be living happily here, there, wherever, but where will Carlotta be?'

'I honestly don't care. It isn't as if she has no one else.'

'But she has, by default, become part of our family and that can't last, or I imagine that's what she thinks right now. Sooner or later, Carlotta's going to be very much on her own, and that's as scary for me as it is for her.'

'So tell your son to provide her with loads of grandchildren!'

'That's not the same, is it? And, look, how do you think I'd have coped with Ma if it weren't for Carlotta's support? She's been my sanity, and a good friend too.'

Marina put her hands to the face she couldn't see. 'You know, if it weren't for your mother and Carlotta, I probably wouldn't love you as much as I do.'

'It's good to hear you say that, because I won't leave Carlotta out in the cold.'

'Is this your way of asking me if she can live with us in perpetuity? Because I'm not even sure that *I*'m going to live with you in perpetuity.'

He drew back. 'Eh? Why the hell not?'

'For one thing, you haven't asked.'

'I didn't think I had to. I thought it was a given – but, hey, I'm asking.'

'I haven't made up my mind,' she said primly.

'You need a formal proposal, is that it?'

She thumped him playfully. 'I don't need any such thing.'

'But if I don't propose, how will I get you to marry me?'

'I . . . you . . . *what*?'

He kissed her nose. 'You haven't thought about it?'

'Thought about it? Luke, I have the dress bought! And it's *gorgeous*, and absolutely gi*nor*mous! It was only thirty-five thousand euro, and it's got, like, sixteen skirts and a train and, oh, the train is fifteen metres long, but that'll be okay, because I'm going to have, like, *loads* of bridesmaids. I thought they could line up, you know, and carry the train between them, like a carpet; and as for venues, well, I was thinking maybe Clooney's place on Lake Como, I mean, he's almost your neighbour. A bit of arse-licking should do it.'

Luke rolled her on to him, laughing, but she rolled right off again. 'And I want you to wear a peach-coloured suit, shiny, like, and –'

'Whereas what *I* had in mind,' he said, rolling her back on to him, 'was a tent in the Sahara with a couple of camels for witnesses.'

She stopped babbling. 'That sounds . . . perfect.'

'We'll get married, then? Have we at least reached consensus on that?'

'Don't get ahead of yourself. I mean, you're not much of a bet, are you? One broken marriage, several failed relationships –'

'Don't forget the interesting mother.'

'Seriously,' she said. 'Does it have to be marriage?'

'No, but I'd like it to be. And we need it. Think how often you've slipped away from me – long ago, and again at Marrakech, and again in Essaouira.'

'You need a rope, not a marriage.'

'Please, Marina.'

'All right, but not yet and not all the time. We can do it our way, can't we?'

'At the moment we don't have much choice.'

'And this has to stay between us until further notice.'

'Whatever.'

'And we get to keep our houses and pensions separate, right?'

'Christ, is there a lawyer under the bed? Because it might be quite pleasant to make love right now, you know, perhaps lend a certain depth to this significant life-changing moment. Or are you going to whip out the old pre-nup from under the pillow?'

She snorted. 'Of course I'm not going to whip it out from under the pillow! Pff! It's over there on the dresser.'

'Marina?'

'Yes?'

'*Finally*. I got her to say, "Yes."'

Jacquie tossed. And turned. Tossed again. Threw off her duvet, pulled it back on because her feet were cold, and stared upwards for as long as she could stay still. The mere mention of his name. She was done for; hammered; taken. Hit her like a shock when Luke said, 'Nico sends his best.' His best. Nico. Sends to her. He could have been there, with her. Instead he went to Rome. For the sake of form, she wondered, or because he missed his fiancée? Or to do *her* a favour? Just as well, just as well, just as well, she thought. Must stop thinking, she thought. One kiss, that was all. Deep, deep, but just one. The rings of Saturn. White, not pink. So deep, and demanding. Carnal. The rings of Saturn. The way it was always easy, and good. The way he didn't come for Easter when he could have. How could that not be significant?

Another toss. Another turn. Damn, damn, damn, she thought.

Marina stood in her kitchen, clearing the sink and watching Bridget kneeling on a mat by the flowerbed, shoving the trowel into the dirt. No doubt she thought the garden was a disgrace . . . No. That would be Carlotta's reaction, not necessarily Bridget's. Besides, the garden was beyond reproach. Marina had pulled every damn weed before they had arrived – except for the one Bridget had found.

Marina squeezed washing-up liquid into her dishcloth. Instead of having Bucks' Fizz for breakfast, she was wiping up grease and crumbs. The night before, in a fit of giggling, she had agreed to marry Luke. It still made her chuckle. On the one hand, it seemed she had gone completely mad, while on the other, it was the only sane thing to do. They were, in effect, already married. When Luke had stepped into Hamid's shop, he had also stepped into her and become her second self. Might as well do the job properly. Buck's Fizz wasn't necessary. 'Jesus,' she said out loud, 'I'm getting hitched again.' She swung round to make sure no one could have heard her.

She looked again at Bridget: her future mother-in-law. As she watched her gardening she was reminded of her own father, when he had arrived in France after his stroke and set to in their overgrown garden with his one good arm. Wiping her hands, Marina went outside. 'How are you getting on, Bridget?'

'I used to garden, you know,' she said. 'You'd miss it in Italy. Oh, they have the weather, but the soil is so dry, not good and muddy like this. I do keep a few plants on the terrace, but it's not the same, is it, as getting your hands dirty?'

'Not the same at all,' said Marina, thinking this could be it – a common point of interest. They could talk gardens. Carlotta, surely, had never in her life got her hands dirty. Marina could even take Bridget to visit some public gardens. Fota, for instance. Yes, they should do that. Take her there that weekend and, with a bit of luck, bore Carlotta to death. 'Be careful you don't tire yourself,' she said, going back inside. With a kick in her step, she ran upstairs to ask Luke, her fiancé, if his mother would enjoy Fota. As she opened her bedroom door, he was standing by the closet in boxer shorts and a shirt, buttoning his cuff. 'I was just thinking,' she said, coming into the room.

Carlotta was sitting on the end of the bed, still in her silk dressing-gown, arms languidly crossed over her knees.

Luke looked over. 'You were thinking?'

'Excuse me, Carlotta?'

'Yes, yes.' Carlotta uncrossed her legs. 'I must dress. It's getting late.'

As she left, Marina turned to Luke. 'What's going on?'

He closed his other cuff. 'We were talking about going out for dinner. Carlotta would like to invite us. Kind of her, seeing as there are – how many of us? Eight, is it?'

'But this is my room. And you aren't dressed.'

He looked down. 'I'm decent enough, aren't I?'

'How long had she been here?' She kept her voice low and measured; Carlotta must not hear them arguing. 'What were the two of you up to?'

'Oh, come on, as if we'd be getting up to anything here.'

'Why? Does it happen somewhere else?'

Luke reached for his trousers. 'Of course not.'

'So what was she doing in my room?'

He gave her a look. 'Nothing.'

'With all her prissy manners, she doesn't have the basic decency to respect my privacy. This is my bedroom!'

'I think we've established that this is your room,' he said drily. 'Marina, you're behaving like a jealous shrew. Don't you trust me?'

'I don't know. Should I?'

'I'd love to say you're incredibly beautiful when you're angry, but you just look scary.'

'So would you if you came in and found me in my knickers chatting to Matthew.'

That hit a chord. Luke blinked. 'Point taken.'

'Ding bloody dong!'

'Yeah, but you can't trust a man with an underdressed woman, whereas Carlotta, well, she's . . . you know.'

'So she often wanders in, does she, when you're getting dressed?'

'I suppose . . . sometimes.'

Marina stood, staring at him.

'All right,' he conceded, raising his hands. 'I know things have to change, but it can't be done overnight. It'll take an adjustment for me to notice and for her to back off. It's just the way things have always been,' he said, coming over to her. 'It isn't meant to upset you.'

'Then you need to cop on to yourself! When I got involved with you, Luke, I didn't expect your ex-lover to be all over me like chickenpox.'

'Easy,' he said, and his tone had changed. 'She isn't all over you, Marina. She is, as often as she can be, wherever my mother is, but since it bothers you so much, here's a plan: why don't I move back here with my mother? I'd do it, if it would make you happy. Then you and I could look after Ma together.' He held her eye. 'What do you think?'

He knew very well what she thought. She didn't reply. He had made his point.

Kitt found it mesmerizing – the jingle-jangle, the snaking arms, the undulating midriff. 'Please, please teach me,' she begged. 'It's so cool.'

'So pay for the classes and come along,' said Jacquie.

'But that'd be a waste of money when you can teach me.'

Jacquie, wearing a long skirt with a scarf tied tight round her hips, went to change the CD. Every time she moved, the coins sewn on to the scarf tinkled.

'Can I watch?'

Go away, Jacquie was thinking, but she nodded. She'd moved the table in the bay window, which offered a perfect space to dance. Kitt sat watching, her hands trying to imitate Jacquie's movements. It was so girlish, and so strangely obedient, that it worked. 'All right,' said Jacquie. 'Get up.'

Kitt was wearing low-slung jeans and a small T-shirt. Jacquie tied a scarf round her hips. 'Over here. Arms up. Now . . .'

When the others came back from a walk, they stood in the doorway. The girls, unaware that they had an audience, were giggling as Kitt tried to get her hips to move independently of the rest of her. Jacquie shimmied swiftly across the floor, everything rattling. When Kitt tried to imitate her, the two of them cracked up.

'Wow,' said Luke. 'Impressive.'

The girls turned. Jacquie rushed to switch off the music.

'Is this appropriate on Good Friday?' Bridget asked. 'Music and dancing?'

'I'll get tea on the go,' said Marina.

Carlotta followed her to the kitchen. 'Perhaps I should help.'

'You could do a tray, thanks.'

'I keep forgetting there is no Maria.'

'I prefer to do things myself.'

'I must say,' said Carlotta, 'Kitt has excellent rhythm, don't you think? A real instinct for that music. Very impressive, as Luke said.'

Bitch, thought Marina. Carlotta knew very well he'd been referring to Jacquie.

As Carlotta sniffed her way round the kitchen, looking into mugs and even returning some to the shelves before inspecting another (objectionable tea stains?), Marina struggled to retaliate. Getting at Jacquie, even indirectly, was the easiest way to hurt her, but it was impossible to bite back without sounding competitive. She wanted to say, 'Actually, Jacquie is the best in her class,' or 'Actually, Jacquie's excellent sense of rhythm has been commented on by her teacher.' The urge again – she hadn't had it for years – to sink to that level, in the meagre hope of regaining ground. Instead, she tried to take comfort from Carlotta's insecurities. Hearing Luke compliment Jacquie was obviously so challenging to her that she had been forced to take a dig at Marina. Trouble was, she was so very good at it. It was a talent too many people enjoyed – coming up with slicing comments off-the-cuff. An art form, Marina decided. A cruel one, but an art just the same. It made her weary. Did she really have to tackle it again, to go back to that low, low place, from which it was so hard to rise?

The harsh fact remained: bullying worked.

Afternoon tea was a repeat of the day before. Bridget reminded everyone, lest they had forgotten, about Maria's marvellous scones and that it was Carlotta who had made them possible. Luke tried to redress the balance by saying, 'As far as I'm concerned, these are the best scones I've ever had,' but that served further to depress Marina. Her worth had been reduced to a few grams of wheatgerm.

Matthew arrived on the Saturday, coming through the airport like a lumberjack on a mission. Marina had insisted on picking him up. Anything to get out of the house.

'So my loving daughter didn't come to greet me,' he said, on the way home.

'She's gone to the cinema with friends and I don't blame her. She's been set upon by Bridget and Carlotta. They're trying to put manners on her, and I am delighted to report that, thus far, they have failed. Otherwise they would crow.'

'I can't wait to meet these women.'

Marina smiled. 'And Luke. You'll like him. You have nothing in common, but you'll like him.'

'I take it Natalie hasn't had much luck finding an apartment?'

'They're all horrendously expensive, and right now, I'm just as glad. I don't know how we'd have got through the last two days without her and Kitt. They're diluting the tension. I've never been so grateful for Kitt's self-obsession.'

Matthew also had a dramatic effect on the house-party. He had no sides, no agenda. He was so cheery he made everyone else relax.

Bridget was instantly charmed. Matthew's low, husky voice rather did it for her, and he was a source of loads of useless information that she could stack away in her filing-cabinet brain. He told her that moose can sometimes be seen crossing streets in Anchorage; that Alaskans refer to the rest of America as 'the Lower 48'; and that the state can grow giant vegetables, like eighty-five-pound cabbages, because of the long summer days. Bridget drank it all in, asked questions, and didn't once lose her train of thought.

Carlotta also, when seated next to Matthew at dinner, seemed to find this slightly unrefined man good company. He had no grasp of the arts, appeared to have read no books, but he could talk shipping. 'After all,' he said, 'I come from a town called Anchorage.'

Later on, Marina wandered alone to the end of her long garden to enjoy the spring evening and a few moments' peace. The birds chattered, someone was mowing a lawn in the dimming light, and the purple clematis on the shed had already sprouted.

Matthew ambled down the path towards her. 'You never said she was beautiful,' he said.

'Who? Carlotta? Have you been flirting with her?'

'Just trying to keep her sweet.'

'Thanks.'

'But if they give you any more gyp,' he said, 'bash 'em. That's what lads do.'

'Tempting, I'm sure.'

'Or ask Carlotta to repeat herself every time she has a go. Then she has to say it again when everyone's attention is on her.'

'That might actually work.' She gazed up at the pale sky, breathing in the evening.

'This is so great,' Matthew said softly. 'I love being here.'

'Don't you miss your beloved Anchorage?'

'Not really.' He pushed pebbles about with his boot. 'You know, Reen, Kitt's Gas-station Moment was a real turning point for me. While I was laid up in plaster, I had plenty of time to dwell on it and it's kind of weird the way so much of my past came together in that one event: Ireland, Natalie,

Kitt and you.' He got down on his hunkers and pulled at some grass. 'And I realized that my life since then – since you all left it – had been pared down to almost nothing. Lads, beers, bears and affairs. Good money, a nice fourplex, great sports, but anything of substance had been whittled away, until it all came back to me in that one phone call from Cashel.' He looked up at her. 'Everything flipped over. Now Kitt talks to me when I call. There's no connection, not yet, but she talks to me without asking for money. And when I have time off, I've got somewhere to go, somewhere other than interesting glaciers, people to visit other than my barmy family . . . The fact is, I'm happier than I've been in a long time, and that's down to you.'

Marina smiled.

He stood up. 'You know I love you, don't you?' She touched his arm. 'I mean, you were always pretty major in the scheme of things and now you've come back centre stage again, and it's like we're family and I just hope you know how much it means to me.'

'Yesterday,' she said vaguely, 'Jacquie danced with Kitt. I wish you'd seen them. They were so beautiful.'

'Jacquie's very special.'

'So is Kitt.'

'We're lucky, I guess.'

Marina looked back at the house. Luke was standing by the double doors, watching them.

Later that night, when everyone had gone to bed, Marina stood by the kitchen table. She had asked everyone to give her what they had so she could lay it out for the morning. Easter eggs were spread from one end of the table to the other. It looked great: Italian extravagances, American atrocities, big eggs and small ones, humble chocolate bunnies, ribbons and chicks, cotton wool and painted eggs. She smiled. 'And now we are nine.'

'Can I help?' Kitt asked, coming into the kitchen the next day. Jacquie, Marina and Natalie were rushing around, getting lunch. They stopped. 'What did you say?' asked Marina.

Kitt looked sheepish. 'It's scary in there.'

Marina gave her a short nod. 'That's why we're hiding in here.'

Kitt smiled.

'What you need to do, Marina,' Natalie said, in her haughtiest voice, 'you see, what you need to do is marry him.'

'Is that so?'

'Yes, it makes perfect sense. She's trying to knock you out of the picture, so marry him and secure your holding.'

'What – you think I should ask him over Sunday lunch?' Marina asked.

'Might liven things up,' said Jacquie. 'Kitt, can you get a jug of water?'

'Where's the jug?'

'Jesus, you'll be asking next where the water comes from!'

'Here's a dilemma,' said Marina. 'Who do I ask to carve? Matthew or Luke?'

'Mum! You'll ask Dara!'

In the dining room, things were certainly stressful for Kitt.

'Do you get a lot of schoolwork, dear?' Carlotta asked her.

Kitt sighed. 'No,' she said, pointedly. 'I'm in Transition Year. We do creative stuff, like fashion shows and musicals, and we go out on work experience and take on community projects instead of doing exams.'

Carlotta was disconcerted – schooling that didn't involve studying? 'How . . . interesting.'

'Yeah, it's great,' said Kitt, warming to her subject. 'It's an Irish thing. You get to do, you know, really cool stuff, like orienteering, and we even went surfing and we're going to Paris and –'

'Yes, yes, but what of your studies? Our students, in Italy, work *so* hard. They cannot even stop at weekends.'

'There's plenty of that in other years,' said Marina. 'Transition Year gives students time to discover themselves a little.'

'What a very strange system.'

Natalie was staring at Luke's mother. Bridget tended to dive into her food, and eat and eat until it was gone, at which point she looked up to see where she was.

Matthew and Luke were talking about Ireland's economy, and how they'd both left the country to find work, thereby missing its economic boom.

'But is it not true,' said Carlotta, 'that Ireland's economic success relies heavily on migrant workers?'

'Same as every other economy,' Dara muttered.

'Oh,' Marina said, over him, 'couldn't have done it without the immigrants, because we're, like, completely useless. Couldn't organize a piss-up in a brewery.'

'Did you know,' Matthew said loudly to Bridget, 'that they've found a new breed of leopard in Sumatra? A new Cloudy Leopard. It's so shy, nobody knew it existed.'

Marina could feel Luke's eyes on her. Odd how he reacted to her sarcasm but not Carlotta's. His silent reproach made her lose track of the conversation until she heard Carlotta say, 'I have a proposition for you, Kitt. I will invite you to my house in Orta for the summer holidays.'

There was a general gasp, which concealed Jacquie's horrified grunt.

'This would be good for you, to experience another country.'

'I've experienced other countries,' said Kitt. 'We lived in Spain.'

'You lived in Málaga, surrounded by tourists. I am speaking of Italy. There is no comparison. You could learn so much.' She glanced down at Kitt's plate, her knife and fork askew, and brought them together. 'You have a very beautiful mother and, with a little refinement, you too might be beautiful. Although you would have to stay with Luke. He has a bigger home.' She leant sideways to catch Luke's eye at the end of the table. She wasn't used to being so far away from him. 'That will be all right, won't it, darling?'

'Sweetie,' Matthew said to Marina, 'would you be a honey and pass the butter?'

Luke cleared his throat. 'Of course. You must all come.'

Easter Monday was hot – a day for the beach, not gardens – so they set off early for Ballyrisode, one of Marina's favourite spots. Natalie volunteered gamely to go with the Italian party, but when they arrived at the cove, she tumbled out of Luke's hired car with crazed eyes and ran down to the sea.

It was a short strand on a squiggle of coast, where creamy sand curved round rocky outcrops, and the water, when it came in, sliding between the fingers of rock that stretched into the bay, was the colour of blue ice. A large island-rock was parked in the middle of the cove.

'It's like Greece,' said Matthew.

Carlotta smiled at him. 'Yes, the sea is just like the Aegean.'

'Not when you get into it, it isn't,' said Dara.

They unpacked the cars and carried their baskets and rugs on to the beach, setting themselves up next to a high rock at the foot of a low, grassy headland.

Luke and Matthew took off like boys, clambering across a belt of rocks that pushed out into the bay.

'Look,' Natalie said to Marina, 'the two men in your life are bonding. Or trying to. I think they're finding it all a bit difficult.'

'How so?'

'They have different bits of you, don't they? Luke has the future, Matthew has the past, and they both want what the other's got.'

Reaching the end of the promontory, the two men sat down on a large rock. 'Let's go and annoy them,' said Marina, 'before they bond too much.'

They hopped across the pools, and as they climbed up to the men, Luke reached for Marina. She loved the squeeze of his hand, the way his arm took her weight as she lowered herself to his side.

'This is spectacular,' said Matthew. 'I swear, Marina, you've given Ireland back to me.'

Luke nodded. 'That's what I said.'

'Me too,' said Natalie. 'I know I'm English, but somehow, when I got here, I felt like I'd finally arrived home.'

They sat for a while, in the warm sun, listening to the sea flap against the lower rocks. On the other side of the bay, on a slip of sand, red cattle stood looking at the sea as if they'd missed a ferry and it wasn't even their fault.

'I'd better get lunch on the go,' said Natalie. 'Come on, Matthew, lend a hand.'

When they'd gone back, Luke lay over Marina to kiss her. She jumped. 'We're in full view of everyone!'

'I'd make a wild guess that your children have come to terms with the fact that we've gone beyond the hand-holding stage. Anyway, they can't see where my hand is.'

She put her arm round his neck and made him kiss her again. Then he sat up and looked back towards the beach. Carlotta was paddling, carrying her gold sandals behind her back, her white skirt held up, a loose gold belt round her hips.

'What do you see,' Marina asked, 'when you look at her?'

'Someone very lonely. And I wonder what the hell I'm going to do about it. It was easier before I met you. There were two of us in it.' They watched as Matthew came alongside Carlotta to walk with her. 'She has a way of alienating men,' Luke said. 'She tries to mould them into being her. It never works.'

Marina sniggered. 'Can you imagine her trying to mould that hunk of frontier brawn into Italian elegance?'

He smiled.

'Why didn't you marry her?'

'Because she wasn't you. Because I knew you had to be there, somewhere in the world, and I figured I had as much right to one successful love affair as the next person. I'd done the marriage, the divorce, the kids, the affairs, the sex, even the ongoing interminable relationship, and even though one miserable affair after another led back to Carlotta, I knew there had to be something else. That's why I'd really like you to marry me.'

'Does it matter that much to you?'

'Yes. I'd like to be able to say I got it right in the end.'

'You sad romantic.'

There was a screech. Everyone turned.

Kitt, in a bikini, was running towards the water. 'Oh, she isn't!' said Marina, sitting up. 'It'll be perish –'

But she did. With a huge splash, Kitt threw herself into the near-Arctic waters.

Natalie lifted her arms over her head and clapped. Matthew joined in, as did Luke and Marina, standing on the rocks, and Jacquie went, 'Yay!' Even Bridget clapped, and when Kitt emerged squealing from the freezing water, Jacquie ran down with a big towel and threw it round her like a cloak.

'We'll make this work, my love,' said Luke. 'Yours and mine . . . and hers and theirs.'

And perhaps they were getting there, Marina thought, later that afternoon when she and Carlotta were sitting together watching the others play soccer. Bridget was dozing against the rockface. It was the first day Marina had spent in Carlotta's company that she had actually enjoyed. They had never revisited, not for one moment, their giggles in the middle of the night in the Saharan dunes.

'Why did you do that?' she asked her. 'Invite Kitt to Luke's place.'

Carlotta gazed along the bay, her elegant hand holding her plastic cup in an elegant manner. 'I hate waste, you see. It distresses me that a young life should be so . . .'

'Aimless?'

'Yes. Look at Natalie. So intelligent, and yet with no fulfilment. A shop assistant. So many bad decisions. Her daughter should not end up like that.'

'Natalie was more a victim of circumstance than of her own decisions. She's thriving now, and so is Kitt.'

'But how long has Kitt been in Cork? Seven months? And still she does nothing. Says nothing. Makes nothing of her day.'

'She just jumped into the water, which is more than the rest of us would do.'

'But you know what I mean.'

Marina did know what she meant. There was sincerity in what Carlotta said, a connection almost. Marina didn't even feel that this was some dig at her own failure to make progress with Kitt. Was it too much to assume that Carlotta acknowledged what she had done and simply wanted to join in? She did, after all, have a good heart.

As if reading her mind, Carlotta went on, 'Thank you for

this charming weekend. It was kind of you to extend your invitation to me also, and so very pleasant to be with your family. Cristina, you know, is in Rome with Nico. They have their own lives.'

No audience. No Luke to hear her. This was genuine, and this was where they had to get to – a point of honesty and respect that might, one day, lead to friendship.

Marina wanted to marry the man who had just tripped over his own foot and landed on his shoulder, and when she did so, she wanted to enjoy it. 'Any time, Carlotta. You're welcome here any time.'

# 17

The house was empty. Jacquie dumped her bag on the hall floor. No muffled television. No voices, music, footsteps. It was familiar, this emptiness, from another time. She had hated it then; she needed it now. There was so much to think about, and never any space to do so. Twelve months before she'd had nothing except time to think. Way too much of it and, worst of all, nothing to think about.

But now she had decisions to make. Her boss needed to know about summer holidays. It was easy, really. Jacquie wanted to go to Orta and stay in that apartment and swim in that lake. Her mother was planning to spend most of the summer there, so all Jacquie had to do was decide on dates. She made tea, grabbed some chocolate (Easter had delivered way too much into the house) and pulled a garden chair into the suntrap to the right of the kitchen door. But it was still chilly in the breeze, so she went upstairs for a duvet. She wanted to sit in complete comfort and stare at their garden and decide – not on dates, but on whether or not she should go to Italy at all.

Decide.

Dad, Dad, Dad, she thought, help me get this right.

The decision was close to the surface. It was perfectly clear what she should do. Nico had not sent her a text for a week. It felt so raw not to see his name in her inbox that every minute of every day had become wretched. If she could not live without his text messages, she must not see him again until these feelings passed. He was committed to someone else; he was likely to become her stepbrother; he was the one she must never have, who would probably be in her life for ever. And from where she sat, that felt like a life sentence.

Nico, presumably, had come to the same conclusion. Hence his silence.

She could not go to Orta in the summer. It was the only fair thing to do – for him, her mother, Cristina, and for her own survival. So she would put down dates, any dates, for her holidays and see if her college friend, Katrina, would be interested in taking a charter to Portugal. Spain. Anywhere other than where Nico was and where she wanted to be. Rather than count the days until her return to Orta, she would count the days until she no longer craved him.

She was still there, wrapped up, when she heard her mother get in from covering for Suzanne in the shop for the day. She was chatting to someone. It sounded like Luke.

'There you are,' Marina said, coming out to the patio. 'Look who's here!' And Nico stepped out behind her.

Jacquie stared, too bundled up in the duvet and too low in the deckchair to be able to get to her feet, even if her legs would have held her. 'What the hell?'

'Hello,' he said, with that familiar, and now, she realized, apprehensive gesture – pushing his specs against the bridge of his nose with his middle finger.

'Where did you come from?'

'I decided to come over with Dad,' he said, 'like you told me to.'

'But he isn't here till next week, is he?'

He shrugged. 'So I came ahead.'

'I'll make tea,' said Marina. 'Or coffee? You'd probably prefer coffee.'

'Tea's okay,' said Nico. 'Here I am Irish, not Italian.'

Jacquie chuckled, managed to untangle herself, and got up to kiss him. 'Sorry, but you've never looked more Italian. When were you last in this country, anyway?'

'Probably ten or twelve years ago.'

'That's a disgrace.' She looked past him into the kitchen at her mother, who could hear every word. 'How long are you here for?'

'Ten days. I'm on holiday!' He beamed, as if the holiday concept was a novelty.

Jacquie sat down. 'It really has started, hasn't it? The to-ing and fro-ing. Us going over to you, you guys coming here. Happy families.'

He stood over her, hands in pockets, linen jacket flapping round his wrists.

'You didn't come for Easter,' she said.

'Cristina and me, we had things to do.'

'You missed quite a party.'

'I heard.' He lowered his voice. 'I thought you'd be glad I didn't come.'

'I was.' Jacquie glanced over her shoulder into the kitchen again. 'So why now?'

'You.' He took a few steps towards the low stone wall, then wandered to the right so that he could no longer be seen from the kitchen. 'I thought,' he said, lightly and quietly, 'that I should tell you I haven't been able to think about anyone else for the last five months, and that I know it's complicated, but what the hell am I supposed to do when I had this feeling about you, from that very first day, when I was reading the newspaper and you had purée all over your face?'

She grinned. 'My squirting-brioche moment? *Must* you bring that up?'

Marina came out and placed a tray, with packets of biscuits and tea-stained mugs on the wall. 'At least with you, Nico, I don't feel I have to whip out fresh-baked cakes.'

Jacquie tried to function normally while they had tea, but she was deeply moved, not only by his declaration but by what followed: the three of them sitting together, munching biscuits, as if this was how it was meant to be. Her mother was relaxed, not fussing but treating Nico like one of her own, which he almost was.

Without her mother, Jacquie thought, she would never have met him; because of her mother, she might never have him.

Nico became an unwilling tourist, hiring a car and setting off every morning with Marina's maps and instructions, to Kerry and Baltimore and Kinsale, but ending up, every lunchtime, outside Jacquie's building, ready to whisk her off to a pub. Every evening, they met in town for a drink. They didn't hide in dark pubs where they wouldn't be seen, but they didn't divulge what they were doing either – not that they were doing much, beyond enjoying one another's company and taking in the neat little moves and quirks that make a person dear. Jacquie noted the shape of his fingernails, how much sugar he took in his coffee and the way his eyes went still when he was listening to her; for his part, Nico told her he loved the way she bit the side of her thumb when she was thinking and the way she looked both wild and glamorous when strands of her hair fell loose.

Jacquie was holding tough. His knee was always close to hers but, like his eyes, his arms, his mouth, never close enough. There was already a depth to this, and neither of them could afford to drop any deeper, even though they acknowledged, in everything they did, that they were in freefall. They didn't talk about it much. She didn't see any point. He wanted to let it come, and promised her he could be a very patient man.

'Where will patience get us?'

Nico rolled his tongue under his lower lip. 'Our parents might split up. That would be good for us.'

'I cannot believe you said that.'

'But it's true. We have the rest of our lives to think about. This is more important for us.'

'Quite the opposite!' Jacquie argued. 'We have the rest of our lives to meet someone else. This might be their last chance. Mum will never meet someone like Luke again. She used to say she'd never marry again because losing Dad was too painful and she didn't want to go through anything like that a second time, so if this doesn't work out, she won't even look at another man, and she'll be lonely and wasted for the next thirty years. Coming back to an empty house. Saturday nights watching telly. Going off on dreary holidays by herself. I couldn't bear it, honestly.'

'Me too,' he said, 'I don't like to contemplate how Dad would manage without her, but, Jacquie, every day I find it harder to contemplate living without you.'

Marina was delighted with the way Nico's visit was going. He was witty and warm, and they got on well together. He would be a super stepson. He blended into the slightly mad jumble they lived in and graciously went along with whatever plans they made for him – as when Jacquie insisted on taking him to West Cork that weekend to show him one of their favourite spots.

And so, that Saturday afternoon, on the rock at the foot of Knockatee, the two of them sat, their arms round their knees, facing the sea. Jacquie couldn't help feeling emptied out, even though she was full to her chin with longing, and other erratic emotions. She hoped they could sit in silence and let the landscape do its work, but Nico had not come to Ireland to look at the countryside.

'I wish you would not be so concerned about Cristina,' he said.

'How can I not be? And everything else is stacked up against us too. We need to get past the attraction, Nico.'

'You can't make this go away, you know, because it doesn't suit you.'

'I can try. We can talk ourselves out of it.'

He gave her a doleful look.

'Anything is possible,' she insisted. 'It can be dampened, like a mood. Flattened.'

'You don't think love is bigger than the people it takes?'

'You're Italian. You would have a romantic slant on it.'

'True. But the Irishman in me thinks love is a parasite. Once it's in there, you won't get it out that easily.'

'Stop talking about love! You love Cristina, remember? This, us, is chemistry, that's all. Just like any of those casual affairs you've had.'

He pushed up his spectacles. 'This is not an affair. For five months now this has not been an affair. And it isn't casual either.'

'Whatever it is, giving it up won't kill us.'

'No. Hunger will do that.'

She smiled. 'Sorry. I forgot to bring food, but there's chocolate in my bag.'

After fetching the chocolate, Nico sat right behind her and brought his legs and arms round her. He fed her a square of chocolate, his fingers touching the side of her mouth, and took one himself.

Jacquie stared resolutely at the ocean. '*Must* you breathe into my ear?'

'It's working, isn't it?'

'Nico, please.'

He tipped her back against his chest, kissing her temple. Once again, he had her surrounded, but this time there was nothing for it: she relaxed into him.

A lamb bleated. They were all over the hills, little white dots following their mothers. The sea wasn't glittering or flickering; it seemed, under the grey sky, to be rather dour, waiting to see what would happen with the couple on the rock.

'This was *so* not part of the plan, Nico.'

'Not for me either, but there never is, you know, a plan.'

'I didn't even fancy you in January.'

'I didn't take you seriously at all.'

She laughed.

'Now I like you very much,' he said.

'In case it's slipped your mind, you're engaged, remember? Or maybe we have different interpretations of the word. I must look it up in the dictionary and see if it means the same thing in Italian as it does in English. What is "engaged" in Italian, anyway?'

'*Fidanzamento* – but that's very formal.'

'*Fidanzamento*. Lovely word, but you're not very good at it. I feel for your *fidanz* . . .'

'*Ragazza*. Cristina and I can break up, you know,' he said casually.

'I can't be the cause of your break-up! Can't you see that?'

He rubbed his chin along her cheek. 'All right, but if I promise not to upset your mother's happiness, would you give me a chance?'

'But you can't make that promise. Mum will never be okay with this, Nico – not only because of Cristina, but because there's a big blot in her own family, relatives getting all tangled up in all the wrong ways . . . Mum's pretty cool, but –'

Nico's mouth was working its way along the side of her face. She tried to pull away, to concentrate on the cuddly lambs and not on the lips light on her neck, but she failed and gave in. It was the worst and the best thing she had ever done. They lay back, and he kissed her as if he was taking possession of her, inside and out. The sky curved over them, like a great dome, and the rock beneath them was like the back of a whale. Jacquie felt as if she was riding the ocean on a humpback. The grey sky let loose a solitary drop of rain that plopped on to her eyelid. She jumped, and blinked.

'You look like you're crying,' said Nico.

'I probably should be.'

'Don't say that. Listen, here is my suggestion.'

'Oh, excellent. Someone has a suggestion that'll make this okay?'

'We'll run away to Australia.'

She snorted.

'Why not?' he said.

'Anything else cooking? Plan B, maybe?'

'Time,' he said seriously. 'We see how Luke and Marina get on. Where their affair takes us.'

'And Cristina?'

Nico sat up and looked down into the valley. 'I should tell you about my engagement.'

'I thought you had.'

He shook his head.

She sat up beside him. 'Oh?'

'The whole thing,' he said, not looking at her, 'is a fake.' He fiddled with his watch-strap. 'Cristina is my best friend, like my sister. But the marriage idea, that was the families'. Not so much my parents, but Carlotta's side, and Cristina's father's family. They see us together and, of course, they think, Romance. It must be romance; they must get married. It was never what we wanted.'

'You've never actually been together?'

'Of course we've made love,' he said, sounding more Italian than ever. His accent seemed stronger in Ireland and his mannerisms more foreign. 'But only . . . like that. Because it was good at the time.'

'But why did you go along with the engagement?'

'Because Cristina is with someone else.' He clenched his fist. 'Really together with someone. In love. For two years now. But her family would never accept him. Her father is very conservative, from the south, and he is the mayor in a town in Piedemonte. He wants her to marry a professional like me, a lawyer or doctor, and have a lot of clever children.'

'But Carlotta isn't conservative.'

'She is worse than that – she's ambitious. She wants her daughter to conform, to have a good family environment.'

'But if Cristina is with someone else, whether her family likes him or not, why pretend to be engaged to you?'

'We didn't pretend, but we didn't disagree. This engagement is a presumption. "Of course they'll get married, they've known each other all their lives." That always counts in Italy. We Italians like connections. And we can't pretend not to adore each other, because we do. So we haven't said anything against it because it suits Cristina. She asked me this, that I should go along with it, to take attention off her life in Rome.'

'And her real boyfriend, why won't he do?'

'Because he's an immigrant from Mali, with two kids and a wife.' Nico sighed. 'I wish for her it was different, but what can they do? They live together. If her parents knew, they would be so fucking angry . . .'

'So you're like a foil?'

'She just asked me to go along, not to disillusion them, but it became more than we expected. She is more in love than ever and is finding it hard to leave him, and now Carlotta is pushing us to make an announcement.'

'Why doesn't Cristina just tell her she wants to marry someone else?'

'Because it can't succeed, this affair. He can't abandon his wife, who has no work, no Italian, no relatives. It's hopeless for all of them. So she asked me for a little time. With a fiancé in place, there have been no questions about why she is not finding a husband, dating, bringing home prospective sons-in-law. It has meant she could have this love affair without interference. But in the end she will leave him.'

'And then what happens?'

'*Then* we will marry.'

Jacquie pulled away from him.

Nico smiled and kissed her. 'I don't know what will happen.'

'You're not writing it off, though, are you? Marrying her?'

'I can't read the future any more than you can. What matters now, today, is that I am unofficially unattached. I wanted you to know that we're not hurting anyone.'

Jacquie set her eyes on the expansive view, the blues and greys and blips of white, her head spinning.

'I could break it with her now, Jacquie. She always said I should, if something serious happened for me.'

'No, don't do that. It wouldn't be fair, not when I'm unsure about things. Besides, she's our security blanket. As long as you're spoken for, no one will suspect, and that gives us time too. Maybe we can ride this out, you know, get over each other before this gets any messier.'

'That isn't going to happen for me.'

'It might.'

Nico looked up at Knockatee. 'Not when I'm this much in love with you.'

When they got back that evening, Luke had arrived, having deposited his mother with her sister-in-law in Skeheenarinky. They were having dinner with Suzanne and Ronan in the kitchen; Dara had friends in; Kitt and Natalie were watching a movie in the living room. There seemed to be nowhere for Jacquie and Nico to go, so she led him upstairs to her bedroom.

It was an L-shaped room, with a double bed squashed behind the door and a broader space to the left, with windows looking over the garden. It had one exceptional feature: an open fireplace. During the winter, in lonelier times, her open fire had been a friend, a presence in the room, crackling and chatting to itself. Its moods reflected hers – sometimes roaring, hot, vibrant; at other times, simmering and subdued, giving little heat or light. Through tough times, when her heart was straining, this room had offered her a retreat. It protected her, held the world at bay.

While she set about lighting the fire, Nico wandered to her desk by the window and looked at the wall of shelves. 'All yours?' he asked, of the books.

'My father's too.'

He put his jacket on the back of the chair, then leant into the mantelpiece above her. They watched the flames worming their way among the twigs. How nice it would be, Jacquie thought, to make love by the fire, but there could be no lying naked in the raw heat on this occasion, not with so many people in the house. Instead, they sat cross-legged on the floor, waiting for the flames to take.

Nico's eyes reflected the flickers of light. He opened two of her shirt buttons.

'Don't. Dara could break in at any minute.'

'How can I go back to Italy without making love to you?'

'You'll have to.' The back of his fingers ran down her neck, across her breast. 'I wish you'd stop.'

'Do you?'

'Not really.'

His other hand moved under her long skirt, over her knee and along her inner thigh. She squeezed his arm.

'Jacquie!' her mother called. 'I've heated up some supper for you. Are you and Nico ready?'

Nico grunted. 'For sure.'

The next morning, Luke and Marina persuaded Nico and Jacquie to join them for a walk. They took the car down to Blackrock and walked along the Lee to the castle. Nico made a point of walking with his father, Jacquie with her mother, and when they got to Blackrock, they wove through the streets to a pub, where they had soup and chips. On their way back along the river, Luke and Marina fell behind. Their children took off at a brisker pace.

'How are we going to shake them off during the summer?' Nico muttered. 'It won't be easy to be together, especially with me working all day.'

'I still think it would be best if I didn't come.'

'Of course you'll come,' he said. 'We'll go away. Take a trip somewhere.'

'I can't leave Mum stuck with Carlotta.'

Nico stopped, then caught up with her. 'What did you say?'

'Nothing. Nothing at all.'

He touched her elbow. 'There is a problem between them?'

'Not so far as I know,' she said airily, walking faster.

'But you said it.'

'I shouldn't have said anything.'

'Tell me.' He made her slow down. 'If we're going to be brother and sister,' he teased, 'you can share things with me.'

'Brother and sister? Do you know something I don't?'

He looked back at their parents. 'It will happen, I think. This has become very serious for Dad. He is completely in love. I've never seen it before.'

'Never? Not even your mother?'

'That, I don't remember.'

'What about Carlotta?'

His eyes narrowed. '*Che cosa*? Marina thinks my father is in love with Carlotta?'

'No, of course not. It's just that she gets a bit stressed trying to fit in over there.'

'I see.'

He did see. He saw it all, she thought, thanks to her big mouth. His interpretation could only be that Marina was jealous and clingy, that she didn't want this wonderful family friend around, in spite of all Carlotta had done for them. Marina would hang Jacquie off a bridge by her toenails if she ever found out what she had blurted.

Nico put his arm through hers as they walked on. 'She can be . . . possessive.'

'She isn't possessive. Not a bit of it. But she's on very new ground and –'

'Carlotta,' he said. 'I mean Carlotta can be difficult. Many women come and go.'

'How do you mean?'

'Pa has had a lot of affairs, but they always end. Carlotta is used to that. They come and go, but nothing changes for her.'

'But that's exactly what worries me! That Mum will be one of the ones to *go*. Carlotta is so intimidating.'

He nodded. 'My mother hates to be in the same room as her, even though they were friends once.'

'*Really?* But that's great! Mum thinks it's just her.'

'In some respects it might be. Cristina probably wouldn't agree.'

'They don't get on?'

'If *you* find Carlotta intimidating, you should try being her daughter. Only she knows what is right for Cristina.'

'And that would be you, I suppose.'

'I suppose.'

'You know what I think? I think *you* are Carlotta's means of hanging on to Luke. If you and Cristina marry, Luke will always be a part of her life.'

Another Italianate shrug. '*Certo.*'

'Oh, God, please tell me *someone* has succeeded in standing up to that woman!'

'Pa has.'

'Excuse me? She virtually lives in your house! She runs it!'

He looked over his shoulder. Marina and Luke had fallen a good way behind. 'He has kept her at a distance. Between them, there is distance.'

'Nonetheless, she has a lot of power over him.'

'Because he feels guilty.'

'About what?'

Nico flinched.

'Aha! You see how easy it is to let the wrong word slip? But you've said it now – so out with it.'

He took a deep breath. 'They were engaged once. He ended it.'

She stared. 'Why doesn't Mum know that?'

'That's between them.'

'*Shit.* Now I know things about Luke that Mum doesn't! This is why this is a disaster. You and me, him and her, confidences going back and forth – it's all wrong!'

'Don't tell her.'

'But if Luke broke off his engagement to Carlotta that gives you no hope at all. You'd be murdered if you did the same thing to her daughter!'

'You think I don't know that?'

*

'I'm afraid we need groceries,' Marina said, on the way home.

Jacquie, in the back of the car with Nico, groaned. 'We can't all four of us go traipsing round a supermarket.'

'You mean *you* don't want to go traipsing round a supermarket.'

'Not the teeniest weeniest bit.'

'We'll go,' said Luke. 'We'll drop you two home.'

Jacquie's stomach clenched. She took out her phone and sent Nico a text.

His phone beeped, he opened it and read: 'Don't think there's anyone home.'

They waved off their parents, then scurried up the path, burst through the front door and hurled themselves up the stairs into her room. Releasing themselves into the bliss of privacy, their hearts whacking against their ribs, they threw off their jackets. Nico lifted her top over her head, but it was tight and jammed on her shoulder-blades, so that her head and arms were stuck inside it as he was trying to yank it off. The seduction became a battle – Nico pulling, Jacquie squirming, both too turned on to find it funny. When the top finally released her, they tumbled to the bed, shoes kicked off, mouths searching. With every creak in the house, they stopped – looking towards the door, before resuming their scramble.

'How long have we got?' Nico asked.

'About half an hour.'

'So let's slow down. Here, get under the cover.' With a kind of reverence, he kissed her breast, her belly-button, her hip, while she pulled at his shirt.

'Why do men always get caught in their shirtsleeves?'

He shook himself free of it, then stretched across to where his jacket had fallen on the floor and, without leaving the bed, grabbed it and pulled a condom out of his wallet. Then he looked at Jacquie. 'Too soon?'

'Way too soon.' She took it from his hand, undid his belt and pushed off his jeans.

Forty minutes later, they were in the kitchen, a little flushed, but helping their parents unpack the groceries with sibling tenderness.

They slipped up only once. After dinner, when everyone was sitting in the kitchen, Jacquie sent Nico a text. At the far end of the table, he read it, then looked up, directly at her.

Natalie and Marina were having breakfast when Jacquie stumbled down to the kitchen the following morning. 'Mum, guess what. I have the best news.'

'What?'

Jacquie pulled her dressing-gown round her. 'It turns out that Nico's mother cannot bear to be in the same room as Carlotta!'

'How is this good news?'

'It means it isn't just you. She's alienated Luke's ex as well.'

Marina looked at her blankly. 'Note: Luke's ex-wife, with whom he has two children – despatched. What hope does that give me?'

'Well, Nico thinks you might be the exception to all the other women who went running.'

'Oh, God, how many has she repelled exactly?'

'The way he tells it, you're the only one Luke has really cared about. Ever.'

Marina glanced at Natalie.

'Ever,' Jacquie repeated. 'And there's something else.'

'It's rather handy,' her mother said with mock sarcasm, 'that you and Nico get on so well. Means I can find out what's going on in my life.'

'This might not be such good news. Apparently Carlotta and Luke were engaged.'

'Yeah, I know,' said Marina.

'Oh, phew! I wasn't sure whether to say anything or not.'

'It's okay, Luke told me.'

'You have all the luck,' said Natalie, with a great wistful sigh. 'Why couldn't it have been me who went to Morocco and found a sweet, non-sleazy man with property in Italy?'

Jacquie brought her toast to the table. 'Yeah, Mum, how's it done? It's, like, you went away and came back silly in love with a guy you barely knew, and nine months later he's stone-crazy about you and it's still all roses.'

Her mother pulled a face. 'Aren't you forgetting a rather large thorn?'

'Apart from her. I mean, how come you were so sure about Luke from day one?'

'Search me, but the moment I saw him, I knew it was going to be good. Maybe there are just some things we're sure about.'

Jacquie bit into her toast, and said, munching, 'See, I don't buy that love-at-first-sight stuff. How can you love someone you don't know?'

'You have to listen to what's going on inside your head,' Natalie said to her. 'Tune in. We have amazing intuition but we don't use it, and if we'd only pay attention to all the sensory stuff that's going on inside us, we'd have a much better idea of where we're headed. You have to block out all the noise.'

'Is that what you did?' Jacquie asked Marina.

'I don't think so.'

'But you still have no doubts about him?'

'I'm not naïve,' said Marina. 'I don't pretend it's straightforward but, no, I've no doubts whatsoever that, given the circumstances, we'd be fine.'

'Shouldn't circumstances be irrelevant?' Jacquie asked.

'You'd like to think so, wouldn't you? But when love affairs don't work out, it's usually because of other people. Circumstances are stronger than love and always have been. If they weren't, there wouldn't have been a broken heart in all of history.'

'But circumstances can still be overcome, can't they?'

'That's what I'm trying to do, love – overcome the circumstance that is Carlotta!' Marina got up, poured coffee for Luke and went upstairs with it.

Natalie watched her go. 'Love really is blind,' she said to Jacquie.

'How so?'

'She thought we were talking about her, when all along we've been talking about you.'

Jacquie busied herself with the crumbs on her plate.

'I really don't want to pry, but I think I know who it is.'

Don't move, Jacquie was thinking. Don't look at her or blink or sigh or give her any indication of anything.

'If I can be of any help . . .'

'Thanks.'

End of conversation, she hoped. Incorrectly.

'But I have to say – not the wisest move, Jacquie.'

Marina put Luke's mug on the bedside table. 'You really are a dark horse.'

'Hmm?'

'Pity I had to find out from our kids about your engagement.'

He blinked. 'How did they find out?'

'Not *our* engagement. *Yours.* To Carlotta.'

He reached for his coffee. 'Oh, God.'

'Indeed.'

'It was too insignificant to mention.'

'Funny, I thought you'd say that.'

'No, really. It lasted all of twenty-four hours. Or was it forty-eight?'

'It isn't insignificant now,' she said. 'In fact, it explains a heck of a lot.'

'Like what?'

'For one thing I now know I'm dealing with a disappointed woman.'

'You already knew that, I imagine.'

Marina sat on the bed. 'I suppose I did.'

Unable to sleep that night, Jacquie got up to fetch the inevitable glass of water. It had nothing to do with thirst, but that was what people always did in the movies when they couldn't sleep – went for a glass of water. It worked too. As soon as she opened the door, her thoughts escaped the confines of her room, stretched out in all sorts of directions, and stopped banging against the inside of her head. She considered sneaking up to Nico's bed, to settle her body as well as her mind, but felt her way downstairs instead.

Someone was still up. There was music in the kitchen – the husky voice of Ray La Montagne, her mother's current favourite, singing her favourite song, 'Within You' – but the room was dark, except for one candle on the table. Luke and her mother were standing by the window. Jacquie stopped. Back up, back up, she thought, but her feet wouldn't move. He had his arms round her waist, her hands were against his chest, and they were sort of dancing, and quietly talking. Marina was arching away from Luke, and yet inviting him, as he leant towards her. They made a gentle curve, against the outdoor light behind them, and it was one of the most beautiful things Jacquie had ever seen.

It was one of the most beautiful things she'd ever seen – her mother with someone other than her father. She felt a sob rise in her chest and had to get out before it reached the surface. She stumbled into the living room, where she sat in the dark until the CD came to an end and she heard them making their way upstairs, their whispers full of laughter, but the sob was still there. Silently Jacquie let it out. What was this sudden rage of emotion? Was it the music – that song, that lament about answers? Was it happiness for her mother? Grief for her father?

Or was it love? Because it wasn't Marina and Luke whom Jacquie had seen in the window. In their shapes, in their language, in the way they held one another, she had seen herself and Nico, as clearly as if she was seeing the future.

# 18

'Assisi?'

'Yes, *cara*, Assisi. It's the home of St Francis.'

'I know that, Carlotta.'

'We're all going!' said Bridget. 'Isn't it wonderful?'

'We are?' Marina looked at Luke.

'Carlotta thought you'd enjoy it,' he said, 'so we're driving down this weekend.'

'We must go before it gets too crowded, you see,' said Carlotta.

'I see.' Barely off the flight and Carlotta was organizing her life already.

'You don't mind, do you?' Luke asked.

Marina did not mind, and nor should they. 'Not at all, but I think I'll skip it.'

'Skip it?' he said.

'How could you not want to see Assisi, *cara mia*?'

'Oh, I do want to see it. Just not this Friday. I've barely arrived.'

'But it's all arranged,' said Luke. 'I thought you'd be pleased. You wanted to see some of the country, you said.'

'I do, and I will, but not this weekend. I've just dragged six students through their Leaving Cert French and I'm knackered.'

'How disappointing,' said Carlotta.

'Devastating,' Marina muttered.

'I haven't been there since the earthquake,' said Bridget.

'Apparently you can see cracks in the frescos. And there are lovely teashops, Marina. You'll like those.'

Marina smiled. 'I will like those,' she said, patting Bridget's wrist, 'some other time. Excuse me.' She left the house, crossed the road and went down to the terraced garden.

As intended and expected, Luke followed. 'Marina?' he said, coming down the squeaky cast-iron steps.

She was standing by the low wall. 'It would have been nice if you'd asked me about this little excursion. I'm not some visiting au-pair, you know. I don't need to be taken round the sights. What did you expect me to do? Clap my hands and say, "Oh, goody, they're taking me out cos I've been ever such a good girl"?'

'I really loathe it when you're sarcastic,' he said.

'I come here to be with you, not St Francis.'

'Yes, but Carlotta mentioned it to Bridget before she said it to me, and they thought it would be great to take you there. By the time I came in on it, it was sorted. *Fait accompli.*'

'Or a coup.'

He walked to the end of the short wooden jetty that jutted over the water, his shoulders tense, tight, as if he was holding something in.

She looked beyond him. How beautiful the lake was in summer! Deep, deep blue, sailboats moving listlessly, and fresh, clear water slapping against the wall below her . . . This could not be spoiled. She went to Luke and put her hand on his shoulder. 'I don't mean to be churlish, but with all due respect to St Francis and his birds, getting into a car for a long journey with Bridget and Carlotta is my idea of hell.'

'Ma will be so disappointed if we don't go. She's all geared up now.'

'So go. I'll stay here. You want me to feel at home, and feeling at home means feeling free to do as I please, right?'

'I can't be away from you on your first weekend. I won't be.'

'You should have thought of that before committing us to Carlotta's itinerary. This is well thought-out, Luke.'

'She isn't as devious as you think.'

'Maybe not, but she is deeply manipulative, and I decided before coming back that I cannot allow myself to be twisted about any longer. That's why I won't do Assisi.'

'But the whole weekend has been planned with you in mind.'

'The whole weekend was planned with a view to interrupting our time together.'

'I can't back out. Mother would have a fit. Won't you even come for me?'

'Sorry, no. If I don't assert myself, Luke, this will go on and on.'

'How very peculiar that you will not come with us,' said Carlotta, when they were having coffee on the terrace after dinner. 'Bridget is so disappointed, aren't you, darling?'

Bridget beamed. 'In his email, Matthew says that the forget-me-not is the official flower of Alaska. Who'd have thought they'd have any flowers up there?'

Carlotta turned to Luke, who was standing against the balustrade. 'Do you remember when Cristina was ten and went through that phase of refusing to go anywhere? You were the only person she would listen to.'

This one he heard, loud and clear. 'Are you comparing Marina to a stroppy child?'

'Not at all. It just came into my mind, like that . . .'

'If Marina doesn't feel inclined to travel, that's understandable. In fact, I'd quite like to put off the journey myself.'

'But I've arranged to meet Father Frank!' said Bridget. She

turned to Marina. 'He's a Franciscan friar from Waterford. I can't let him down.'

Carlotta sighed. 'I fear you will have to disappoint him, Bridget.'

'Not at all,' said Marina. 'You must go and I'll stay. Then nobody will be disappointed.'

'Except me,' Luke muttered.

They left that Friday. Marina missed Luke even before he'd left, and he looked like a boy who was being sent away to school. Bridget was as excited as a nun going to a papal audience, and kept calling Carlotta into her room to see if she should bring this dress or that. Marina couldn't help wishing she might ask, just once, for *her* opinion.

'You'd think she had a date with St Francis himself,' Luke grumbled.

Before Bridget got into the car, she said to Marina, 'I'll pray for you, dear.'

'Thank you, Bridget.'

'I will. I'll pray for you and Luke.'

They drove off, leaving her alone on the driveway in the shade of the big house. It was a good thing there were tenants making noise upstairs, throwing their towels over the railings, and coming in and out, their footsteps on the gravel. She might otherwise have been spooked, alone in the villa.

Luke was miserable. All evening, texts kept coming: 'Bridget thinks we're going to the grotto in Knock. She's going to be v. confused.'

'Cursed traffic.'

'Cursed fucking traffic.'

'Hope you're having an aperitif and enjoying our splendid view,' he wrote at seven. To which she replied: 'Young lover has just gone to get me aperitif, thanks.'

He was right: the view was splendid. In the evening light, a blue hue settled on the landscape – the hills were blue-green and getting darker, the water grey-blue and shiny. Only the cream of the seminary and the campanile stood out, and the lime trees along the water's edge added a snap of green. Marina sat with her drink, listening to the voices passing below, usually arguing – Italians seemed always to be in animated debate – until Maria served her gnocchi, and said goodnight. It was a long one. Marina had once been used to spending evenings on her own. As the lights came on round the shore, and more and more pedestrians made their way to town for an evening meal, she felt lonelier than she had in quite some time. If forcing them to go without her was some kind of victory, it was a hollow one.

Before she went to sleep, she received a final text from Luke, after they had arrived in Assisi: 'Bridget thinks we're in Lourdes. She's wondering where the sick people are.'

Maria had agreed to take the Saturday off, which meant that Marina woke in an empty apartment for the first time. She took breakfast outside, feeling brighter than she had the night before, and enjoyed hearing English voices in the flats above while watching a few boats on the lake. Every half-hour, the tourist train puttered by in one direction, tooting, then came back in the other, with tourists grasping their handbags and cameras, and wearing the aimless smiles of the holidaymaker.

As she sat there, a stubby white motorboat came across from the island, heading for the jetty next to Carlotta's cottage. When it came in, Marina peeked over the railing to see a bunch of nuns in full-length black habits climbing out and coming up the steps, carrying handbags, briefcases and shopping bags: a rare sight. They were rumoured only to leave the island to vote or in coffins. The first, older and austere, was clearly Head Nun, and she hurried her jolly little flock along the road, while the boat, with another nun at the wheel, skidded back across the lake. Marina reached in for the binoculars Luke always kept by the doors and pointed them towards the quay on the island, where another clump of nuns was waiting. She could almost see their excitement as the blur of habits scuttled towards the incoming boat.

After breakfast, she went down to the garden. It was framed by a boathouse on one side, and Carlotta's cottage, with its terrace and slipway, on the other. The jetty was too high above the water to allow Marina to put in a testing toe and, fearing the Alpine waters, she wasn't too keen on taking her chances with a great leap, but further along, an iron ladder hung off the stone wall, so she could always get in like a little old lady when the time came. Meanwhile, she pulled up a sun-chair and stared across the water. Stillness. No Carlotta, no Bridget, no Kitt. Bliss. Marina closed her eyes, felt the sun on her eyelids and its warmth seeping into her bones, and looked around inside her head. Random streams of thought flitted about, scrambling for attention: scenes from a siesta the day before – the languid love-making of a warm afternoon, with none of the encumbrances of higher latitudes; Italian tomatoes, Italian breads; Bridget sitting at the computer in the study, talking at it. Marina opened her eyes again. Carlotta would no longer get to her. This, she thought, is a new start for Orta and me.

For lunch, she walked into the village, had a small plate of pasta in a café on the square and stayed on, sitting in the shade, as it grew quieter in the early afternoon. In the dead heat, she walked back along the winding street with its silver cobblestones, and lay again by the lake, enjoying the solitude even more than she could have expected. When she went back up to the house to make tea, she put on loud music and jived around the kitchen, hoping the tenants wouldn't complain to the landlord. How lovely it would be, she thought, if she and Luke could have the villa to themselves, but that would be to wish away their past lives and the people who had come aboard along the way.

As evening came in, the space around her grew emptier. Assisi would have been interesting. She'd always wanted to go. It had been pure stubbornness on her part. She remembered again how she had coached bullied schoolgirls not to sink to their tormentors' level by taking cheap shots. Was this not a cheap shot? Was there any integrity to be had in staying back just to get one over Carlotta?

To clear her mind, she went outside with a gin and tonic, put her feet on the railing and allowed the view to seep into her thoughts. How beautiful Lake Orta was at sunset, the pink, quasi-orange shimmer on the water and the buildings on the island turning a gentle grey as the sky dimmed and the sun fell off behind the hills to drop into space. Black spread out from the dark corners of the lake, creeping over its waters like an inky tide.

The memory came at her from nowhere: her hands shaking as she tried to fold her things, and the room emptying, item by item, into suitcases, the room where they had laughed, fallen asleep in the same bed, spilt hot chocolate on the shaggy carpet. She remembered picking up those suitcases, could almost feel their weight on her arms, and saw again that there was no one in the hall – not Matthew, who might have stopped her, or Gwen, or any of the friends who had shared that house with her. Only her father, waiting outside. They had crawled away in his car. At home, he had made her tea; she drank it at the kitchen table, tears flowing, flowing, not stopping. 'Ah, now, pet,' her dad kept saying. 'Don't upset yourself. It'll blow over. These things do.'

Marina took her feet off the railing and put them on the

warm tiles. She should never have left that house. It was a capitulation, almost an admission. She should have said no. But it was guilt that had made her leave, not Gwen. She regretted it now, the way she'd skulked away, like an outcast turned out of the village, only to end up at her dad's kitchen table, dripping into a mug of tea, too strong to drink, that her helpless father had made.

Odd, really, how it still hurt.

The looming house behind her, the bats flitting about in the dark and too many unsavoury thoughts loud in her head made her reach for her phone.

He answered straight away. The sound of his voice made her smile.

'Can you hear me okay?' she asked.

'I hear you fine, Reen. How are you?'

After telling him why she was alone, she said, 'It reminds me of the day Gwen threw me out.'

'How do you mean, threw you out?'

'Of the house.'

'But . . . you wanted to move home, didn't you?'

'That's what she told you?'

'In so many words, yeah.'

'It makes sense.'

'Gwen asked you to leave?'

'That sounds so polite. She froze me out, then kicked me out, and the thing is, it's happening again. Here. I'm allowing it to happen to me again, and I'm terrified it'll take me somewhere I really don't want to go. Like it did last time. I've sent Luke away for three days just to make a point. No matter what way you look at it, I'm the loser.'

She could hear Matthew move round his kitchen, could even hear the coffee percolating across the world. 'You want to be careful, Marina. You can't let her get to you like this.'

'But I don't know how to stop it without upsetting everyone.'

'You have to play dirty. I mean, hell, she's not playing fair, why should you?'

'Because I won't sink to her level. I want to be a bigger person than that.'

'Turning the other cheek and all that crap?'

Marina put the phone to her other ear. A couple, both dressed in yellow, were walking along the street below holding hands. 'I wish you were here,' she said.

'I will be in a few weeks. Can't wait to see the place.'

'I feel like I'm seeing it for the first time now I'm on my own.'

'You're still mad about him, right?'

'Totally.'

'So why are you wishing I was there?'

'I don't know.'

When Luke fell through the door on the Sunday night, he looked like a convict who'd been let out of jail. He was sweaty and smelly, but she endured his embrace and showed him the shower. He was still frazzled when he got out. 'You look like you've been through a butter churn,' she said.

'I have. It's called the Milan bypass on a Sunday night. Come on, I need a walk.'

They wandered along the dark street and sat for a while on the wall beneath a lime tree, talking about their respective weekends. 'It was good,' Marina admitted. 'Gave me the chance to get a feel for the place.'

'And?'

'I love it.'

'Excellent, because this weekend was the last straw. Enough messing about. We've done the courtship, we've taken the familiarization course. I can handle your family, you can handle mine. Let's settle this.'

'How do you mean?'

'I seem to remember that we sort of got engaged.'

'We did.'

'Right. So we need to work out how this is going to work out.'

The Assisi adventure had only minimally undermined Carlotta. The sweeping put-downs kept coming (in Luke's absence) and for all Marina's ducking, the daggers were hard to avoid. Much of it was trivial stuff, as when Carlotta gushed over Marina's new shirt – 'How nice to see you at last in good Italian clothes' – but went on to point out that red was absolutely not Marina's colour, and a glance in the mirror in the hall proved her right. 'Quick, quick,' she said, 'run upstairs and change before Luke sees it.' And Marina did run upstairs, like a perfect idiot, because she couldn't bear him to see her looking like a bad shade of cheap lipstick.

Nor did she get anywhere when Carlotta found her reading in the drawing room. She was always coasting about the apartment, never staying longer than two minutes in one place. 'What a lot of time you spend reading. Always lost in a book.'

'The best place to be,' Marina replied, without looking up.

'*Certo!* I only wish I had the time. I have not one minute in my day when I can relax and sit down.'

'Well, that's what holidays are for, aren't they? And this week I am on holiday.'

'Ah! Holiday. A word I scarcely know.'

Marina groaned inwardly. When was she going to stop walking into these too-obvious traps?

'I say to Luke,' Carlotta went on, 'I say to him all the time, "One day, *caro*, I will take a holiday."'

'Wasn't Morocco a holiday?'

Only fleetingly stalled, Carlotta hurried on, 'Yes, but I was always on the email or the phone. Luke has made me promise that the next time we go away, I will not bring my computer.' With which, of course, she left the room. In her wake a neat image of herself and Luke having a lovely holiday together – without computer – lingered.

Marina's book dropped to her lap. Damn. What *was* the answer? Why was Carlotta always three steps ahead? Marina's father had once said ruefully that such people always had an answer. 'If you threaten to upstage them, they'll tell you they had the pope to dinner!' he'd said.

'Oh, Dad,' she said out loud, 'where's *my* pope?'

Luke was teaching her Italian, usually after they had made love, when they were relaxed and unlikely to get snarly. He went through the verbs and she constructed short sentences with her limited vocabulary. During the day, she memorized new words. The last thing she wanted was Carlotta trying to teach her. She had threatened it several times. 'You must make an effort. You'll never learn if you let everyone else speak for you.'

Marina knew that, but wouldn't dare speak a word of Italian for fear of being condescendingly corrected, and yet without it, she remained at a disadvantage. For one thing she could not communicate with Maria, and as long as she could not do that, she could make no inroads into the household. She could barely get a foot inside the kitchen as it was, let alone suggest what they might have for supper or do any cooking. Maria was fierce about her territory. She worked six days a week, left a cold plate for them on Sundays, and deferred to Carlotta on absolutely everything. Marina had to find a way in, a side avenue that would allow her to take her place, somewhere between Bridget and Maria. If she did not, she would only ever be a guest, for whom everything, from what she ate to what time she ate it, was decided for her.

'Maybe we could give Maria a night off,' she suggested to Luke one evening. 'Or even two, and take turns cooking, you and me.'

'Hmm, not a bad idea. We really don't need her all the time, do we? I'll speak to Carlotta about it.'

'Surely you need to speak to Maria.'

'Maria will think we're offloading her. She's bound to think you're trying to take her place. It'll have to be handled sensitively.'

'I'm sure you and I are capable of doing that without consulting Carlotta.'

'Still. Best left to her.'

'Luke, where is it exactly you expect me to fit in? Am I to become some kind of permanent guest?'

'Of course not, but I do like seeing you take time off. You've been looking after other people for years. Isn't it nice that here you can have things done for you?'

'Yes, but I only need a few weeks' holiday a year. If you want me to spend more time here, what is it that you imagine I would do? Because if I'm to feel in any way at home, I have to be able to go into the kitchen to make a piece of toast when I want one!'

'All right, all right,' he said, throwing down his newspaper. 'Don't get shirty.'

'You're the one getting shirty.'

'I'm just trying to point out that we can't do this whole thing your way. I must have some say in it.'

'Fine, but I *had* hoped you might appreciate that I have a number of other balls in the air.'

'So I'm the ball that gets dropped, am I? I'm supposed to sit back and be decorative, is it, whenever I'm in your life?'

'I don't interfere with yours!'

'You never stay longer than five minutes! I'll be here for most of the summer.'

He sighed. 'I just hoped that you and I could cut free of all this domestic stuff.'

'That's romance. We live in the real world – don't we?'

'I wish we didn't. I wish we could live in bloody Morocco, away from your lot and my lot and the whole damn cocktail party!'

Carlotta was totally opposed to cutting back Maria's hours, and therefore her earnings, which was not what Marina had been suggesting. Luke let it go. They needed Maria for Bridget, and could not afford to alienate her.

All right, Marina thought. *Noted.*

But she had left herself open to Carlotta's condescension. One morning, when Marina was sneaking back to their bedroom with breakfast, Carlotta came out of Luke's study and followed her up the stairs. 'Really, Marina, it would be better if you did not involve Luke in household affairs.'

Because she was holding a tray, Marina could not turn at the bedroom door and block Carlotta, who marched in behind her. She put the tray on the bedside table.

'He is not good at managing that side of things,' Carlotta went on. 'That is why I have been doing it for him for many years, and you need not concern yourself with things that have worked very well for us for a long time.'

Marina glanced around: an old and friendly bra was thrown over the back of a chair, her bikini was hanging over the railings, three of Luke's socks were on the floor, and the box with her diaphragm lay on the bedside table.

Carlotta looked around also.

'I was simply trying to give Maria a few hours off,' said

Marina. 'She works an extremely long week. Or haven't you noticed?'

'Maria is a very treasured member of this family.'

'She ought to be, the hours she works!'

Carlotta left the room in a puff of indignation. Marina beamed. A rare victory.

There was another domestic disagreement when Marina, fearing that Carlotta might at some point suggest she was sponging off Luke, tried to give him money towards household costs. He refused point-blank to take it and the row that followed was loud and crushing, especially when Bridget came in, having heard most of it, and suggested Carlotta might be able to do the figures and work out what exactly Marina was costing them.

There were other jolts. One day, Marina hooted with laughter when she saw Luke in his tight black shorts, synthetic T-shirt and cycling gloves. 'Oh, you may scorn,' he said, 'but I have been known to cycle all the way up Mottarone!' She followed him down to wave him off, and found Carlotta, in similar get-up, standing outside with her own mountain bike. No wonder she was so bloody slim. They cycled together.

But Marina and Luke had their own pleasures. Often, after he'd had a cooling swim, they went for a wander, and one late afternoon, they went up to Sacro Monte, dipping under an arch half-way into the village and climbing the back steps, which were hewn out of the rock and curved their way up the hill between high walls and wild gardens, full of tall yellow and pink flowers. Over her shoulder, Marina glimpsed a slice of lake beyond the red and grey roofs. It was steep at first – Luke put his hand on the small of her back to give her a gentle push – but the steps broadened as they reached the higher road at the back of the town. Here, elegant villas and modern mansions commanded a breathtaking view of the island. Marina kept turning. 'You never quite get used to it, do you? I want to see it from every perspective.'

Luke stopped beside her, panting slightly. 'From up here, I often think it looks like a word on a blank page, a word that says everything about beauty and architecture, nature and religion.'

'I keep expecting it to sail on by and disappear.'

'Come on, we're not there yet.' They carried on along the cobbled road that led to the wooded plateau at the top of the peninsula, where twenty tiny chapels dedicated to St Francis were nestled among the trees.

'It's like a religious theme park,' said Marina, walking around.

Inside the dim chapels, frescos representing significant stages in the saint's life provided a backdrop to ghoulish statues standing in the naves, like figures in a museum. Mosquitoes nibbled so persistently at Marina's ankles that she abandoned the shady chapels and headed for the sunlight in the walled cemetery, where they wandered among its white-gravelled graves, reading about Orta's dead.

'I was thinking about easing the boys in on our plans,' Luke said, 'mentioning to them that we'd like to get married. Ma too.'

Marina kept her eyes on the headstones, her hands linked behind her back. 'But then I'd have to tell my kids.'

'Yes. Why not?' He tipped her elbow to make her look at him. Those deep eyes ate into her. 'You're not reconsidering, are you?'

'Let's get back.'

They headed out of the graveyard and back down the gently sloping path.

'Marina?'

'Luke, doesn't it worry you that I'm not happy in your home?'

'It totally freaks me out,' he said quietly.

'So perhaps before talking to your mother and the boys, you should talk to Carlotta. Have you told her we plan to marry?'

'No. It doesn't strictly concern her.'

'For heaven's sake, your home is more hers than it is yours! I'd have to play third fiddle in the scheme of things. She still treats me like a passing fad.'

'On the contrary, she knows you aren't a passing fad. That's why you're getting the wrong end of her. She's nervous about her own situation, but once it's out in the open, she'll be fine. There is a warm individual in there, you know.'

'Well, I wish she'd come up for air more often, because the present incumbent makes me extremely tense. Every time she comes into the room, I'm worried about how I'm sitting, what I'm wearing, what *one* thing she's going to pick on, and I can't challenge her because I'm a guest. I can't be myself around her. The thing about bullies is, they give you no right of reply.'

'I really wish you wouldn't call her that. She's a deeply unhappy woman.'

'And she's making me unhappy too, Luke. Her entire purpose right now is to make me feel like I don't belong with you. I don't cycle, I don't speak Italian, I don't understand property –'

'None of which matters a jot.'

'It *does* matter when someone's trying to freeze you out. It's grist to her mill. I love it here, I do, but I'm squeezed between you and Carlotta, and have no room to manoeuvre, no room to breathe, and if you don't make more space for me, I'll be squeezed right out!'

They were coming down towards the yellow church at the back of the village. The house on the corner was wearing its wisteria like a great long beard, flowing down from the high cloister and spreading out across a lower roof.

'Carlotta is my mother's friend and carer, Marina,' Luke said abruptly. 'My hands are tied.'

'And isn't that just so convenient for the both of you?' she snapped. 'Because you can't *quite* give each other up, can you? After all, you've never had to. You're safeguards to one another – standbys. Carlotta isn't just your ex, Luke, she's all of your exes. I mean, when was the last time?'

'Oh, for fuck's sake.' With a broad stride, he went down several steps.

'No – tell me. When was the last time?'

He stood sideways on the path below her. 'About . . . I dunno . . . three months before I met you.'

It hit Marina like a brick. They'd been together so recently?

'It doesn't mean anything,' he said.

'Of course it does. It means you turn to each other when you're lonely, or randy, or in need of comfort. What if you and I have a row? Will you run to her then?'

'This is unreasonable,' he said, his voice measured. 'It's all very well for you, Marina. You've had that one joyful marriage so many of us aspire to. You've known true companionship. But you have little experience of the alternative and, believe me, when you're on your own long-term, it's important to stay close to the people who know where you've come from. What is *so* wrong for a single person to keep such friends close by?'

'Nothing, until that person is no longer single. You can't behave like a bachelor any more, Luke. I'm here. Account for me. Act *for me*. Carlotta has no intention of relinquishing an inch of her claim to you and it's up to you to make sure she does!' She came down and marched past him.

'I won't ask someone to whom I am indebted to stand aside, Marina,' he said, raising his voice, 'no matter what it costs me.'

Marina stopped, turned, and walked back to him. 'Luke, what is it, exactly, that she's holding over you?'

# 19

Orta San Giulio was like the bright corner of a dark room. Climbing up to her bedroom, after a long day's travelling, was like arriving in her own personal shelter. Jacquie was hot and sticky, and the evening sun was scorching the terrace when she stepped out, but the expanse of water, so different in summer from winter, looked fresh and cool. The gentle evening light made the buildings on the island glow and a broad beam of sunlight lay on the water like a fluttering ribbon. The hills were hazy, the air warm, and the sheen on the surface of the lake was broken only by the wake of a plastic see-through motorboat moving across it.

It was good to be back. Since Nico's visit, she had been living in a mist of longing and confusion, of secrecy and subterfuge. For the first time, she was keeping something significant from her mother, something that could make things immeasurably worse for Marina, if the affair were ever discovered. Yet Nico, through emails, texts and phone calls, was clear in his conviction that they must follow their own path or risk losing their way.

And so she had come again to Orta, when she almost certainly shouldn't have.

That evening, Marina and Luke took Jacquie to dinner in the square. It seemed a different place from the one she had walked across in the snow with Nico, when the island, rising out of a dim mist, had looked like a Gothic shrine. Now, all was brightness and elegance, and the eerie winter silence had been replaced by the lazy buzz of July. Three sides of the square were graced by cream buildings, with frescoed walls and bursts of red flowers on their balconies. The town hall stood at one end, like a room on stilts. Holidaying families flowed back and forth, and it was good to breathe it all in – the languid sway of people enjoying themselves in slow motion, the women's impeccable clothes, the attractive men, the prevalence of children. One man went past wheeling a pushchair with his small sleeping daughter curled up in it as if she was in her cot. Another child had fallen asleep on a plastic bag full of shopping and was stretched across two chairs put together for him, while his parents had an evening coffee. A tourist was making her way round an enormous ice-cream piled high with fresh cream, but the more she licked, the thinner became the tower on which sat the cream, until the cream inevitably fell off and landed on the ground in a great splat.

Luke talked about how many apartments had been rented out and how great it would be to give one to Natalie and Matthew for their first 'family' holiday. With such a good season lined up, he was happy to relinquish his penthouse to Jacquie.

'But you shouldn't have to do without income on my account,' she said.

'It's fine,' Luke insisted. 'In fact, henceforth I think I'll keep the penthouse free for you and Dara.' He glanced nervously at Marina.

They'd had a row. That was clear. They weren't making eye contact and were slightly formal with one another. Jacquie wasn't bothered. They'd sort it out. These two, she knew, were in for the long haul. They were entitled to their tiffs, same as anyone, and besides, she had her own preoccupations.

Nico had still not appeared and had not yet sent a text. He probably didn't want to be too obvious, rushing over as soon as she arrived. Besides, she needed to find her bearings and steady herself before she saw him. She was glad of this breathing space, this peaceful evening, spent with Luke and her mother. It crossed her mind that Nico might be having second thoughts; she almost wished he would, while knowing with certainty that he had not.

Her first day was long and lazy, and she intended every other day to pass in exactly the same way: breakfast with her mother, morning spent by the water, retreating to her penthouse to read and snooze in the afternoon before returning to the lake for more swimming and reading, followed by whatever happened to be going on with whomever happened to chance by . . .

But nobody did chance by, not least Nico. It was extraordinary in view of the pressure he had put on her to come in the first place, and it was disconcerting that he wasn't even texting. She heard Luke telling Marina that Nico was flat out at work, but he didn't show, that day or the next. What *was* he up to?

Late on the second afternoon, after a cooling dip, she lay face down on the wall to dry off. In the distance, she heard the roar of a sports car. Nico, perhaps, in his little blue car? Being in lust, as well as in love, was exacerbated by the sun, the sweaty heat. She imagined Nico in her room, in her bed with the sheet thrown off and a box of morning sunlight lying across his body. She wished they could have the freedom, in this warm, romantic place, to lie naked, with no fear of intrusion, then shower together, dress up and saunter into town hand-in-hand for a long dinner.

The gate squeaked and the steps rattled – her mother coming down for her evening read. A fly landed on the small of Jacquie's back. She waved it away. It returned. It felt like a finger running down her spine. It *was* a finger. She swung round.

'*Come vai*?'

'Nico!'

When he smiled, he bit his lower lip, showing a hint of tooth. 'Welcome back.'

Whether it was the nature of her daydreams, or his summer clothes and light tan, he looked better than ever, but she had to play it cool. 'Thanks. How are you?'

'Very well,' he said. 'Busy. We've been working long hours. You?'

'Very busy, too.'

'Yes, I can see . . .' He tied the straps of her bikini gallantly, allowing her to sit up.

'I *am* busy,' she said, 'enjoying your sunshine and lake. The water's so warm.'

'Is it? I need it to be cool. It was so hot in the office today.' He was already in board-shorts, but he pulled his shirt over his head, took off his specs, and made his way to the end of the jetty. There was a loud splash.

She followed along the wooden slats, waited for him to swim out of the way, then jumped. That cooled her down pretty quick.

'Fantastic,' he said, 'I've been planning this all day.'

Little waves bobbed round them. The water was different from the sea. Softer. Jacquie could see her legs, like spaghetti, dangling beneath her.

'So what have you been doing today,' he asked, 'while I've been working hard?'

'Umm, let's see. I had breakfast and a swim, then lunch and a swim, then a rest and a . . . swim.'

'Ach, poor you.'

'Hey, I've earned it. Going into that shitty office every day.'

'So, what do you want to do while you're here?'

'I want to have breakfast and a swim, lunch and a swim, do as little as possible and swim. Why? Do you have other plans for me?'

Nico swam over to Carlotta's slipway and sat on it, half in the water, half out. Jacquie joined him. 'It's good to see you,' he said quietly. The formality was piercing.

'You took your time about it.'

'I'm sorry, Jacquie. I'm sorry about everything. I shouldn't have gone to Ireland.'

Here it was then. She wanted to sink to the bottom of that deep, cold lake.

'You were right,' he went on, though she wished he wouldn't, 'in everything you said. If Carlotta found out something had happened between us . . .'

The past tense.

'. . . she would make it very difficult for you and your mother.'

Droplets of water ran from his shoulder down his upper arm. His nipples stood out with the cold, but her insides were as hot as cinders. She needed him to touch her. 'You talked me into this,' she said, 'and now you want to forget the whole thing?'

'We have to, I think?'

'We shouldn't have damn well started it! I told you –'

'Yes, yes, I know. You told me. But it was hard.' He looked at her. 'It's still hard.'

'Is it?'

'*Che cazzo*, Jacquie! Don't say things like that.'

'I'll say what I bloody well like. Because this is a bit bloody predictable – as soon as we have sex, you go off the boil! All in the chase for you, is it?'

His eyes were cold, angry. 'That is . . . not it.'

'So why this change of heart? And *why* didn't you damn well tell me before I got here?'

'Pa is . . .'

'What?'

'I think things are not going so well. The atmosphere,' he threw his head towards the villa, 'is not so good.'

'Tell me about it.'

'Pa is worried your mother won't stay. I can't make that worse. If she knew about us . . .'

'Oh, if Mum knew about us, she'd be gone. One complication too many.'

He squinted at her. 'That doesn't make her sound very committed to my father.'

'You know very well she adores Luke.'

He raised his eyebrows, looked across the water. 'Not enough, maybe.'

'And maybe your father could do more to make her feel comfortable around here. *Chez* Carlotta.'

'I'm not going to fight with you about them.'

'Fine.' Feeling sick, Jacquie threw herself into the water and swam towards Luke's garden, paddling extra hard so that her heart wouldn't sink her. There was cement in her guts; an extra weight dragging her down. She had to get out of the water. Fuck him anyway, she was thinking. She had let him in, against her better judgement, had allowed something to start, and had spent the last few weeks thinking only of seeing him again – and all for the great pleasure of being dumped on arrival. But he was right, of course. It was better this way, she thought with every stroke. Better. Better. Better – for everyone else.

The following morning, around midday, Carlotta was sitting on her slipway in a red bikini, throwing bread to the ducks. Marina swam towards her. 'Don't alarm the ducks,' Carlotta called, but Marina, seeing an opportunity and smelling courage in her own blood, ignored her. Bridget was surfing the Internet, Luke at work, Jacquie engrossed in a novel. Carlotta was exposed: she was in her own humble home, not prancing around in her silks and beads, commanding attention in the big house. She watched warily as Marina crawled on to the slipway and sat near her. Sure enough, this act of defiance, of trespass, caught Carlotta unprepared. She tore up more bread and flung it at the ducklings. For such an imposing presence, she had a very slight figure, thin, and she was deeply tanned.

'Carlotta, we need to clear the air a bit.'

'Clear what air?'

'Between us,' said Marina. 'It's not as if we get on very well, is it?'

Carlotta looked at her doubtfully.

Marina liked her own tone. She'd found the right voice for this, light and nonchalant, so she continued, 'I feel you try quite hard to undermine me and, to be honest, you mostly succeed, but I am not about to be chased away, so it seems silly to go on like this.' Carlotta was already protesting, her mouth opening, closing, but Marina went on: 'You seem to feel threatened by my presence here, so I just wanted to say that I have enormous admiration for your friendship with Luke. You've been invaluable to one another over the years, and I will never come between you. I respect your claim to him, Carlotta, but I would ask that you might also respect mine.'

Carlotta's countenance changed. The ripping of bread stopped. 'I assure you, *cara mia*,' she said, with a coarse chuckle, 'that I am not at all threatened. I have no reason to be. Luke and I, we have things between us that you could not even imagine.' She moved her sunglasses some way down her nose to look over the top of them. 'It is a pity if you have a problem with the way I take care of him and his family, but that is how it has always been.'

'Except that he no longer needs you to look after him, if he ever did. We can manage quite well by ourselves.'

'And will you manage Bridget?' she asked, her voice so deep it almost sank.

There was no upper hand to be gained here.

'Will you take her to Mass every morning, Marina? Will you bathe her and comb her hair? Do you love her that much, as I do? Do you love her at all? Because I am not going to abandon Bridget simply because Luke has fallen in love. I didn't before and I will not now.'

'I'm not asking you to abandon Bridget. I'm simply pointing out that I have a place here too, and if Luke's happiness matters to you, then –'

Carlotta laughed throatily. 'Oh, I can take care of Luke's happiness! Darling Marina, I always have. Bridget, Nico, Francesco, Cristina and I, we are his family. That has always been and will always be.'

It was such a lost cause that Marina got cheeky. 'So, umm, why doesn't he just go right ahead and marry you? Sounds like a plan, doesn't it? I mean, if you're all one big happy family, it seems obvious that you two should hitch up. No?'

Carlotta's lower jaw shifted to the side. 'That is not . . .'

'What he wants?'

'That is not the nature of our . . .' And here Carlotta failed to complete. Marina knew that she had hit on something, but it had nothing to do with the marriage jibe. Carlotta pushed her large sunglasses up the bridge of her nose. 'You think you know us. You do not. You cannot. If you are uncomfortable here, Marina, it is not because of me.' She got up, pulled up her bikini top, and went into her house.

That afternoon, Marina and Luke walked into the village, through it, in the shade of high buildings, and out the other side, emerging again on the waterfront where the path skirted the walls of two old villas before it went on round the rest of the peninsula. They spread their towels near a tree that leant over the water and sat with their legs dangling off the wall. Edginess had settled between them. Marina now actively reproached Luke for his uncompromising stance on Carlotta, even though she could see for herself that his options for manoeuvre were limited, but she longed to regain the ease they had always enjoyed in one another's company.

Water flapped round her ankles; she kicked it about, her hands under her thighs, and stared across at the far shore, where windows flickered with silver flashes of sunshine and the hills seemed remote under the white sky. 'I spoke to Carlotta earlier,' she said. 'It got me absolutely nowhere.'

'Oh. What did she say?'

'Lots of stuff I didn't follow. She has an impenetrable view of you all as an indestructible unit.'

'Hmm,' said Luke. 'I'm in the process of dismantling that notion.'

She frowned at him.

'I've been gradually . . .' he struggled to find the right word '. . . *disengaging* her.'

'How do you mean?'

'We own a property together – an investment property – and I've told her I want out. I've also told her that that I'm planning to take you and Mother to Verona at the end of the month, and that we'll be out for dinner on Friday, so she shouldn't make plans on our behalf.'

Marina winced.

'Too much?' he asked.

'A bit.'

'Oh. That's unfortunate, because I've also spoken to Maria about her hours.'

Marina stared at him, aghast. 'Does Carlotta know?'

'Not about Maria, no.'

'Your life could well be in danger.'

'So be it,' he said. 'I'd be in a lot more danger if you left me.'

She put her hand on the side of his neck. 'Don't be silly.'

'Is this the kind of space you meant?'

'Yes,' she said. '*Yes.*'

'I can't afford to hurt her, Marina. She's had her share of that. And I won't interfere with her and Bridget. You hear them, same as I do, their sing-song voices in the morning when Carlotta's helping her to dress. I can't stand in the way of all that.'

'I don't want you to, and I don't want to see her hurt either, Luke, or excluded. I just want her to stop hurting *me*.'

'I'll make sure of it,' he said. 'Look, I do accept that she's way too embedded in my life, but at the moment, with Cristina away and work demands not being quite what she'd like you to think, she simply doesn't have enough going on to use up all that emotional energy of hers – so it's being directed into us. She needs a distraction. A wedding would do it, if only Nico and Cristina would get their act together.'

'Or a love affair,' said Marina. 'If she fell in love, she'd leave me alone. Why don't you set her up with someone?'

'I've tried, but she's picky and, let's face it, it would take someone fairly robust.'

A flotilla of swans came by. Marina edged herself into the water and paddled backwards, looking up at the neat pink villa behind them. 'That's my favourite house round here. We should buy it and live here after we get married, away from them all.'

Luke watched her. '*Are* we still getting married? Because I've been living on a wire these last weeks, Marina.'

She smiled. 'We're engaged, aren't we?'

He lowered himself into the water. A swan hissed at him. 'Hiss off,' Luke said to it, taking Marina into a long, tight hug.

*

Jacquie was falling into a rhythm, lazy and indulgent. She had all the necessary requisites to cure a broken heart. From her perch at the top of the house, she absorbed the calm and quiet, and had an opportunity to reflect; in the village, she could enjoy distraction, diversion and good ice-cream. The combination was bound to heal. Eventually.

But idleness gave her too much time to think. Every morning, when she retreated to the lakeside, she couldn't take her eyes from the water. It seemed to be coming for her, the waves heading straight at her, as if to engulf but not drown her. She thought and thought and thought, feeling stupid, stupid, stupid. She should have known better – no, she *had* known better. That was what really got to her. She'd known it was a non-starter, and yet allowed it to start, and now this thing had attached itself to her – the parasite, Nico called it – this useless, redundant love, and she didn't know how to get rid of it. It had nowhere to go, and yet that was all it could do – go. One day. Some time.

She frequently drifted off, imagining that Nico kissed her, held her, loved her; that they woke together in the mornings and that their union was intense. It was comforting, in the still heat, to go there, but actuality would always drag her back to where she didn't want to be, where the unpretentious lake was trying to cure her, and where she was, once again, without him.

Every day, after lunch, Marina and Luke retreated to his room for their siesta. Jacquie wished they wouldn't. *She* was the one who should have been taking a lover to her bed, not her widowed forty-seven-year-old mother, who emerged every day around four, her hair tousled and her face glowing, looking for tea. Instead, up in her loft, Jacquie could only sleep and read and fantasize in the early afternoons, but whenever she looked up, her eyes were drawn again to the water. She could see the lake from her bed. It had become her comfort zone, always there, like a painting on the wall that drew in her thoughts and made them well, when they were black and gritty and no good to anyone.

The late afternoon was busier in the lakeside garden. Marina and Jacquie leant against the upright posts of the jetty, with their books or not, talking or not. After his day's work, Luke joined them, and sometimes Bridget too, and they'd treat the lake like their own private swimming-pool, with their own set of ducks. They came very close to the wall, the resident ducks and ducklings, including a big black bird with a scarlet beak and a pure white mother, who herded her charges away from the swimmers. Jacquie often saw them from her terrace too – this family of ducks, off in the distance, spotting the water like bits of litter.

One evening, when Jacquie was coming back through the house, wet and refreshed, she passed Marina in the hall.

'Hurry down when you're dressed. Nico's here,' Marina said.

He'd been keeping a very low profile, which had made things easier for Jacquie, and probably for him too. 'So?'

'With Cristina.' Her mother made eyes at her, but carried on in her usual tone, 'Carlotta's daughter.'

The bottom fell out of Jacquie's stomach. She took her time on the stairs, thinking, Shit, oh, shit. Cristina was not so much a rival as an ally, and yet, seeing them together, this cosy couple whom everyone thought so perfectly matched, was bound to be excruciating.

It helped that Nico winked at her when she came into the room, but that was the highlight of the evening. The rest was torture. He was wearing an exquisitely tailored slate-grey suit, and his sort-of-fiancée matched him in every respect – intelligent eyes, warm smile, a healthy, tanned complexion and clothes to die for. Her yellow dress, perfectly fitted, showed off her just-so figure, white sandals flattered her delicate feet, and her shoulder-length nearly-black hair would not have gone astray in an advertisement for conditioner. When they were introduced, she flashed Jacquie a girlish smile. Her English was weak, but she giggled at her mistakes and always looked to Nico for help. Jacquie had expected someone tougher, more hard-edged like her mother, but this businesswoman with a married lover was all gentleness and grace.

'It is a pity Cristina's English is not so good, Jacquie,' said Carlotta.

Marina was astounded – criticism of the Blessed High-achieving Cristina?

'But you see,' Carlotta went on, 'she also speaks German and Spanish, so English has been left a little behind.'

Right.

Over dinner they spoke mostly Italian, with insets in English from Nico and Luke. Jacquie couldn't follow the conversation. She was aware only of the tightening in her pelvis and across her shoulder-blades. She had a headache and backache and a physical craving so severe that she felt as if she was being squeezed into a bottle. When people spoke of the pain of love, she'd never realized they meant actual, physical pain. She kept stretching her neck to ease it, and berated herself again for allowing Nico to get inside her heart like this.

'Are you all right, love?' her mother asked.

'Yes – why?'

'You keep twisting.'

'I'm fine.'

Nico threw her a look of compassion. She wanted to touch him, but he was with Cristina, probably for ever. They were indeed made for each other. Perhaps they were the only two who couldn't see it. Who could he be, Jacquie wondered, this Malian man who had taken Cristina's heart when she so evidently belonged with Nico?

After dinner, when everyone sat over their coffee in the drawing room, Nico and Cristina stood by the window, leaning over the sill, their backs to the room. Her waist was so slim, her voice so soft. Nico tilted towards her, listening, a glass of wine in his hand. He shook his head; his voice took on more insistence, urgent, but firm. Cristina leant against his shoulder. He kissed her forehead, put his arm round her waist and squeezed her.

The next morning, Jacquie and Marina went over to Isola di San Giulio. It was a short hop from the square, and as they motored across, the old waterside villas, with their porticoes, arches and jetties, seemed simultaneously inviting and standoffish, while the huge seminary was like a priest in a pulpit looking over their shoulders. They climbed ashore and wandered through an archway into the Way of Silence, a meandering pathway, with private villas on one side and the religious buildings on the other.

The Way of Silence was not so silent. Vehement family exchanges poured through the windows of the houses, so close that anyone passing could have joined in.

'It's like being part of an argument,' said Jacquie.

'I feel like saying, "Well, *I* don't know where it is, do I?" '

Every few metres, hand-painted messages dangled from walls. The first one read 'In the silence you accept and understand.'

Further on, a man on a red ladder was weeding a huge stone wall that rose to their left. 'Listen,' Jacquie said, stopping, 'someone's beating cream.' From a window high up in the seminary came the sound of a whisk hitting the sides of a bowl through the slurpy consistency of ever-thickening cream. 'Now *that*'s what I call a spiritual sound!'

Marina read the next sign: ' "In the silence you receive all." '

'Receive all what?'

'God's grace, I imagine.'

Her daughter snorted. She took a photo as they came to an S-bend where the path curved round a small tower.

'Poor Bridget,' said Marina. 'She cannot understand why I don't go to Mass. She keeps putting it down to things – I must be unwell, or tired, or unable for the heat.'

'"Silence is the language of love." That one could be true, I suppose.'

'You're very grumpy this morning.'

Jacquie shrugged. 'Slept badly.'

'Again? What's going on with you?'

'It's the heat. And the mozzies.'

Marina was looking up. 'Is that the campanile that wakes us every morning?'

'Yeah, pretty noisy place, all in all.'

It took less than twenty minutes to arrive back on the quayside, where they sat on steps to wait for the boat, their feet dipped in the lake. Marina took a couple of brioches from a brown-paper bag.

'Yum,' said Jacquie. 'Thanks.'

'So, what did you make of Cristina?'

'Lovely. Not a bit like her mother.'

'I know, and just as well too, if she's going to marry my stepson.'

Jacquie turned. 'Excuse me?'

Marina's hand went to her mouth.

'Ooh, that slipped out, didn't it? Come on – let's have it. What's the story?'

Marina ran her hand through her curls. 'We've been thinking about, you know, maybe . . . getting married.'

'Mum! That's so great!'

'Yeah, but not, you know, I mean, I'm not prepared to give up Ireland, not totally, so we'd spend quite a lot of time doing our own thing.'

Jacquie gave her a hug, her eyes brimming. 'Congratulations.'

'You know it has no bearing on Dad? He's still with me every day. He's my fifth limb, even if no one else can see it.'

'*I* can see it.'

Now Marina was welling up. 'Can you?'

'Always.'

'It's just . . . I wanted to meet someone, I did, but I never thought about actually falling in love again, and now I have, and it's like acquiring a possession – it has to be put somewhere. It has to find a place, and marriage is something Luke very much wants and –'

'Mum, it's okay. It's great. I mean, yeah, I wish you and Dad could have had the time that you and Luke have to do things, but there's no point you missing out just because Dad had to. And you were right – he would like Luke.'

Marina squeezed her wrist, nodding.

Jacquie sniffed. 'So, will you mostly live here?'

Marina's reply was to look across the water at the villa's upper corner poking out from behind trees. They could just see Jacquie's terrace.

'I take your point.'

'Are you sure you wouldn't mind?' Marina asked.

'If I were in your place, I'd do it. I'd move.'

'But a few months ago, you –'

'Yeah, but I had to get used to the idea. Now it's nice to think of you here. It's nice to *come* here.' A wave of nausea passed over her. How *would* she do it – come back, year in, year out, watching Nico and Cristina having their babies and living happily ever after? As for their wedding – what an ordeal that would be! She would rather eat centipedes.

'How do you think Dara will feel about it?'

'Same as me.'

A shrill voice behind them made them turn. On a terrace

off the convent, a nun was hanging over the railing, her hand pressed under her veil. She was on the phone. 'So much for silence,' said Jacquie.

Marina took out tissues. 'Well, if you're all right with it,' she said, 'you and Dara I mean, we thought we'd have some kind of celebration when the others arrive.'

'An engagement party! Cool!' Jacquie's overenthusiastic reaction shaded a flush of irrational, but nonetheless intense, mortification. She had had sex with her soon-to-be step-brother.

Up behind them, the nun shrieked with laughter.

Natalie, Matthew, Dara and Kitt arrived that evening and were greeted by the lady of the house as if they were the Holy Family arriving on Christmas Eve. Jacquie and Marina, standing by the balustrade, exchanged a glance. 'Standard,' Marina mumbled. 'Flatter someone else, anyone else, to undermine me.'

'At least you were able to wrest control of supper. The buffet looks delish.'

'I thought it would be more pleasant out here, instead of sweltering inside.'

'Scuse us, Jacquie.' Luke edged Marina off to the side. 'Nico's on his way over. Everyone will be here who can be here. Mother's primed, so is Jacquie. Are we set?'

Marina glanced at Matthew. Did he also need to be primed? 'Have you said anything to Carlotta?'

'No need to single her out. She'll be delighted.'

Marina touched his face. 'You're so deliciously naïve. I love you so much.'

'So, let's get formal. Please. Now, with our families.'

She looked over his shoulder. Odd how Natalie, Kitt and Matthew had become her family. 'I haven't even met Francesco yet.'

'He'll be home for Christmas. I'll call him now, then tell the others, okay?'

'Keep it low key. No big hoopla.'

'Party-pooper.' He went inside to make the call.

Nico appeared, took a drink and stood back, leaning against the balustrade. He was subdued, not as chirpy as usual. Jacquie went over. 'So,' he said, 'how are you?'

'Bearing up. You?'

He stared at the gathering. Behind him, in the dimming light, Lake Orta looked like a sheet of polished zinc.

'You know,' she said, 'everybody's right. You and Cristina make a lovely couple. You'll be perfect together.'

Nico turned his eyes on her, hurt. 'Why do you say these things?'

After most of them had finished eating, Luke tapped a glass with a knife, but when everyone turned to him, he became diffident, unconsciously taking small steps backwards, towards Nico, just behind him, as if for protection. Marina stood nearby, plainly enjoying his bashfulness, his discomfort at having all eyes on him – his mother's, peering up from a bowl of zabaglione; Matthew's, flashing between Luke and Marina; Natalie's and Dara's, bright and expectant, and Kitt's – bored.

Carlotta, displaying a beam so broad she looked like a gargoyle, was perplexed. '*Caro, cosa fai?*'

'Ah, well. I have some news, but I've been asked to, um, exercise middle-aged restraint, which seems a shame. I mean, I'd like to shout it from the rooftops myself . . . not least because I don't quite understand how, well, someone like me, someone like her, it's hard to credit, actually –'

'Get to the point,' said Dara.

'Yes, well, we, that is, Marina and I, or should that be me and Marina –'

Everyone groaned.

'She's agreed to have me, all right? To do the deed and all that.'

'Do you mean you're getting married?' Natalie asked, her voice deliberately arch.

'I do. I do mean that.'

Everyone cheered. Luke smiled the coy smile Marina adored, and turned to his son, who embraced him, but then Carlotta was upon him, saying she knew, she knew, right from the moment they'd met in a Land Cruiser, she knew that Marina was the one. Moved to tears, she then turned to Marina, saying how happy she was, how very wonderful, while Natalie and Jacquie were jumping around Marina, squealing.

Luke leant over his mother. 'Ma, did you hear me? Marina and I are getting married.'

'Why?'

'Because we want to.'

'Want to what?'

'Get married.'

'Why should I get married?'

He hugged her. 'Enjoy your zabaglione, Ma.'

'Did you know . . .' She looked up, her eyes watery and grave, and Luke sensed, for the first time ever, that she wasn't quite sure who he was. 'Did you know that most of us don't really understand the rules of rugby?'

'Who told you that?'

'Dara. Nice boy, but you won't be having any more children, will you? You have quite enough as it is.' She waved round the terrace.

'They're not all mine, Ma.'

'They are now.'

'Marina.' Matthew held her hands, kissed her. 'I . . . Yeah. Speechless.'

She was flushed. 'To tell the truth,' she said, 'we decided to get married the moment we met. We just didn't tell each other.'

'Have to say, I'm kinda surprised.'

'Really? I don't think anyone else is.'

'Or maybe not so much surprised as devastated.'

Her smile dropped away.

'I guess life really is a bitch,' he said quietly. 'The very moment you and I come back into each other's lives, *he* comes along too. Go figure.'

'Matthew . . .'

'And you know the worst part? I reckon you would have had me. Not in college or even before then, but this time round, we could have made a go of it – if it weren't for him.' He gripped her elbow. 'Tell me that much. If I have to stand here celebrating, can you at least tell me I'm right about that?'

'You are right, yes.'

He backed away, as if she had stabbed him, and went to the drinks, just as Natalie sidled up to her. 'Carlotta did *not* see that coming. I saw her face. She thought she had the situation under control.'

'A backlash can be expected, no doubt.'

'Don't worry. We're here. We'll sort her out. One thing, though.'

'What?'

'She *does* have something on him. I can feel it.'

'And are your heebie-jeebie vibes telling you what it is?'

Natalie shook her head. 'No, but you should maybe get to the bottom of it.'

Luke was pouring himself a drink. 'No Champagne,' he said to Jacquie. 'I should have had Champagne on standby.'

For the first time, Jacquie hugged him. 'Well done,' she said, tearful again.

'I hope those are happy tears?'

'Of course they are. You're an embarrassment to all of us, you and Mum, with your puppy love, but I know you'll look after her.'

'I will, love.'

The endearment made Jacquie worse. The tears became fuller. She moved to where Nico was once again leaning against the balustrade, his back to the party. 'We have no chance now,' he said bitterly. His glass of wine was shaking in his hand.

'We never really did. This doesn't change the fact that you're already spoken for. But all things considered, it's just as well we let it go.'

He didn't look at her. 'You must think me very dishonest. Weak. Allowing everyone to believe something that can never be true.'

'No,' she said warmly. 'On the contrary, I think what you've done for Cristina is generous and loving – and even now, when it's hurting you, you're still being true to your promise to her and holding back for Mum and Luke. I admire you for that. A lot.'

'Even though I hurt you?'

She wanted to comfort him, to hold him. 'Time can get us over anything.'

'Then I wish time would stop this minute.'

'By the way,' Marina was saying to Luke. 'I've remembered where we first met.'

He raised his chin. 'You have?'

'Yes.'

'Go on, then. When? What was I wearing?'

'But you already know,' she said, drifting off.

'Yeah, right. Remembered, my arse!'

*

Carlotta was at the breakfast table with Bridget the next morning, making a list. She was a list person, always ticking off jobs done and jobs to do. 'I'm making some notes,' she said to Marina, when she came in. 'If there is to be a wedding, we have a lot to organize.'

Before Marina could respond, Kitt came in, wearing a bikini and a towel.

'Oh, my dear, that is not at all appropriate,' Carlotta said to her. 'Run along and put some clothes on for breakfast.'

Kitt glanced at Marina, who nodded, then left the room, her mouth turned down, like a child's in a cartoon.

'Luke and I plan to marry very quietly,' Marina told Carlotta.

'But that's nonsense. We must have a wonderful party. That's what you'd like, isn't it, Bridget?'

Bridget, looking up from her brioche, said to Marina, 'I thought, you see . . . You see, all this time, I thought I understood the rules of engagement.'

'There are rules?' Marina asked, thinking, Rule One: the bride and groom shall make their own arrangements.

'Oh, yes. Many more than I knew about,' said Bridget, earnestly.

'Like what?'

'Well, for one thing, if a player is lying on the ground, he can't throw the ball, Dara says.'

'How can you resist our beautiful church of San Bernardino?' Carlotta asked Marina. 'Couples come from all over Europe to marry there.'

'We won't be marrying in a church, Carlotta.'

'Gracious me, why not?' said Bridget, as disconcertingly part of the conversation as she had not been moments earlier.

'Because Luke has been divorced, and we are neither of us religious.'

'But I'm praying for you, dear. I am.'

'I know you are, Bridget. Thank you.'

Marina slouched in her chair, drained already. What *had* she done? Marrying into *this* lot? She glanced over her shoulder at the lake, the hills, the blistering sunshine. Anchorage would be cool, fresh. There would be air to breathe in Anchorage. Air to breathe, and moose in the garden. Matthew's chunky body . . . but, oh, those fleecy shirts! No. Not possible. Still, she was curious. She, too, wished Matthew had appeared a little sooner than Luke, because it would have been interesting maybe to sleep with him, at least once, and then she could have had them both. On the other hand, the reason she was so quickly drained by these two women this morning was that she had already been feeling weak. Before Luke got up for work, they had celebrated their engagement in a torrid and extremely delicious manner. Their love-making seemed to get better, deeper, ever more satisfying. Carlotta could have their wedding. She could line up the Pope for all Marina cared. Just so long as she got the man.

Kitt reappeared in a tiny sundress and sidled into one of the big chairs, her eyes wide – croissants, rolls, silver teapots, and she wouldn't even have to tidy up afterwards because they had a maid. She beamed at Marina. 'This place is cool.'

'Thank you, dear,' said Carlotta, without looking up. 'Marina, I really do believe Luke would enjoy a very big party. A proper celebration.'

'It's the second time for both of us,' said Marina. 'It should reflect as much.'

Carlotta went on, 'We should have the reception at the Villa Crespi.'

'Whose wedding is it?' Kitt muttered.

'Not mine, I hope,' said Bridget.

'You have to get married in Cork,' said Kitt, then she looked at Marina and asked with a cheeky guffaw, 'Hey, are you going to wear white?'

Before Marina could open her mouth, Carlotta retorted, 'Oh, I hope not! It's so vulgar when older women try to look like young brides.'

'Maybe she wants to wear white!' Kitt protested. 'God, how come everyone says I'm rude? I'd never say something like that.'

The heat thickened. Temperatures were going relentlessly up. Mosquitoes were feasting on ankle bones, nights were sweltering, and Natalie and Kitt were bronzing like there was no such thing as skin cancer.

The backlash was in full swing. Carlotta was grinding Marina down. She took Kitt shopping in Milan, tried to be Natalie's best friend, and flirted with Matthew. Once again, through a strange quirk of time and place, he was part of the equation. He was being used, kept on the other side of the jetty, his presence elsewhere intended to hurt Marina, as it had done with Gwen. And once again, she could not demand his loyalty, because Matthew had his own reasons for keeping his distance. Whenever Marina came into a room, he left it, and he spent more time on Carlotta's slipway than in their own garden. It infuriated Marina, as had his untimely declaration, which had unsettled her when she was already feeling anxious about their own announcement. It didn't help when she then came down with a dose of homesickness – she'd been away for more than a month – and flurries of doubt harried her. The worries were always at their worst during the middle of the day, when the heat was at its tightest, and she found herself wondering if she really liked this wonderful climate. She longed for rain, Irish rain, and the thundering sound of it, so lively compared to these still afternoons and their rigid silence. She longed for the cool luxury of sitting down with a cup of tea in front of *Oprah* on a cloudy afternoon, her feet curled under her. Tea, here, gave her hot flushes, and she never curled her feet under her because the straight-backed furniture wouldn't allow it.

Jacquie and Dara helped her keep the faith. They so clearly loved Orta. They got up late, swam, ate, slept and ate, and went clubbing with Nico and his friends into the small hours. Jacquie had cheered up. She'd been quite surly on arrival, and Nico had not been as attentive as previously, but that had changed when Dara arrived and they all went out together. Her children seemed to embrace their new connection to Nico and the prospect of their tiny family expanding.

And although the days could be a struggle, the evenings were a balm on Marina's concerns, when Luke came in, sweaty and tired, but always with a smile. He loved his work. He was so passionate about Italian architecture that his job was as satisfying to him as heat to a cat. Whatever came on to his books – grand villas, apartments in old blocks, stone cottages on hillsides waiting to be done up – received his enthusiastic dedication. While he showered, Marina often stood by their bedroom window, listening to the ducklings honk with panic as they hurried across the water after their big white mother, and just as often, Luke came from the shower, cool and hot, and cajoled her on to their starched white sheets. She wasn't marrying Carlotta, or Bridget; she was marrying him, and there could be no doubt about his love for her.

Later, when the whole crew gathered, they usually wandered into town, a large contingent, and took the longest table in the square, sometimes joined by Luke's ex-wife and her sister, Nico and his friends. These were good times. There was a lot of laughter, a lot of spraying of feet to ward off mosquitoes, and street performers to entertain them. Jacquie looked well, Dara ate, drank and argued, and Luke had an aura of contentment about him. An inner well-being. Marina was sure that her own inner peace would return, if only the heat would break.

Before they went back to the house, Kitt always insisted on going down the road to the Arte del Gelato, which served the best ice-cream, as far as she was concerned, on the planet. She planned to work her way through every flavour in Italy.

'Here's a good one for you,' Nico said one night, with a mischievous glimmer in his eye, handing her a chocolate cone.

Kitt took a great long lick. Her eyes shot out on stalks. 'Ow! Agh!'

Nico laughed.

'What is it?' Jacquie asked.

'Chocolate and chilli.'

'*Chilli* ice-cream? You're so mean!'

'My mouth's on fire!' Kitt screeched. The man behind the glass counter was also chuckling, but he handed her a cup of cool white sorbet. She groaned with relief and waved the ice-cream at Nico. 'I'm not eating this. It's hot!'

'I'll have it,' said Dara.

Dara and Kitt walked back through the crowds towards the square, where jugglers were playing with fire for those children that still remained upright, and on through the town. Jacquie and Nico fell behind, and still further behind, their elbows touching so often that they were finally digging into one another. Stopping at a window to admire a display of glass jewellery, Jacquie felt his arm brush along her back and almost leant into him. They stared at the red and gold pendants, the black and silver earrings, their breathing audible and shallow, then moved on, slowly, reluctantly, until they came to the archway that led through to the back steps. Nico steered Jacquie under it and hurried her up round a bend. As soon as they were out of sight of the road, they fell on one another, and also fell over. There were weeds on the steps, probably bugs getting into Jacquie's hair, and her elbow had been grazed when he came down on her, but she didn't care. She moved her legs to better feel his weight. He nuzzled her breasts and pressed against her, and then, as suddenly as they had started, they stopped, knowing they'd run out of time. He helped her to her feet, caught his breath, kissed her. 'I'll come to your room tonight.'

'Better bring your telescope.'

They hurried along the street until they heard Kitt and Dara's voices up ahead, then slowed to a stroll. Couples were sitting on the wall between the lime trees, cuddling.

'At least we tried,' said Nico.

'Not hard enough, apparently.'

'It hasn't been hard for you?'

She stopped. 'Jesus, what do you think? I don't fall in love with my otherwise-spoken-for-soon-to-be-stepbrother every day, you know.'

He touched her arm. 'You love me?'

'It would seem that I do.'

Dara called back at them to hurry up.

'I thought it was bad,' Nico said, 'when things weren't going well for them, but now they're getting married, it's more difficult for us. I'm not sure what we should do.'

'I should go home, that's what, and give us a chance to forget this.'

'That would only work if we never had to see each other again.'

'An option we no longer have.'

'I'm glad. I've tried to be without you. It's impossible. We'll find some way.'

At the villa, Nico made a big performance of bringing the telescope up to her terrace. A mistake. They hadn't thought it through. Kitt, Dara and Matthew were fascinated, so they trooped up to the penthouse and wouldn't decamp. The stars explored, they sprawled across Jacquie's couch watching television. Nico dismantled the telescope. 'It's late,' he said, when he and Jacquie were alone. 'I have a meeting at eight.' He glanced inside. 'But we must get some time together.'

The following evening, when no one else was in the garden, they threw themselves into the lake and swam under the jetty, where Nico grabbed Jacquie from behind. Her face went momentarily under. His chest was against her back, his mouth on her shoulder. Kicking to keep her head above water, she turned and put her arms round his neck. They both sank a little as they kissed.

A sudden thudding overhead resulted in a great splash at the end of the jetty. They pushed off each other and kicked frantically backwards. Luke emerged from the splash.

'Where's Jacquie?' Marina called from the wall. 'Her stuff is here. She hasn't –'

'I'm here.' Jacquie paddled into view.

'Oh, I thought maybe you'd drowned.' Marina went to the end of the jetty and sat against an upright to read.

Jacquie climbed up the ladder. Nico had to dally a bit longer in the water, until he had quite cooled down, before joining her. He dried himself off. 'We have to do something about this soon,' he said quietly, 'or people will see me glowing in the dark.'

'Easier said than done. We live in a circus.'

'We'll go away. We could pretend to go to Rome. Cristina would cover for us.'

'Mum would expect photographs when we got back, of all three of us.'

'Florence?' he suggested. 'I could take you there for a weekend?'

'Great idea. Dara and Kitt would love to see Florence.'

Nico pulled on his shirt. He looked stressed; he needed a shave. She wanted to tell him it'd be okay, but their relationship was like Cristina's – it had a short lifespan and nowhere to go. 'What about your place?' she asked. 'Doesn't your flatmate ever go out?'

'Alfredo? Not often. He's always working on his thesis.'

Luke was swimming around by Marina's feet, threatening to pull her in.

Nico glanced at his watch. 'But wait – he works until seven. We'd have a little time if we leave now.'

'Now? But I'd have to go and change, and what would we say?'

'Marina?' Nico called. 'We're going into Omegna for a while, okay?'

'Okay. Will you be back for dinner?'

'Nah, we'll pick something up.' He smiled at Jacquie. 'Easier than we thought.'

Omegna was squashed between mountains at the northern tip of the lake. Nico's apartment was in an old building overlooking the canal, the Nigoglia, which flowed out of Lake Orta. The main room was dim but tidy. 'Lovely,' Jacquie said, when he showed her in. 'It's such a relief that you're neat. Dara's a right slob.'

Nico cleared his throat, flicked his head in the direction of his bedroom and opened the door to reveal such a panorama of untidiness that it took her breath away. It was clean mess, almost orderly, but she couldn't even see the bed, there was so much piled on it. Shirts, jackets, shoes and towels were spread across the room; boxes, folders, portfolios, piles of magazines and papers. 'Oh.'

Nico gestured helplessly.

She looked at him. 'But you're . . . so well turned out.'

'Ah,' he said apologetically.

'This,' she nodded towards the mess, 'isn't because your mother's been doing everything for you all your life, is it?'

'I intend,' he said firmly, 'that my mother will live with me always.'

'Now you're scaring me. Your mother's Italian and your father's Irish – not a great domestic combination, is it? Can you cook?'

He brought his finger and thumb together. 'The finest *zuppa di pesce* you will ever taste.'

'I don't like fish.' They were still standing in the doorway, considering one another. 'You really are Italian, aren't you? Have you ever had a pint?'

'I am not a tidy person, okay, but I don't scratch my belly while drinking beer and watching foot –'

'Shut up,' she said, kissing him. 'We don't have long.'

'We'll do it like in the movies,' he said, approaching the bed, 'and pretend it's a desk.' With a great sweep of his arm, he pushed the entire pile of clothes on to the floor, then lifted Jacquie and threw her, laughing, across the bed. His chin scraped against her collarbone, which made her squirm, so he kept doing it, finding her ticklish bits and making her squeal, until they slid off the bed on to the cluttered carpet.

Nico looked up, across the mess. 'Somewhere here . . . is a packet of what we need.'

# 20

The dinky railway station of Orta-Miasino provided little in the way of concealment when Luke dropped Jacquie outside and offered to come to the platform. She said, no, no, no need, and waved him off with a sigh of relief. There was no sign of Nico's car: he had had the sense to park elsewhere and was himself out of sight, at the far end of the platform, to the side of the building. He peeped out, picked up his bag and came towards her. They kissed formally, cheek to cheek, and stood by the track, waiting, in the mid-afternoon sun.

'How did you arrange it?' he asked.

'By lying to my mother, which I do a lot, these days.'

'This is turning us into schoolchildren. Sneaking around, being bad.'

'At least, you're hoping we'll be bad . . .'

When the train slid in, they clambered on and took seats side by side. Nico flattened her hands between his. 'What did you tell Marina?'

'I said I wanted to go to Florence for a few days, and she said, "Great idea, why don't we all go?" So I told her I wanted to be on my own for a bit, if only to escape Kitt's incessant dive-bombing into the lake. That, she understood. But here's the good news: when Carlotta heard I was going alone, she insisted on booking me into a former monastery turned *pensione* in Fiesole.'

'*Porca puttana.*'

'She knows the owners, and simply *has* to be in control of everything. How are we going to get round it?'

'I'll think of something.' He kissed her. 'Relax, will you?'

'I can't. If this was Ireland, we'd run into at least three people we know. In fact, we probably will run into some Irish acquaintance. Did you say where you're going?'

'If they notice, they'll think I've gone to Cristina.'

'Does she know about me?'

'Not yet,' he said. 'If I told her, she would feel responsible and end her relationship. I don't want that. Not until there's good reason for her to do so.'

'What sort of good reason?'

'Knowing you are committed to this.'

'How can I commit to it, Nico? We have two engagements to worry about now – yours and theirs. You're as good as married and we're as good as related.'

'So we tell them.'

'Yeah, right.'

'Why not? They can be together and we can be together – who cares?'

'I care. I feel like I'm moving in on Mum. On her life. That I'm sort of invading her love affair. "Anything you can do, I can do better" kind of thing.'

He was smiling. 'You make me laugh. You always look on the bleak side. Your mother might be happy for us.'

'Hardly. She'd be rightly pissed off with me for taking someone else's bloke and making a cheat out of you, but with or without Cristina, I can tell you for sure she would not be ecstatic about this. Especially since she thinks she's brought this wonderful big-brother figure into my life. She thinks we're bonding.'

'We are.'

'Like siblings! She's so chuffed about that. Look, what are we going to do about Fiesole? If word gets back to Carlotta that I turned up with someone . . .'

'I told you. I'll think of something.'

'Or you could stay somewhere else.'

He clicked his tongue, shook his head, and kissed her at length, so seductively that she could no longer contemplate him staying elsewhere any more than he could.

It was late when the taxi drew up at the *pensione* in the hill town of Fiesole. Florence lay below them, like a glittering magic carpet that at any moment might lift and hover away. Jacquie rang a great clanging bell and they stood in total darkness outside the door, waiting. A crumpled old woman let them in. '*La signorina* ffrench? *Irlanda*?'

'*Sì.*'

Nico gave her an admiring look. 'You speak Italian so well.'

'Feck off.'

The woman looked at Nico. He explained, all politeness, that they had shared a taxi from Florence when they'd realized they were both coming to Fiesole, and he wondered if there might be a room for him. The woman said they were completely booked up. Nico said that, since it was late, he wasn't fussy; anything would do. The woman suggested something; he agreed.

'Will you be all right?' Jacquie asked him politely, as she was led off to her room.

'Thank you, yes.'

'Goodnight, then.'

In her room, she got undressed, slipped into bed and curled up, thinking about that kiss, the way they had jolted with the rumble of the train, but had gone on kissing and kissing, like it was their first time. 'Shit.' She sat up. They'd come away to be together, to relieve some of the frustration they dealt with every single day, and here she was in a former monastery, alone, with no idea where they'd put Nico. All thanks to Carlotta.

She closed her eyes; opened them. Got up. It seemed only right to make sure he was okay down there in the dungeon or wherever they'd dumped him. Nightlights lit the winding staircase that led down to the front hall. She was trying to decide which way to go when a dark figure came upon her. She yelped.

Nico grabbed her. 'Shush!'

'You scared me! What are you doing?'

'What are *you* doing?' he whispered.

'I came to see if you're okay.'

'I'm okay.'

He had a hold of her, his arm tight round her.

'Where have they put you?'

'In a kind of storeroom. Come on, I'll show you.'

He led her through an office and another room to an anteroom with a camp bed in it. Jacquie giggled. 'Aw, the things you'll put up with for me!'

They lowered themselves on to the iron bed, which squawked, but Nico's hands were on the move and her flimsy dressing-gown offered little resistance. She pulled at his shirt buttons, nibbling his collarbone and shoulder. She loved his neck. His palm came over her hip and across the small of her back.

'Stop,' she said. 'I'm sick of this – hurried gropes and being quiet and afraid of being caught. It's too much like home. Why did we bother?'

Nico slumped down beside her. 'You're right. This is not the place. Tomorrow we will find a hotel.'

'No way! Carlotta will be so insulted if I skive off after she's organized this. I feel watched . . . You don't suppose she knows, do you? That she did this deliberately?'

'Even if she did, I'm not letting her destroy our weekend. We'll move tomorrow. You can tell her you saw a rat in the dining room.' His hand stroked her thigh. 'I'll show you

Florence quickly tomorrow, then we can relax. So get up early. You have a date.'

'I do?'

Her date was standing on a pedestal in the piazza outside the Uffizi Gallery.

'That's him?' she said. 'The *David*? The most famous statue in the world and they leave him out in the cold to be shat on by pigeons?'

'That's not the real one. But this is where he first stood.'

'Got cold, did he, and went inside?'

'And that's the Uffizi,' said Nico, marching her across the square, away from it. 'We'll do it later. I have the tickets.'

Teasing glimpses of the Duomo quickened her step, especially since she had seen, from the extraordinary vantage-point of Fiesole early that morning, the cathedral's red dome sprouting out of the city's roofscape like a rare bloom on its best day. Now it kept slipping and sliding out of sight, as if it was peeping at her and running ahead, so that she had to get to the next corner, and the next street, coming ever closer, before emerging right beside the cathedral. 'It looks like the whole thing is covered in mother-of-pearl.'

'Come on,' said Nico. 'Not now.'

'But –'

'*David* first. You have to book for a specific time. We must go to the Accademia straight away.'

'It *is* true,' she said, hurrying along behind him, 'that we don't have long to take in the many treasures of Florence, but at this pace, I'll be dead by teatime.'

They had to dive and duck between the crowds, as they made their way through the streets until they came to the Galleria dell'Accademia that housed *David*. Nico was in such a hurry that Jacquie practically slid along the floor of the main hall until she reached the alcove where he stood, magnificent and bathed in grey light.

'Gawd, he's huge.'

'Five metres, I think.'

'And look at the veins in his hand . . . and that expression. He's . . .'

'Apprehensive?'

'I was going to say determined.'

'Like me,' said Nico. 'Apprehensive, but determined.'

'You don't quite have his body, though, do you?'

In that gallery, and later in the Uffizi, through vast corridors and stately rooms crammed with art, they hurried round, Nico pointing at masterpieces and dropping the names of too many masters – Giotto, Botticelli, Raphael, Michelangelo – in case someone should ask her about them back in Orta.

It was sticky work, and it was fun. Florence was beautiful, Nico good-humoured and generous. She took photos of the sights, but longed to photograph Nico – looking up at the Duomo, hand on his waist, or grinning at her as she walked backwards ahead of him. Fearful that this weekend might be all they would ever have together, she wanted to capture these moments. At one point, they were sitting on a low ridge against a wall, licking each other's ice-creams when a Japanese couple asked politely if they would mind taking their picture. When it was done, the gentleman offered to reciprocate, reaching for Jacquie's camera. 'No, no, thanks, no.' The couple scuttled off, glancing over their shoulders.

'You could have let them take one, no?' Nico said.

'You know what it's like with digitals – everyone wants to see them as soon as you walk in the door. Not like the good old days when you could take out the incriminating prints you didn't want anyone to see and hide them in a bottom drawer.'

'You could have deleted it, right here.'

'If I had a photo of us, looking like we do at the moment, I'd never be able to delete it.'

'How do we look at the moment?'

'Happy.'

They checked into an old, slightly shabby hotel, a former palazzo, on the Arno. The room was Spartan; the view grand. Jacquie leant out the window, allowing her eyes to settle on the Ponte Vecchio further along the river. 'The only bridge,' Nico said, 'the Germans did not blow up when they were retreating at the end of the war.'

Jacquie sighed. 'It's just too beautiful.' A tight confusion of tourists could be seen on the only open part of the crowded bridge, beneath the three high arches, on either side of which disorderly extensions, cream and yellow and pink boxes, hung off the outer walls, like bees clinging to a honeycomb. It was framed by a backdrop of green – cypress trees and hills. 'You know,' she said, 'I like Cork, with its river and hills, but I don't think it likes me. I've tried to blend in, to be a part of it, but it always feels as if I'm just outside. In two years, I haven't put down any really good times there, and that's what makes a place home, isn't it? I can't imagine it'll ever feel like home.'

'Good,' said Nico. 'At least I wouldn't be taking you away from your home.'

'If only you *could* take me away.'

He pulled her over to the bed. 'Now we have so much time,' he said, as they lay down, 'I don't know where to start.'

'We must ring Carlotta at intervals to let her know how we're doing.' She could feel him smiling against her mouth when he kissed her. She took off his glasses and set them aside. 'You have a Roman nose and Irish eyes.'

'You have everything I want.'

*

They had dinner in a trattoria on the pavement. Motorbikes whizzed by with young women on the back, hair trailing behind them, and little Fiats honked at one another, interrupting conversation. Jacquie stared across the street, fork in hand, meal untouched, eyes glazed. 'It's so unfair,' she said, 'that the happiest two days either of us has spent in a long time will have to be lied about when we get back to Orta.'

Nico reached across for her hand. 'Cristina and I will break up.'

'I'd hate to have that on my conscience.'

'... and then there is nothing anyone can say. Carlotta can blame no one. As for our parents, they fell in love. Why shouldn't we?'

'Ask Carlotta.'

'The step-thing, you know, is just someone else's contract.'

'But it's still there. It's still *something*. If we were a couple, I can imagine people asking, "So how did you two meet?" and I'd have to say, "Em, he's my stepbrother." ' And they'd say, "Ooh, incest!" '

'But it wouldn't be!'

'I *know* that, and nor was it incest when my grandmother ran away with her cousin, but that didn't stop the whole town muttering about it. People aren't rational about family. Loads'll be creeped out by us. I mean, how do you suggest Mum introduces you? "This is my stepson and Jacquie's boyfriend." Dara would probably go, "Gross!" And Natalie's already said, "Not the wisest move, Jacquie." They won't be able to see past it.'

'Jacquie,' Nico squeezed her wrist, 'are *you* able to see past it? The others don't matter.'

'My relationship with my mother matters. It was hard for her, you know, starting again, but she did it, and it's like I'm coming along and stamping all over this whole new life she has and making it about *me*.'

'Right from the start you have thought only of them. Now it's time to –'

'Because they deserve it. And I seem to remember you dumping me because you were concerned about them too.'

Nico sat back, letting go of her hand, and gave the once-over to a young woman in a miniskirt getting on to a moped. Then he turned to Jacquie. 'You've made a lot of sacrifices for your mother already. Your life in France. Your life with Didier. I don't want to be another sacrifice.'

They had intended to spend the weekend making some kind of plan, but the only conceivable plan involved risking Cristina's love affair, and resolving to do so in the midst of their own deep passion proved too hard. Instead, they walked, all the next day, seeing more in each other than they did in Florence. They held each other's hands and arms, as if they feared that, should they let go, the other would be gone.

And Jacquie *would* be gone – back to work – within a week.

Before they went for their train, they came across a curiosity shop backing on to the Arno. It was bursting with souvenirs, curiosities and tourists, so they took refuge on a cloister at the back, also crammed with stands and postcards. Jacquie took photos of the Ponte Vecchio, and leant over the wall at the corner of the terrace where there was still sunlight. Nico pulled at the collar of his blue shirt. The tips of his fingers touched the tips of hers on the warm wall. The murky river below ambled by, tourists fought for space behind them, and in the evening light the Ponte Vecchio turned gold.

## 21

Nico pulled on the oars, let them drip, then placed them inside the boat, which gulped at the water, like a dog drinking from puddles. He had barely said a word since he'd rowed up to Luke's garden, in Carlotta's little boat, and told Jacquie to get in. She'd put on her skirt and shirt, let herself down the ladder, and he had rowed straight out into the lake in the early-afternoon heat.

'Won't she mind you borrowing her boat?'

'I often take it. Anyway, she's in Armeno.'

Jacquie had never seen him like this – cross and bossy. 'What's wrong? Why have I been brought out here on a scorching afternoon? I don't have my hat.'

'We need to talk. We can't in there.' He gestured towards the villa.

Jacquie's fingers tightened on the bench. Time had come. He was going to bring this to an end. It was proving too difficult, too stressful, but she didn't want him to say it, or to say another word. Better they sit in silence, drifting, dying a bit. Kissing under the jetty when their parents were right over their heads had been a close call, too close, but since Florence, they had become even more reluctant to throw off the camouflage of his engagement, as much for themselves as for everyone else. The atmosphere in the villa was taut again, and Nico didn't want to provoke a crisis they might later regret.

Everyone was edgy, not least Jacquie's mother, who was visibly straining in the face of Carlotta's strategic presumption. Carlotta had handled the news of Luke and Marina's engagement as she handled everything, by taking control. She had purchased their wedding wholesale and owned it outright within twenty-four hours of the announcement, as if it was hers to conceive, plan and execute. She talked about it so frequently – harrying them for a date, a location, pressing Luke to get Marina a ring, and even suggesting a double celebration for father and son – that the subject became such a sore point between the happy couple that neither dared bring it up. Marina had been driven to announce that she didn't want an engagement ring, which wounded Luke, who, with Jacquie's help, was in the process of designing one with the posh jeweller in the square. He told Carlotta not to mention the wedding again, thereby making it taboo for everyone else.

After the McGonagles left with Dara in early August, the house felt eerily empty, in spite of a full quota of tenants, but Jacquie, who should have left before them, had refused to go home. When it came to it, returning to that job was beyond her, so she had sent off her resignation instead, with Luke's support. Marina wasn't so sure: she was afraid, she said, that Jacquie would end up drifting and settle nowhere. But Luke reassured her that there would be plenty of opportunity, come the autumn, for Jacquie to find work, either in Cork or Italy. If it came to it, he was convinced she could make use of her languages in Milan. Jacquie suspected that, with all the changes that lay ahead, he liked the idea of keeping her close to Marina, unaware that it also kept her close to his son.

Jacquie was living in a state of suppressed elation. This secret affair was the joy of her days, the heat of her nights, the shilly-shallying of her heart when no one else could see it. Even if there was no easy place for it, this was love as she had never known it, and never wanted to know it again.

Yet Nico sat opposite her on the boat, looking as if their lives were about to end.

*

Marina leant against the window frame, arms crossed, heart heaving. It didn't add up that she could meet such a man, who fitted into her like a made-to-measure joint, and yet struggle to hang in, hold on. Carlotta could not be removed from the equation; she was stuck to these people like a limpet, and announcing their engagement had changed nothing. Carlotta did not reveal her warm, embracing side, as Luke had hoped, nor was she contained by the news, as Marina had hoped. She had been wrong: in marrying Luke she would indeed be marrying Carlotta; it was a deeply challenging prospect.

Her attention was drawn down to the right – a boat coming out from under the overhanging tree. Nico and Jacquie, in Carlotta's rowboat. Marina frowned. Where were they off to? There was something weary in Nico's rowing, and Jacquie was stiff, her hands gripping the seat. They weren't speaking. Oh, God, she thought, they must be having a tiff and it's probably about us and the mess this has become . . . It wouldn't do if they fell out. If she was to stick this out, she needed these two supporting her.

Her eyes lifted and moved across the lake, so still in the mid-afternoon, and so quiet. How, she wondered, could such a vast body of water make so little sound? Miles long, miles across, all but silent. She looked back at the boat. What were they thinking, heading out there in the dead heat? Nico had pointed the boat straight out, away from the shore. Her eyes wandered again, but kept returning to the two of them, as they got smaller and smaller, and the lake got deeper and deeper beneath them.

'Hallo.' Luke came in behind her. 'What are you looking at?'

'Nico and Jacquie. That's them in the boat. They've gone way out . . . Good day?' she asked, without turning.

'Good enough. I was talking to Roberto earlier – the friend who owns the place in Essaouira – he says it's free from October if we'd like it. I thought we could go, the two of us, and maybe,' he added tentatively, 'make enquiries about getting married there. Some time in the new year, perhaps?'

She glanced over her shoulder. 'With a couple of camels as witnesses?'

'And Hamid, of course. In fact, I've booked flights.'

Marina's gaze drifted back to the lake. 'For when?'

'October. That's some scorcher out there,' said Luke.

'I hope they're all right.'

'Leave them be.'

Instead she reached for the binoculars.

'Marina!'

'I want to make sure they're okay.'

Nico was no longer rowing. They were just sitting there. 'I hope she's got sunscreen on.' Marina turned the glasses to the shore. On the terrace of a raspberry-cream mansion surrounded by trees, a man was standing, shirtless, gazing out. 'I wonder who he is. Big house, all alone. Maybe he'd like a woman in his life. A woman like Carlotta.' But the binoculars, almost of their own volition, swept back to her daughter. 'I wish those two would come in. It's the only boat on the whole lake.'

'Leave them, would you? It's a bit intrusive, isn't it?'

Nico glanced at the villa and said, 'Cristina is coming back.'

'What?'

'She's leaving him, and moving to Omegna.'

Jacquie stared at him, trying to add this up and come out with a neat equation in her favour. From his expression, this was not good news. 'She wants you back?'

'She wants a family. There's no hope for her in that

relationship, and even if they tried to make it work, they would make problems for everyone else.'

'I know *that* feeling.' Jacquie put her hand in the water. 'So your engagement is about to be reactivated? Marriage and babies, here we come?'

'Ah, Jacquie,' he said wearily, 'I know we have operated in strange circumstances, but please don't talk to me like this. Cristina is leaving Rome, coming back to live here. My purpose as her shield is no longer necessary.'

'But you've often said you would probably marry, eventually.'

'That was before you.'

'Isn't it all the more important now that you two present a united front?'

'I've played my part and kept attention off her life in Rome. She never asked for more. Now she will return and we will make it clear we no longer wish to be together.' His intensity, Jacquie now realized, had not been anger but suppressed excitement.

'How will that go down?'

'On my side, no problem,' he said, 'but her parents will blame me.'

'Even if Cristina says it's her choice?'

'They'll make it my fault. Which is okay, I don't care, as long as it ends, now.'

'Are you sure she doesn't want to be with you?'

'There is only one thing Cristina cares about – if she can't be with the person she loves, she wants me to be with the person *I* love. I brought you out here to tell you I'm free and that . . .' Nico's arms were hanging between his knees so that his hands were almost on the planks '. . . I can't continue without you. It's like . . .' he looked past her '. . . having nothing to drink. I feel, you know, dried up.'

'Scorched. Me too.' She put her bare toes on his feet.

He held her wrists. 'At least now we have a chance. After Cristina and I have ended things, we can get everyone used to the possibility of you and I being together. It'll take time, but we can do it. As for everyone else, I don't care. They can deal with it or not. Cristina will be here this weekend to tell them her plans.'

A speck of hope flickered in Jacquie's mind. 'It certainly eliminates the Carlotta factor.'

'For you, anyway,' he said. 'She'll punish me for the rest of her life.'

'But she won't be able to blame Mum, or me.'

'Exactly. This is the beginning for us, if you want it. So I was thinking – you should go home, for a month maybe, then come back when this stupid engagement is over, and we'll take it from there. I'll tell Dad. He'll back us up with your mother.'

'You think he won't mind about us?'

'Come on, I know him. He's a reasonable person. And so is your mother.' They sat there, bobbing about.

'Jacquie? What do you think?'

'I think . . . I think I'm absolutely thrilled your fiancée's leaving you. I told you she would. It's nothing less than you deserve!'

He smiled, putting his hands under her knees and pulling her towards him.

'Careful. We could be seen – two blobs blending into one.'

'*Ma voglio baciarti.* I want to kiss you so much.'

'Me too, and I know just the place.' She stood up and jumped. The water was cold and deep, but something rejoiced in her as she came to the surface, ducking sideways to avoid Nico as he jumped over her. She squealed, and reached out to him.

Hidden behind the boat, they held on to the rim with one hand. Jacquie wrapped her legs round him and pulled him against her. 'Take these off,' he said.

Marina raised the binoculars. 'They've jumped in! I hope they'll be able to get back out again.'

'I'm going for a shower,' said Luke. 'Quit snooping.'

The empty boat immediately caught her eye. It looked like her own, pale blue and red. Carlotta slowed down, pulled into the side of the road, and lifted her sunglasses. It *was* her boat, and it was drifting far from the shore. How had it slipped off the jetty? And how had it got so far? It was leaning to the left. She climbed out of the car and shaded her eyes. The afternoon sun was staring straight at her.

Two people were hanging off the side of the boat.

'*Porco demonio!*' She jumped into the car and skidded out of the lay-by.

Marina heard Carlotta's quick footsteps coming across the hall, going along the corridor to Luke's study, and coming back towards the drawing room. She looked in, nodded curtly at Marina, and hurried upstairs. Uneasy, Marina went to the door and listened, then also went upstairs. Hearing a mumble of voices coming from Luke's room, she made her way through the alcove, half expecting to find Carlotta sitting on the end of their bed, watching Luke get dressed. But she wasn't there.

Her voice was coming from the bathroom. Marina's gut seized.

They were in the bathroom.

The door was ajar. She stepped towards it and pushed it fully open.

Carlotta was standing in front of the bath, her hands on her hips, ranting at Luke in Italian. He was standing in the shower, his body clearly visible behind the frosted glass.

Marina gathered her voice. 'Get out.'

Carlotta glanced over her shoulder, but continued babbling at Luke.

He looked round the partition. 'Carlotta.'

'Please leave our bathroom,' Marina said.

'One minute!' said Carlotta. 'I have to speak with Luke.'

'I don't care if you need to speak to God! You will not do so in our bathroom.'

Luke snapped at Carlotta. She snapped in Marina's direction, like a dog snapping at something behind it.

'Oh, say it in whatever language you choose,' Marina retorted. 'It amounts to the same thing. You are an overbearing, arrogant bitch in any language!'

'Marina!'

Unfazed by Luke's reprimand, she stepped towards Carlotta, her throat dry. 'You should be very careful, Carlotta, because the chances of me sticking around for another little threesome in the shower are pretty thin at this point, and if I do leave, I don't think Luke will ever forgive you.'

'My boat has been stolen!' Carlotta shouted. 'Luke must get it back.' She grabbed a towel and handed it to him.

'Get out,' he said to her.

'Oh, your boat hasn't been stolen,' Marina said dismissively.

'It has! There are two youngsters pushing it away. There could be an accident!'

'It's Nico and Jacquie. They're bringing it back in.'

Carlotta turned, her face glowing white like a full moon. Muttering oaths, she rushed from the room.

Luke dried himself off, shaking his head reproachfully at Marina.

She raised her chin defiantly. 'It can only be a matter of time before I wake up and find her in bed with us.'

'Marina . . .'

'Don't bother with the towel,' she said, going into the bedroom. 'We're all friends here.'

Carlotta was still there, standing at the window, her hand covering her mouth.

'For God's sake,' said Marina, 'could we *please* have some privacy?'

Carlotta turned. Her eyes were darker than usual, and still.

Luke came out, a towel round his waist, another in his hand.

'He is engaged to my daughter,' Carlotta said to him, in a half-whisper.

'I'm aware of that. Now, could you allow me to get dressed?'

'Why, then, is he kissing *her* daughter?'

'Don't be ridiculous.' With a nervous glance at Marina, Luke went to the window. 'He isn't doing anything of the sort. They're rowing in.'

'I saw them from the road! In the water. I didn't know who it was!'

Luke blanched.

Marina sank on to the end of the bed.

Jacquie and Nico, stuck into their wet clothes, came up the steps, still laughing about the ungainly struggle they'd had getting back into the boat, and squelched across the hall. The drawing-room door was open. They went in.

A tableau confronted them, like a vast painting, colourful, still, throbbing with words just uttered. Marina was sitting on a couch against the wall. The tissue in her fist drew Jacquie's eyes to her face, but Marina would not look at her. Carlotta stood by the window, arms crossed. Only Luke looked at them face on, with a piercing expression, challenging them in a way the women would not.

'Nico,' he said.

'*Che sta succedendo?*'

'Perhaps you'd like to bring us all into the picture.'

'What do you mean?'

'It seems,' Luke said, with a slight nod towards Carlotta, 'that Carlotta here has fairly powerful eyesight.'

With one glance at her daughter, Marina knew. Jacquie looked straight at Nico, and he at her, which was enough to tell everyone what they wanted to know.

'While we appreciate that this is, strictly speaking, none of our business,' Luke struggled on, 'we're nonetheless confused. Aren't you quite seriously committed to Cristina?'

It was Nico's opportunity to say, 'No,' but he hesitated. He had to. He could not pre-empt Cristina. Not yet. Especially since there could be no retrieving, now, the neat severing of their engagement. It was gone. Too late, now, for Cristina to announce that she was leaving Nico of her own volition. They would only believe that she was doing it because of Jacquie, so there was nothing to be gained in blowing her cover.

'Committed?' Carlotta hissed at Luke. 'What kind of word is this? They are engaged to be married. Just like you and I were – before you did exactly this!'

They started yelling at one another in Italian. Old gashes spread open.

Nico watched them.

Marina got up, walked past them and left the room.

Jacquie felt ripped. Torn. For the first time, her loyalties were divided. She knew she should go after her mother, yet felt a strong, and deep, inclination to remain with Nico. But the lonely click of her mother's sandals on the marble steps was too much. She followed. 'Mum?'

'Not now.'

'But I can –'

'I don't want to hear it, and I don't want to see you.'

Closing the bedroom door behind her, tears flowing, Marina found it hard to stand up.

On a plate. Her head. Handed to Carlotta. By her own daughter.

Voices rose from below – Carlotta screeching and Luke trying to calm her now, soothing, soothing, and then the bang of the drawing-room door, followed by a greater bang as the front door slammed.

Luke's voice again, shouting at his son this time – English, Italian, English, he didn't seem to know which language he spoke – and Nico shouting back in Italian.

Marina stepped out to her balcony, where she could hear more clearly.

'Fucking hell,' Luke growled. 'Just when I'm trying to bring it all together, you pull this off! Don't you see that I'm holding on to Marina with both hands? Trying to keep her here against the odds? How many women do you think would put up with your barmy grandmother and another woman hanging around this place like a fucking tapestry? Do you know how many women would put up with it? None. Zero!'

Nico retorted in Italian.

Luke talked over him. 'If you no longer had feelings for Cristina, why maintain the engagement? Why the duplicity? What purpose did it serve? Because it'll fuck things up good and proper for me. Could you not see what would come of it?'

Marina dithered. She should go down to him – he sounded as if he was breaking up – but she had to hear this. Nico spoke, more quietly. Something about Cristina.

'As if that will make any difference now,' Luke said, 'even if it were true.'

'It *is* true!'

'Then why didn't you say something? Nico, I have forced Marina to endure Carlotta's condescension because I was trying to protect *your* relationship with Cristina!'

Marina stepped back, as if she had stepped into view. How had she not seen that? Luke never taking her part, never properly challenging Carlotta – how could he, when his son's long-term happiness depended on their continued friendship?

'The only relationship you have been protecting,' Nico said in English, 'is yours with Carlotta. At Marina's expense.'

Luke didn't respond. Marina, listening so intently her ears wanted to crack, sensed that he wasn't sure where Nico was going and couldn't afford to lead him. Natalie had been right, of course, about Luke and Carlotta. There was more. Marina gripped the railing, bracing herself. It was coming at her, like a great wave off the lake.

'*Senti, Papà*,' Nico's tone softened, 'I've known for years, okay? And I'm sorry for you, really. But you took a lot from us, from me, and I wonder about that sometimes. About who . . .' Emotion had crept into his voice. 'You paid a hard price, but don't pretend you did anything for me, and don't make Marina part of the price you pay. Cut her loose, because you know, as I do, that Carlotta will never do the same for you.'

In spite of a tremor in her limbs so severe that she could barely walk, Marina began to pack. Taking her things one by one, folding them neatly and placing them in the suitcase she had thought not to see until the end of the summer, if then. Her room drained into her bags, item by item, tears plopping on to the backs of her hands. Take me back to that hospital bedside, she thought, to the man who couldn't think or speak or feel. She closed her eyes and imagined herself by Aidan's side, on that narrow hospital bed, and whispered, 'Take me with you.'

She could not stay. She would never live it down. Whatever about Carlotta, Bridget's scorn would be unendurable, as would the disdain she would heap upon Jacquie for taking another woman's fiancé. Just as Luke had broken his engagement to Carlotta, so Nico had broken his promise to Cristina. It was a mess, a wretched mess, even worse than it had been. Whatever was going on between their children, the damage was comprehensively done, in one vicious blow. She couldn't do it, couldn't pack, so she stood by the window and waited for Luke.

She stared across the lake to where the boat had been. She had known. It had been in the stillness of the afternoon and on the stillness of the water. The only ripples disturbing it had been spreading out from that one boat and coming all the way to the shore. When she'd seen them row away like that, she had known something was about to blow. Luke had too. He kept telling her to leave them, to come away from the window. Was that premonition on his part? Or something else?

When he came quietly into the room, she said, without turning, 'Did you know?'

'I . . . suspected.'

'Why didn't you tell me? Why didn't you speak to him?'

'I didn't believe him capable of it with so much at stake.'

'What made you suspect?'

He handed her a whiskey, then sat on the bed, leaning over his knees, his hands clasped round his glass. 'They'd become like mirrors to each other. When one was low, so was the other. When one was giddy, flushed, the other was too. I'd only just become aware of it. I would have told you otherwise, but I'm not sure I would have done anything. I'm not sure we have the right to interfere.'

'What about Cristina?'

'He says they had an understanding, but it was quite different from what we presumed. He's not at liberty to say further. I'd like to believe him, but . . .'

'The fact remains that he's been cheating on her. He's –'

'Your daughter is not entirely innocent.'

'At least she's single!'

'She knows he's spoken for.'

Marina leant against the window frame. 'Arguing about them already. Taking sides. We haven't a hope now, if we ever did.'

'I don't accept that but, then, I'm not as inclined to give up as easily as you are.'

'You think this is easy? Carlotta will blame me, so will your mother. He'll be the golden boy, seduced by the vixen, my daughter. You said as much yourself just now.'

He ran his fingers across his forehead.

She paced in front of the window, cutting that peaceful evening vista, so incongruous a background to this fractured display, shouting voices from every window, people pacing in the lake's view.

'Packing already?' Luke asked.

'I've got to get out of here. No wonder your mother's losing her marbles.'

'Every which way you turn, Marina, you see an obstacle. It makes me wonder if you're looking for a way out.'

'You don't think this is an obstacle?'

'I think it's two young people enjoying themselves.'

'My daughter with your son! That would never work, even if we did stay together. *Especially* if we stayed together.'

'There you go: one more excuse to leave – my exes, my mother, now my son.'

'I'm not making this up, Luke!'

'I know!' he roared. 'And I know it's bloody difficult, but we cannot allow our children to dictate what we do. As far as I'm concerned, they can do what they bloody well like, but I won't blame you, now or ever, for anything that happens between them. But can *you* say the same?'

'No. I *can't* promise that I wouldn't take it out on you if he hurt her. It's the way of things. We'll side with our children, they'll side with their parents – it won't work for any of us.'

'From what I can see, Jacquie and Nico are siding only with each other. We should do likewise.'

Marina could barely get the question out. 'Do you think it's serious?'

'Nico claims to be deeply in love with her.'

'Oh, God.'

'Look on the bright side. Carlotta will, as you say, never forgive us. We'll probably never see her again.'

'Don't kid yourself. This will empower her. She's got you in a vice now. Our children have ruined her daughter's happiness.'

Without looking up, Luke reached out. She gave him her hand. He pulled her down beside him. 'We can get over this.'

'I just want to go home.'

'We're supposed to be a couple, Marina. We're supposed to stick together when the going gets rough, but you were never that keen on sharing the rough stuff, were you?'

'This,' she said, 'from you? Who doesn't share at all?' She went back to the window. 'You expect me to live with only one half of you, Luke. The other half isn't even up for grabs.'

'It is now.'

'Too late, I think.' She stared out, shaking her head. 'Love and circumstance. You'd think it'd be easier, somehow . . . This should have been easier.'

'Sit down,' said Luke.

'Why?'

'I want to give you the other half, even if it is too late.'

She sat on the chair near the window. Years ago she'd seen a ballet. Towards the end, the dancers had peeled away the garments of one of their troupe, layer by layer, until he was all but naked in the spotlight. She felt like that dancer – other people tearing away her protective layers.

The ice cubes in Luke's glass rattled when he wiped his mouth, no more ready now than he had ever been to speak of things of which he had rarely spoken. He took a slug of whiskey. 'There was a baby. I mean,' he corrected himself quickly, 'a pregnancy.'

'I don't think I want to hear this.'

'I'm sure you don't, and I don't want to tell you. I'm breaking a long-held confidence by doing so, but if it'll make you understand . . .' He hadn't looked at her since he'd come into the room. 'Carlotta became pregnant . . . It was a . . . We'd had a . . .'

'Oh, for Christ's sake, I know how it happens.'

'It would have been disastrous. For both of us. Nico was eight months old.'

'God, you were married,' she whispered. 'Jesus, Luke.'

'Yes.' He ran his tongue over his upper lip, then bit the bottom one. 'We were living in London. I came to Orta to do some business for my aunt and, well . . . No excuses. I was unfaithful to Francesca for the first and only time. When Carlotta told me she was pregnant, I came back to see her. She was beside herself, with the usual terrors of the time, especially in Italy: her parents, the community, her studies, her life as she'd planned it. I panicked too – my marriage, my child. Financially I was strapped. I was barely supporting my family, such as it was. And Carlotta, for her own part, was as ambitious as hell. She had big plans, she wanted to do a lot of things, and she was scared of what would happen to her if she didn't achieve it. So we agreed she'd have a termination in London. I arranged it and flew her over . . . But when she arrived, she was having second thoughts.'

Marina bent over her knees. 'You're not going to tell me that Cristina and Nico share a sibling?'

He went on: 'I'd made an appointment for her at a clinic and put her up in a guesthouse in Islington, well away from where we lived . . . Carlotta asked for more time. I exerted some pressure, a lot of pressure. I had no faith even then, and my suffocating rural upbringing and my mother's rigid holiness made me determined to suffer no Catholic guilt at all. But Carlotta had faith, a deep faith, as she still has, and if discovering she was pregnant was devastating for her, making that decision was worse. It was very hard on her.' His voice was strange. The words were coming out as if he was pressing buttons on a computer to bring the correct word forward. 'She said she had an Italian friend in London and wanted to speak to her, so I backed off for a couple of days so they could talk it through . . . But her friend urged her to keep the baby. She told her about a convent somewhere in Italy where she could spend her pregnancy and then have the child adopted. I couldn't handle that, couldn't countenance it. You can't draw a line under adoption. There's no . . . ending in it. Or that was the way I felt at the time. So she was being tugged in one direction by this devout friend and in another by me.' Luke's voice grew even quieter. 'It was an intolerable position to put her in. Everything I did at that time was contemptible and I don't excuse myself at any level. Nor do I expect you to. Nor should Carlotta ever forgive me.'

For several moments, neither of them moved or spoke, until Marina finally asked, 'What did she do?'

'She had the termination.'

Marina put her hand over her eyes.

'I spent a few days nursing her – pretended to be away on business – then put her on the plane home and went back to my wife, relieved. Saved. Off the hook, like so many men before me. Nico was sitting on the kitchen floor beside a chair, a white kitchen chair, gripping its leg with his little chubby hands, and Francesca was at the table, crying as if her heart were breaking.' He took another deep breath. 'There's something I've never told you about Francesca. She was the love of my life. Before you. She was my greatest success and my worst failure.'

'She'd found out about you and Carlotta?'

'No, that wasn't why she was crying. She was crying because . . .'

Marina went to sit with him. He was trembling.

'Because she'd had an opportunity to prevent an abortion and had failed. Failed, failed, failed, she kept saying. A baby had died because she had not been able to persuade the mother to keep it. A friend, she explained, had come to her in great distress, but she had failed her, and herself, and God. That was the way she saw it.' He was whispering now. '"Here are we," she said, weeping in my arms, "with one healthy, loved child and trying to have another, but in a bucket somewhere in this city . . ."' Luke took more whiskey and rubbed his eyes. 'That was when I realized what I'd done.'

'Why did Carlotta go to her? Of all people?'

'Because she needed a friend and she knew she could rely on Francesca's discretion. She also knew that Francesca would never suspect me.'

'Did she ever find out?'

He nodded. 'Years later, after Frankie was born. I confessed. It was too big to carry around and I thought enough time had passed . . . But with Francesca there would never be enough time for such a thing, so she left. Not because I'd cheated, she could forgive me that, but because I had blood on my hands. My own.'

Marina shivered, and wiped her cheekbones.

'Carlotta would say, often says, it was the right decision,' said Luke. 'She was single. Her family was deeply conservative. I was deeply married. She could never have given the child away, could never have managed as a single parent . . . It was a terrible decision, but it was the right thing to do at the time, she says now. That's the game we play. But the thing is, Marina, it was more than a decision. It's a burden, a cross she carries every single day. She prays and goes to church and hopes for forgiveness, but she doesn't believe she'll ever receive it. Her conscience is black, and mine even blacker, because I *gave* her that bad conscience. I coerced her when she was vulnerable. Because I didn't have any faith, I didn't value hers, and now she thinks she's a sinner, and I'm the one who gave her that sin. She never really enjoys anything, because she doesn't believe she deserves to, and the only thing she feels she ever got right is Cristina. That's why, no matter how unreasonable she is, I can't hit back. For as long as I can, I'll do everything to make her life the way she would like it to be, so that carrying the penitence around might be a little easier for her.'

'Why didn't you marry her? That's all she wants.'

'No, you see, she doesn't want that. She loves me, but also loathes me. You're right about her wanting to sabotage our relationship. Of course that's what she's been trying to do. Why should I have such happiness if she can't?'

'So if I were to marry you, I'd have to take on this sin of hers as well?'

'You already have, my love.'

Bridget burst in. 'What's this? What is Carlotta telling me? Jacquie and Nico? What about poor Cristina?'

Bright as a button, of course, just when Marina needed her to be confused and thinking about the cliffs of Dover.

'I believe the engagement is off,' Luke told her.

'Whose? Yours?'

'No, Nico and Cristina.'

Marina stood up. 'Ours is also off.'

Luke shot her a look so sharp she recoiled.

'Of course Cristina has ended it, poor thing,' said Bridget. 'What choice does she have? Carlotta is devastated, Marina. *Devastated*.'

'I'm sorry. Nico rather swept Jacquie off her feet.'

Bridget's jaw tensed. 'Don't be ridiculous! He's been in love with Cristina since they were this high!' She marched out of the room.

'And you really think,' Marina said to Luke, 'that I could stay?'

'Yes. I do. This will sort itself out.'

'But that depends on what Nico and Jacquie choose to do,' she said, 'and that is out of our hands. Luke, I love you, I do, and I'd love to stay, but I'm drained and done in, and I don't have the courage required to take on those two women, especially now that their backs are up.'

'All right,' he said, defeated. 'I'll book you a flight, get you back to Ireland for a bit, but I'm not giving up, Marina.'

Nico and Jacquie were chasing cars. They headed north, winding round the lake to Omegna, then taking the long straight road towards the Swiss border. It was a beautiful evening. The sky was high and blue. They drove past a tumbling river, bluey-white with cold. The jagged slate-grey mountains were so much like a set of pointy teeth that driving towards them was like heading into a mouth whose sabre-like gnashers were about to crunch down on them. They didn't speak, but played a CD very loudly, in an attempt to block out the last hour. Nico was driving too fast. Jacquie stared up at those ominous peaks and wished the bite would come down on her, because she was cold on this hot day and she wanted to weep. She shivered.

Nico reached over, undid the top button of her shirt and put his hand over her breast. 'Take it off. Let it dry.'

So she pulled off her shirt and held it over her head to dry in the wind.

Snow Patrol was beating out 'Chasing Cars'.

Nico nodded, in time and in agreement. 'We'll be okay. Like the song says.'

'Will we?'

'I won't accept anything else.'

'Will *they*?'

Jacquie turned up the music. Nico stared hard at the road ahead, looking angry, cheated, and a bit scared, like her. The pain of her love for him shot through her. His arm stretched to the steering-wheel; the cuff of his shirt turned back; with one finger of his other hand he pushed up his spectacles. If they never went back, if they went on driving, driving to loud music, she wondered, would they ever arrive in a place where they could be? Whatever happened, she would never let this pain go. Not ever. No one could have it. Or take it. It was hers for keeps. Even when she died, she would take this pain, this love, with her, because it was everything she had become.

Nico's hand moved across her midriff. The mountains spiked the sky. The car purred. A perfect day. Could have been. The song tore at her. Chasing cars. They were chasing only themselves. Trying to catch up. To hang on to what they'd had, even though it had gone ahead without them.

Suddenly, with a skid of gravel, Nico pulled off the main

road and followed a minor road under a bridge and along a rural backway until they came across a dirt track. He followed it into a field, where they were shielded by corn as high as a bus. They tumbled out of the car, Jacquie in bikini and mini-skirt, and Nico pulling off his shirt as they crashed into the long yellowing grass at the edge of the crop, shoving off the necessary clothes so they could finish what they'd been trying to do in a hundred and forty-three metres of cold Alpine water, unseen even by Carlotta's powerful eyes.

Side by side, they lay in the grass afterwards, staring at the deep blue sky. 'Lucky I have my credit cards,' Nico said.

'Where will we go?'

'Somewhere.'

'For what it's worth, I love you.'

*'Ti amo anch'io. Sempre.'*

*'Sempre?'*

'Always. *Sempre e per sempre.* Always and for ever.' His eyes looked inwards, as if a thought had suddenly stopped behind them. '*Porco puttana.*'

'What?'

'I've just come up with Plan B.'

'Which is?'

When he told her, Jacquie laughed; she looked up at the sky, and laughed like mad.

## 22

Natalie put the pot on the table, fetched mugs and sat opposite Marina. 'Before we take this any further,' she said, 'I ought to tell you something. You'll probably throw me out.' She poured. Marina reached for the mug and held it with both hands, close to her face.

'I knew,' said Natalie.

Marina's eyes flickered. 'About Nico?'

'I should have told you, maybe.'

'Carlotta and I seem to be the only ones who missed it. Something in common at last. How did you know?'

'A look, that's all. From one end of the table to the other. Too tender to have been platonic. When he was here in April.'

'*April?*'

'I tried to talk to her. I pointed out the difficulty it could create for you –'

'As if she cared.'

'She did care, Marina. They were trying to pull it down, I'm sure of it, but it must have been bigger than their best intentions. It wasn't as if they could walk away from each other.'

'It's such a slap in the face,' Marina said quietly. 'In spite of all Carlotta's provocation, I managed to behave with dignity, only to be shown up by a daughter with no scruples. The ground went from under me.'

'Would it help if I said I suspect they might be in love?'

'That doesn't help at all. I'm also in love. How many chances can Luke and I hope to have? Jacquie'll be having love affairs for years yet. Why did she have to fall for Carlotta's future son-in-law, my future stepson?'

Natalie went round the table to her. 'Because we don't choose it, do we? It chooses us.'

'I don't think much of its choices. I mean, why couldn't I have fallen for Matthew, for example? He's so uncomplicated.'

'But then you'd have Kitt for a stepdaughter and *me* for an ex!'

Marina laughed half-heartedly. 'At least there are no sides to Kitt. What you see is what you get.'

'You just concentrate on Luke, all right?' said Natalie. 'Matthew's all very well, I'll grant you, and he earns a lot and he's good in bed, but –'

'*Is* he?'

'Fabulous, actually, but –'

'See, why didn't I ever take advantage of that?'

'Because you've never been in love with him, remember? A small detail, but one worth noting nonetheless.'

'Oh, Natalie, why was I so short with Jacquie? I wouldn't hear her out. I didn't give her a chance and then they took off. What if I don't get her back? We might never see them again!'

'Oh, stop it.'

'But no one knows where they are.'

'They're off licking their wounds, as well they might, after the chaos they've caused. And maybe they're saying goodbye. I can't see Jacquie sticking with this, not when she knows what it's cost you.'

'If only they'd come to us – we might have been able to do something before Carlotta found out. But to find out *from* her!'

'Listen, as soon as you found out, you left Luke. No wonder they kept it quiet. Speaking of which, why did you leave him?'

'Because I needed air. I needed to breathe.' Marina's eyes glazed over. 'The thing is, I know how Carlotta felt. When Didier dumped Jacquie – after she'd waited so long and staked so much on him – I wanted to string him up by his earlobes, and if there'd been a third party involved, I would have damned her to hell. So I feel for Carlotta, especially when she has so much else . . .'

'So much else?'

'He told me what it is, the thing she has on him.'

'Oh.' Natalie sat back. 'How bad is it?'

'Bad enough, but it was a long time ago. A youthful mistake. A panicked type of mistake.'

'So why is she still making him pay?'

'I'm not sure she is. I think it's him. He feels he hasn't made up for it yet. He believes he never will.'

'Does it make a difference to you? Can you forgive whatever it was?'

Marina didn't say anything for a long time. She'd been thinking about those events in London, night and day, but the only emotion they brought out of her was compassion for Luke and his wife, and a deep compassion for Carlotta. 'It isn't up to me to forgive him,' she said, 'but I can excuse it. It's left a terrible mark on them, which would make Carlotta even harder to handle because now I can't blame her any more. I understand why she needs to control everything. If she's in control, nothing like that can happen to her again.'

'If you don't blame her, can you live with her?'

'Can't seem to, can I? I've spent months and months trying.'

'This isn't over, you know,' Natalie said, after a moment. 'With Luke. There has to be a solution to this problem and I am going to find it.'

Marina stood up. 'I have a plot booked in the local cemetery.

You'll find me there when you've come up with your solution.'

Jacquie turned up when no one was expecting her. She didn't ask to be collected at the airport, didn't let anyone know she was coming, simply let herself into the house a full ten days after Marina had got home, late in the evening when they were finishing dinner.

'Well, look what the cat dragged in,' said Dara, when she came into the kitchen. 'Proud of yourself, are you?'

Marina turned. Jacquie put down her bag.

'Can I have more chicken?' Kitt asked.

'No,' said Natalie. 'You and I are going upstairs.' As they passed Jacquie in the doorway, Natalie smiled. 'Welcome home.'

'Thanks.'

Dara shot her a disapproving look as he, too, left the room. 'I seem to remember you rushing to Orta to smooth things along for Mum. Great job!'

Marina couldn't say a word, but everything felt a little better already. Seeing Jacquie, having her back, made everything else bearable. These were the people who mattered – Jacquie and Dara. Nothing else in the world was of any consequence. Not Bridget or Carlotta or Luke. All could be sacrificed as long as Jacquie and Dara were okay. But that, somehow, didn't stem the hurt or the anger. It still had to be resolved, and now at last Marina could have the furious argument, ask the questions, and quell the screaming that had been going on inside her head for almost two weeks. She began with 'Tea?'

'I'll get it.'

Marina grabbed the kettle, filled it, banged it on to the stove. She pulled out the teapot, flung some tealeaves into it. They had a long night ahead. By morning, perhaps, the anger would be gone and she would be a normal mother again.

Her daughter sank into a chair. Marina wanted to hug her, and blame her. But for what? For falling in love with a lovely and decent young man?

'I'm sorry, Mum.'

'Are you?'

Jacquie looked away. 'Have you spoken to Luke?'

'He called to say you were both all right.'

'Did he mention that Cristina had broken off the engagement three weeks ago? They just hadn't told anyone.'

'There's been a lot of that going on, hasn't there?' said Marina. 'Not telling people things.'

'The point is, it wasn't a proper engagement. It wasn't even a relationship. I knew that all along.'

'The problem, Jacquie, is that nobody else did.'

Music pounded down from Dara's room.

Marina sighed. 'I thought you wanted things to work out for me. I thought you kept coming to Orta to help with Carlotta, and all along –'

'That *is* why I went!'

'– all along in the background, you were sabotaging any hope I had of ever fitting in there.'

'We're not responsible for your happiness, Mum. Go back to Luke. There's no reason not to. I'm going to bed.'

As the door closed, Marina picked up the teapot and smashed it on the floor.

Jacquie went to her room; it was dark and cold. She lay down. Her stomach was a jumble of jitters. A long day; a desperate day. She smelt the back of her wrist. Nico had held it as they had walked through the airport car park, gripping her as if he would always pull her forward like that, by his side, even though it was the end of such a week.

A week of love and catastrophe. An insignificant catastrophe, Nico kept saying – a controlled disaster, affecting only those closest to its core, who were nonetheless ragged and wounded. They had wandered about, the two of them, staying in small towns and villages, lying in strange beds and beside gushing rivers, wearing clothes newly bought.

'What do you think will happen?' she had asked him one day, when they were sitting in some place somewhere, having coffee, after hearing from Luke that Marina had left.

'Pa will go after her. He'll get her back. I don't know how, but he doesn't give up.' He took off his glasses to rub his eyes. 'And they'll live happily ever after.'

'And us?'

He put his glasses back on. 'You know what the story has to be for us.'

Back in Ireland, dropping sideways on to her pillow to sleep alone for the first time in twelve days, Jacquie was mesmerized. The best time of her life had also been one of the worst. The most companionable had been the loneliest. Days of tenderness were days of hurt inflicted on others, until one morning she woke to see Nico at his laptop, booking her flights home. It had simply been a question of one of them finding the guts to do it. Then he got into bed and said he asked only one thing of her: if their parents did not reconcile that she would pack up her things and come right back to him.

'And if they do get back together,' she had said, 'as you think they will?'

He rolled on to his back, sighed, and stared at the ceiling.

Jacquie pulled the duvet over her without even undressing. Back to the cooler Irish nights. Away from that stifling twenty-first-century heat-wave, back to where there was air. In the sticky room of their *pensione* that morning, they had made love before dawn. At the other end of the day, she had gone to bed fully clothed and alone.

'This is not the way it is going to finish,' Nico had said that day in the grass. 'This is not the way it is going to finish.'

Marina was a wreck. She'd given it everything, had been browbeaten all summer, and had still come out the other end without Luke. It hurt to lose him, to know he was hurt. No matter which way she turned, it hurt. If love could still make you soar in the middle years, so it could also make you drop, hard, to the ground, like a novice. She ought to have known better. Naïvely, she had imagined that with experience and age would come an ability to assuage the ravages of heartbreak.

The doubts were still there, but they were now the flipside of the ones she'd had in Orta. They came at night, in the dark. Night terrors, when the room got smaller and the air thinner, and panic rose in her throat. The idea of living without Luke terrified her, and she dreaded the life that, only a year before, had been so clearly mapped out: work, family, holidays alone for the ageing widow. She had perhaps avoided that other scenario: Bridget growing more infirm, more gaga, and making no sense at all, until one day Marina and Luke would have found themselves old and gaga, their best years well past, with Carlotta looming over them, flapping her mortal sin. Instead, Marina could see herself living with Natalie, the two of them getting cranky and crotchety together, maybe with Matthew thrown in, old geezers nobody wanted. Except that Luke *had* wanted her and, short of tying his mother and Carlotta to a lump of cement and dropping them into the lake, would have done anything for her. She was the one who had not been prepared to do anything for him.

No one believed it was over. The others were in cahoots to get her back with Luke. Jokes about how to handle Carlotta became ruder and more outrageous. 'I'll take her to rugby,' Dara suggested, 'and put her in the scrum – that should take care of her.' And Natalie kept drumming her nails on the table, saying she'd come up with a plan, some plan . . . Jacquie didn't get involved in the hoopla about how to deal with the Terrible Two and kept to herself. She was distant, and obviously lonely, but Marina didn't know how to breach the gap, mostly because she could not bring herself to say the one thing she probably should: "You didn't have to give him up for me." And she did not say it, because she did not want Nico in their lives. He would be too painful a reminder – his eyes, his body language, his voice, all so much like his father's. She couldn't be expected to stand by and watch them make a life together. One day she might get past it, but it was too soon to be so generous. Jacquie suffered, but Jacquie was young. She would heal more easily, Marina told herself, then probably meet somebody else.

'But you like Nico,' Suzanne said one day, when Marina was sitting on the pouffe in the shop, staring out at the grey September afternoon. 'Jacquie could do a lot worse. And if you're not with Luke . . .'

'If I don't have Luke, having Nico around would be like water-torture.'

'Okay, but let's say, for argument's sake, that you and Luke got back together. What then?'

'I don't know. I mean . . . what if they broke up?'

'Why would they?'

'Because it got off to a bad start, and because they'd have things to deal with other couples don't – like Carlotta, for example. And because Jacquie's young and restless . . . she might hurt him. They might hurt each other, and then Luke and I would have to handle this fractious ex-couple, step-siblings who used to be lovers.'

Suzanne shook her head lightly. 'Funny thing is, if they'd met first – if you and Luke had met through them, none of this would bother anyone.'

'I know, I'm making no sense. I accept that. Anyway, it's irrelevant now. Both relationships are over. Somehow, we've all managed to become victims of Carlotta's past. No wonder I had such a bad feeling the first time I saw her.'

Luke made his move in late September when a small package arrived in the post addressed in his neat hand. A set of keys fell out. She held them in her palm, in the grey light of the hallway – a Chubb and a latch key.

'I'm pretty sure they're for that house in Morocco,' she told Natalie and Suzanne later that day, when they were sitting on the patio. 'We were due to go in October. My flights are still booked for next week. This must be his way of telling me to go without him.'

'Or maybe he hopes you'll meet him there.'

The front door banged. 'Oh, God,' Jacquie said, coming out. 'The coven's sitting.'

'Do have some of my brew,' Natalie chortled.

'If Dara ever moves out,' Jacquie said, 'we'll end up like some ghastly spinster sorority.' She poured herself a mug of tea and, as always, retreated to her room.

'She's so limp,' said Marina. 'She tries to be cheerful, but it's like she . . .'

'Can't unfold herself,' said Natalie.

'I should be able to help, but . . .'

'You need to mend first,' said Suzanne.

Natalie tapped the keys. 'And here's the way to do it. Take him up on this, Marina, but persuade him to meet you there, as planned.'

Marina's phone beeped. 'Speak of the devil. Luke.' Holding it at arm's length, because she didn't have her glasses on, she read, '"Did you get my parcel?"'

'Just say, "I did,"' said Natalie. 'See where he's coming from.'

When she did so, he replied: 'I've taken the house for a month, but we could have it for a year. We could meet there. Away from them all. As often as possible. Whenever we can. What do you think?'

'Not a bad idea,' said Natalie.

'If he said he was going to put those two women on to a shuttle and send it into space, you'd say it was a good idea!' Marina looked at the keys again. '*Damn* him! What kind of a relationship is "whenever we can" and "as often as possible"?'

'More of a relationship than you have at the moment,' Suzanne said drily.

'A long-term foreign affair? A holiday fling in perpetuity?'

'Not in perpetuity. Just while the dust settles,' said Suzanne.

'But what if I commit to it and can't keep it up? I'll hurt him again. And anyway, I'd . . . I'd . . .'

'Go on,' said Suzanne, 'say it! You'd feel guilty, right? Guilty that you'd got your man when Jacquie had to give up hers for your sake. You don't want to be happy at her expense, right? Cos that's what we bloody mothers are like. You know how much she's in love with him, so you're blaming yourself and punishing yourself by not going back to Luke.'

Another text came through. Marina's delay in replying prompted Luke to save her the trouble. 'Never mind,' he wrote. 'Consider it yours for October. Your place of contemplation. I'll send the caretaker's number. If you want me to join you there, just make my phone go off. I'll be standing by.'

The two women stared at Marina. 'Make his phone go off,' Natalie pleaded.

She put her phone on the ground, and looked down along her garden. 'No.'

*

He was standing there, leaning against a car, when Marina came out of the local shop the following afternoon. She walked towards him, smiling. He wrapped her in an all-embracing hug.

'What are you doing here?'

'Damsel in distress,' said Matthew. 'Couldn't resist being your knight in shining hire car.'

'You came all this way?'

'Please don't be impressed. I'm only trying to make up for past misdemeanours, including July, about which I am still losing sleep.'

She patted his chest. 'Excellent.'

'I was way out of line. Ruined your special night.'

'Well, it seems you were right. I *was* making a big mistake.'

'I didn't think you were making a mistake. I never said that.'

'Still. Coming all this way just because I'm in the dumps is pretty dramatic.'

'Sure is. But then Natalie told me you wanted to sleep with me. What's a man to do?'

She slapped his arm. 'Oh, Matthew, your long trip has already been worth it! You've made me laugh for the first time in weeks.'

'Let's get a drink.'

In her local pub, he brought drinks over to the table, saying, 'So, on a scale of ten, how horrible has it been?'

'It'd be bearable, I suppose, if it weren't for Jacquie's involvement. And the awful paradox – that Luke and I have maybe prevented the two of them having something worthwhile. They're in love, apparently. So being with Luke would now involve not only dealing with his mother and Carlotta, but also seeing our children having a relationship and waiting for the fall-out when he leaves her.'

'She might leave him.'

'Even worse. I'd feel horribly guilty, wouldn't know what to say to Luke, *and* I'd have to pick up the pieces of my stepson's broken heart.'

'Or they might not break up.'

'In which case my daughter becomes my stepdaughter-in-law.'

'Don't get hung up on labels. If being with Luke is what makes you happy, you should be with him. The rest will fall into place.'

'It had a year to fall into place, Matthew, but none of it did. Instead of gaining anything, I've lost whole parts of myself. Even my relationship with Jacquie has being compromised by those people. How much more do they want from me? I mean, when I met Luke, I was still kind of depleted, empty, and now Jacquie wants to date Nico, like we're all living in an American soap opera, and I'm expected to be reasonable and generous, and give, give, give and not mind.'

'So do some taking. Take Luke back, for a start. As long as the two of you are apart, you can't think straight, so you can't get a handle on the Jacquie-Nico thing. If you could look at it together, I reckon you'd find it easier to be objective about it.'

'Who is ever objective about their kids?'

He finished his pint. 'Can I get you another?'

'Let's not.' Marina looked hard at him. 'How jet-lagged are you exactly?'

'Why?'

'It'd be great to get out of town. Go for dinner down the coast, stay somewhere.'

'Stay somewhere?'

She raised her eyebrows, and smiled.

'If that's meant to be seductive, it is.'

'Well?'

'Don't tease, Reen. I didn't come all this way to be your rebound.'

'Oh, relax, you old fuddy-duddy. I'd only be using you.'

He sat back. 'You'd really do it?'

'Would you?'

'You know I would.'

She smiled.

'With one proviso,' he added.

'Oh?'

Matthew hesitated. 'I've met someone.'

'Matthew! That's fantastic. Who? When? And – oh! How *dare* you consider cheating on her?'

'Wouldn't be cheating cos there ain't nothin' happening.'

'I see. So the way would be clear for a bit of casual sex between old friends, then?'

'My God, you *are* serious.'

Marina sighed. 'Not really. But I'd like to be. I just want to stop thinking – you know? Stop my head whirring. Sex is good for that.'

Marina hadn't meant it, that was the odd thing, but the suggestion had been made, aired, and when they were strolling back to their guesthouse after a boozy dinner in Rosscarberry, it tailed them, hanging back like a reprimanded child they didn't know what to do with. Then, simultaneously, they decided what to do with it, and their pace quickened. They called goodnight to their landlady and went upstairs. Matthew took Marina's key and opened her bedroom door, saying, 'Don't turn on the light or I'll never be able to do this.' He didn't give her much time to think about it. He held her, as he often had, tightly, as if he was about to leave for the airport, which wasn't a great start because they got locked into the familiarity of it, and almost got stuck there, in their friendship. Marina was about to say, 'Never mind, bad idea,' when she felt his mouth on her neck. It sent a current through her. Yes, she thought, this is what I need. She wanted to be carried, to know the blank-out that was arousal and its resolution, to believe that nothing mattered other than where he would next put his hand, his mouth, his tongue. And Matthew took her there, to that thoughtless, pleasured state.

The next morning, there were no hangovers, neither alcohol-induced nor regret-laden. So they did it again.

'Natalie was right,' Marina said afterwards, curled up against him. 'You *are* very good at it.'

'So are you. My God.'

'A good marriage will do that for you. Followed by a very experienced lover.'

'Aw, don't mention the opposition.'

'There's always been an attraction between us, I suppose, but don't tell Suzanne I admitted to that.'

'At least there'll be no more what-ifs.' Matthew blinked. He had very long eyelashes. 'You know, this last year I've been a bit preoccupied with you. Your voice, on the phone, did terrible things to me. I thought I was in love with you.'

'I know you did, but I knew you weren't.'

'How?'

'Because I was also looking at a man who really was in love with me. You were like an infatuated teenager by comparison.'

He smiled, but his eyes drifted across the room. 'Yeah, and that felt good, somehow, whereas now I feel completely shite.'

'Because of this new woman? Is it hopeless?'

'More or less.'

She put her finger on his chin. 'Matthew McGonagle, I do believe you're in love.'

'Reckon so, but I haven't lost my appetite. You hungry?'

'Very. And that was the best night's sleep I've had in weeks. You've really restored me.'

'Good. But let's not get into a habit of consolatory sex like Luke and Carlotta, okay? That's a really bad scene.'

'How do you know about that?'

'You must have told me.'

'No,' she said. 'I didn't. Carlotta must have. Did you get that cosy with her?'

'The point is, it can happen way too easily.'

'Clearly,' said Marina. 'Maybe I've been unfair to Luke about that.'

'So we're agreed? That was a once and only?'

'Twice and only.'

'And that third time when you were asleep.'

Marina elbowed him. 'We're so bad.'

'Bad and hungry.'

'Now that you've sorted me out, will you help me with Jacquie?' she asked. 'Help me put it right?'

'Sure, but there's something else we need to sort out first.'

They walked, Gwen and Marina, in the gentle amble of those who walk only to talk. Certain words, certain thoughts stopped them mid-step, and they dallied in one spot. The tide was out, the sand hard. The waves held back, like sprinters on a starting line, waiting for the tide to turn.

Gwen's expression was neither welcoming nor conciliatory. Still beautiful, her features were enhanced by some graceful silver hairs and the facial dents of experience. They had already struggled through the small-talk. An hour before, when Marina and Matthew had arrived, unexpected, on her doorstep, having spent much of the day driving around looking for her cottage, Gwen had not welcomed them as the long-lost friends they were, but seemed resigned to the chore of making them tea. Matthew, it transpired, had been trying to find her for months, and had a ream of emails in his laptop from people they'd known, who concurred that she lived near Clonakilty.

When she suggested a walk on the beach, Matthew had made a discreet retreat, saying he had to call his daughter and would pick them up later. He parked on the headland. Marina was momentarily distracted by the yellow sweep of beach, the pale sun and the sharp blue sea. Who needed Orta, she wondered, when they had this? The air was so warm and the light so gentle, she believed this encounter had to end well.

'So why bother, after all these years?' Gwen asked. 'You're not dying or anything, are you?'

'No. I just want to fill in some gaps.' She stopped a few steps behind Gwen, her thoughts further back again, her eyes on a downy green headland where the tip of Ireland sloped into the ocean like a majestic lady slipping into a swimming-pool. She had started a process that might upset them both and make her feel worse, but if it went well, it would calm the unhappy memories that had been revisiting her since Matthew had called.

The friendship was long buried. Marina didn't seek its revival – it had been too long lingering in murky depths. She wanted only to bring her latent defence to the bench and perhaps to get some acknowledgement that she was not all bad. This was the screw that still twisted into her: that a spark of loyalty had been taken as its absolute reverse.

'Look, Marina,' said Gwen, 'I'm really not interested in rehashing ancient history or granting pardons. You did what you did. Don't come asking me to clear your conscience.'

'Actually, my conscience *is* clear. I've long since apologized for squealing on you, but I've never explained why I did it, and you never asked. Haven't you wondered?'

'I was too busy dealing with the consequences.'

'Well, you should know the circumstances. The context.'

'I can't see that it'll make any difference,' said Gwen.

'Really? You cheated on one of my best friends and I got thrown out of the house for it. I've never been able to add that up. Where was *your* loyalty, Gwen?'

'Easy, there. Loyalty isn't a word you can afford to bandy about.'

Even on this warm evening, at this remove from events, the *froideur* reached Marina's bones. The sun was still bright enough to make them both look jaundiced. Gwen's restless eyes skimmed across the landscape.

'So here's what happened,' Marina began.

When she got to the bit about Aisling, she glanced at Gwen. No reaction, so she went on, and when she came to the end, she said, 'I'm sorry I said it, more sorry than you can imagine, but I was taunted and I snapped.'

'My affair with Selim was not yours to divulge,' Gwen said flatly.

Her attitude was beginning to grate. 'I am well aware of that,' said Marina, 'but what would you have done in my place? How would you have handled the strutting if it had been at *my* expense? Would you have joined in? Laughed? Should I have said, "Wow, what a lad!" and patted Matthew on the shoulder for being unfaithful to you? He expected me to stand by him, instead of by you. That's what riled me. The presumption that *he* came first. So I snipped off his cock-feathers, and you cut me out of your life.'

They had come to the end of the beach, where the sand dipped into a channel that curved its way slowly towards the town, and the sea swirled and sucked its way into the inlet.

They turned back towards the rocky outcrop at the other end of the bay.

'You shielded Matthew and exposed me,' Gwen said.

'They were scorning you. My hackles rose. I hit back.'

'You hit *me*,' said Gwen. Some heat, at last. Marina was almost relieved to see that Gwen, too, was still hurt.

'Yes, but you and Matthew were hardly Romeo and Juliet before we went away. You were going to break it off.'

'You had no right to tell them. No amount of context changes that.' Gwen pressed her fingers into her lower back. 'Matthew and I broke up because he never got over it. He never trusted me again.'

'Well, I'm sorry about that, but I'm not the one who slept with Selim.'

'No, you're the one who told him about it. Why didn't you tell *me* about Aisling?'

'Because you fell in love with him,' said Marina.

As the tide turned, the waves became more purposeful. They stepped back quickly to avoid them. 'So you're with Matthew now,' said Gwen.

'I'm not with Matthew.' Marina saw him sitting on the bonnet of his car, on the phone. She could have lived in Anchorage; she would not have been widowed; she would have laughed a lot . . . 'Anyway, that's all I wanted to say. No malice was intended. I couldn't read the future, Gwen. I couldn't know that you and Matthew would leap from infidelity to grand passion.'

As they headed back across the strand, Gwen muttered, 'Aisling – of all predatory cows! Hypocritical bastard.'

'She was livid when Matthew went back to you.'

'*Good*.'

In the car park, Gwen stopped in front of Matthew. 'Aisling, huh?'

He smiled sheepishly, but Gwen got into the back of the

car. They drove in silence. Marina might have made the effort to chat, but couldn't be bothered.

'Actually, drop me here,' Gwen said suddenly. 'I want to call in on someone.' Matthew pulled in. 'Thanks,' she said, and got out.

Marina was driven to jump out as well. 'Nothing to say? At all?'

'Not really,' said Gwen. 'Everything you say is true. I shouldn't have cheated. He,' she gestured towards the car, 'shouldn't have cheated. We all shouldn't have cheated. And if the lads drove you to do it – fine, I didn't know that. But the thing is, instead of telling me about him, you told him about me, so don't kid yourself that you were doing me any favours, Marina. He was always more important to you than I ever could have been.' She turned and walked back along the verge.

Marina got back into the car. 'Phew.'

'Okay?'

'Fine.' She reached over to him. 'Are you? That must have been hard.'

'Actually, not really.' He glanced in the mirror. 'She's a barrel of laughs, isn't she? And to think I might have married her.'

'Maybe we didn't know her very well. She looked at me a couple of times with really cold eyes and I realized I'd seen that look before.'

'When?'

Marina was staring ahead.

'Marina? When?'

She was frowning, as if she was trying to identify something a long way down the road. 'We were about fifteen and . . . someone got hurt, and everyone was trying to help, but Gwen just kept reading . . . *my God*,' she whispered.

'What is it?'

She came back to the moment. 'Nothing. I just . . . It's been a while since I thought about that day, that's all.'

'I'm sorry,' said Matthew. 'This wasn't one of my better ideas.'

'It was a great idea. I won't be mourning *her* any longer. And you know what the really odd thing is? She was right all along. I *didn't* lash out at you guys out of some grand gesture of loyalty to her. I did it for you. I was pissed off with her for cheating on you and I wanted to punish her for it.'

'Umm . . . thanks. I think.'

'Drive on. If we sit here any longer, she'll think we want to abduct her.'

'But here's the thing,' said Matthew. 'Are you going to let Carlotta boot you out of Luke's life, the way you let Gwen boot you out of mine – only to discover years down the line that she really isn't worth it?'

'I've got it!' Natalie came rushing into the kitchen when they got home. 'I told you I would, and I have.'

'It won't work,' said Dara.

'Shush!' said Natalie.

Dara looked deadpan at his mother. 'Won't work.'

'Sit down, both of you,' said Natalie. 'Matthew, you're here for a couple of weeks, yeah?'

'Yeah.'

'Okay, so just do this for me, would you? Go to Morocco, the two of you. Marina, please. You're already booked and it'll be easy with Matthew. Go and enjoy this little house, get some sun, take advantage, have some long walks on the beach, swim –'

'This could go on all night,' Marina said, wryly. 'There's a lot to do in Morocco.'

'Please.'

'This is your solution? A holiday with Matthew?' Marina glanced at him. 'You're not trying to match-make us, are you? Because that won't work.'

'Give me some credit,' Natalie said crossly. 'It's far more devious than that.'

'But Matthew's here to spend time with Kitt.'

'Well, that's lovely, isn't it? Only Kitt never notices.'

'This is not devious, Natalie,' said Marina. 'It is completely transparent. You're going to tell Luke I'll be there and try to get us back together.'

'That's not it,' said Dara.

'It isn't?'

'Why would I tell you to bring Matthew if Luke was going to turn up?'

Marina frowned.

'Please, Marina. It's only a little thing. You have those keys, and you can clear your head and come home, fresh and rested, for the winter.'

'Fresh and rested sounds good.' A place of contemplation, Luke had said. She turned to Dara. 'Why won't it work?'

'Actually, Morocco isn't a bad idea,' he said. 'It's the rest of the plan that sucks. I mean, wide of the mark, Nat.'

'I'll put money on it,' she said.

'You're on,' said Dara. 'Fifty euro.'

She turned back to Marina. 'Anyway, you kind of have to go. You kind of have to go because I've kind of booked Matthew on to the same flights you're on.'

Marina sat by Jacquie's desk, fiddling with the spines of the books on the shelves. 'You wouldn't come with me, would you, instead of Matthew?'

'No, thanks. Anyway, he'll be more fun.'

'Have you any idea what Natalie's up to?'

Jacquie shrugged. 'She had some sort of lightbulb moment. Something to do with the summer.'

Marina couldn't look at her daughter when the summer was mentioned. 'Will you be okay?'

'Fine.'

'But you're not fine, really, are you?' Marina went over and squeezed her shoulder. It was the first gesture of affection to pass between them in weeks. 'We should never have got involved with that stupid family. They weren't good for either of us.'

'They were very good for me.'

Marina swallowed. 'If he means that much to you, you can keep in touch with him, can't you?'

'What do you mean? Emails?'

'No, I . . . Jacquie, you're twenty-four years old. I can't stop you having this relationship if you want to.'

'Somehow you don't sound like you mean that.'

'Yes, but if he's important to you, no one else really matters. I mean, that's the view you took, isn't it?' Marina could have bitten out her tongue.

Jacquie's eyes went cold again; she turned back to the window.

'What I'm trying to say is, if you're this miserable without him, maybe you could continue at some level . . . without it being . . . whatever it was.'

'It can only be what it was. And you wouldn't be able to hack that, would you?'

'You think I should find it easy? You over there, seeing Luke, being with Luke? It would tear the heart out of me. And having Nico here would be even harder. You must be able to see that.'

'But if you'd married Luke?'

'Well, that's a bit academic now, isn't it?' Marina snapped.

'Besides, you didn't give us the option, did you? To know how we'd feel about it without . . . all this. I don't think I'll ever forget the look on Carlotta's face, that day at the window, and she isn't going away, you know. You'd have to deal with her, the two of you. With her anger and disappointment. Her sense of betrayal. She's good at that, and she can make it drag out for a long time. As for me, for what it's worth – call me daft, call me unreasonable, but no, I would not have relished having my daughter sleeping with my stepson.'

'But we're completely unrelated! There would be no real connection. A piece of paper that doesn't even matter!'

'It would matter to me.'

'More than I do?' Jacquie eyeballed her.

Marina stared back at her. 'Right at the beginning, when you met Nico, I asked you not to let this happen.'

'And I tried, Mum. I really did. All I wanted was for you and Luke to be happy, and I still do. That's why I'm here. That's why I came home. But I don't understand why you don't want the same for me, and shag the rest of the world!'

'Because you're pressing on a fresh bruise, Jacquie, that's why.'

'But bruises clear up, Mum. Bruises clear up.'

## 23

Holding the silver pot aloft, high over their glasses, the waiter poured mint tea. A passing group of schoolkids, teenagers, started tapping handheld drums and clapping and dancing on the square, the girls ululating. It felt, to Marina, like a welcome. It was good, sitting there. Perhaps coming back was the way to move forward. It might give her the chance to cross out the last year and start again from the very point at which things had changed: Essaouria, in the autumn.

'I've never been much of a tea-drinker,' said Matthew, 'but this stuff is magic. Must be the way they pour it.' He looked around. 'So this is where Jimi Hendrix liked to hang out?'

'Yeah. There are still a few hippies around.'

'Noted.' Matthew nodded towards a middle-aged couple near them. The bloke had long, matted dreadlocks, and a multi-coloured cap perched on top; his wife had short curly hair laced with paper flowers.

'Is it bringing stuff back, being here?' he asked.

'Yeah, but it also reminds me that there was always something elusive about Luke. It was as if he wasn't really available, though he desperately wanted to be.' She looked at the dancing teenagers. 'No regrets, though. I loved being with him.'

'So Natalie was right – that coming here would clear your head?'

'Maybe, but that doesn't explain where you come into it.'

'She had a dream about me,' he said. 'About me being in Morocco. That's why she wanted me to come.'

'Really?'

'Yeah, apparently I still had my bust leg and I was running after some woman who kept dipping into alleyways, and Natalie was trying to catch up with me, but couldn't. What with the cast and all, I must have been pretty fast. And then I vanished, so she sat down and had a cup of coffee.'

Marina laughed. 'That'd be Natalie, all right.'

'When she woke up, she had this urge to tell me I'd get the woman in the end.'

'Have you told her about your new love interest?'

'As a matter of fact, I have. She told me to go get her.'

'Why haven't you?'

He sighed. 'Other people. Complications.'

'*Jesus.* Stay clear! Learn from me. You've seen what other people can do to relationships.' Marina stood up. 'Come on, I want to show you a very special shop.'

The smell of Hamid's place, when they stepped inside, got to her; the memory was too sharp. 'This is where Luke and I met,' she told Matthew.

'Madame,' said Hamid, coming forward with a broad smile. 'Welcome, welcome.'

'You remember?'

'Of course.'

'But that was over a year ago.'

Hamid glanced at Matthew.

'Oh, this is my friend, Matthew.'

Hamid's lip seemed to turn up. 'Your other friend?' he asked politely.

She smiled. 'Kaput!'

'*Non, non. Pas possible.*'

When she explained that Matthew wanted to buy some jewellery for his daughter and her mother, the chests were opened and the kettle filled. They sat for a long time, drinking tea, while Matthew picked out rings and necklaces. There was a beautiful silver ring that he kept coming back to, but his final choice didn't include it.

'And this,' said Hamid, holding it up to him, 'for someone special?'

Matthew shook his head. 'There's no one special,' he said, and for the first time Marina saw his loneliness, which was not a lot different from hers, yet neither could do anything to relieve the other.

Hamid put the ring into the bag anyway. 'Soon you will need it.'

Marina raised her eyebrows at Matthew. 'You'd better believe him. He's usually right.'

The house belonging to Luke's friends was in a narrow alleyway that smelt of cat pee. Beyond the low arched doorway, the whitewashed house rose upwards, like a funnel, towards the light. Thick walls and windowless bedrooms, with beds elevated on cement platforms, made it a cool, almost secret, place to be. It was narrow, but the steps went up and up, until you came out into a small enclosed courtyard, where Matthew served breakfast every morning, and more steps led to another high-walled terrace, which, although it had no view, was an ideal spot to take the evening sun.

'So if Hamid is usually right,' said Matthew, when they got home, 'I guess it follows that he must be right about Luke? About it not being over.'

'Could be.'

'You believe him, but none of us?'

'He knows things. He's so confident about the good things in life that it gives you hope even if you don't want it.'

Matthew offered her a plate of sticky pastries he'd picked up in the town. 'You've really mellowed since you got here.'

'I know.' Marina lifted her face to the sun. Maybe it was the white brightness of Essaouira, but she could see light ahead. She didn't know, yet, where it was coming from, but she was heading towards it.

'So are you going to call him?'

'I've thought about it,' she admitted, 'calling and asking him to come, as he hopes I will.'

'If you got back with him, what would you do about Carlotta?'

Marina sniffed. 'I have absolutely no idea.'

'You could take consolation from the fact that she doesn't want you there any more than you want her there. You could cancel each other out.'

'True.'

'And Jacquie?' he asked, more tentatively.

Marina glanced at the gliding gulls. 'I'm hoping she won't ever want to go back to Nico, but if she does, there isn't a damn thing I can do about it.'

'I imagine she knows that, but she left him anyway.'

'Yes. She's always been more generous than I am.'

'How much would it rankle, really, if they were together?'

She took off her sunglasses and placed them carefully on the bench beside her. 'We just want our kids to be happy, don't we?'

'More than ourselves.'

'And I know too well the choking feeling of helplessness when you see your children submerged by sadness and you can't protect them . . . I had a dream a few months ago. A nightmare. Jacquie was drowning. The sea was brown, opaque, so Aidan couldn't find her, reach her, in the deep murk . . .' Marina picked up her sunglasses again, put them on. 'This time I could reach out to her.'

'And will you?'

'What do you think?'

Matthew kissed her on the mouth. 'You know what I think.'

On their fifth day, in the late afternoon, they were sitting on the top terrace, reading, when they heard voices. They looked over the tops of their books, but the surrounding buildings were so tightly pressed together that whenever anyone moved in any of the adjoining houses it sounded as if they were in the same one. They went back to their books, but there was no doubt about it – people were coming up their own steps, and when they looked over the wall, the voices were unmistakable.

Matthew grabbed Marina's wrist. 'Don't bolt!'

When Luke came through the arched wooden doorway, Marina's stomach leapt, then twisted – Carlotta was behind him. They looked around the courtyard, with its small tiled table, unaware that Marina and Matthew were staring down from the upper level. Carlotta saw them first, and gasped. A mixture of anguish and warmth crossed her face. When Luke saw Marina, his eyes brightened, then darkened; he looked as if he might throw up. No one said anything.

*Then* Marina bolted.

The steps were high and uneven, but she flew down, crossed behind Luke, and went on through the house, past Matthew's bedroom to her own. She grabbed her handbag and ran.

Children were playing in the tight, narrow alleyway and, at the corner, the man who tanned pelts for drums was hard at work. She ran past him, not certain where to go, and found herself in the main thoroughfare, ducking through the crowds, heading down to the square where tourists were reclining over coffee. Marina would be a sitting duck for Luke if she stopped in a café, so she headed down a side-street to the ramparts, climbed up, and there, leaning against the old wall, caught her breath. The sound of the sea calmed her. Boys and tourists sat on the crenulated walls, and even on the cannons that still pointed at the ocean, watching the sun, impeccably round and striped with pink and orange as it dallied above the horizon before its final decline of the day. Marina was shaking. To recover from her hare-like dash, she sat in one of the breaks of the wall. At the base of the ramparts, white waves fussed round the rocks, and a man lay asleep on a slanting rock, his scarf over his head. There had been a moment – one fractional instant – in which she had known that it was over. When Luke had come through that doorway, she knew with certainty that being without him was no longer an option: their separation was over. It had failed. And then Carlotta had appeared.

When her limbs steadied, she wandered along the rampart. The façade of white houses that stood behind the wall glowed orange, like the rest of the town, and two white cockerels postured on a railing. Marina was stunned that Luke had reverted so easily. Telling her to come here, that it was hers, her place of contemplation – then coming himself and bringing his lover . . .

In the port, as if to exaggerate her loneliness, families were out in force, enjoying what seemed to be a traditional Sunday-evening outing. On a low white wall, a row of women – twenty or more – sat chatting, side by side, old and young, in their pink, and red, and white *jellabahs*, like a multicoloured identity parade, their scarves tight across their foreheads and some mouths, while their children played around them. Further on, men and boys stood about, smoking and jousting, and a fisherman fed scraps to cats on the rocks, to the outrage of the seagulls. In a small harbour, dozens of blue rowboats were lined up, like tubs in a freezer. Marina couldn't go any further and couldn't go back to the house, so she walked across the square, through the arch and went over to the Riad Skala. She needed to close herself in, to think and wait. Luke, she hoped, would have the decency to take Carlotta elsewhere.

'Thank you,' she said to the man who showed her to a room. She closed the door and lay down. How contented they had looked, Carlotta and Luke, wandering on to the terrace like that, chatting. He had told Marina the house was hers if she wanted it, had given her the caretaker's number . . . Perhaps her silence had made him think she wasn't taking up the offer.

Her throat was tight with sadness. That one glimpse of him had squeezed her out, left her dry and rotten on the inside, like an old tree. If he had ten mothers like Bridget, she would have had him back, but she, and Jacquie, had thrown him into Carlotta's arms. In the end, he had indeed returned to his lover.

There was an urgent knock on the door. 'Reen?'

Matthew. He knew the place. She'd taken him to dinner here. She got up, opened the door, and before she could react, Luke had stepped in and closed it behind him.

'Please don't,' she said, backing away.

'Marina.'

'You send me keys, say it'll be my own little bolt-hole, for me, mine, for the taking, and then . . . in a blink, a damn blink, you bring *her*! I knew you and she would resume your European ways eventually, I just didn't think it'd be quite so quick. I was right. So right to get out of this.'

'What about Matthew? You brought *him* to a house I'm paying for.'

'Yeah, my mistake, but don't worry, I won't be doing that again. Now, please go. This room is my room, paid for by me.'

He stepped towards her.

'Please leave.'

'No.'

'Just go back to her, Luke. She's waited long enough. Go and nurse your little sin together.'

'Fuck off,' he said, still coming towards her.

Marina had backed herself into the bathroom. Luke stepped in too. 'There's nowhere else for you to go now.'

They stood there, in the terracotta room, almost on top of each other, and every word they spoke rebounded off the walls. Marina felt everything tighten – her chest, her fingers, her tongue. In the cool room, she felt only heat, as if she were feverish, and she loved the man who stood before her so thoroughly that beyond this little room there was no life for her, only despair. She had tasted something so sweet that no day henceforth would bring anything close to it. Beyond that bathroom door was darkness.

Luke was panting slightly. He must have been running to find her, and he was stressed. 'I didn't come here to be with Carlotta,' he said. 'I came because Natalie told me to. She sent me a text insisting I come immediately. I thought it was pretty clear what she was up to – that you'd be here – so I didn't need much persuading. But I sure as hell didn't expect to find Matthew looking down at me.'

Marina rubbed her arms. She was feeling cold now.

'This is Natalie's doing,' Luke went on, 'so don't take it out on me.'

She shook her head, her mouth in a bitter line. 'If you wanted to be reconciled, why did you bring Carlotta?'

'Because Natalie told me to! She said it was all part of the plan and that you'd understand.'

Marina shook her head. *What?* Natalie knew that she would *never* understand Carlotta turning up. 'Jesus,' she muttered. 'She said the plan was devious, but it's plain deranged.'

'Maybe she was trying to get you and Carlotta together,'

Luke suggested, 'away from Orta. Maybe she thought it would . . . smooth things over.'

Marina sat on the loo, thinking. He stood in front of her, arms dangling.

Thoughts flew about her head . . . Dara saying, 'That's not it.' Saying the plan wouldn't work . . . She tried to think like Natalie. In her wildest moments, Natalie could not have imagined this would turn out like an international conference in a neutral location where disagreements were ironed out, with Matthew and Luke acting as arbiters. There was no romance in that. Natalie liked romance.

'Either way, we've been set up,' said Luke. 'That's obvious.'

'No, that's not it. Dara said so.'

'So what are we all doing here? What conceivable purpose could there be in throwing us together, apart from it being enormously painful for you and me?' She glimpsed the pain behind those eyes. 'Did she think, I don't know, that I'd see you don't care for Matthew and you'd see I don't care for Carlotta?'

'But she knows we know that already.' Two things came into Marina's head simultaneously. 'Wait . . .'

Luke watched while she thought it through.

'*We* haven't been set up,' she said. 'Matthew and Carlotta have.'

'Come again?'

Marina was nodding. 'She was always saying . . . that if Carlotta were happy, if she were distracted, if someone loved her, she'd get off my case.'

'*I*'ve said that. *You*'ve said that.'

'Yes, but we missed the vital ingredient.'

'Which is?'

'Matthew.' Marina was still working it through. 'When they

were in Orta . . . Remember all the time he spent with her? I thought he was avoiding me, but . . .'

Leaning against the sink, Luke said, 'Matthew and Carlotta? She's trying to set them up? She really is deranged. And it amounts to the same thing – getting you and me together.'

Marina glanced at him. 'What do you think?'

'About us?'

'About them. Did you see the way they looked at each other just now? And Matthew told me he'd fallen for someone. Someone unattainable. It must be her! But she'd never go for him . . . would she?'

Luke crossed his arms. 'I'd never have thought it, but it isn't impossible. Her complete opposite. Someone she can spend the rest of her life trying to tame.'

'Natalie is such a chancer!'

Luke bit his lip. 'Yeah, fairly inspired, all right. It might have worked too. Maybe it will, between them. But as for making it work for us,' he looked at her, 'it won't.'

She gaped. What? This was her call, wasn't it? Hadn't he been hounding her to reconsider? Hadn't he said he would never give up?

'Look,' he said gently, 'you know I love you. Always will. But when I was running around just now, looking for you, I saw families hanging out in the port, old and young, kids and parents, and it struck me that you left me because my ageing mother needs me, because I won't abandon a friend, and because my son loves your daughter . . . But that's a total contradiction of the way you live your life, and a rejection of the way I live mine. To me, mothers and friends and kids falling in love are blessings. That's my wealth, Marina. That's what I have to offer. And it's also what you have to offer me – your apparently difficult mother heading our way, the ghost of a husband I can *never* hope to better, and a daughter who wants to be with my son. What's the difference? This is what we've both accrued, what the average life accrues – losses and mistakes, regrets and delights. Isn't that why people get married? Isn't marriage supposed to be an act of forgiveness, a mixing of families, a shot of hope? Isn't that what we're all supposed to be looking for?'

'*Yes,*' she said emphatically.

'Except I'm prepared to take it on, and you're not. And that,' he said, pushing himself off the sink, 'about puts me in my place.' He reached for the door. ''Bye, Marina.'

And he left. Just like that. The door closed behind him.

Incredulous, Marina had to gasp for breath. She bent over her knees and wept, glad of the thick walls, so that no one would hear the sound of her cries.

She stayed in the bathroom for so long that she scarcely knew if it was bright or dark outside. Dark, she presumed. The prospect of the night ahead, of finding Matthew, getting their bags and driving to Marrakech, only to return to Cork to her large empty house, full of people, was so horrible, she couldn't move. She couldn't begin, and didn't want to. But neither could she start another day in this place. She forced herself upright, thinking about the one place in the world she wanted to be – Lake Orta, looking back at her like an eye, blinking and holding on to her. She imagined it, seeing it from Luke's garden wall, her feet dangling over the water, the wooden slats of the jetty cutting into her thighs, the ducklings honking. How blessed she would have been to care for him there, and for his mother, and his wounded friend. How unlonely it would have been. How large their Christmases; how full of Easter eggs their Easter Sundays . . .

Instead, she had held on to loneliness as if it was the only safe place to be. With Luke she would never have known where the next bash would come from, the next strike; loneliness had seemed a more predictable companion. But she had made the wrong choice, and had the rest of her life to regret it.

She wiped her face with cold water, hating the sight of the wretched hag in the mirror who, weeks before, had been desirable and beautiful in the eyes of some. Courage was needed now, and a lot more courage than she would have required had she stayed with Luke. With a fortifying sigh, she opened the door and stepped into the rest of her miserable life.

'I forgot to tell you . . .' a voice said in the dark.

Marina swung round. Luke, just visible in the gloom, was leaning against the wall behind the bathroom door.

'. . . where it was that we met.'

Half turned towards him, she didn't move. 'I told you I'd remembered.'

'But you hadn't. You were chancing it.'

'Yes. I hoped you'd blurt. But I do remember now.'

'Do you?'

'It was the cows, wasn't it?'

He slid down the wall on to his hunkers. 'Yes, it was the cows, God rest them.'

Jittery and weak, she slithered to the floor beside him. 'It came back recently, when I saw Gwen again . . . We were fourteen or fifteen, I think, and we were on our way to Dublin, and the train ran into a herd of cows that had strayed on to the line. We hit them . . . just as the cute guy across the aisle who'd been chatting me up was standing on the armrest, reaching for his bag on the overhead shelf, and when the train suddenly braked, he went flying. Hit the back of his head off another seat and knocked down a girl who was carrying steaming coffee. Am I right?'

'Yes.'

'I remember the train going bump, bump, bump. It was horrible.'

'I remember that,' said Luke.

'I thought he was dead, your friend.'

'Me too.'

'What was his name?'

'Keith.'

'You'd barely said a word to me before it happened.'

'You couldn't take your eyes off him.'

'True,' she said. 'I hardly noticed you.'

'Yeah, I made a really big impression.'

'No, you did. When he was hurt, you were so calm, laying him flat, not letting people crowd him. You called for a doctor, I think, and told me to get cold water for the girl's burns . . . Gwen just went on reading. You looked after him so well while we had to wait – how long did we wait?'

'Two hours before they got him off, and another two before we were shunted back into Kent station.'

'Was he okay?'

'Fine. Broken clavicle and rib, concussion. He lives in China now.'

'I remember how they wouldn't let you go with him in the ambulance. I thought that was terrible.'

'I didn't try too hard. I wanted to stay with you.'

'But you still didn't say anything,' said Marina.

'Never was much of a talker.'

'Funny, but I don't remember *seeing* you, only being aware of the cute guy's friend.'

'Baseball cap,' said Luke. 'The shy person's protection. Very little eye contact.'

'Did you really remember me all this time?'

'Not consciously. You stayed with me for days afterwards. I kept thinking, That's the kind of girl I want – gentle, pretty. A bit flirty. Then time blurred you, but when I saw you in Marrakech, I was pretty sure you were the same person. I even remembered your name. Those curls are hard to forget. And then you chanced across my path in Essaouira. I couldn't believe it.'

'Hamid would love this story.'

'*I* love this story. Our story. I love you.'

'So why did you just leave me?'

'How could I leave you when we aren't together?'

'I wish we were. I want us to be . . . if you can forgive me for being such a selfish brat and trying to have everything on my own terms.'

'No, no, don't say that. You've had a lot to put up with. Carlotta's been a bitch, our children are probably lovers, and my mother's trying to bring you back into the Church. Above all, I appreciate that coercing someone into an abortion isn't a great calling card. I expected way too much from you.'

'That's not quite what you said a while ago.'

'Standing in the dark for forty-five minutes will do that for you.' He reached out for her hand; she gave it to him. 'I got frazzled coming here,' he said quietly. 'I felt like a blinking idiot running after you, as if I was desperate, as if it didn't matter that you came here with Matthew, whom you've known for ever and loved for longer, and I thought, Fuck, why am I trying to rope someone else into my life, someone else I can't make happy, whom I've already failed and will fail again, like I did Francesca and Carlotta and the boys, and the sibling they were never allowed to have? I arrived here feeling like a small kid trying to jump at something he won't ever reach, and I couldn't bear to hear you say it – that you *were* out of my reach and that we weren't going to make it, so I said it first. But as soon as I'd put one door between us, I couldn't put another. So here I am. Stuck in the vestibule.'

'Thinking about cows and trains and how I've known Matthew for ever, when the truth is that you've known me longer than he has.'

'The truth *is*, Marina, that I *am* desperate, because I can't do it.' His voice cracked. 'I can't leave this room because I can't be without you. Please don't ask me to.'

She kissed the back of his hand and held it against her. 'If you'd stayed in the bathroom long enough you'd have heard what I was actually going to say.'

'Which is?'

'We need to line up a couple of camels.'

He let his head fall back against the wall.

They sat on the cold floor, holding hands, like two people who had driven through a long stretch of dense fog and had pulled into the side of the road to recover. In time, Marina kissed him and said, 'The others will be worried. We should get back.'

'On the other hand,' he said, 'we could send them a text. Ask if they'd mind keeping each other company for tonight and . . . tomorrow. And maybe the rest of the week.'

'Do you think it'll take? Matthew and Carlotta?'

'I have no idea.'

'Hamid,' Marina said, getting to her feet and pulling him with her. 'Hamid will know if they'll work.'

'Let's go ask him.'

# 24

Jacquie sat at the table, waiting. It was raining. Dismal. The drops came down on the tarpaulin, and it was chilly, but she wanted to be outdoors. Her phone vibrated in her pocket. Here it is, she thought, reaching in for it. The call to explain why he hadn't come.

But it was her mother. *Christ.* Had she been found out? 'Hello, you,' Marina said warmly, when Jacquie answered.

'Hi,' she said, trying to sound cheery. 'How're things in the unpronounceable place?'

'They're good, love. All good. Or, rather, they will be.'

'Bad line. Can't hear you very well.'

'Okay, Jacquie, listen, this isn't the ideal way to, you know, clear the air . . . but I'm really sorry for being so . . . I mean, I think you know why –'

'Mum? Hello?' The line broke up and went dead. Jacquie breathed a sigh of relief and put her phone down. She looked left again, to where the street came into the square. Natalie had been right. Morocco seemed to be working its magic. Her mother already sounded lighter, less stressed. She was bound to call back when she had a better signal, but how the hell, Jacquie wondered, was she going to respond?

He came, at last, with great purposeful strides, saw her immediately and headed over, a slight grin hidden behind a tight mouth. Beautiful, she thought. Working clothes – good suit, thin tie, white shirt, and that confidence. She didn't stand as he came to the table. He motioned to the waiter for an espresso.

The rain tinkled on the lake. Across the grey, singing water, the island seemed grizzly and crotchety, as if it didn't want to be there.

Nico sat back, his hands clasped. 'I shouldn't smile.'

'No, you shouldn't.'

'But she *has* turned down Dad's offer, yeah? To get together in Morocco?'

'Yes, not that it makes much difference now.'

'I thought it was a clever plan,' he said, with a shrug. 'A place where they could get away from us all.'

'She's taken Matthew there instead.'

Nico winced. '*Cazzo!* I mean, fucking hell, that hurts!'

'Yeah, I thought it was a bit cruel. I hope Luke never finds out. How is he?'

'Living in a fog.'

'I hope I don't run into him.'

'You won't. Carlotta's taken him away for a few days.'

Jacquie gaped. 'Is that a fact? So Mum was right – the status quo has been re-established. Carlotta's got him back, and it's all thanks to me. No wonder Mum hates me.'

Nico kissed her fingertips. 'Don't, now,' he said kindly. 'Don't get upset.'

She motioned towards her phone. 'But here she is, phoning to apologize to me.'

'She apologized?'

'Almost. She got cut off. I should be the one apologizing to her.'

The waiter brought his espresso. He knocked it back in two gulps. 'Come with me.'

He paid; they left. They walked to the end of the square under the arcade, then hurried up the sloping steps, past the Shakespearean set, to the yellow church at the top of the rise, the rain wetting their shoulders and heads, and ran into the sombre interior.

'You want me to go to confession?' Jacquie asked, moving along the nave.

'You might have to, you know, if we had a church wedding.'

She shivered. Nico took off his jacket and put it round her. 'A church wedding? But isn't the civil ceremony –'

'The important bit,' he said, 'yeah. You can have the civil without the church, but not the church without the civil.'

Jacquie looked up at the dome. 'Would have been sweet, wouldn't it? In another life, where you and I had met at some conference in Geneva or somewhere and then introduced our parents to one another at our big happy wedding in a beautiful church?'

'My mother has no daughters,' said Nico, his voice low but resounding in the quiet apse. 'She's counting on her sons for church weddings.'

'You really want to do this?'

He grinned. 'I will if you will.'

Jacquie kissed him. 'We are *so* going to upset everyone.'

'They'll get over it. Soon as we present them with a few grandchildren and great-grandchildren, everyone will be happy. Mostly me.'

Her phone went off, three times in a row. 'Must be Mum's full confession. She'd be quick to retract it if she could see us now.'

'Let's get out of here.'

Back in the café, they ordered wine.

Jacquie took out her phone. 'Better see what Mum's saying.' She read it, pushing the button down, and down again, as the message went on.

'*Allora?*' Nico lifted his chin.

'Christ.'

He took the phone from her. Marina's message read: 'As I

was saying, sorry for being such a horrible grump recently but Luke is here with me now in Morocco and all is well. Sorry it couldn't work out with Nico . . .'

'You told her it didn't work out?' he asked, looking up.

'Nope.' She half laughed. 'Never said a word, but they assumed. All of them. Maybe they couldn't imagine anything else.'

He read on. '. . . but as you'll see, it's probably for the best. Stand by!'

The rain came down, heavier again.

'What's he doing in Morocco?' said Jacquie.

Nico looked equally perplexed. 'What happened to Carlotta?'

'God knows, but they're obviously back together.'

He inhaled sharply. 'Sounds like it.'

Her phone went off again. Then his did too. 'Here it comes,' she said.

Their respective parents had sent the same message:

'Hi, kids, we're sitting in our favourite café in Essaouira, hoping you four (and some others!) will join us here on 1 Jan for a lovely Moroccan wedding. Lots of love, Marina and Luke.'

Nico and Jacquie placed their phones on the table, side by side, like a couple in a bed. 'Happy ever after,' she said. 'Like you predicted.'

'It's good, really,' he said.

'Of course it is.'

They sat a bit longer. Jacquie pulled his jacket round her. 'What now?'

'You'd be walking away now, wouldn't you? If you could.'

She smiled. 'Wouldn't you like to know?'

'We need to congratulate them,' he said. 'We'll do that, and then we'll think.'

So they did that.

'Mum, so happy for you! What great news! Of course I'll be there, and so sorry for being a horrible grump too. Love you lots.'

'They're sitting over there in their favourite place,' Nico said thoughtfully, 'in the sunshine, and we're sitting here in the rain, and we didn't know they were together and they certainly don't know we are.'

'Mm. I wish I could take a snapshot of them, right now, and one of us, and capture this for posterity. Especially with the four phones.'

Her mother's reply came a few minutes later. Marina wasn't nifty at texting and had yet to use prescriptive text or abbreviations, but she wrote, 'Thanks. We're so excited and happy. I know the step-thing will be hard for you and Nico but you both have to be there. Will you be okay with everything?'

Luke replied to Nico along the same lines, but was both more specific and more compassionate. 'Apologies for turning the girl you love into your stepsister but I hope being together as a family won't be too much of an ordeal for you guys for too long.'

'This is getting worse and worse,' said Jacquie.

'I know.' Nico took a pen from his shirt pocket. 'Let's write things down.'

'Our options?'

'Yes.'

'That should be fun,' she said drily.

Wine glasses and coffee cups took up most of the table, along with napkins that had been scribbled on in her writing, and his. He'd drunk so much espresso that his hands were shaking; she'd become less constructive, her suggestions more ridiculous. They finally settled on what to do. She punched the agreed text into her phone, read it, and sent it to Nico. 'How does it read?'

He opened the message and pulled back as if it was news to him. 'Maybe we should phone, speak to them.'

'No. I *really* don't want to talk to them yet. And this way they'll have time to let it sink in before they have to say anything.'

He squeezed her wrist. 'Come on.' Reading from her phone, he keyed the same text into his.

'Right,' she said. 'Ready?'

'Wait.' Nico reached over, took his wallet from the inner pocket of his jacket, unzipped a compartment and took out two rings. 'These,' he said, taking her finger and holding her eye, 'are never coming off again.' He pushed her wedding band back on. She did the same for him. They chinked their glasses, drank a shot, picked up their phones and simultaneously hit 'Send'.

'Don't worry about the step thing,' read the messages that went to Morocco. 'We'll never be steps. We got married last month instead.'

Jacquie smiled at her husband, switched off her phone, walked out into the square and stood in the pelting rain.

# *Acknowledgements*

With warmest thanks and appreciation to my excellent editor, Patricia Deevy, for her exceptional patience and forbearance, my wonderful copy-editor, Hazel Orme, and all at Penguin Ireland – Michael McLoughlin, Cliona Lewis, Patricia McVeigh and Brian Walker; and Ann Cooke in London. Thanks also to friends and acquaintances who helped along the way: Alisdair Luxmoore, of Fleewinter UK; Bruno Busetti of the Italian Cultural Institute, Dublin; Romeo Quartiero, Milan; William Schwitzer, of Holiday Homes at Lake Orta; Forrest Schroeder-Einwiller, Anchorage, Alaska; Hachim Youssef, Essaouira, Morocco; Charlie Sheil, of the Clarion Hotel, Cork; and, for many years of technical support and assistance, Colie O'Brien and Paul Murray, of Specialist Office Services, Cork. As ever, Finola, Tamzin and William.

Finally, on this, the publication of my fifth novel, special thanks to my agent, Jonathan Williams, who has put up with me for ten years now.

Denyse Devlin
Knocknamarriff, Co. Cork
November 2007


WITHDRAWN FROM STOCK